ALSO BY VASSILY AKSYONOV

The Colleagues

Half-way to the Moon

The Steel Bird and Other Stories

The Island of Crimea

The Burn

Say Cheese

In Search of Melancholy Baby

Generations of Winter

The Winter's Hero

THE
WINTER'S
HERO

Vassily Aksyonov

TRANSLATED BY JOHN GLAD

RANDOM HOUSE

NEW YORK

The poetry appearing on pages 45, 46, 47 and 50
was written by Yevgeny Yevtushenko.

Library of Congress Cataloging-in-Publication Data
Aksenov, Vasiliĭ Pavlovich.
[Ti͡ur ́ma i mir. English]
The winter's hero: a novel / Vassily Aksyonov; an authorized
translation by John Glad & Christopher Morris.
p.   cm.
"Volume III of the trilogy Moscow saga."
ISBN 0-679-43274-4
1. Soviet Union—History—1925–1953—Fiction. I. Glad, John.
II. Morris, Christopher. III. Title.
PG3478.K7T5813   1996   891.73´44—dc20   95-24409

Printed in the United States of America on acid-free paper
Book design by J. K. Lambert
2 4 6 8 9 7 5 3
First Edition

In memory of my parents,
Pavel Aksyonov and Eugenia Ginzburg

The Story of
Generations of Winter

The family of famous Moscow surgeon Boris Gradov, who may count among his ancestors many physicians back even to the days of Peter the Great, lives in a large, old house in the capital's Silver Grove suburb. It is 1925, the heyday of the so-called NEP (New Economic Policy), a relatively tame period of Soviet history, when private enterprise was partially and temporarily restored in order to ease the privations caused by the Revolution and the Civil War.

Dr. Gradov enjoys life in a house filled with love and the music of his wife, Mary, a woman of Georgian ancestry who was trained as a classical pianist. To his disappointment, however, his children have been infected by the spirit of the Revolution, and have chosen not to carry on the family profession. His oldest son, Nikita, becomes a senior commander in the Red Army. The second son, Kirill, is a staunch Bolshevik and Marxist philosopher. The youngest child, his daughter, Nina, is an inspired poet and an active member of both the artistic avant-garde and the Trotskyite underground.

Nikita and his wife, the beautiful Veronika, give birth to the first child of the next generation of the Gradov family, a boy who, his grandfather hopes, will certainly continue the Gradovs' medical dynasty. He calls him, half-jokingly, Boris IV.

As the story unfolds, the Gradovs cross paths for various reasons with a number of mostly infamous historical figures: Stalin, Molotov, and Voroshilov, the leaders of the Bolshevik Party; ominous secret police officials such as Menzhinsky and Beria; the military commanders Frunze and Bliukher; and others.

Because of his high-ranking medical position, Dr. Gradov finds himself inadvertently privy to certain Kremlin secrets, particularly those concerning the leaders' internal organs—hearts, stomachs, kidneys, and any other organs they may have possessed. He even learns that Stalin has six toes on one of his feet.

One day, Dr. Gradov, along with other medical authorities, is compelled against his will to endorse a sinister procedure that has been performed on the people's commissar of defense, Commander Frunze, which results in Frunze's death on the operating table. For the rest of his life, the doctor will not forgive himself for surrendering to fear and violating his Hippocratic oath.

By the end of the 1920s all opposition groups inside and outside the Communist Party have been defeated, and Stalin has consolidated all power in his own hands. In order to avoid an imminent arrest, Nina Gradov has fled Moscow, to Tbilisi in the Caucasus, where she finds shelter among her mother's lovely, jovial relatives and colorful Georgian poets.

At the peak of Stalin's ruthless purges, both of Dr. Gradov's sons fall victim to the state-run terror. They are tortured by KGB investigators and then sent to the Siberian labor camps. Nina is spared from the purges due to the efforts of her cousin and lover Nuzgar, who is otherwise a cynical thug and close associate of Beria. Gradov himself expects to be arrested at any moment. Instead, a KGB unit arrives one night to take away his daughter-in-law Veronika because she is the wife of an "enemy of the people."

Thus has the Gradovs' warm family nest in Silver Grove been scattered. Boris and Mary are left with their orphaned grandchildren and a peasant boy, Mitya, who was adopted by Kirill and his wife, Cecilia Rosenbloom, during the cruel collectivization campaign. Ironically, Gradov is given the high honor of nomination to the Supreme Soviet, which he accepts, despite the grave humiliation, for the sake of his remaining family.

In 1941, Hitler unexpectedly attacks his ally Stalin, and almost succeeds in capturing Moscow. During these desperate days, when the capital is on the verge of being captured by Guderian's tanks, Nikita Gradov is freed out of the blue from a prison camp in Kolyma, and his commission is restored. Needless to say, his wife Veronika is freed from the camps too. Placed at the head of a special crack army, Nikita from that moment on enjoys meteoric advancement within the Soviet military hierarchy, and is ultimately promoted to marshal of the USSR and commander of the Reserve Front, which is always sent into the most decisive battles. His career is broken off on German territory, when a lucky shot by a German boy, a fanatical member of the Hitler Youth and Volksturm, kills him. His death comes ten days before Germany's surrender, and on the very day when the KGB planned to arrest him for being overly independent in his honest approach to a group of Polish resistance members.

Before succumbing to this tragic fate, Marshall Gradov is unaware that his son, Boris IV, member of a Spetsnaz commando unit, is fighting near the position of his own army in Poland. The young man, moved by a sense of patriotism and by an ardent desire "not to miss the great march of History," had volunteered for the army before reaching draft age. To his bitter disappointment, he finds himself in a secret unit of Head Intelligence Operations, which is chiefly engaged in killing Polish independence fighters rather than dealing with the Nazi army.

Meanwhile, Boris IV's childhood friend, the Gradovs' adopted son Mitya, now a prisoner of war, volunteers to join the Russian anti-Soviet Vlasov army fighting on the side of the Germans. Captured by the Soviets, he manages to escape from the execution ditch and disappears into thin air.

By a twist of fate, our former revolutionary and Trotskyite, poetess Nina Gradov, becomes a superstar during the war for her song "Clouds in the Blue," which stirs emotions equally on the front line and on the home front. She cannot forget her husband, Savva, a surgeon missing in action, but by the end of the war she falls in love with a Georgian painter, Sandro Pevzner.

Love was not totally suppressed by the atrocities of war. Marshall Gradov's widow, the still-beautiful Veronika, finds it too, this time in the person of a middle-aged bachelor, American diplomat Kevin Taliaferro. Trying to escape from the KGB's persistent attentions, she leaves Russia with him for the United States.

The story leads us from the battlefields to the wild voids of Kolyma, where the late Marshal Gradov's younger brother, Kirill, is still serving his ten years' term in the labor camps. A major spiritual transformation has overwhelmed the one-time Marxist philosopher, who has converted to Christianity and joined an underground group of fellow believers.

Thus, old Dr. Gradov, who has spent the war providing medical services for the army, finds himself in almost total solitude and disillusionment after the war. He is getting old, and in his house in Silver Grove in the dead of night can sometimes be heard groans of anguish.

Here the story flows into the novel the reader holds now in his hands. Continue, dear reader, and see if you can make out who were the real heroes of that seemingly endless winter.

Contents

The Winter's Hero

And God came driving by in five automobiles.
BORIS SLUTSKY

The author of the lines quoted in our epigraph, while having distinguished himself among the poets of the mature Soviet era by his talent, never attained the clarity of a Khlebnikov, and therefore, like the author of the epigraph in this work, Lev Nikolaevich Tolstoy, requires a certain amount of explanation.

It goes without saying that Boris Slutsky was a man brought up on the ideals of collectivism, materialism, internationalism, and other such communal ideals, and in calling Stalin "God," he used the name in a purely negative sense. It is, of course, not God, the Creator of all that is, whom he had in mind, but rather some sort of pagan idol, a usurper of the shining ideas of the revolution, a tyrant who had sneered at the inspiration of the young literary-institute types and established his cult over the cursed people's democracy. This is why he provided his "god" with a paradox that is staggering from the point of view of the materialist: the god traveled in five cars at the same time! We have before us a scene to make the skin crawl: the Arbat by night, and a pagan idol that had propagated himself into five automobiles was driving along in some unknown direction. He was in no hurry at all. One would say that he didn't even like going fast. After all, what can you expect from a non-Russian?

In the 1960s, one of these five machines was parked in a garage at the Mosfilm studios. It was perhaps the most important of them, the one to which the fundamental part of the idol, his body, had moved and had its being. It was a custom-made, armor-plated Buick with thick windows. Even with the most powerful of motors, it would be difficult to imagine such a monstrosity dashing along. Its movement was unhurried and steady and inspired unimaginable horror. The other four black creatures rolled along before and behind. Together they formed a single whole, the "God" of the Communists.

From time to time, the writer who sets two opposing feelings, fear and valor, alongside each other may be tempted to say that they are manifestations of the same magnitude. Fear, however, is more comprehensible, being closer to biology, to nature. In principle, it is akin to reflex. Valor is a more complicated business. That, in any case, is the way things present themselves to us at the moment this volume begins, at the end of the 1940s, when the country that so recently had demonstrated marvelous bravery was in the grip of the stupefying fear of Stalin's five-car embodiment.

Chapter 1

━━━━━━━━━ ☆ ━━━━━━━━━

MOSCOW SWEETS

The *Felix Dzerzhinsky* was sailing into Nagaevo Bay. An immensely proud bird of the sea, it might even have been called a true "stormy petrel of the Revolution." It is not usually the profiles of such crafts that come to mind when one thinks of the Sea of Okhotsk with its slave ships and stumpy old boats like the crumbling *Jurma*.

The *Felix* made its appearance in these latitudes after the war in order to become the flagship of the Dalstroi fleet. Various rumors about the giant from abroad circulated among the recently freed convicts. Some even spread the story that the craft had belonged to Adolf Hitler himself and that the ill-fated Führer had made a gift of it in 1939 to our "Great Guide" to strengthen the bonds between the two "socialist" countries. Maybe Hitler had presented it as a gift and maybe he hadn't, but then he had gotten greedy and taken it back and nearly snapped up Moscow in the bargain. History, of course, punished him for his treachery, and now the old boat was ours again, fortified for all time with the proud title "Knight of the Revolution." According to the fanciful version, nearly the whole Great Patriotic

War had broken out because of this tub. There's no telling, though, what yarns former zeks will spin when, with a blizzard raging outside, they gather in the barracks over chifir, a kind of drug made of incredibly strong tea. It was natural, of course, that they would pin to any such story the name of their favorite hero, a man nicknamed "Ivan and a Half."

"Ivan and a Half" was powerfully built, a superb specimen, young and statuesque. Yet at the same time he was a mature, animallike zek. He had been given terms that, all told, added up to 485 years and included four death sentences, rescinded at the last moment by the great Stalin himself. It was in fact "Ivan and a Half," and not some admiral, whom the Great Guide had entrusted to bring the *Felix* to Kolyma with its living cargo. How had a zek come to be given command of a convict shipment? The secret lay in the fact that 1,115 former Heroes of the Soviet Union—that is, a restless lot—were sitting in the hold of the *Felix*. "Get the bastards to Kolyma," Stalin had said to "Ivan and a Half," "and you'll become a hero yourself, you'll write your name in gold in the annals. Where? In the annals, you asshole, in the annals! And if you don't get them there, I'll shoot you myself, or get Lavrenty Pavlovich Beria to do it."

"Your assignment will be carried out, Comrade Stalin," replied "Ivan and a Half," and he flew off to the Far East with a great war ace, Pokryshkin. What happened then? The *Felix* tied up at the American port, "Sanitary Frisco." President Heinrich Truman was there to meet it. Each hero was given his rank back and a million dollars. Now they're all living well in America: fed, clothed, and shod. As for "Ivan and a Half," Heinrich Truman forked over $10 million for betraying the USSR and gave him a dacha in Argentina as well. No, "Ivan and a Half" said at this point, I didn't betray the Motherland, I was saving my comrades in arms. I don't want your money, Citizen Truman. And he took the *Felix* back to his native shores. While he was still sailing, Stalin received word of the affair and was unabashedly delighted: there's the sort of people we need, not scum like you, Vyacheslav Mikhailovich Molotov.

An MGB regiment was sent to the Far East for the execution of our hero. A cameraman filmed the end of "Ivan and a Half," and the scene was shown to every member of the Politburo individually. In fact, it was of course a double who had been shot, while "Ivan and a Half" was invited by Stalin to eat roast mutton and drink a samovar full of spirits. After that, "Ivan and a Half" put on the uniform of a colonel in the MGB, took off for Dalstroi, and disappeared for a time into one of the far-off camps.

★

Such tall tales sometimes reached even the captain of the *Felix,* but he was not interested in this sort of folklore. In fact, it was unclear just what he was interested in. Standing on the bridge of his vessel, which had once been a cable layer in the Atlantic—the Nazis had seized it from a Dutch company, and it had ended up in the Soviet Union in the form of a war trophy—the captain surveyed without interest yet attentively the steep cliffs of Kolyma, which continued without interruption to the bottom of Nagaevo Bay, the small waves of which were now dancing up and down in concert, like a crowd of zeks trying to warm themselves. The combination of deep and vivid hues—the crimson of some of the rocks and the leaden coloring of some of the passing clouds, for example—did not interest the captain. The weather conditions, naturally, he followed with keen attention. We arrived on time, he thought, it would be good to get away on time as well. In the past, the bay had been known to become icebound in a single night.

As he gave orders in a temperate voice to the machinists, nimbly mooring the great hulk to the piers of the "jackal country," as he always called Kolyma in his mind, the captain tried not to think about his cargo or, as the load was referred to in countless accompanying manifests, the "contingent." Throughout the war, the captain had taken goods across the Pacific from Seattle as part of the Lend-Lease program. He was quite content with his lot and had no fear of Japanese submarines. Our captain, not old at all, had been an entirely different man then. In those days, absolutely everything about the Allied country across the sea interested him. He had no trouble finding a common language with the "Yankees," since already he knew English. Life at sea back then had been a delight. "Eh, if only . . . ," he not infrequently now said to himself in the solitude of his cabin. He always stumbled on the stone of that hopeless subjunctive, though, and never continued the thought. When all is said and done, my job hasn't changed, it's still ship transport. What they load into my holds at Vanino is none of my business, be it bulldozers or a living workforce. There are other people who take upon themselves the obligation of transporting this living force—call them "zek haulers" if you will—but not me, the captain of a 23,000-ton-displacement craft. I'm under no obligation at all to poke my nose into the other meanings of these trips that have nothing to do with navigation. Those other meanings don't have a damned bit of interest for me.

The one thing that did interest the captain was the light Studebaker that always went along with him in a specially created compartment in the hold. He had bought the vehicle in Seattle, in the last year of the war, and now, during stopovers in Vanino, and in Nagaevo as well, it was lowered onto the pier like a swan and the captain would sit down behind the wheel. There was nowhere for the captain to go in either port, but nevertheless he drove, as if affirming his role of international seaman and not a despised "zek hauler." He loved his "Stude" even more than his own wife, who seemed to have forgotten all about him, living as she did in the midst of a large number of sailors in Vladivostok. On the other hand, it looked as though quite a dirty business was coming to a head over the car: more than once the question had been raised in the Party Committee as to whether the captain was abusing his position in the service, setting himself apart by his attraction to foreign trash. In the year this story begins, 1949, a thing like keeping an American car for one's personal use could lead to unpleasantness. To make a long story short, this experienced navigator, the captain of the zek hauler *Felix Dzerzhinsky,* was in a chronically depressed state of mind, which had already come to be accepted by those around him as a character trait. This did not prevent him from displaying exceptional professional qualities and, in this instance, carrying out the mooring to the Nagaevo harbor wall without a hitch.

The mooring lines were fastened and the gangplanks let down, one from the upper deck for the crew, another from a hatch slightly above the waterline for the "contingent." Around the latter were already standing the ranking officers of the guard and guards with rifles and dogs. A brigade of civilian workers from the delousing unit stood idly behind the chain. Among them was supply clerk Kirill Borisovich Gradov, born in 1902, who had served his sentence to the bitter end, and then another six months "pending special instructions." He was now settled in Magadan, having been deprived of his rights as a citizen for a period of five years. One of Kirill's "brothers in arms" from the collective fur farm had gotten him the job in the delousing unit. After his adventures in Kolyma, the work was a sinecure. The pay was more than enough to buy bread and tobacco, and he had even managed to scrape together enough for a black overcoat fashioned from a secondhand pea jacket. The most important thing, however, was that in one of the barracks a clerk was provided with something that Kirill had forgotten even how to dream about, and the words for which he often pronounced with a certain blissful sigh—"a separate room."

He had recently turned forty-six. His eyes retained their former brightness but seemed to have somehow changed in color, tending to a cool Kolyma blue. His eyebrows had grown bushier for some reason, and strands the shade of aluminum had made their appearance in them. Wrinkles ran down his cheeks, lengthening his face. In his baggy, ludicrously short clothes and felt boots, he looked like a typical Kolyma bum and had long ago stopped being surprised when someone shouted "Hey, Pop!" at him on the street.

In theory, Kirill could buy a ticket at any moment and leave for the "mainland." Of course, he could not get permission to live in Moscow or its environs, but he could—again in theory—find a place to live at precisely the 101-kilometer limit. In practical terms, however, that was out of the question, and not only because the price of the ticket seemed astronomical (though both his father and his sister would send the needed sum of 3,500 rubles straightaway) but basically because a return to the past seemed to him entirely contrary to nature, like entering into some sort of pastoral scene depicted on a Gobelin tapestry.

He wrote to Nina and his parents that, yes, of course he would come, just not right now, because the time was not right. Just when the time would be right, he did not specify, throwing all of them in Moscow into a panic: Was he really going to sit out his whole five-year term of deprivation of rights? Meanwhile, a so-called "second wave" was breaking over Magadan. They were arresting those who had only just finished their sentences and come out into supposed "freedom." Kirill was calmly awaiting his turn. His Christian faith had become firmly rooted, and collective suffering now seemed more natural to him than the joys of individual "lucky types." With his separate room, he considered himself a "lucky type." He took pleasure in every minute of this so-called freedom, which in his mind he no longer thought of freedom per se as such but rather as the absence of armed guards. He delighted in a trip to the store or the barber shop, not to mention the cinema or the library. He had been "free" for a year and a half now, yet he was still unconsciously ashamed of himself for being so impudently successful at evading work. In his heart of hearts, and particularly in his dreams, he felt that the natural place for a suffering man was not all at the milk-and-honey buffet of freedom but in the columns of prisoners under guard being led slowly toward their doom. He remembered that it is difficult for a rich man to enter into the kingdom of God, and he now considered himself a rich man.

In all of Kolyma, in all of that country of millions of imprisoned laborers, there was probably not a single copy of the Bible. A civilian worker would have been pulled out of Dalstroi or even thrown into a cell for such an act of sedition as reading the Bible, and as for a zek, he would be sent straight off to the mines of the First Directorate—the uranium mines, that is.

And yet, here and there in the barracks among Kirill's friends circulated the fruits of the camp's creative spirit: tiny books that occupied no more than half of the palm of one's hand, sewn together with needle and thread, covered with a bit of burlap or a scrap of a blanket, in which the newly converted Christians wrote down in indelible pencil what they remembered from Scripture, snatches of prayers, or simply retellings of the works of Jesus; everything they could remember from their pre-Bolshevik childhood; everything that had survived the journey through three decades of godless living and their own atheistic delirium, as it now seemed to them.

One day, someone called out to Kirill on the creaking wooden planks of Magadan's streets. Kirill's head began to spin—the voice had flown straight from the tapestry of an unreal country, from Silver Forest. The stubby figures of two former zeks in trousers padded with cotton wool who had met by chance as they were racing past each other now slowly, with amazement, turned toward each other. From a graying frame of disheveled locks and a beard, from a tanned, wrinkled face, the eyes of Stepan Kalistratov, Imaginist poet and unfortunate husband of his sister Nina, were peering greedily at Kirill.

"Styopka, you survived?"

As it turned out, not only had the former bohemian survived, he had somehow landed on his feet. He had come out of the camps well before Kirill, since he had been arrested earlier. He was working as a security guard at an automobile repair shop—that is, doing nothing at all except writing poetry, just as he had done his whole life. What, you managed to write poetry even in the camps? A shadow came over Stepan's face. No, in the camps not so much as a line. Imagine that, ten years and not a single line of verse! And now here we are in the middle of an opulent Pushkinesque autumn. Aren't you afraid of being arrested again, Stepan? No, I'm not afraid of anything anymore: everything important is behind me now, my life is over.

Stepan introduced Kirill to his friends. Once a week they gathered at the quarters of two ladies from the literary circles of Petersburg who were now working as nannies in a day nursery. They sat on rickety stools, with their legs crossed as though they were in the drawing room of the House of Writers. They talked of the early symbolists, of Vladimir Solovyov and the cult of Sophia.

> Not Isis thrice-crowned
> Will save the souls of mortals
> But she the eternal, radiant
> Virgin of the rainbow portals. . . .

recited someone with a phenomenal memory, a former fellow at the Institute of World Literature who now handed out basins at the city bathhouse.

What else, then, could a man who had left his Marxist beliefs in the convicts' burrows of Kolyma—like a shed snakeskin—need? No more armed guards, his daily bread, the joy and humility of a new faith, mystic poetry in a group of refined intellectuals—and a renaissance of the Silver Age using Dalstroi for cover at that! Kirill couldn't shrug off the feeling that he was out of place in the paradise of Magadan. He felt almost as though he was stealing something, as though he had come looking for a free handout at the engineers' campfire, where it was warmer. Meeting the new formations that arrived in endless streams, seeing them off to the mines of the North after disinfection, he pictured himself in their ranks. That was what he, Kirill Gradov, had been made for, and not for anything else—to depart in the company of all those who were suffering and to disappear with them.

At that moment, then, watching the group of prisoners emerging from the belly of the *Felix,* he felt a strong desire to break through the chain of soldiers and join the stinking crowd tormented by the stench of the hold. He had never learned to regard these unloadings as a quotidian task. At every unloading, as the human mass emerged from its steel container to go off to the expanses of the labor colonies, he heard the sound of a symphony playing, an organ with an orchestra, the tragic echo of an unknown temple.

Now they were coming out and greedily gulping at the abundance of the God-given atmosphere, seeing the clear skies and the gloom of the new earth, the prison to which two thirds of them, if not actually three quarters, would go forever. One way or another, though, the days of being half suffocated, of the rocking boat and nausea, were behind them. While they were being assigned to camps, they could enjoy a dose of oxygen well above the normal ration. They moved to and fro, swayed back and forth, supported one another, and looked around at the new shores. Perhaps these minutes held nothing but routine for the soldiers and the officers of the guard, but for the zeks, for every new formation, every moment was charged with significance. Wasn't it because of this that Kirill heard the tragic yet invigorating music? Eleven years ago, when I scrambled out of the hold of the *Volochaevsk,* light-headed from the air and the open spaces, I felt the same thing, a sort of awed inspiration I'd never felt before. In those days I didn't want to think that it might mean I was coming closer to God.

The formation with its rucksacks and cases bound with string gathered on the pier at the feet of the bridge cranes. Here and there could be seen remnants of foreign uniforms—an overcoat that was not of a Russian cut; a hat that one could see had once been a square Confederate headpiece; a Finnish Army fur cap. Even among the civilian odds and ends there was an occasional glimpse of something that had miraculously made it over from a stylish European shop—a hat made of fine felt, a checkered alpaca scarf, loafers quite out of place in the frozen muck. . . . From time to time through the steady hum a non-Russian name was heard, or the sound of languages from the banks of the Danube. . . . A strangely rapturous look now began to shine forth from faces almost obscene in their torment, a look that was not necessarily foreign: perhaps there were still Russian eyes that had not lost the ability to shine.

The soldiers pushed the male prisoners from the *Felix* out beyond the rails. Now the female sector of the cargo began pouring forth. The register of sounds immediately shifted. It was obvious that this time the women were mostly Galician peasants. Their common lot, it seemed, lent boldness to their voices, and they chattered away as though they were in an open-air market. They too were crowded off to the other side of the rails, right up to the base of a jagged mossy dormant volcano, and there the guards began sorting them by categories.

Kirill and the rest of the workers in the medical brigade waited for orders from those in command. The degree of lice infestation and the number of infectious diseases would determine the level of disinfection of the clothing. Owing to the constant shortage of overalls, they would also have to decide how many jackets, pairs of trousers, and boots to issue, and according to what principle, as well as the amount of time the items of clothing would last: most of these jackets, trousers, and boots had been patched time and time again. They were mere rags that had come down to those arriving from people who wouldn't be needing them anymore. The question of whom to give clothing to, and whose would hold out until they reached the camps and the mines, was being decided. Though he was forbidden to speak to any of the prisoners, Kirill nevertheless explained to many of them that they might be given something of better quality once they reached the camp, while if they took these rags from the disinfection station, they would have no hope of a replacement. Once in a while he also talked with the greenhorns, telling them it seemed like only yesterday when he had been in their shoes, and that he had knocked off a ten-year sentence and then come out, a survivor. The newcomers peered at him with great curiosity. He gave many of them hope by this bit of information—here's a man who's still alive, he made it through. That means that we've got a chance that this place isn't as hopeless as they say in that song "Kolyma, Kolyma, planet of wonder, here winter rages all twelve months, then the rest is summer." Someone, though, would look on with horror: ten years, from start to finish, like this old man! Can it be that our ten-, fifteen-, twenty-year terms will go by the same way, that there will be no miracles, that our dungeon won't crumble away?

There was plenty of work to be done. The guards were running about with papers, calling out surnames, serial numbers, and articles of the Criminal Code. There still remained the task of separating the so-called "special settlers" from the skeleton of the formation, from that group to pick out the "special contingent," and then, within that group, to determine who was "socially harmful" and who was "socially dangerous." The free workers circled the guards smartly, taking orders. Kirill hustled about with a notepad and a ring of keys, one of which, incidentally, was to a storeroom where leg irons for particularly important "guests" were kept. On the whole, a certain solicitude aimed at keeping the living cargo alive was shown by the authorities. Otherwise, what would be the point of hauling them all in this way? Showing a profit was one of the principles of socialist construction.

Today's formation was proving to be a particular headache for the bosses. Half the group was made up of those classified as "socially nonalien"—thieves, in other words. Among them, according to rumors and reports from various "mother hens," was a band of "monks," the faithful of one of the two warring cliques of criminals in the gigantic camp system. Once upon a time, in the old, perhaps even Leninist, days, the world of prison criminals had been divided into two camps. The "monks" had been faithful to the thieves' code and had not squirmed or humbled themselves with work in the camps, hadn't played cat and mouse with the bosses; they had gone mad, they had rebelled. The "bitches," on the other hand, had schemed, informed, done anything to get by, even stooping so low as to go out on general work assignments—in other words, they had gone crawling. As a consequence, an enmity based on ideological grounds had sprung up between the two groups, as it might have between two factions of the Social Democratic movement. Later on, though, all codes had been forgotten, and the enmity had degenerated into hostility for its own sake. Some six months or so ago, one of the camps in Kazakhstan had been chosen as a battleground. By means of the complicated system of the camps' internal migration, powerful forces of "bitches" and "monks" had been brought in. The "monks" had triumphed in the bloody clash. The remaining "bitches" had mingled with the regular shipment of convicts and, by means of bribes, extortion, and threats, had made their way to Kolyma. The rumor was that they had established themselves solidly there, particularly in the Magadan-Nagaevo quarantine camp. Now the Northeastern Corrective Labor Camps Directorate (NECD) had gotten word that "monks" had begun arriving, both in scattered groups and individually, and with a single aim in mind—to wipe out the "bitches" once and for all. It hardly needs to be said that the story couldn't get along without "Ivan and a Half," who was, of course, the cleanest of the "monks," maybe even some sort of marshal of the underworld. It was whispered that he had come in one of the formations in the guise of an ordinary zek; or that he had flown in on an Il-14, passing himself off as a personal friend of General Vodopyanov; or that he had been dragged in with the leg-iron crew; or that General Nikishov, head of Dalstroi, had met him, and that Nikishov's wife, Second Lieutenant Gridasov of the MVD—Ministry of Internal Affairs—had made a bed for him in their private house on Stalin Prospekt.

In any case, "Ivan and a Half" was here. One way or another, NECD took these whispers, reports, and chatter quite seriously—a slaughter could significantly undermine manpower. This was why the guards had an added headache on this day: now they had to pay serious attention to sorting out not only the politicals but the thieves as well.

Suddenly, in the midst of all the fuss, a sailor leapt over some packing crates and shouted to Kirill, who at that moment was hurrying along on the other side of the barbed wire enclosure, "Hey, buddy, do you know some prick called Kirill Gradov?"

Kirill stopped in his tracks. "As a matter of fact, Kirill Gradov, that's me."

"As a matter of fact," mimicked the sailor in a mocking voice. Then he squinted comically. "Well, then, come on up here, Pop, there's a passenger come for you, a dame."

"What do you mean, a dame?" Kirill asked in surprise.

The sailor had said the word "passenger" with particular scorn. It was clear that he felt awkward about doing a favor for some "passenger" by looking for some Gradov, who turned out to be some lousy old man, a Trotskyite from the looks of him. Kirill sensed this tone in his voice and for some reason fell into a state of great agitation, as he had on that day twelve years before when the NKVD investigator had asked him to "step in for a chat."

"All the passengers are already in the landing area," Kirill said with an air of absurdity, making a gesture in the direction of the barbed-wire compound in which the crowd of prisoners was assembled.

The sailor guffawed. "I'm talking about a real passenger, Pop, not a zek!"

He pointed with his index finger back over his shoulder in the direction of the gray-blue wall that was the starboard side of the *Felix* and then walked away.

On the verge of understanding what the business was about and refusing to believe it, Kirill cautiously—as if by caution he could still avert whatever was coming—went off in the direction of the pier. He carefully skirted legs of cranes and stacks of cargo, and then suddenly, thirty feet away, he saw a familiar old woman coming down the main gang plank.

At the first instant, he felt as though a weight had been lifted from his heart: it was not her, after all, only some woman he had known in a previous life, as it were. It couldn't be Cecilia—why, it simply wasn't possible. . . . The next moment, he realized that it was indeed his lawfully wedded wife, Cecilia Naumovna Rosenbloom, and not just some "old woman."

Stooped, bent down by an unimaginable quantity of sacks and string bags filled to the bursting point, she swayed awkwardly down the gangplank, her skirt askew as always, her skinny legs encased in an improbable pair of boots; even more incredible was a touch like something out of a painting by Rembrandt—a velvet beret, from beneath which protruded disorderly reddish locks of hair heavily streaked with gray. Her weighty breasts could not be contained by an overcoat that was manifestly too small for her. It seemed as though she would collapse at any moment beneath the weight of her bags, and her bosom, and the whole stunning moment. Sure enough, when she took her first step on Kolyma's soil, she tripped over a log and became entangled in a cable. Everything went flying into a puddle, and she fell to her knees in the dirt. Dangling behind her back in a string bag and striking her between the shoulders as she fell was an object the size of a head of cabbage. It was a bust of Karl Marx, whose features protruded from the openings in the string bag like a zek from behind barbed wire. Naturally, the swine on the deck watch of the *Felix* roared with laughter, and the guards on the pier guffawed as well. Kirill rushed forward and grasped his wife beneath the arms. She looked over her shoulder and, immediately realizing who it was, opened her mouth wide, spread her lips, absurdly smeared with lipstick, and let out a long, heartrending cry like the whistle of a steamship: "Kiri-i-ill, my da-a-arling!" "Celia, my Celia, you've come, my dearest. . . ." he muttered, kissing what he could of her, given the difficult position he was in, that is, her youthful ear and her flaccid cheek, which gave off a strong smell of hamburger fried in onions.

It would have seemed that this was the time for the young people to laugh at a love scene being played out between two scarecrows from a vegetable garden, yet for some reason the ship's crew and the guard detachment simply went on about their business, leaving the two alone to revel in their meeting. In order for mockery to enjoy any kind of success, of course, the object has to react in some way, has to get angry or burn with shame; but the object in this case, the man and wife, were so so oblivious to their surroundings that making fun of them would not have been interesting at all. Then again, one has to reckon with the possibility that this pathetic scene tugged at the heart-strings of some of the younger guards, dimly reminding them of the unending, unceasing misfortune of the Russian penal system. At any rate, everyone minded his own business, and two sailors on duty quietly and without further comment brought the most important of Cecilia's belongings down onto the pier—two carpetbags she had inherited from her father and a box full of classic Marxist tomes.

Man and wife were unable to move from the spot. Her eyes shining with inspiration, Cecilia put her hands on Kirill's shoulders and began to speak as though she were declaiming from the stage. "Kirill, my beloved, if only you knew what torments I have suffered these twelve years! If anyone has told you any stories, don't believe them! I was faithful to you! I turned away all other men, all of them! And there were many, you know, Kirill, there were many!"

Kirill still could not come to his senses. "What are you saying, Celia? What are you talking about? I don't understand. How did you come to be here, on this . . . on the *Felix Dzerzhinsky*?"

She laughed triumphantly. It turned out not to be so complicated after all. She had come on an assignment from the Department of Political Enlightenment. The what? I'm now on the faculty of the Evening University of Marxism-Leninism, my dear! Audacity can conquer cities, that's how it's done! She had gone to the Central Committee to see Nikiforov himself, and after a long discussion he had given his approval. No, no, there was nothing of what you're thinking of, unless you count, well, a few eloquent glances on his part. In the end he had realized she wasn't one of those and she was taking a genuine and Party-minded approach to a serious matter.

The most terrible thing was here in the Far East. You know, everything is growing here at a frantic pace, new buildings going up all over the place, streams of young people, unfeigned enthusiasm, the lines of transportation are overloaded. She had cooled her heels in Nakhodka for a week, trying to get a passage on a Dalstroi steamer, but it was no use. Then she had been told that the *Felix Dzerzhinsky* was sailing from Vanino to Magadan, and she had rushed off to Vanino. No one had wanted to talk to her there, so she had thrown herself on the captain. What else could I count on except womanly charms? Not a thing! And here was the result: she had sailed on the *Felix,* and the captain, a strict gentleman of the sea, had invited her to lunch in his cabin. Of course I kept everything within certain bounds, and our relations never went beyond those limits. . . .

Cecilia swung back and forth between muttering and shrieking as she babbled out all of this, taking no notice of anything around her, only looking at "her boy" with beaming eyes. She did not even seem to take any notice of the profound changes that had occurred in him. Cecilia Rosenbloom belonged to that comparatively small number of people who do not notice details and live only in the world of fundamental ideas.

In the meantime, Kirill's surname, accompanied by strong interjections, had begun to reach his ears from the other side of the nearby barbed-wire enclosure: "Gradov, goddammit! Where is that Gradov screwing around? Where the hell has that fucking Gradov got to?"

I have to get away from these guards—they're no better than a pack of jackals. The thought came to Kirill all of a sudden, as though the work at the delousing unit had long been more than he could bear. Now that my wife has arrived, I can't stay here any longer. I'll find a job as a stoker in a schoolhouse, God willing, or in the House of Culture—or anywhere where there's a boiler, for that matter.

Just then a certain Philip Bulkin, a scoundrel of a sort one doesn't meet every day, came walking by. Though he had nothing to do in the port that day, he of course couldn't let the arrival of a steamer and a shipment of prisoners pass him by, because there might be a way to profit from the situation. Kirill promised Philip a bottle of grain alcohol to take his place. "My wife has just arrived, you see," he said. "We haven't seen each other in twelve years."

"Interesting wife you've got there," said Bulkin, with a quick glance at Cecilia and her motley outfit and a more careful look at the bags lying in a heap around her. Philip Bulkin belonged to that class of people who concentrate entirely on details and pay no attention to fundamental ideas. "Tell me, did she happen to bring a phonograph needle with her?" When he learned to his surprise that Gradov's wife had not brought with her one of these scarce items, which changed hands for a ruble apiece in Kolyma, he agreed to take over the shift. This was, of course, sufficiently profitable to be to his liking.

After prowling the waterfront jungle for a while, Kirill found an unclaimed wheelbarrow and loaded Cecilia's things into it. One of the tightly packed string bags came into the "passenger's" field of vision, and she immediately pounced on it. Newspapers that were wrapped around some of the sacks flew everywhere like the feathers of a chicken being plucked. "Have a look at what I've brought for you, Kiryusha, Moscow sweets! I'll bet you've been missing them terribly!" In the course of her two-week journey, all these Moscow sweets had been crushed, soiled with grease, turned to liquid, or petrified, depending upon the consistency at which they had begun the journey. Nevertheless, she went on tearing at the sacks, breaking off pieces and stuffing them into Kirill's mouth. "Here are courabe, here are some grillage, here's some USSR marmalade for you, some Feinkuchen, strudel, Eirkuchen. . . . They're so tasty—why, you used to love all of this so, Gradov!"

He looked at her tenderly. It was obvious that his absurd wife by means of these sweets, which were in fact unimaginably delicious, if a bit moldy, as well as by addressing him by his surname in the Party fashion, just as she had many years ago, was trying to tell him that everything can be fixed in this best of all possible material worlds.

They arrived at the gates of the port. His mouth was stuffed with a sweet mixture. "Thank you, Rosenbloom," he managed to mumble, and they both laughed.

They had to slow down at the gates. The first column of male prisoners was passing. The zeks had removed all their belongings from their rucksacks and were now carrying them in their arms to the delousing point.

"Who are these people?" Cecilia asked in amazement.

An even more amazed Kirill forced himself to swallow the candied lump in one gulp. "What do you mean 'who are these people,' Rosenbloom? Why, you came with them!"

"Beg your pardon, Gradov, but how could I have come with them? I came on the steamer *Felix Dzerzhinsky*!"

"They were on board, too, Rosenbloom."

"I didn't see any of them there."

"You mean you didn't know . . . you didn't know . . . who it is that the *Felix,* that bird of good fortune, brings here?"

"What are you babbling about, Gradov?" she exclaimed. "It's such a wonderfully clean ship! I had a tiny cabin, but it was perfect. A shower off the corridor, clean sheets . . ."

"Out here that ship is known as a 'zek hauler,' " said Kirill, looking at the ground, which was not difficult since they were now climbing a hill and the wheelbarrow was heavy.

"What sort of jargon is that, Gradov?" she asked severely. Then she began to speak quickly, tugging at the nape of his neck endearingly, pinching his cheek: "Stop it, stop it, Gradov my darling, my dear one and only, there's no need for it, no need to exaggerate, to make generalizations."

Kirill halted for a second and said in a hard voice, "This steamer transports prisoners." When all was said and done, she had to know the way things really stood. After all, one could not live in Magadan without knowing the way things were done there.

This little tiff passed quickly without casting a shadow over their meeting. They went up the hill along a decrepit road barely sprinkled with macadam, pushing her belongings in front of them, and beaming at each other like Hansel and Gretel. Meanwhile, it was growing dark, and here and there among the pathetic huts and warped barracks of Magadan, for some reason all painted in the same dirty pink color, lights were being turned on. Cecilia finally began to take notice of the reality around her. "So this is Magadan?" she asked with artificial cheerfulness. "And where are we going to spend the night?"

"I have my own room," Kirill replied, unable to keep the pride out of his voice as he uttered the words.

"Now that's what I like to hear!" she sang out. "I promise you a hot night, my dear Gradov!"

"That's something I can't promise you, Rosenbloom, I'm afraid," he said, squirming guiltily and thinking, If only she, my dear old woman, didn't smell of hamburger fried in onions.

"You'll see, you'll see, I'll rouse the beast in you!" she said with a tigress grin, shaking her head at him. Her teeth were in a lamentable state.

They continued on up the hill for several more minutes and stopped at the crest. From there a view of the city of Magadan, lying in a broad dale between dormant Siberian volcanoes, spread before them. They saw its two wide intersecting streets, Stalin Prospekt and the Kolyma Highway, rows of five-story stone buildings, and clusters of small houses.

"This is Magadan," said Kirill.

At that moment, the streetlights on Stalin Prospekt were turned on. Through the clouds, the sun, just before setting behind the dormant volcanoes, threw a few rays onto the windows of the large houses in which the families of the Dalstroi administrators and camp bosses lived. At that moment, the city, viewed from the hill, seemed the embodiment of well-being and comfort.

"Very nice!" a surprised Cecilia said, and for the first time Kirill suddenly felt a certain pride in this city built on bones, in this clump of shame and sadness.

"This is the city of Magadan. The place we've just come from was only the village of Nagaevo," he explained.

A car drove by, snorting in low gear, its foreign headlights illuminated. On the steering wheel rested a pair of gloves of some fine animal skin with five round holes baring the knuckles. The captain's English nose in all its rigorous serenity sailed by.

The further they walked, the further they left behind the fashionable part of Magadan and the more terrible the maze of the criminals' settlement seemed to Cecilia: contorted barracks walls, guard towers, barbed wire, rubbish pits, streams of nightmarish liquids, clouds of boiler steam. From time to time something encouraging, something connected at least partly with life-giving modernity, sprang up: a playground with a figure of a Soviet fighting man; a sign reading SHAME TO THE WARMONGERS!; a portrait of Stalin over the gates of a construction materials depot. Kirill, however, went on pushing the wheelbarrow. They left those scattered buoys of socialism behind them and plunged into the chaos of the life led by zeks after the camps. Then, without any warning, swirls of snow came hurtling down straight out of the black skies, sudden and breathtaking. "That's the way it always happens here," Kirill explained. "The first snowstorm starts all of a sudden. But we're already here."

Illuminated by a hysterically flickering streetlight was a low, pink, shattered wall, from which protruded all kinds of refuse. The snowstorm was hammering at the door. Kirill had no small difficulty in pulling it open, and then he began to drag her things inside.

The floor of the long corridor in which Cecilia found herself seemed to have survived a major earthquake. Here and there planks were arched into humps, while in other spots they had fallen in or stuck out to one side. At the end of the corridor were the "public conveniences," from which emanated an odor that was a mixture of excrement, chlorine, and overcooked seal fat. The corridor was lined with at least thirty or so doors, each one deformed and protruding in its own fashion. The sounds coming from behind the doors ran the gamut from timid flatulence to the sublime voice of the diva Pantofel-Nechetskaya, performing an aria from the opera *Natalka-Poltavka* on Radio One. Somewhere, the threat of "I'll bite it off!" was repeated over and over in a strange, monotonous tone. Whether it was a man's voice or a woman's was impossible to say. The mournful and ominous voice mangled the first two syllables of the disagreeable words and then shrieked the third and fourth in identical fashion each time, so that what emerged was sounded something like "I-i-i-lll b-i-iite it o-o-ff!"

Sprawled in the corridor was a motionless body, which Cecilia tripped over, naturally.

"Well, it's not exactly Moscow here, you understand," Kirill muttered with embarrassment, removing a dangling padlock and opening the plywood door that led into his "separate room." An "Ilych lamp" with a long hanging cord made shorter by having several knots tied in it illuminated an area of five square meters which could barely contain a bunk covered with a ragged blanket, a bookshelf, a small table, two chairs, and a bucket.

Well, go on, sit down. Where? Right here. All right, I've sat down, and now I'm lying down—turn off the light! What, you mean right away, Rosenbloom? I've been waiting eleven years for this, Gradov! I chased away all comers, and there were so many of them! Well, you know, Celia dear, as they say, I'm completely . . . No, that doesn't happen, it's never "completely . . ." Here take it and squeeze it, squeeze it, and before you even notice it . . . There you go, there you go, there you are, Kirillchik, there you go, honey, there you go now . . .

It's a good thing it's so dark, thought Kirill, so that I can't see what an old woman I'm having it off with. Suddenly, in a dim band of light he glimpsed the string bag with the bust of Marx. The rounded features of the founder of scientific communism were turned toward the ceiling of the barracks dug into the earth. The presence of the founder somehow lit a fire in Kirill. The smell of the masticated cutlet vanished. The gamut of sounds around him, including the monotonous "I'll bite it off" was muted. Blue-blouse, Komsomol girl, 1930, the year of the great turning point, of the great fuckover, electrification, close ranks, training! Cecilia shrieked exultantly. My poor little girl, what has happened to you!

In the silence that followed this pathetic scene, someone groaned so close by that the voice seemed to come from the same pillow.

"Kiryukha's brought a dame in," said the lazy voice.

"Can it really be that Kirill Borisovich has found himself a tart?" a woman's surprised voice added.

The wall shook as Kirill turned lazily, and at the foot of the crumbling plywood door he saw a black heel belonging to the inhabitant of the neighboring "private room."

"My wife has arrived from the mainland, Pakhomich," Kirill said quietly. "My lawfully wedded wife, Cecilia Naumovna Rosenbloom."

"Congratulations, Gradov," said Pakhomich, obviously now lying with his back to the wall. "And welcome, Cecilia Rosenbloomovna."

"I promise you, soon we'll have a real private room," Cecilia whispered directly in Kirill's ear.

Her whisper produced a tickling sensation that traveled through his ear straight down into his nose. Kirill sneezed.

"Want a drink?" asked Pakhomich.

"We'll drink tomorrow," Kirill replied.

"You bet," Pakhomich sighed.

Kirill explained to Rosenbloom's youthful ear, "He's from our Tambov Province. He's a good man. Received a sentence for armed rebellion . . ."

"What stupid jokes, Gradov," said Cecilia with the dismissive wave of a tired belly dancer.

They would have to unpack her things, of course. Kirill set about the task, trying to avoid the direct gaze of the old woman puttering about next to him. In fact, she wasn't really an old woman. After all, she's two years younger than I am, which makes her forty-four. A good woman is like a good wine, she gets better with age. Who knows, maybe Rosenbloom will recover at least some of the bloom of her youth.

"What's all this, Gradov?" Cecilia suddenly exclaimed. She was standing, hands on her hips, in front of his bookcase, on the top shelf of which stood a sort of miniature altar, a triptych containing icons of the Savior, the Virgin Mary, and Saint Francis of Assisi with a wild goat beneath his arm. These makeshift icons from the Susuman camps had been a gift to Kirill from Stasis the medic before they had parted: he had still had another three years to serve on his sentence.

"Those, Celia, are the dearest things I own," he said quietly. "You still don't know that when I was in prison I became a Christian."

He was expecting an explosion, a flaring up, a furious outpouring of Marxist faith. Instead, however, he heard only a strange clucking of her tongue. My God, Rosenbloom is crying! Almost blindly she extended a hand and placed it on his head like Saint Francis petting his brother the wolf and whispered, "Poor boy, my poor dear, what has happened to you? Well, it doesn't matter," she said, straightening up. "You'll get over it!" With a vigorous gesture, she untied the cord around the bust of Marx and set it gingerly on the shelf next to the icons. Now we'll see who wins out! The two of them laughed in relief.

Now then, isn't this idyllic? An electric teapot from Moscow is boiling. A package of "Georgian tea, first class" is open. Lumps of stuck-together sweets are scattered on the table. The first snowstorm of the autumn of 1949 is blowing outside. The decrepit dug-in barracks is silent except for the voice of the opera singer Sergei Lemeshev coming from a radio somewhere: "Will I fall, shot through with an arrow?" Next door, Pakhomich and his girlfriend, "Beer Belly," inspired by the example of their neighbors, are going at it themselves.

Cecilia pulls out a twelve-year-old photograph taken on the veranda at Silver Forest after their wedding reception. Everyone was there: Bo and Mary, Pulkovo, Agasha, their fourteen-year-old kulak orphan Mitya, Nina and Savva, eleven-year-old Boris IV, and Nikita the young division commander, more amused than any of them, together with the irresistible Veronika, who was wearing a white dress with enormous printed flowers at the shoulders. Ah, Veronika . . .

"That bitch!" Cecilia hissed abruptly. "They could have set you free in '45, set you free and rehabilitated you as the brother of Marshal Gradov, the hero of all peoples, but that bitch, that prostitute buggered off with her American, with that spy. She took off for America without waiting to hear any news about her son. Don't even talk to me about her, she's a bitch and a whore!"

"Don't, Celia, don't," Kirill murmured, stroking her hair. "After all, we all loved each other then, just look at how much we loved each other. There was such a moment, here's the proof. It never flew away, it still exists right here alongside us."

When she's angry, her nose and her lips seem to stand up straight, like some sort of enormous comical rat. But now her face is smoothing itself out again—it looks like she's not mad at Veronika anymore. . . .

"You say we all loved each other, but I had eyes only for you."

Chapter 2

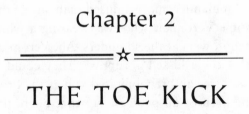

THE TOE KICK

From the squalor of Kolyma, dear reader, which has been following us so faithfully for over two books, my foreign pen, purchased here in Washington, D.C., at the corner shop for one ruble and seven kopecks and emblazoned on the side with the mysterious inscription "Paper Mate Flexigrip Rollen-Micro," will lead you to that huge city, Moscow, that over the centuries has alternately fallen into abject poverty and shabbiness and, with equal rapidity, manifested its age-old inclination toward gluttony, debauchery, and a strange sort of luxury that was as palpable as it was fantastic.

As before the war, housewives fling pots full of cabbage soup at one another in the kitchens of communal apartments and young people sleep on folding beds beneath tables in the same room with three generations of their revolting families. As before, half the monthly salary goes to purchase shoddy "fast-stepping" boots, while the sewing of a winter coat is an operation equivalent to the construction of a battleship. As before, the lines for the bathhouse begin forming early in the morning, while the bus stops resemble a wrestling free-for-all. As before, drunken war invalids hang around the train stations, while the blind and those who pretend to be ride the trains singing a fierce and unending adventure song called "I Was the Battalion Scout." As before, the inhabitants shudder at the sight of the black vans at night, and as before, everyone is careful not to open the door at the sound of meowing, so as not to let in the Black Cat Gang headed by, rumor has it, the powerful and mysterious bandit "Ivan and a Half."

Famine, on the other hand, is no more. As a matter of fact, it never existed in Moscow at all. It may not have been much, but the system of supplying the population of the capital by means of ration cards worked. After the currency reform of 1947, the ration cards were done away with, and baguettes, pretzels, challahs, French rolls (renamed "city rolls" a couple of years later in order not to spread the infection of cosmopolitanism), bagels, flat breads, and every imaginable sort of bun, along with at least half a dozen different rye breads, made their appearance in the bakeries. . . . In the pastry shops, in addition to a generous sprinkling of candies, whole fortresses of cream sprang up, reinforced by imposing collections of square and oval chocolates. In the delicatessens, in the cheese departments, one could now spot not only those who would gobble down anything, but connoisseurs—well, by that we mean any stout Muscovite, face marked by the past, explaining to a more simple-hearted neighbor, "Good cheese, my dear, is *supposed* to smell like old socks."

As for the meat department, well . . . make no mistake about it, ham and suckling pork filet gladdened the eye by their proximity to meat loaves and sausages of different shapes and sizes, some cut in exquisite cross sections so as to lay bare the mosaic of delicious items they were stuffed with. Frankfurters hung from the tiled walls, attached to them with some sort of tropical garland. Herrings of different sizes, some fatter than others, splashed about in pots that drew lines over the heads of the customers, lines that formed invisible yet perceptible trajectories heading for the spirits department. And there the patriotic eye was met with the spectacle of guard units on parade, from run-of-the-mill bottles of vodka to damask-clad liqueurs. Caviar was always to be had, in enameled cruets that disconcerted simple folk but were the joy of Stalin Prize laureates. Crabs preserved in jars were everywhere, for an affordable price, but there were no takers for them, in spite of the neon advertisements that crackled in the night.

The same could be said about cod liver, and anyone whose youth was spent in the glow of the static and unending blaze of Stalinist stability—"Tasty, nutritious cod liver!"—will confirm this.

The simple folk had their own pleasures: "Mikoyan" meat pies at six kopecks apiece, the aspic that lay on baking sheets everywhere and sold for a price that was practically symbolic, that is to say as close to communism as possible.

Here and there across the city, some of the best-known beer halls were still open. Let's duck into Yesenin's Place, for example, beneath the Lubyanka Passage. Comrade waiter immediately puts a plate down in front of you with the obligatory zakuski, without even asking: lightly salted rusks, soaked peas, a scrap of ham or bacon. And the beer, the beer! Draft or bottled, at your service! Zhiguli, Ostankino, Moscow by the half liter, Double Gold in small, spiraling vessels of dark glass!

Where had it come from, all of this Stalinist gastronomic abundance, and so soon after the ruin of the war years? Subsequently, it would be revealed to us that the cities enjoyed their abundance only by plundering the countryside, and we agree, though we permit ourselves to suppose that this is only a partial explanation.

There was order then! camp guard veterans invariably bark at us now. There was no stealing! There is truth in this, too, or, let us say, partial truth. The fact of the matter is that our Russian folk had been brought to such a state by the Cheka that they were afraid to steal. For a sack of corn ears from a freshly plowed field, for some rotting potatoes that were no good to anyone, you were sent off "by decree" to hack at the frozen tundra for ten years. It didn't matter what you took, a string of sausages or gold bars worth a hundred thousand dollars, anyone charged with "misappropriation of socialist property" got a long sentence at hard labor, and sometimes even the firing squad if there were aggravating circumstances. To the camps were sent even the bumblers who showed up late for work—in other words, who commited a crime that amounted to sabotage of reconstruction. On the whole, it's hard to argue: there was order.

Nevertheless, to fully explain the grandiose stabilization and the extension of authority that occurred at the end of the 1940s and continued on through the first half of the 1950s, we will have to jump from the well-worn rails of realism into the quagmire of metaphysics. My goodness, doesn't it seem that all that happened was this: by that time the organism of socialism (which we now know has to be compared with an ordinary human body, if only because of its life span) had reached its peak, pure and simple? Doesn't it appear that way? That is, socialism, if we regard it as a biological form—and why shouldn't we?—had reached the peak of its development, and that is why it ran for a while without a hitch.

Indeed, in those days, it was just past thirty years old—the prime of life for the average body. A limit to development is in the nature of any body, and of the given body, that is, socialism, in particular. Finally, a perfect social equilibrium had been attained: twenty-five million in the camps, ten million in the army, and as many again in the state security forces. The remaining sector of the working population was occupied with self-sacrificing labor; the state of mind and reflexes in all of them was impeccable. The maximum, and as it would later be revealed, final stage of geopolitical expansion had been reached. The other socialist countries, which had sprung into being nearby like a garland of inflated bags, were striving to keep up with the Russian metropolis by purging their cells. By the beginning of this volume, that is, in the autumn of 1949, each "People's Democracy" had already carried out its own "Great Purge": the "Rudolf Slánský band" was responsible in Czechoslovakia; the "László Rajk band" in Hungary; the "Traicho Kostov band" in Bulgaria. . . . Only one band of former friends had managed to squirm out of the Stalinist embrace, "the band of Josip Broz Tito and his vile satraps, his orchestra of American spies, murderers, and traitors to the socialist cause." The hatred directed at Yugoslavia was so intense that it undoubtedly bore witness not only to the state of an aging tyrant's gallbladder but also to the vigor, that is, the perfection, of socialist processes. The vilification of the traitors did not cease for a moment—neither in the press nor on the radio nor in official pronouncements. The Kukryniks brothers and Boris Yefimov vied with one another to see who could come up with the lewdest caricature of Tito. On one occasion, the obstinate marshal was shown as a female bulldog, with a fat backside, on a leash held by a long-armed Uncle Sam, with its nails, of course, dripping the blood of patriots; elsewhere, he was depicted as a cushioned stool flattened out in sycophantic delight beneath the bony bottom of the same insolent Uncle Sam. The fat haunches of the Yugoslavian Communists were constantly alluded to, as well as something effeminate in the features of Tito's evil face. Yet no matter what crimes and evil intentions the man was accused of, his most heinous intention was never mentioned. The fact was that the leader of the South Slavs was leaning not only toward a break with the camp of peace and socialism but also toward a rapprochement with the other side. As early as 1946, the "Tito clique" had proposed to Stalin that Yugoslavia join the USSR as a federal republic, with the entire "clique," naturally, becoming voting members of the Politburo. Stalin trembled more at that moment than he had in 1941. The "faithful friend of the USSR" would show up in the Kremlin with his haiduks, and at night we'd all be strangled in our offices and bedrooms. That's why he's so obstinate—the bastard wants to become the ruler not only of the South Slavs but of the Slavs as a whole.

It's curious that this conspiracy against progress, on the whole one of the most terrible ever, was never mentioned in the Soviet press. It was simply too great a sacrilege, the very idea of an attempt on the life of the great Father of the Peoples and his most precious child—the Soviet Union.

On the whole, not many specific crimes of any sort were mentioned, particularly when it was a question of slander directed at the Soviet Union. Yury Zhukov, for example, one of the best "warriors of the pen," wrote from Paris that there was an "explosion" of slander in the imperialist press. What these slanders were, however, he never stated, only that they were "vile calumnies, filled with zoological hatred for the bulwark of peace and progress." In this absence of names, this failure to mention examples was deemed the apogee of socialism, its fullest flowering, because the New Socialist Man had no need at all for details in order to be filled with righteous wrath.

And all of the most important Soviet writers, particularly those employed internationally in the struggle for peace—Alexander Fadeev, Boris Polevoi, Konstantin Simonov, Nikolai Tikhonov, Nikolai Gribachov, Anatoly Sofronov, Ilya Ehrenburg, Alexei Surkov—knew perfectly well that there was no need to be specific in talking about malicious slander. On the whole, the Party had arrived at a mutual understanding with the writers of that era. Literary public-minded-ness rejected any notion of conflict within Soviet society as sheer fiction fabricated by decadent cosmopolitans. Some time later, some unwise people tried to discredit the theory of the absence of conflict as a distortion, yet such a theory was itself another expression of the youthful maturity of the body of socialism, indeed its veritable apotheosis.

Every mature body ought to be inwardly healthy in every respect. However, socialism also needs a powerful external enemy. We had such an enemy, and not someplace called Yugoslavia, but the most odious, the most treacherous, and, of course, the most surely doomed of all: America! All other foes, even England, were less odious, less treacherous, and even less surely doomed, because they were weaker than America. It was in this standoff with America that our socialist body enjoyed significant successes: first it broke her monopoly on the atom; then it raised an indestructible barrier in Germany in the form of the Republic of Workers and Peasants; after that it carried out a mighty attack against the American satraps in Korea: "Time is moving faster. The tank drivers of North Korea are bringing freedom to the plowed earth on their armor," said Sergei Vasilievich Smirnov; fourth, it shortened the long arm of reaction in Western Europe by means of the peace movement; fifth, it did away with corrupting Atlantic influences at home once and for all.

Before us, then, basking in the triumphs of these glorious years, lies the city lauded in song by Satanic choruses—huge, yet nonetheless surprisingly alive, an eating, spitting, running, marching, drunkenly staggering city, and we shall look at it through the eyes of a sixteen-year-old youth making his appearance on Sretenka Boulevard from a godforsaken backwater in Tatarstan and those of a twenty-three-year-old young man returning to Gorky Street from the Polish taiga.

☆

Where had the invalids of the Great Patriotic War gone to? There had been an amicable joke about them among the people: "No arms, no legs, no luck—but, man-oh-man, they sure do fuck!" And then, one fine day, they had all simply vanished. The Kremlin had been worried: there was no reason for these limbless people to display themselves on the beautiful streets of the capital and in the marble halls of the metro.

In those days, the decisions of the city fathers were carried out with 100 percent efficiency in instantaneous and stunning fashion. The invalids of the GPW could live out the rest of their days perfectly well in places that did not have such great symbolic significance for the Soviet people and for all of progressive humanity. This was particularly true of those who had been literally cut in half and who moved about on ball bearings attached to little platforms lashed to their legless bodies. These truncated comrades had a tendency to get blind drunk, shout wild, reckless words, and fall over, their wheels spinning off on one side and thereby doing nothing to further the spread of optimism.

Drunkenness was not especially frowned upon as a general rule, so long as it was something indulged in by healthy, serious people on their off-hours from work or on holiday. Drink was of good quality and available everywhere, right down to the humblest dining halls. Even in the dead of night, one could pick up vodka, wine, and zakuski in the sparkling clean twenty-four-hour grocery store on Okhotny Ryad. By the beginning of the 1950s, all of the huge Moscow restaurants had reopened, and they didn't close until four in the morning. Many of them had first-rate orchestras. The struggle against Western music slacked off after midnight, and exciting cascades of sound of "Gulf Stream" and "Caravan" rang out beneath chic prerevolutionary chandeliers. Lighting effects were quite the rage, as well: restaurants would turn off the house lights, leaving only a few lamps projecting rays of various colors across the ceiling and through a many-faceted glass sphere. Beneath the patches of light given off by the sphere danced the youths who had survived the front lines and the only slightly younger up-and-coming generation. At moments such as these, it seemed to all the dancers that the charms of life would only keep on growing and would never turn into a wretched, impoverished hangover.

A whole corps of doormen was in full flower in Moscow, their chests as broad as their backsides were large, stripes down the sides of their trousers, and galloons, too. Not all of them were swindlers and swine; some proudly carried on the traditions of their profession, marking with satisfaction a turn, in aesthetic terms at least, in the direction of imperial values. The doormen were particularly pleased by the introduction of uniforms for different levels of society: black tunics for miners and railroad workers, gray jackets with velvet chevrons for lawyers of different classes. . . . As light manufacturing became more and more successful, it became obvious that soon the whole country would be wearing uniforms and then it would be easier to judge the clientele.

For the time being, of course, some anarchy did occasionally crop up. Moscow lads, for example, loved to walk around with their collars turned up, wearing eight-paneled bouclé caps cocked sharply to one side. Trendsetters particularly valued the long oilcloth raincoats that came from Germany as part of reparations. Czechoslovakian velvet zipper jackets were extremely popular, as were little suitcases of domestic manufacture with rounded edges. A portrait of the young Muscovite of 1948–49 would include: a bouclé cap, a zipper jacket, an oilcloth raincoat, and a small suitcase in one hand. As for details in the way of noses, eyes, and chins, you can supply those yourself.

The ideal of the young people in those years was the sportsman. The prewar words "physical culturist" were now used in an ironic sense to indicate another's lack of professionalism. A top-ranked bearer of the title "sportsman" was a professional or a semiprofessional (though, by contrast with the decaying West, professional sports in the Country of the Soviets did not exist). A sportsman received a stipend from the State, the precise amount of which no one knew, since it came under the heading "top secret." In extreme cases, when the authorities could not manage a stipend for a sportsman, he was supposed to receive coupons that could be redeemed for special foods. The sportsman was unhurried and laconic, measuring his words carefully in public, moving from place to place with a certain languor, concealing his colossal explosive force. The true sportsman, of course, had outgrown the German reparation raincoats. He appeared in public in streaming silver gabardine or in a pilot's leather jacket. He usually kept the bouclé cap, though, and sometimes even cut away the brim to remind him of his younger days as a hooligan.

Chief among the sports heroes were the big-league soccer players, particularly those from the Central Army Team and the newly created Air Force Club, supervised by, rumor had it, none other than Lieutenant General Vassily Iosifovich Stalin. Great popularity was also enjoyed by those who played a game that was called "Canadian hockey" at first and then renamed "hockey with a puck" in the course of the "anticosmopolitan campaign." Quite frequently, the football players and hockey players were one and the same—in the winter, when the playing fields were covered with ice, the "masters of the leather ball" donned skates, planted cycling helmets with metal rings that encircled the skull, or even tank drivers' helmets, on their heads, and then all hell would break loose: the puck whistled, skates scraped, powerful officers' bodies slammed into one another with oaths flying like sparks.

Lieutenant Seva Bobrov was one of those who in a soccer match could turn on a dime and plant the ball between the posts from sixty feet away; while in hockey, after executing a one-of-a-kind turn around the goal, he would slap the puck in right under the keeper's ass. And the young man had pleasing features as well: well groomed at the back of the neck, a lock of hair across his forehead, a square face the way Russians like them, and a smile that was at once shy and insolent. That was Seva.

Hockey games at Dynamo Stadium, temperatures well below zero. Clouds of steam over the mighty players, none of your heated stadiums with artificial ice. Veteran fans with sheepskin coats over their topcoats, a small glass factory in their pockets: quarter- and half-liter bottles of vodka. What Russian doesn't love fun on ice, after all!

The people of Moscow were mad about skating rinks as a whole. In Kazan, say, or in Warsaw, they didn't have such a thing. But in Moscow the evening crowds of young people carrying skates of all sorts—Norway Blades, Snow-Whites, Scalpels—came out of the Park of Culture metro station and crossed the Krymsky Bridge in the direction of the ice-covered park. There, on the frozen tree-lined walks, beneath the streetlights, dates were made, slippery courtships were set in motion, and there was even the occasional fight that drew blood. "I'll catch you, I'll catch you, you won't get away from me!" sang the girlish voice of a popular songstress over the loudspeakers.

Basketball was popular as well, but didn't have as wide a following. Older school-age children and college students had a particular fondness for this American game, which was still called *basketbol*, no patriot having managed to come up with a more Russian-sounding name. A provincial from Kazan who had himself recently begun to play and already knew how to dribble the ball and take a jump shot nearly went out of his mind when he saw the dimensions of basketball life in the capital. What wouldn't you give for Baltic players alone? The Estonian team, real European athletes, would come onto the court in Moscow with leather kneepads and carefully brilliantined and parted hair. They all smiled, sucked up to the referees, no swearing, wheezing, or spitting, and then won "with ease and elegance," as the newspapers put it. Or the Lithuanian giants, whirling around in the so-called eight formation before the astounded players from Kirghizia. Final score: 115–15 in favor of the big people from the small country.

Meanwhile, the ideal Moscow woman of those days was quite a long way from being a sportswoman. That ideal consisted of a combination of traits of the singer Klavdia Shulzhenko and the movie star Valentina Serova. The ideal promenaded around Moscow in platform shoes with straps that wrapped around the ankle and white felt three-quarter-length jackets. The glance of this ideal promised an eye-opening fulfillment of any romantic fantasy imaginable to mature men and growing boys alike. Our Pole, who had been extremely reserved in the complicated circumstances of his work abroad, found his head spinning in Moscow. One day he was buying a small orange pack of Ducat cigarettes on Sretenka Boulevard, when every man at the tobacco kiosk turned his head in the same direction. In the midst of the stubby Emkas and war-trophy BMWs, a huge green Lincoln with its top down was gliding by, with a dream of a blonde in the back seat. "They're taking Serova to the Kremlin for a fuck," one of the smokers announced by way of explanation in a tipsy bass voice. Whether it was Serova or not, and whether she was being taken to the Kremlin, and if it was really for a patriotic mission, no one knew, but our Pole for a long time afterward searched the tangle of the Moscow traffic for the green Lincoln with the serious intention of jumping onto its running board next time to get the dreamboat's telephone number. He never saw it again, though, and even at that instant on Sretenka Boulevard doubted the reality of the moment; wasn't it just a dream transferred by a trick of memory to Sretenka Boulevard?

There was one more curious aspect to this little scene worth mentioning: the offhand, informal mention of the Kremlin in the context of Moscow whoring. The drunken smoker did not, of course, represent the majority of the population, rather only the scattered and tattered "Moscow Men's Club." This club had not been wiped out yet and continued to shoot pool, bet on the horses, swill vodka and beer with sardines and pickled cabbage or, at the opposite end of the spectrum, take fine cognac with salmon on the starched tablecloths at the Hotel National and go womanizing from room to room.

As for the Kremlin, it was somehow difficult to imagine that such a graceful, pretty girl would be headed for that gloomy fortress. All right, maybe under the cover of darkness, in a Black Maria, they might drag in a girl with a gag over her mouth to be humiliated. . . . After all, they say He sits up at night, thinking about the fate of peace and progress. . . .

Walking along the Sofia Embankment one night, the "Warsawite" could not take his eyes off the Kremlin hill. The ruby stars were shining brightly and seemed to be turning against the dark autumn sky, while everything below the level of the towers was motionless and terrible. Suddenly a blazing light appeared and slid by. Most likely it was the headlight of a patrolling motorcycle, and yet our "Warsawite" trembled: it was difficult to avoid thinking that it was the eye of a dragon passing by in the darkness.

No one seemed to notice that the "Warsawite," who had been tried and tested and had seen all sorts of things, was trembling. The embankment was deserted, not a soul around except for a young man huddled under an arch some ten paces away. He had not noticed anything, either, it seemed, perhaps because he himself had shuddered when the gleaming eye passed along the Kremlin hill.

What sort of a strange young fellow is this? What's he doing here alone, and why is his gaze riveted on the residence of the head of the government? In Poland, he would be turned face to the wall and searched. . . . "Got a match?" asked the "Warsawite."

"I don't smoke," the man from Kazan replied.

Strange type, thought the first, it's not as though I asked him whether he smokes or not.

After all, he didn't ask me about smoking, thought the second, and blushed. What a disgrace, I'm turning red in front of some guy.

What's he blushing for, this kid?

"Aren't you cold?" The guy had in mind, of course, the kid's dubious-looking clothes. The wind was whipping up his sateen shirt like a sail. True, he did have something on underneath, but, whatever it might be, it didn't look like enough for a night in October. The Pole didn't know, of course, that this "something else" was the kid's secret source of torment. For some incomprehensible reason, the kid thought his shirt was just the sort of thing for a "end-of-the-'40s youth" to be walking around in, while the "something else" was just not chic: a jersey sewn by his grandmother. He had put on the warm, well-stretched garment of no particular color underneath his shirt and thrust it deep into his trousers so as not to spoil the line from behind. When he walked, though, the jersey gathered in lumps at the rear and sides, thereby depriving the population of the capital of the chance to admire his irreproachably youthful silhouette. A smartly cut, padded jacket could have resolved the problem, but in Moscow, in contrast to Kazan, these padded jackets were more often worn by janitors than by "end-of-the-'40s youth." That was why this kid had gone out in subfreezing weather in his best shirt, beneath which his ugly, shameful jersey lay concealed.

"No thanks, I'm not cold," he said to the young stranger.

They were about to go their separate ways, but they lingered for a second as though they wanted to remember each other. The lad in the black overcoat with the turned-up collar, dark red hair, and hard, light gray eyes enthralled the fellow from the provinces. There he is, the ideal modern Moscow youth, such self-confidence, must be an ace sportsman, thought the out-of-towner. Somebody should give a sweater to this snot-nosed romantic, thought Boris. He had brought a half-dozen heavy sweaters from Poland. But it would be strange, somehow, to give a sweater to some kid he didn't even know.

They parted. The provincial kid walked up to the corner of the embankment at an unhurried pace, afraid that the other man, if he turned back toward him, might think he was cold. At the corner he looked back. The young man was sitting on a motorcycle. His hair was blowing in the wind, but he restored order with a ski cap he produced from one of the saddlebags. If only I'd had an older brother like that, suddenly thought the provincial, who had turned the corner and then had begun to run for all he was worth, forgetting about the doubtful state of his shoes, which he thought about all the time, to be perfectly honest. He raced toward the Novokuznetsk station and the warm bowels of the metro to get out of the wind, but from time to time he seemed to become one with it, as though he were taking off in ecstasy.

His older brother had died in Leningrad during the siege. His father was serving a fifteen-year sentence in Vorkuta. His mother had only just been released from Kolyma and was now living in Magadan. Considering himself a representative of the "end-of-the-'40s youth," however, this provincial was thinking not about the millions like him who were registered where such things were noted as "children of enemies of the people" but about those who played basketball, soccer, and hockey; who roared by on motorcycles, both made at home and captured abroad; who danced the rumba and the fox-trot, whirling their partners, stunning Moscow girls, around with assurance and ease.

In fact, Moscow was a stopover for this provincial on his way to Magadan. Until this trip he had never been out of Kazan, where he had aspired with all his young heart to become an urban romantic. Taking no notice of the poverty all around him, he gazed at the twilight silhouettes of the towers and rooftops, the dried-up fountains and boarded-up windows of the *belle époque*. And then suddenly he had landed in the great wide world, in the whirl of everyday life in the capital, where Kazan is just a city that Vladimir Mayakovsky, that bard of cities, found nothing better to say about than: "Old and cross-eyed, there stands Kazan . . ."

From Moscow, he was supposed to fly to Magadan with his mother's patron, a woman who lived in Kolyma as a free citizen and was returning from a holiday. The woman had extended her stay in connection with some family business, and in the meantime he spent his time wandering the streets of Moscow, in the workaday crush and in the nocturnal emptiness, falling in love ten times a day with faces flashing by, scribbling verses on the cover of *Soviet Sports:* "The nighttime fog soundlessly struck a blow without a quiver / On the other side of the skyline's barricade at dusk fell the last sunset communard," and on the whole behaved as though he had completely forgotten who he was, as though no one could take away his youth, and as if the thought never entered his head—with the exception, perhaps of that moment at night when the dragon's eye came creeping along the Kremlin wall—that this city was permeated with lies and cruelty right down to the last brick.

And yet, it was Moscow. . . .

Chapter 3

—————☆—————

A LONELY HERO

"Why is it I feel drunk on Indian summer, Indian summer," sang one of the Moscow bards in the sixties. In the Indian summer of 1949, the same feeling came over our twenty-three-year-old motorcyclist, who, though he did not yet know this song, seemed to have a premonition that it would appear. He was riding along on a war-trophy Zuntag motorcycle on jam-packed streets in the evening rush in the city's Boulevard Ring quarter. The sky at dusk was beginning to turn the color of hammered bronze, opening itself up as the sun dipped below Sretenka Boulevard. For some reason it filled him with excitement, as though some enchanted meeting awaited him just around the next corner, as though it were opening up not before a veteran commando from the Polish forests but before some naïve kid from the provinces. The whole business has to do with broads, thought Boris IV Gradov. Come to think of it, he had already been madly in love with all the women of Moscow for a whole year now.

☆

At the same time, a black limousine with bullet-proof windows was driving slowly along the Garden Ring, staying close to the sidewalk. Two men were sitting in the back seat. One of them, Major General Nugzar Lamadze, was a bit over forty, while the other, Marshal Lavrenty Beria, vice chairman of the Council of Ministers, head of the Atomic Energy Project, member of the Politburo, in charge of state security and internal affairs, was just fifty. The latter, too, one might say, was in love with all of the women of Moscow, though in a somewhat different manner than our motorcyclist. Parting the cream-colored curtains of the limousine slightly, the marshal trained his glassy eye on the passing female representatives, for the most part careworn, of the toiling population of the capital. This act of glancing made his massive body turn itself around into an unnatural position, and the bare nape of his twisted neck reminded one of a centaur's thigh. The marshal's left hand played in the pocket of his trousers.

What a swine, thought Nugzar, he doesn't even let my presence embarrass him. What has he turned me into, the dirty jackal! What a disgrace, the second in command of a great power and the things he gets into!

He pretended to pay no attention to his boss and, holding a folder full of documents on his lap, separated pressing matters from those that could wait. The marshal's hand, meanwhile, crept out of his trousers, dragging after itself a large checkered handkerchief that was stiff as starch in some places, and mopped his damp balding head and the back of his neck.

"Ai-yi-yi," the head muttered. "Just look at what the new generation is offering us, Nugzar. Oh, Moscow girls, where else in the world will you find such apples, such melons, such berries. . . . We can be proud of this kind of youth, wouldn't you say? And look how she jumps puddles, eh? You can just imagine how she would jump at . . . hm . . . Well now, see here, Nugzar! Are you going to stop pretending, finally?"

The major general put the folder to one side, gave a feigned sigh of reproach, and eyed the marshal as one might look at a naughty child; he knew that the latter loved to be on the receiving end of such glances.

"So who is it that has struck your fancy, Lavrenty?"

It was forbidden at moments such as these to address the omnipotent satrap by his name and patronymic, much less by his rank: a simple, friendly "Lavrenty" recalled the good old days of the blissful bacchanalias back in Georgia.

"She's stopped!" shouted Beria. "She's looking at her watch! Ha, ha—must be waiting for some stud! Stop the car, Shevchuk!" he ordered his driver, a major in the state security.

The lumbering, armored Packard, which struck fear into the heart of every cop on the beat in Moscow, came to a halt not far from the Park of Culture metro station.

An accompanying ZIS limousine drove up behind them and pulled in at the curb. Beria took out a pair of Zeiss binoculars, specially mounted in the Packard for the observation of the best representatives of the local masses.

"Well, Nugzar, give us your expert opinion!"

The major general moved over to the folding seat and peered through the slit in the curtains, at first without the binoculars. Some fifty yards from the car, a slender girl in a fairly chic, wide-shouldered jacket was standing by a newspaper kiosk, reading a paper and eating an ice cream. In other words, she was doing what comes naturally to a modern Soviet citizen: trying to enjoy two pleasures simultaneously. In the deepening shadows, she seemed to be about twenty years old, but the way she was slapping her knee like a child with a music folder threw one's calculations off.

"Why are they taking so long to turn on the lights?" an indignant Beria asked. "It's an outrage, people are walking around in the dark!"

The metro was thirty feet from the girl's right shoulder. Streams of people were flowing in and out of the revolving doors. She wouldn't need more than two seconds to disappear, thought Nugzar. She'll turn around, vanish, and there'll be nothing left for the bastard to do but jerk off. He won't be content with that, of course. He'll look for another one, and of course he'll find one, but at least it won't be that beauty. But she's not leaving. She's standing there with her ice cream, the silly fool, as though she's waiting for him to dispatch Shevchuk, or . . . or even me, Major General Lamadze . . . it's more likely that he'll send me than anyone else, "not on official business, but as a friend." Why doesn't anyone ask me to kill him?

Over the last year, Nugzar's hatred for his boss had reached its apparent limit. He realized that time was ticking away and that Beria would never allow him to climb to the next rung on the ladder, to occupy a more independent position in the system. The general's star so unexpectedly bestowed by Stalin in a difficult year for the armed forces was still shining all on its own. Then again, was it really a question of rank? Majors general in the system sometimes were in charge of entire directorates, accomplishing a tremendous amount of work, receiving the satisfaction that comes with creation, and accumulating authority. Beria, however, had closed all avenues of advance to Nugzar. Obviously, he had already decided on this back in 1942, after the dinner in honor of Iosif Vissarionovich. A rat can always sense danger—young Lamadze must be stopped! Of course, he could simply have had him taken away, as he had done with scores of others in his entourage. Who knew better than Nugzar that Lavrenty liked to do away with dangerous careerists personally, in his office, with an unexpected shot to the back of the neck in the course of a friendly conversation? In those days, though, he had not been able to make up his mind to get rid of Stalin's protégé by this favorite method, and now he had clearly decided that any need for using it had disappeared. He would destroy Nugzar Lamadze by keeping him as close to himself as possible. What sort of a position is this, "assistant" to the vice chairman of the Council of Ministers? Maybe it's a man of unheard-of influence, who gives himself over entirely to all of the most important affairs of the state . . . on the other hand, maybe he's just an adjutant, a flunky they send after broads.

The bastard would never forget the black marks in Nugzar's service record. Oh no, he'd always remember how Nugzar had saved that Trotskyite, his beloved Nina Gradov, from state security by shuffling her dossier from one filing cabinet to another. A sexual liaison with an enemy of the Party, my dear Comrade Lamadze, more often than not leads to ideological ties. But I'm only joking, he would giggle. What, don't you have a sense of humor?

And then there was the whole business with the wife of Marshal Gradov—the same damned "relatives" again! The "organs" clearly hadn't come out of that affair smelling like a rose, either; that's how he sees it, the good-for-nothing. Why, what do you mean, Lavrenty Pavlovich? Here's her signature on the document. We've got her where we want her, we can activate her anytime we want. Well, Nugzar, here you are again, poking your nose into official business. It would be better if you told your old pal how you stuck it to her and how you got your member, so to speak, involved with the American intelligence service. Come on, now, Lavrenty, I break into a sweat from jokes like that. Come on yourself, Nugzar, can't a man even make a joke anymore? You really are short in the humor department.

Nugzar admitted to himself sometimes that the matter of Veronika and Kevin Taliaferro had been far from clear in 1945. The psychological profile of the operation had looked irreproachable, but it hadn't taken into account one thing: Russian female hysteria. On the second or third day after their proposal, Veronika had signed the agreement to cooperate without any fuss or screams, even with a certain degree of arrogance. Maybe the beauty has opened up to her boyfriend about this, maybe she's playing a double game, Nugzar had thought at the time. He had not communicated his suspicions to the higher-ups, though. In the first place, he hadn't wanted to muddy the waters all over again, to lessen the value of such a beautiful business as putting his mark in the bed of an important American military specialist. In the second place, he'd felt a bit sorry for Veronika, whom on some human level he liked. She would never survive a second arrest. If they were simply to "lower the boom," it would be even worse: the great beauty of Moscow would end up with her head in a bottle.

At first everything had gone unexpectedly smoothly, from Nugzar's point of view. First of all, Lavrenty, who at the beginning had directed the operation personally, had suddenly lost interest in it. In the second place, it appeared that the top Allied brass, almost right up to General Eisenhower himself in Germany, had appealed to Stalin—maybe through the Allied Control Commission, maybe even through Zhukov himself—not to place any obstacles in the way of the wedding of Colonel Taliaferro and the widow of a twice-decorated Hero of the Soviet Union. For one reason or another, Beria had stopped asking about the affair and simply waved off any direct questions: do as you like, he would say, it's not of any great importance. It was only when the two lovebirds had crossed the ocean—the latest reports had them living in New Haven and having nothing whatsoever to do with state secrets—it was only then that the marshal had begun to make ominous jokes about sexual relations with American intelligence agents. Now the scoundrel had made another forking maneuver: on the one hand, he says it's an insignificant matter, so there's no need to promote Lamadze; on the other hand, it smells slightly fishy and you could draw the wrong conclusions.

As far as smells went, the chief had been giving off a few bad odors himself over the past few years. His wife was sick and tired of his constant little affairs and had stopped keeping an eye on his underwear. He wasn't noted for being fastidious, either, getting loaded just before sessions of the Politburo. ... All in all, certain eccentricities had begun to be observed in the monster. All of a sudden, he was nuts about sports, and particularly about his beloved Dynamo soccer team. Even during the war, he'd had players from the Spartak team tossed into prison so that they would not prevent the success of the "organs' team." Now he had gone completely off the rails: he went hunting for sportsmen, luring them away from army teams or sometimes simply having them kidnapped. He was particularly irked by the new Air Force squad, which was under the aegis of Vassily himself, Lieutenant General Stalin. Now he would begin to fly into a rage for no reason at all. So you think the intelligence services have committed a blunder or that something is not quite right in Iran or Berlin or that some hitch has developed in the Leningrad affair? "Vaska" is to blame—he's been siphoning off hockey players for his teams again.

★

So now, all of a sudden, something not entirely rational, not to say irrational, was beginning. Not long before, Nugzar, upon coming into the office, had found Lavrenty Pavlovich reading *Soviet Sports*. He saw immediately that the boss was unhappy with something in that rag, that something had gotten under his skin. Is something not quite right, Comrade Marshal?

You could say "something's not quite right." Just take a look at what these bums are printing. A finger resembling a small member in a wrinkled condom rested firmly on a poem entitled "On Red Square." It was an ordeal for Nugzar to read:

> The marshal reviews the parade,
> Onto the square in a stream of columns,
> To the sound of a march well played,
> The banner of daybreak follows.

"Read it aloud!" Beria snarled.

Nugzar trembled: a shout like that, even without a gun, could rob a man of his voice. Nevertheless, he plucked up his courage and spread his arms apart: sometimes one has to display the character of a Cheka agent. "I don't understand, Lavrenty Pavlovich, what is it you want me to read?"

Beria laughed loudly but nervously and snatched the paper away. "You don't understand? Then listen, I'll read it to you with feeling, with meaning, and with the pauses in the right places." He started to read, stopping constantly, pressing a line with his finger, looking at Nugzar, and going on, in the heat of some strange madness, often putting the stress on the wrong syllables of the Russian words.

> This day astride the Kremlin walls
> The sportsmen
>   I will know
> By their courage,
>   youth,
>   ability,
> See the tight
>   formations go.
>
> The tread of the columns is light
> And the leader
>   of all the eons
> Stands high above
>   shining Red Square
> On the
>   marble
>   mausoleum.
>
> Throughout the expanse of our Fatherland
> The captains
>   are setting sail
> For the Kremlin,
>   communism to build
> According to
>   Stalin's will.

The distances bright
>>are thrown open wide
And like the dear
>>name of our homeland
There are two other names
>>in which we take pride:
Lenin and Stalin!

"There you are." Beria concluded in a sort of state of exhaustion. "What do you say now?"

"I still don't understand, Lavrenty Pavlovich," his assistant replied without the slightest sympathy. He did not, in fact, understand what the point of all of this clowning about a poem was. After all, no one else was present in the room.

"You don't understand, Nugzar? That's too bad. If even you don't understand, then who can I count on? Only on my own intuition?"

"Forgive me, Lavrenty Pavlovich, but what is there to find? Everything there seems to be as it should be . . ."

"Oh Nugzar, Nugzar, you're not being a pal. . . . How many times have I told you not to call me by my name and patronymic when we're alone, Nugzar, my friend? I'm only ten years older than you, and we've been working together all of our lives." He flung away the copy of *Soviet Sports* and began to pace back and forth in the office, walking as though he would stop at any moment and pull out a gun. "Nobody in the goddamned office understands me except Maximilianich!" He was referring to Malenkov. "What's the matter with you, Nugzar, can't you read between the lines? Can't you see how much mockery there is in it? He's jeering at us, at everyone, the SOB! What's his name, already? Look how it's signed: Yevg. Yevtushenko. Yevtushenko, what kind of a family name is that? No one with a name like that should be published in the Soviet press!"

"Lavrenty, my friend, what's wrong with this name?" objected Nugzar in the manner that seemed to be expected of him. "It's an ordinary Ukrainian name, and as for 'Yevg.,' it's probably short for 'Yevgeny.'"

"I don't believe this 'Yevgeny'!" Beria flared. "My instincts have never let me down! I have faith in writers like Surkov, in Maxim

Tank, even in Simonov and Antanas Ventslova, but in this one, no! Where did he come from, this 'Yevg.'?"

He crumpled the copy of *Soviet Sports* into a wad and kicked it like a goalkeeper clearing out the ball. "Look into it and report back, Comrade Lamadze!"

The marshal straightened his jacket and with a scowl on his face went to his desk to read the records of the Leningrad interrogations.

Then a thought occurred to Nugzar: the bandit is playing cat and mouse with himself. He's trying to distract himself from the endless killings. Of course, it was difficult to forget that it was in this very office of the Lubyanka that Nicolai Voznesensky, just the day before a member of the Politburo, had squealed like a piglet while being interrogated. How many other "piglets" like that does he have on his conscience? All of us do. We're all evil spirits and devils here, there's no other way to put it. This one, though, wants to get his mind onto other things: girls, sports. . . . Here he is, reading this paper, but the gloom comes crashing down again, he wants more blood—this time, it's some Yevg. Yevtushenko. . . .

And that unlucky chap doesn't even have an inkling of who has taken an interest in him. The publishers pay by the line, and he's trying to string one line out into three to make a living, imitating Mayakovsky. He's probably some ex-LEF writer, some old, overgrown loser. . . .

Nugzar put on his civilian raincoat and a fedora and headed for *Soviet Sports*. The editor there nearly wet his pants in fright when Nugzar entered. He leapt to his feet, stood unsteadily for a moment, and then dashed off somewhere. Soon there was shouting in the corridor: "Tarasov to the office of the editor in chief!" A department head arrived on the run. Here it is: the comrades from State Security are interested in your author. Now, now, calm down, Comrade Editor—why the plural? It's not "comrades" that are interested, it's just me personally who was wondering why you've printed this Yevg. Yevtushenko. He has a ringing rhythm, you say? A youthful style, you say? Interesting, very interesting. He's here right now, you say? Where? Why, right here, Comrade General, out on the stairs having a smoke. Call him in? No, that won't be necessary. Just show him to me. The editor in chief personally opened the door to the landing. A lanky kid in a velvet jacket and a bouclé cap was standing there blowing dove gray smoke from his nostrils and proudly modeling his new artificial rubber soles, all the rage at the time.

"That's Yevg. Yevtushenko?"

"Indeed it is."

"How old is he, this Yevg. Yevtushenko of yours?"

The editor lurched forward from his desk, then, stopped in his tracks by a gesture from his ominous guest, flopped back into his chair. It was difficult to look at such a guest from behind an office desk; one wanted to stand at attention like a cadet at a military school. "Tarasov, how old is your author?"

Tarasov's expression was impenetrable, even contemptuous: fear, most likely, had caused it to lose its obsequiousness. "Sixteen," he muttered, "or maybe eighteen. No more than twenty, in any case."

"Still in school, then?"

"So they say," Tarasov responded with even a certain nasal arrogance. "In one of the upper classes, I think."

Out in the corridor, they saw someone come downstairs from the offices of another publication—*Novy Mir*, most likely—and walk by Yevg. Yevtushenko, who craned his neck in the direction of the passerby, his clear-eyed gaze sparkling with unexpected shrewdness. The passerby laughed and said something that must have been encouraging, since Yevg. Yevtushenko went into a little jig on the landing.

"What is it about his verses that won you over?" Nugzar asked Tarasov. He had not yet paid any attention to the editor in chief. Tarasov was sitting there like the Buddha, almost detached from reality. Nevertheless his mouth opened: "They're so ringing, so youthful . . ."

At that moment, Yevg. Yevtushenko put out his cigarette with his heel and noticed that the door to the office of the editor in chief was open. He immediately rushed down the hall in the direction of the bathroom and looked into the office with immense, all-consuming interest as he passed by. What a kid, Nugzar said to himself. Then another thought immediately formed in his mind: someone like that has no business in jail.

Tarasov took a scrap of paper out of his pocket. Here's another poem that he brought us. There are some unusual rhymes, the ideology is irreproachable . . .

Yevg. Yevtushenko's latest poem was called "The Fate of a Boxer," and it told the story of an American athlete named Gene.

> . . . He remembers the war
> and a Russian soldier,
> Born on Siberia's plain,
> Who gave as a token
> of soldierly friendship
> A picture of Stalin
> to Gene.
>
> Now of everything Gene is bereft
> That photo
> is all
> he has left!
>
> The man who was champion
> so many times
> Crosses the gray
> of the square.
> It's probably now
> that they're ringing the chimes
> In Moscow,
> on Red Square!
>
> There, they breathe like the air
> the freedom
> Of following the Stalinist colors
> Of bright ideals,
> of sports for all people
> That raises them
> up unsullied!

"So where are they, these 'unexpected rhymes'?" Nugzar asked. All of a sudden, the situation seemed quite comical to him. There was somehow a strange randomness in this collection of compulsory words. Could it be that Beria had sensed this? "Freedom . . . Free them, bereft . . . left," Tarasov muttered.

"What about them?"

"They're root rhymes."

"Ah, yes." This generation obviously had no intention of going into the camps. What were they counting on, root rhymes?

"For the time being, Comrade Tarasov, you'll hold off on publishing this poem," Nugzar gently advised. "All right?"

"Whatever you say," said Tarasov.

"Just wait until I give you a call—right now, do nothing. Verses don't go bad in a couple of weeks, after all. Do you remember the poet who said 'For my poems, as for fine wines, a time will come'?"

Tarasov swallowed some saliva and looked away into a corner. You can't let him see that you remember Tsvetaev, she's banned, Nugzar mused. He's probably thinking, Why, even the secret police go about with verses like that on their lips. This Tarasov doesn't know I grew up with poets. Back in Georgia, I had poets by my side, and I grew up to be a killer . . . with poets by my side. That must make me a noble variation on a murderer.

In two weeks, of course, Beria will have forgotten all about the author of "On Red Square." The most important event of 1949 is coming up, the trial run of the atom bomb in Semipalatinsk. They had called several meetings of scientists involved in the top secret project and twisted their insides into knots. Now they're going to make an inspection tour of the installations. They're checking their system of agents of influence in the Western mass media. If the test run goes well, on the one hand, no one must know, but on the other hand, everyone should know. The Master had implied more than once that the new correlation of forces in the world arena depended upon this test. An advance all along the line might be possible.

Beria always received *Soviet Sports* in the morning mail. From time to time, he would pull it from the stack of newspapers, glance at the page containing the soccer scores to see how his beloved Dynamo was faring, bang the palm of his hand down on the edge of the table, either in annoyance or with satisfaction, and then toss away the tribune of the State Committee for Sports. One day, in order to establish an alibi for himself, Nugzar mentioned his visit to the editorial office. Perhaps he did so just at the moment when the boss was least inclined to talk about anything but the atomic installations, but Lavrenty Pavlovich interrupted him, saying, "What are you talking about, General? He can go fuck himself, this *gamakhlebulo* Yevtushenko." From this one could conclude that the excess of rage he had had concerning the poet had more likely as not been a caprice of middle age that ought no more be remembered than any of the satrap's other escapades. So, for the time being, Yevg. Yevtushenko could work away to his heart's content at his "root rhymes" to the glory of the Revolution.

☆

I might as well admit it, he's always made me just his flunky, thought Nugzar, following through the part in the curtains the slender figure with the padded shoulders. Someone to help him indulge his disgusting whims, even though he always asks me to help him as "one man to another." Just then, the streetlights by the metro came on. "There, you see?" Beria said. "Feast your eyes, what a beauty! I'm in love!"

"What do you mean, 'there'?" asked Nugzar. The boss handed him the binoculars. So he's in love. A wild boar in love. It would be good to hit him with a bullet in the forehead, so that his eyes pop out. Nugzar turned the focus wheel. No two ways about it, Zeiss produces good stuff. A delightful childlike face stood out distinctly from the crowd: the bright eyes of a pampered beauty; a steeply sloping forehead that told of an almost unspoiled nature; a fine, slightly long—ever so slightly!—nose; full, rosy lips with a tongue darting between them that resembled a small flame as it demolished the ice cream. All of this was suffused beneath waves of chestnut hair quivering in the rising wind.

"A good one," said Major General Lamadze.

"What did I tell you!" exclaimed Marshal Beria. A smell like the depths of hell exuded from his mouth. He doesn't clean his teeth, this ideological martyr of ours.

"She'll be a good one," added Lamadze, finishing his thought.

"What do you mean by 'will be'?" Beria cried indignantly, in the manner of a repulsive child who has had a bone taken away from him. [Beg your pardon, something doesn't add up, you repulsive asshole.]

"In two or three years she'll be ready," Nugzar replied, smiling gently and falsely. For some reason he could not imagine himself going up to this girl, showing her his MGB identification, and then dragging her to the limousine. Any other one that you want, but not her! Let him pluck out my eye, I still won't go!

"You're not talking like a man of the Caucasus," Beria grumbled, his chin thrust slightly forward. "You remember what age girls are in Azerbaijan when they take them to bed."

Maybe in Azerbaijan, thought Lamadze, but in a civilized Christian country? Never! His own daughter Ophelia, for that matter, was also coming up on "that age." Already has her period, it seems. She may be still hanging on to Mama's skirts, but at any time . . . in a year or so, she'll attract the eye of some obnoxious marshal. His eyes clouded over at the thought. I still have enough killing power in my right hand, a roundhouse shot to the jaw with these binoculars so as to fracture the base of his skull.

"Bring the girl in, Comrade Marshal?" the faithful Shevchuk suddenly asked jauntily from the front.

"Why should you go? Why not Nugzarka to go?" shrieked Beria. When he gets mad, he starts to use bad grammar.

Nugzar laughed merrily. "I just thought, Lavrenty, that according to Russian law . . . ha, ha . . . we are on the territory of the RSFSR, after all . . . we might get run in . . . ha, ha . . . for corruption of a minor . . ."

The idea of being "run in" for a violation of RSFSR law struck Beria as so amusing that he even forgot about the young girl for a moment. "Ha, ha, ha . . . well, Nugzar, you make me laugh. . . . You're not such a wet blanket after all. . . . Did you hear that, Shevchuk? 'According to RSFSR law'!"

At that moment, the whole state of affairs by the Park of Culture metro station changed. A powerfully built young fellow in a cloth jacket of a cut that was not Russian went up to the girl. He gave her a condescending, self-assured pat on the behind. The girl turned around and joyfully threw her arms around his neck, all without dropping her half-eaten ice cream. The lad wiped away the sticky drops from his face with a gesture of annoyance. Taking her by the hand, he dragged her through the crowd to a fast motorcycle parked beneath a streetlight. A few seconds later, the motorcycle had moved away, executed an immediate turn, and headed off in the direction of the Garden Ring. The girl was sitting on the backseat, holding on to the young man by the waist, in keeping with all of the rules of romantic etiquette of postwar Moscow.

"After them, Comrade Marshal?" Shevchuk cried. By the exclamation, of course, he was demonstrating his 100 percent devotion and 200 percent zeal. Would it be possible in Moscow for any spectacle more absurd to unfold than that of the armored Packard of the number two man in the country chasing a frivolous couple on a motorcycle? To give such an order to their escort car would have been preposterous as well: in these few minutes, the motorcycle would have raced far away, and you could search in vast Moscow for as long as you like. In any case, the whole style of Beria's flesh hunts did not call for any fuss, hurrying, or chase. On the contrary, everything was supposed to happen at a pace as slow, inexorable, and hypnotizing as that of the government itself. All in all, the antelope had bolted!

"It's all your fault, Nugzar!" Lavrenty Pavlovich said with annoyance, though fortunately without particular malice. "You felt sorry for her because she's underage, and instead her stud shows up." He suddenly guffawed: "This will make quite a funny story: we'll be run in for statutory rape, you said? Then some young skirt chaser makes off with her!"

Now that the danger had flowed away around one of the capricious bends of the tyrant's mind, Nugzar too burst into laughter and shook his handsome head with its distinguished touches of gray at the temples. "I blew it, Lavrenty, I'm behind the times. I must be getting old."

"Well, go out now and hunt some new game!" Beria giggled happily. "I'll give you five minutes. We still have to go see the boss tonight." He pressed a button. A tray with a bottle of cognac, crystal glasses, borzhom water, and lemons came out of a small cupboard affixed to the backseat. Failure had to be quickly forgotten with a drink and a nibble on a lemon.

They did not have to wait long for the "game." Straightaway, as if made to order, a Moscow Aphrodite with a young plebeian face, the ultimate version of the concubine, emerged from the depths of the metro. Beria nodded. Nugzar climbed out of the Packard and went directly toward the girl.

According to the established pattern for such cases, he was supposed to be extremely polite, which was not difficult considering his generally good Tbilisi upbringing. The rules called for him to salute if he was in civilian clothes, to touch the brim of his soft hat and then to take out—no, not what you think, dear reader—the MGB identification that filled everyone who saw it with fear. Only then would he say in a low baritone voice: "Pardon me for disturbing you, but a person of some importance in the State would like to have a word with you." Without fail, Nugzar did everything by the book, with the exception of the sacramental phrase, which he uttered with his own variations: "Pardon me for disturbing you, but one of the statesmen of the Soviet Union would like to have a word with you." In the final analysis, what difference did it make? Still, it seemed to introduce a sort of murderous irony into the situation. He felt as though he were killing the scoundrel, just for an instant, and saving himself from the nastiest of humiliations by pronouncing the words "statesmen of the Soviet Union." There was no way of knowing how the chief would react if he found out about the "Nugzar variant" of the invitation: after all, until quite recently he had been expecting one of his entourage, and perhaps him in particular, to play a dirty trick on him. Now it looks like he doesn't expect anything from me anymore except the lowest kind of servility. As for the victims, they have no time for plays on words. They lose their heads out of fear and don't remember anything.

The "plebeian," who up to that moment had been carrying herself and her divine figure proudly past the glances of men, cringed at the sight of the handsome general emerging from the sinister limousine and coming straight toward her. The most dramatic moment of her paltry life had arrived. "I remember that I was still young . . ." That will be the tune she'll sing in later years. He saluted, and from his breast pocket pulled out a small case embossed with the initials that reduced everyone to ashes: MGB, the Moscow Geriatric Bottomchasers, or something to that effect.

The sprinkling of freckles on her face suddenly became visible, along with a few pockmarks. No matter, she'll do for tonight.

The girl was so frightened that she could neither say a word nor move a muscle. Nugzar gently took her by the arm. He imagined his chief at that moment already stimulating his system through his trouser pockets.

"There's nothing to be afraid of. What's your name?"

"L-L-Lyuda," stuttered the victim in a barely audible voice.

Nugzar noticed that a cop on the beat and a news vendor were observing the scene intently.

"Don't worry, Comrade Lyuda. Believe me, there's nothing to

worry about. He simply wants to get acquainted with you." He mod-ulated his voice so as to make her understand, the fool, that he just wants to fuck her, not put her in front of a firing squad. Does she un-derstand? . . . Well, she's no cherry . . . no, she doesn't understand, the idiot is shaking. . . . "He's an important state [He almost said "criminal"] leader. . . ."

He led her along carefully, as though she were ill. A door opened—not to the main car but to the accompanying vehicle. Obviously, Shevchuk had already gone running to give the order to the goons: take her safely to the appropriate entrance on Kachalov Street. Clearly the plan was to see the boss first, deliver the report, and then after-ward, as the bastard put it, "go to the kingdom of harmony."

When they were just alongside the car, Lyuda suddenly began to kick, straightened up like a string, and balked so much that something of the man left in Nugzar's frozen soul stirred. Just then, however, Major Galubik jumped out and adroitly lifted the girl by the buttocks onto the backseat. The door slammed. Nugzar's part of the operation had ended in success.

★

Meanwhile, the motorcyclist and his passenger were racing along. Moscow, which would have seemed ugly to, say, a Parisian, seemed to them, a twenty-three-year-old young man and a sixteen-year-old girl, more wonderful and more mysterious than any Paris they had seen at the cinema. If only I had a more mature woman sitting behind me instead of Yolka, thought Boris IV. Let's suppose I had Vera Gorda with her arms around my stomach muscles.

Oh, if only it were a famous athlete, say, Ilyasov the ski-jumping champion of the navy, who was driving me instead of our Babochka, thought Elena Kitaigorodsky, the daughter of poetess Nina Gradov and therefore the cousin of our motorcyclist. To be this close to an athlete, so as to be able to touch his back, could such a thing be pos-sible? The wrap of these delightful arms around the stomach muscles of a man who's not related to me, is it even thinkable? Then again, can you even use "wrap" as a noun?

Today both had promised their grandparents to come to Silver For-est for dinner. Yolka had a private piano lesson on Metrostroevsky Street, and it was agreed that afterwards Boris would pick her up at the Park of Culture metro station. Neither of them had even an inkling that they had been the focus of attention of the infernal band in the armor-plated car.

They drove by Moscow's first high-rise hotel, the Peking. It was still surrounded by scaffolding, yet a huge portrait of Stalin already covered the windows of the tower section that crowned the building. The same personage was visible as a matter of course from any window in Moscow, wherever the eye looked. In some places, above the rooftops, one could see his profile, outlined with neon lights; in others, the full figure rose up: a hero in a uniform of the highest rank one could have, generalissimo, surveying with a paternal eye the world's peoples rejoicing under his protection. "Stalin is the standard-bearer of peace throughout the world!" In a couple of weeks, at the thirty-second anniversary of the October Revolution, his image would appear at the apex of the Moscow skies between fountains of fireworks.

★

When Boris Gradov had returned from Poland the year before, in the midst of the May Day celebration, Moscow had been simply pulsating with outpourings of fire. The Father of the Peoples had been floating over Manège Square, suspended from dirigibles concealed by clouds. All around flashed multicolored fireworks and rockets by the thousands. The Russians had once called such rockets "jesters," but they had long ago lost their facility for jesting and consequently the name along with it. The word "fireworks" no longer seemed appropriate for such a spectacle, either. The invigorating word "salute," which included the accompanying mighty volleys, was in vogue.

After four years in forests and on the edge of cities half destroyed by fire, First Lieutenant Gradov was at somewhat of a loss in the midst of the magnificence of the capital. Thousands of upturned faces with permanent smiles gazed upon the Caesar-like countenance spread out in the sky. Caesar-like, if not more, thought Boris, who was quite drunk. The multicolored dots flying along the cheeks and forehead and occasionally leaving cloudy pink and blue streaks behind clearly hinted at the divine origin of this face.

"Oh, what a beauty we've made of our celebration," an imposing woman standing alongside him sighed loudly. Black whiskers that seemed to have been pasted on graced her upper lip, giving her a substantial appearance. Boris took a swig of vodka from a flat officer's canteen wrapped in a cloth. "He's looking straight down at us, like Zeus, am I right?" he said to the woman. "What are you talking about, young man?" she whispered in frightened indignation and moved away from him into the crowd as soon as she could.

"So what did I say?" Boris shrugged. "All I did was to compare him with Zeus, the father of the gods of Olympus, is that so bad?" Still sipping from his canteen, he left Manège Square and walked up Gorky Street, that is, in the direction of his home, the huge, empty marshal's flat that awaited him on any day at any time. "The marshal's apartment." The marshal had not spent even a week here, all told. Lower-ranking officers had lived here. One day, coming back from a training exercise at an inopportune time, Boris had run to the "library," as he called his father's office, and heard moans that stopped him in his tracks. His mother was sprawled on the couch, her face buried in a cushion. Only a jumble of blond hair was visible. Behind her on his knees, Shevchuk, still wearing his unbuttoned tunic, was laboring away. A hooligan's crooked smile was frozen on his face. Catching sight of Borka, he had assumed an expression of holy terror, then waved his hand as if to say, Get lost, don't keep your mama from having a bit of fun.

That May 1, 1948—that is, immediately following his return from the Polish People's Republic, where he had done his part to establish fraternal socialism by fire and the knife—the drunken first lieutenant sat on the very same sofa in the darkness, taking pulls on his canteen of schnapps and crying.

There's no one here. No one was waiting for me here. She left and took my little sister, Verulka, with her. Now she lives in the land of the warmongers. I don't know whether or not you could call her a traitor to the Motherland, but she betrayed me.

Reflections of the "salute" that would go on until midnight were still wandering along the ceiling and walls. The spent cases of the rockets were landing on the cornice. One of the guns taking part in the artillery salute was firing away nearby, evidently from the roof of the Council of Ministers. He had less and less vodka and more and more self-pity.

During his last year in Poland, Boris had no longer been fighting, with the exception of two or three night alarms when their entire school on the outskirts of Poznań had been put on alert and then been given the order to "stand down" without any explanation. All of the units of the Polish Home Army or, as they were called in the political instruction courses, the "forces of reaction," had been wiped out or had managed to flee the country or had melted into the subdued mass of the population, where the local branches of State Security were now hot on their trail. Boris and a few other MGB and GRU—Military Intelligence Directorate—operatives trained in forest combat had been posted to the school in Poznań as instructors. For a year there, he had given trainees of the Polish secret police—a rather thuggish lot that had to be shown sometimes not only how to defend themselves in unarmed combat, but also how to finish the job—the benefit of his considerable experience as a killer.

In the course of the year he had sent no less than a dozen requests to be demobilized in order to continue his education. Each time, the reply had been identical and thorough: "the question of your demobilization has been decided in the negative." He had begun to think that perhaps he should accept an offer to enter a restricted school for High Command officers, just to get to Moscow somehow, closer to Grandpa with his connections, when all at once he was summoned to the joint Polish-Soviet Directorate and informed that his "demob" had come through.

It later turned out that it was precisely his grandfather, Boris III, who had been directly involved in the matter. Having learned by some unknown channels whose command his mysterious grandson was under, Boris Nikitovich had begun to systematically besiege the appropriate authorities, trying to make the comrades understand that everything has its time, that the boy, motivated by romanticism and patriotism—rather, the other way around, patriotism and romanticism, that's the right order—had given the Motherland and the armed forces four of the best years of his life and that now he needed to continue his education in order to assume his place in the Gradov dynasty of Russian doctors. In the end, it was difficult to refuse the request of a distinguished general in the Medical Corps, a professor and present member of the Academy of Medical Sciences and father of the legendary Marshal Gradov. The unseen authorities went back on their earlier decisions and with a gnashing of teeth gave the grandfather back his grandson, an expert in sabotage and intelligence gathering so valuable to the cause of peace in the whole world.

Finally the blessed day came. Boris IV stuffed his uniform with its shoulder straps deep down into his duffel bag. He headed for the Poznań flea market and bought himself a pile of civilian clothes. He had a drink with the quartermaster, greased his palm, and received for his personal use a huge convertible SS Horch staff car that had been "written off," as it were. He also received a pile of money, both rubles and złotys: the Polish United Workers' Party generously thanks you for your help in laying the foundations of the proletarian state. Then, in Poznań, Warsaw, Minsk, and Moscow, the appropriate comrades had had a series of soul-numbing conversations with him. Gradov, you're an army spy, and even though you're leaving us, you'll always be an army spy, GRU. You could be needed at any time, and you'll have to come, otherwise it's your ass. If you ever betray us, wherever you are, anywhere in the world, you're a dead man. Know what we mean? It's good that you know. As long as you remain our loyal comrade, you'll always have a green light.

It was implied, and rather clearly at that, that never under any circumstances was he to accept any offers from the MGB secret police. They have their people, we have ours. If they put the screws to you, let us know right away.

It was officially declared to him that he would remain on the top secret list of reservists of the Military Intelligence Directorate, GRU. It goes without saying that he had to sign at least a dozen documents to the effect that he would not divulge anything he knew or anything about the operations he had taken part in on the temporarily occupied territory of the Soviet Union or in the neighboring fraternal country of Poland. In case of a violation of this agreement, the severest measures of internal protocol would be applied to him, which was just another way of saying "it's your ass."

Somehow or other, he had made it in the ponderous Horch (loaded mostly with spare parts) to the place of his origins, Silver Forest (we will allow those who have already read our first volume to imagine the emotions that the inhabitants of the Gradov nest must have felt), where he was given the key to the empty flat on Gorky Street. He already knew from vague hints in his grandmother's letters that his mother had taken off somewhere, probably far away. He supposed that she had gone to the far eastern part of the country with some new general or high-ranking engineer, or else—the Devil plays some funny tricks in this life—with that very same petty demon of the nights of his youth, the camp guard Shevchuk. That she might have gone to America he would not have imagined in his wildest dreams. By that time—the spring of 1948—people had invented a new source of amusement for themselves, one that pervaded every aspect of life: the Cold War. Their "buddies" of yesterday, the Yanks, had now become evil spirits from another world. The leader of the Brits, a man given to speaking in metaphors, had coined the term for the new Soviet isolation: the Iron Curtain. Having a correspondence with someone in America was a terrifying thought for even an ordinary Soviet citizen; as for a soldier in a special branch like Babochka Gradov, any attempt to contact his mother would now be equivalent to betrayal of his secret order, whose name sounded like the cooing of doves: g-r-u, g-r-u . . . and at the same time like *grusha,* or "pear," a pear with a fleshy, half-eaten backside.

At first, Babochka's intentions were entirely serious. He had to get his high school diploma. All of the people from his class at school were now finishing their fourth year at university or at an institute, so he had to catch up, catch up, catch up! And then? To get admitted to some prestigious Moscow institute—someplace where he could study steel production or aerodynamics or foreign languages—and to finish in three years. Not some ordinary provincial pedagogical or medical school. His grandfather's line of argument had been useful for getting him out of the army but was now irrelevant to the determined, ambitious Boris IV. Even without making any long-term plans, he simply wanted to belong to the best circles of the young people of the capital and not to the also-rans from the "peds and meds," so common that they had been given numbers: first, second, third. . . . Medical school? Cut up cadavers in the dissecting room? No thanks, Grandpa, I've seen enough corpses. Boris III spread his hands in resignation: that's one argument you really can't refute.

But Babochka's good intentions with regard to practical Muscovite life quickly ran aground. At the night school where he enrolled to receive his high school diploma, he felt like Gulliver among the Lilliputians. Indeed, something Lilliputian showed in the eyes of his classmates whenever he appeared. None of them knew who he was, but all of them sensed that he was not on their level. Even the teachers shrank from him a bit, especially the women: the redhead in the deer-pattern sweater with the impeccable manners and exemplary posture cut quite an odd figure in the down-at-the-heels school for working-class youths. "You have a peculiar accent, Gradov. You wouldn't be from the West, would you?" asked the attractive geography teacher. Babochka laughed, displaying his perfect keyboard teeth.

"I'm from Silver Forest, Ludmila—er—Iliinichna." The geography teacher flushed and began to tremble. Did she really have the guts to teach a man like this geography? After that, every time she met Gradov in the school, she lowered her eyes and blushed, sure that he would have nothing to do with her unless it was because he was fed up with other women above her station, the artists and society ladies.

It would have been premature, however, to talk about Boris being fed up. Once back in Moscow, the twenty-one-year-old veteran of covert warfare began to experience an odd shyness, as though he had returned not to his native city but to the capital of some foreign country. Even his manhood seemed shaken, as though that adolescent of "direct action" had returned, as though all of that Polish business had happened to someone else, as though that kid with the submachine gun and the dagger, a figure nicknamed "Grad," had no direct connection to him and that only now was he returning to his true essence, of which he had no more perhaps than that chap from the provinces whom he met one night on the Sofia Embankment.

It would not be an exaggeration to say that the mysterious, handsome Gradov trembled a bit himself when he encountered the geography teacher. He wanted very much to ask her out on a date, but he was overcome by a childish timidity, where it had come from, he could not understand—as though, if they went out, this geography teacher would begin drilling him on the planet's raw materials!

In the mass of women's faces he encountered his first year in Moscow, one shone forth in the pinkish beam of a restaurant light: the stage singer Vera Gorda. One night he had been sitting by himself at the Moscow Hotel nightclub, smoking Troika cigarettes with their gold-tinged paper and drinking 112-proof vodka—not in great gulps but in small swallows, Polish style. Suddenly Gorda was announced and, with a rustle of her long concert dress, raised slightly in a gesture of greeting by a pair of long, bare arms, a blond beauty appeared, looking like Rita Hayworth in the American film that they had shown in Poznań until the print was full of holes. Beneath the multicolored lights the entire hall swayed to the now falling, now rising rhythms of her song, and Borya, though he had no one to dance with, stood up and began to rock back and forth. It was an unforgettable moment of his youth. She sang that cloying hackneyed verse "In a pack of dusty letters, there was one I happened to find / Where letters tiny as pearls had spilled into a lilac pool . . ." Alone before the microphone amid twenty characters in starched shirtfronts, her sweet eyes half closed, barely moving her sweet lips, flooding the huge, columned hall with her sweet voice . . . what happiness, what inaccessibility . . .

But why should she be inaccessible? he wondered the next morning. She's just some songbird in a restaurant, and you're a retired intelligence agent, after all. Just send her some flowers and invite her to take a spin in the Horch, no problem. Damned easy it would be, too. It seems like just yesterday when you thought there were no complicated situations in the world. Once you've been plugged by bullets and stabbed twice, and if you're not afraid to die, what "complicated situations" could there possibly be? On top of that, I think she noticed me. When I jumped up, she was looking in my direction. . . . He went back to the Moscow, and Vera Gorda stood before him again, arms extended, inaccessible as a screen goddess.

"It seems to me that Babochka is going through the shock of coming back from a war," Boris Nikitovich said one day.

"You're probably right," replied Mary Vakhtangovna. "You know, he hasn't called a single one of his old friends and hasn't gone out with anyone he was at school with."

His grandmother was almost right—that is, she was right, but not entirely. After his arrival in Moscow, Boris had not in fact expressed the slightest desire to see any of his old classmates—the children of "big shots"—from School 175. He had, however, made an effort to learn at least something about the fate of his idol, the former youth boxing champion of Moscow, Alexander Sheremetiev.

He had seen Alexander for the last time in August 1944 on a stretcher as he was being shoved into an overloaded Douglas transport a short distance from Warsaw. He was still alive then, delirious from painkillers, muttering incoherently. Later, when Boris asked what had become of his friend, he had been told not to ask any more questions in the future. The fate of Sheremetiev, as it turned out, was a state secret of the highest order because he had received his wounds in the course of a top secret operation to evacuate a Communist general from burning Warsaw.

In 1948, once he had in his hands all of the documents freeing him, at least partially, from the GRU, Boris ventured to appeal to the inscrutable comrades who were seeing him off: "Really, Comrades, if you could at least just tell me if Sashka Sheremetiev is still alive, and if he isn't, then where he's buried."

"He's alive," the inscrutable comrades said curtly, then added, "That's all we can tell you, Comrade First Lieutenant, retired."

What happened, thought Boris, to make it all so hush-hush when he's alive? Is he still in the service? Does that mean that his arms and legs are okay? But that just couldn't be: his leg was crushed by a steel girder right before my eyes.

With only this small bit of information, Boris IV continued on in solitude. On the whole, he kept to himself not out of arrogance, nor even because of some postwar shock, as his grandfather and grandmother supposed, but simply because he had lost the habit of offering himself to others, if he had ever had such inclinations. Sometimes he caught himself hoping like an adolescent for some fortunate event of luck that would bring him together with some great guys and some beautiful girls.

As far as the first were concerned, the stroke of luck was not long in coming, and it happened quite naturally over motoring. One day two fellows in leather jackets approached Borya—Yury Korol and Misha Cheremiskin. At that very moment he was cranking up his Horch, which had suddenly stalled. He had raised the hood and was poking around in the engine, vast enough to be a metallurgical enterprise all by itself. The two lads stood behind him for a few minutes before one of them proposed taking a look at the "trambler": it was his opinion that a contact had come loose there. That turned out to be the case. When the car was running, the lads looked long and admiringly at the purring eight-cylinder beauty.

"Quite a piece of machinery," one of them said to Boris.

"From the number on the license plate, I gather it's private, not a government car?"

Thus they became acquainted. The two young men turned out to be motocross aces. Their motorcycles were parked nearby—two Harley-Davidsons, of course. "At the moment we're racing on these," they explained, "but when the new season starts we're going to have to move down to something worse. The Sports Committee has issued a decree that only domestic makes will be allowed in competition."

Just then another pair drove up: Vitya Korneev, the undisputed champion of cross-country skiing, and Natasha Ozolin, another first-class athlete. They immediately joined in the conversation. The topic was close to the heart of everyone in these circles. On the whole, admitted the sportsmen, there is a kernel of rightness in this decision. It's hard to see any more imports coming from America any time soon, so something has to be done to encourage industries here at home. Machines like the L-300 or the Comet, if we bring them up to speed, can compete with anything in Europe.

Borya was delighted with his new acquaintances. Luckily for me, I've met some regular guys! And the "regular guys" cordially accepted him into their number, particularly when they learned that he was the son of Marshal Gradov and himself a man with a mysterious military past. Moreover, he had an empty flat on Gorky Street that was always at everyone's disposal; and when it turned out that he knew a fair amount about German motorcycles, they all but fell at his feet.

Naturally, the young man threw himself headlong into the business of motorcycles. The Horch was abandoned except for infrequent nocturnal sorties. Quitting the school of working-class youths entirely, Boris IV now spent all his days in the garages of the Army and Dynamo clubs, as well as on one of the tree-lined walks in Petrovsky Park, where the "motorized youth" gathered on Sundays to exchange spare parts and gossip. He had still not been able to get a Harley, that sign of excellence of a first-class motorcyclist; on the other hand, he had managed to lay his hands on a powerful Wehrmacht Zuntag, which in the days of the Second World War had been equipped with a sidecar and machine gun and which was perfectly capable of carrying three fleshy Fritzes. Meanwhile, the sports club had provided him with a Russian make, a racing DKB with a 125cc engine. Naturally, he began to tune up this machine under the careful tutelage of Yury Korol and Misha Cheremiskin. Soon he began to show decent results on it: fifty-five at the half-mile mark from a standstill and seventy-five miles per hour top speed. "In a year, we guarantee it, you'll be an ace," the chiefs said. I'll be one before then, Boris smiled inwardly.

In the spring of 1949, the motorcycle gang went to Tallinn, in Estonia, for the annual race along the Pirita-Koze Ring Road. They rode at their own pace through the forests of Pskov and Chukhonia, even though the "forest brotherhood" partisan group frightened people there.

Babochka was ecstatic about the event on the Ring Road. No question about it, he thought, I have to win this carousel race sooner or later. For the time being, he was still warming the Army Club bench but was doing well in practice runs. The section of the public that knew something about the sporting scene clearly had its eye on him, as did a certain Iria Iyun, a racer from the Kalev club, a twenty-year-old beauty of pure Baltic stock with huge blue eyes. "It turns out that I feel simpler, more natural somehow, with the women of enslaved Europe," Boris said to her after they had passionately made each other's acquaintance by the light of the moon in the gothic fortress of Toompea.

Fortunately, she didn't understand a word and only laughed. "There are a few decent guys among the damned invaders," she said in her own language, giggling. "What's more, they bring good wines like Akhasheni."

As for the "forest brotherhood," it seemed to the eye of an experienced commando that at least half the crowd at the race were members, and no less than 80 percent of the townspeople. On one occasion, in the early hours of the morning at the Pirita Restaurant, which had been built in the "bourgeois independence" style, Rein Iyun, a basketball guard and the brother of Boris's girlfriend, took Boris aside and showed him the lining of his club jacket. There, in the area of the heart, was sewn a tricolored patch: white, blue, and black—the colors of free Estonia.

"Get the message?" Iyun asked threateningly.

"Got it!" shouted Boris. Everything was perfect: the motorcycles, the break of day, a bit of anti-Soviet feeling. Only, it's too bad I'm not an Estonian, I'd sew on the same patch. So what should a Russian clod like me sew under his own arm—a two-headed eagle? "I understand, Rein," he said to the brother. "I'm on your side!"

"Fool!" said the basketball player. He wanted to have a fight with the Russian, to give him one in the face for Estonia and for his sister. The country is unhappy, his sister laughs, so he wants to give a good fellow, a motorcyclist from Moscow, a punch in the nose.

So the days of a retired officer of the guard were passing, occupied with affairs like this, when one day Ludmila Iliinichna called from school (how had she, the "geography fairy," gotten his number?) and said, hesitantly, "Perhaps you've forgotten, Gradov, that the exams for the high school diploma begin in a week."

The first thing Boris did was to run out and buy some coffee. Then he went to a doctor who gave everyone prescriptions for codeine. This was the fad in student circles: get some codeine into you, and then you can study political economy all night or master any other rubbish you can name. He studied this way for a week, at first drinking coffee until he was blue in the face, then switching to codeine toward morning, so that everything began to blur together before his eyes. Either I'll fail miserably, or get a gold medal! In the end, neither happened. At the school of working-class youths, they tried to maintain a head count, and lapses of memory were simply filled in with the grade of "Pass." Codeine parties at dawn didn't do anything for anyone there, either. The chic, mysterious pupil Boris Gradov received his diploma, but with only mediocre marks.

To hell with them and their kiddy games! I'm going back to the "regular guys," to the bikers! Boris and his friends spent the summer following the motocross circuit—Saratov, Kazan, Sverdlovsk, Izhevsk. By autumn it turned out that he had racked up enough points to receive the title of "Master Sportsman of the USSR." The papers, signed by the coach, went to the committee.

It was then that it became clear that it was far too late to take the entrance exams for the institutes. Well, it's not so bad—I waited four years, I can wait one more. In that year I'll become a champion, and then any institute will be delighted to accept me, even without my taking an exam. Especially since I'm the son of a twice-decorated Hero of the Soviet Union, Marshal Gradov, whose name already graces a fairly smart street in the Peshchany quarter! In any case, Boris made the rounds of the selection committees of the most prestigious institutions—Moscow State University, Eastern Studies, Steel and Alloys . . . and then all of a sudden there arose another unexpected circumstance. It turned out he had better not count on a green light into any of these institutions, that he was not one of those "to whom all roads are open." On the selection committees sat specially trained people who told him that they had "done some checking" and that their advice would be not to submit his application, since in Russia a would-be student can apply to only one institution of higher learning each year. He would be simply wasting his chance.

You're wasting your time, Comrade Gradov. Our work here is to select high school graduates with only the most impeccable records. That is, your personal reputation is beyond reproach, one couldn't ask for better, as they said . . . er, well, you know where . . . but there are blemishes in your biographical information. Your biographical data is strange, atypical, Comrade Gradov. On the one hand, you have your grandfather, a medical luminary, the pride of our scientific community, and your father, a hero and an outstanding military man; on the other hand, however, there is your uncle, Kirill Borisovich, whose name is on the lists of "enemies of the people," and most important, your mother, Veronika Yevgenievna Taliaferro, who lives in the United States, the wife of a professor at an American military school. This, of course, is the decisive factor. . . .

What has happened to you, Boris IV? he asked himself as he paced from room to room at a late hour when no one was around in his huge flat. In nearly every corner could be found a half-liter jar filled with cigarette butts or an array of empty bottles, all left over from the last motorcyclists' get-together, or a pair of wheels for ice racing, or boxes of grease-covered spare parts, or a pile of clothes, or a stack of books. Somehow I don't see the connection between myself today and the person I was just the day before yesterday, whom Mama in her good moments called "my stern young fellow." What became of my patriotism? I can hear the words of my adoptive cousin Mitka Sapunov about "Communist monsters." But I'm one of them now. I joined back then, in the Polish woods, when everyone had to be accepted into the Party. No, that's not what I mean. Patriotism . . . it's not the Party, it's not even communism, it's just the feeling of being Russian, of tradition, "Gradovism" . . . something like that was just beginning to grow within me when I ran away from home like a damned fool, afraid the war would pass me by. It all dissolved in the muck of that punitive unit—yes, that's just what we were in Poland, a punitive outfit, and a savage bunch at that—it evaporated, "the Motherland," and all that was left was a cynical inward smirk. None of the lads ever grinned at the word "Motherland," everyone maintained a respectful silence, but he saw something of that smile reflected fleetingly on every face, as though the Devil himself were grinning right through their faces at the mention of the word "Motherland."

And now I've lost touch with myself in a way or, rather, with the "stern young fellow." Some sort of connection has come undone within me, and I can't get back to myself, assuming that that "stern fellow" was really me and not someone else—that is, if the disconnected person whom I now see myself as, is not my real nature.

I simply can't stay here without my mother, he suddenly thought one night when the flat was deserted. Back there in the forest, I didn't need my mother, but here in Moscow I can't get along without her. Maybe I ride around nonstop on these bikes because I can't manage without my mother. Maybe all-consuming speed is some mad way of reaching out to her. I can't get to her, though. She's in America, a traitor. America is a nation of traitors, of people who abandoned their homelands. She went off with her tall American, whom I hate more than Shevchuk. If we ever met on a battlefield, I'd have given him a good one. She betrayed our crafty, fat-assed country, betrayed Father, betrayed me. And she took Verulka, too. Now I'll never even have a sister.

Still, I do at least have my cousin Yolochka, thought Boris IV, racing down Leningradsky Prospekt on his Wehrmacht Zuntag. She's a darling, holds on to my steel belly with her sweet little fingers. What the hell, in the old days cousins used to get married. In those days I would have married Yolka. It's impossible now. Right now I need a sister more than a wife, maybe. Our Yolochka will find herself some jerk. It's not likely that he'll be a serious guy, a motorcycle ace. More likely some damned fool philologist she meets at the subscription series of concerts at the conservatory.

It was already quite dark by the time they arrived at the dacha. The gates were open: the old folks were expecting them. Boris drove into the yard and stopped opposite the large window of the dining room, where the remaining members of the Gradov clan were gathered around the table: the gray-haired, melancholy patriarch; Grandmother Mary, still upright and proud; the poetess Nina, still young and beautiful, the epitome of style, never without a cigarette in her

hand; and Agasha, who seemed to have no concept of age, all hustle
and bustle around the table, talking constantly in a monotone and still
serving up the same repertoire with which we favored our earlier readers: meat pies, cabbage *à la provençale,* country-style meatballs. . . .
Something new had appeared, however, in her bustling: from time to
time she would come to a stop with a dish in her hands and a philosophical expression on her face that crowded out her usual radiant
benevolence. She seemed to be asking someone a mute question: Is the
meaning of life to be found only in love for one's neighbor?

We should also not conceal from the reader that, after so many
losses in the Gradov clan, an addition had appeared as well, that is, a
sort of broadening—if such a definitive noun can be applied to the
balding, narrow-shouldered, bushy-mustached artist Sandro Pevzner,
whom Agasha referred to as none other than "maybe our husband,
maybe just a friend" in telephone conversations with her old friend
Comrade Slabopetukhovsky, now assistant director for buildings and
equipment at the Gorky Film Studios.

Yolka sprang from the motorcycle, and Borya slapped her roughly
on the shoulders, as a cousin should.

"Seems to me you were hugging me a bit too tenderly, mademoiselle. Where did you learn to do that?"

"Fool!" she replied, waving him away with her music folder. A
thought uncharacteristic for a motorcyclist suddenly flashed through
his mind: if only we could stop things, just to repeat this moment.

A slender girl with such graceful, impetuous movements, with such
a happy, unspoiled face. He looked at her as though he were no longer
young himself, as if he already knew perfectly well that he would
never again experience what Yolka was feeling now, an enchantment
with life and great expectations for it.

✫

She was sixteen years old but only now beginning the ninth grade. The
puritan education given by her school and the general sanctimony of
society, as well a certain lack of attention from her brilliant mother
combined with an overabundance of attention from her stately grandmother, had resulted in Yolka only quite recently coming to understand the strange glances men were giving her in the metro and on the

street. At first she thought that maybe a button had come off her coat
or that her socks were down around her ankles. Blushing, she looked
in a reflecting surface to see what the matter was and why she was on
the receiving end of these intent looks, which more often than not
were combined with wry smiles. One day she had been riding in the
metro with her mother. Suddenly someone fixed them with a stare. It
was a chubby-faced man in a large leather overcoat and white felt
boots with leather trim. Though Mama, as usual, was reading a
book—the diaries of Adelle Omar-Grey, it seemed—she noticed the
man and with a sharp movement tossed her hair back and looked directly and defiantly at him, as she knew how to do. Then something
happened that for both mother and daughter was as engrossing as it
was unforgettable: the mother realized that the man's lustful attention
was directed not at her but at her daughter. Blushing, she turned to
Yolka, whereupon the full meaning of this instant reached the girl
who only yesterday had been a child. Something happened to her then
that she had never known before, the dawning of a feeling that was at
once obscenely agitating and joyfully, musically intoxicating. Her
mother, taking her by the hand and leading her to the doors of the
car—fortunately, they were approaching their stop, the Lenin Library—felt a keen, momentary sadness, if one can call "sadness"
something that stings instantly. Of course, they never said a word to
each other in the days that followed about the whirlwind of emotions
that had descended upon them thanks to some creepy, fat-faced type
in a metro car between Okhotny Ryad and the library, and yet, of the
mass of moments in life that come in throngs and vanish, this was one
that stood out clearly and that neither would ever forget.

In short, Yolochka had grown up, and now after school and before
her piano lesson, she ran home to Bolshoi Gnezdnikovsky Street, to
change from her hated brown school uniform with its black apron to
Mama's jacket with the padded shoulders and put on a bit of eye
shadow to set off the radiant eyes of the Gradov-Kitaigorodsky line.

She had already spent half her life, that is, eight years, without her
father. She remembered Papa as a friend—a giant with whom she had
frolicked and laughed. Small, bright pictures of her early childhood
flared up and then died out: Papa the skier, Papa the swimmer, Papa
the camel—that is, when she rode on his shoulders from the lake to

the train station—Papa the wise man reading and explaining *Don Quixote,* Papa the glutton devouring a whole frying pan full of macaroni and cheese, Papa as Mama's ever-loyal knight giving the poetess Gradov a chinchilla coat disguised as ordinary heavy wool, straightening his coat and tails in the form of an ordinary jacket. The two of them going to a ball at the House of Writers . . .

"Like Sam, like Sam!" she remembered her father shouting.

"What, don't you see that I look like Sam in this outfit?"

Mama and Elena had nearly died laughing. It was only many years later than Yolka found out that by "Sam" her father meant Stalin. That was why Mama had laughed so hard, because imagining Stalin in coat and tails was so impossible to do. Of course, it would have been still funnier if Papa had said simply, "Today I'm like Stalin in tails," but he had been quite right not to say it, because he was afraid that the next day at kindergarten his little daughter would pretend to be "Stalin in tails" for her classmates. He had been right, of course: Yolka remembered that she had indeed hopped around the kindergarten yelling "Sam in tails! Sam in tails!" like a town crier.

The words "killed in action" with which she had filled in the space beside "Father" on the biographical information form for school had never acquired their full meaning for her—that is, she had never pictured to herself her father's body riddled by bullets and decaying in the damp earth. At first, "killed in action" simply meant that he had disappeared; that he was somewhere, of course, but could not reach his one and only daughter. She saw Mama weeping into her pillow in private, and, in imitation, wept into her pillow, too. She did it, however, with the certainty that these tears would in the end help to bring Papa back. As she grew older, she realized that Papa would never come to them again, that he was no more. Nevertheless, the idea of the destruction of his flesh did not occur to her.

Suddenly her big brother appeared—well, not her real big brother, rather, her cousin. But what a great one, Boris IV! They became instant friends, often going together to the movies or skating. Sometimes he even took her along with him to show her off, and then she noticed how obviously proud he was of her before his friends: look what a beautiful sister I've got! There was a funny, affectionate side to their relationship that somehow bore an oblique resemblance to the frolicking of her distant childhood, that reminded her of her half-forgotten father. Too bad he's my brother, she thought sometimes: I'd marry him.

★

So they entered the house, to the great joy of their waiting family. There used to be a dog here, too, our beloved Pythagoras, they both thought at the same time. Recalling the animal was not difficult for Boris: the German shepherd had been in the prime of its life when he was a child. Boris had always maintained half seriously that Pythagoras had played an important role in his upbringing. And yet it seemed to Yolka that she could remember perfectly crawling along the carpet, the old and noble Pythagoras circling and touching her from time to time with a paw.

So they went in, and everyone's face lit up. Even the high-strung Nina beamed fleetingly before plunging into her newspaper again; Sandro beamed as well.

★

The latter had managed to register himself in Moscow upon returning from the war, at the address of his only living relative, an elderly aunt. His happiness knew no bounds. He could scarcely imagine living far from Nina. At first, everything had gone smoothly. His first official exhibition was a success. For that matter, a favorable review in *Culture and Life* had read, "Sandro Pevzner unites the best artistic traditions of the Jack of Diamonds school with deep patriotic content and powerful impressions of his recent martial past." Nowadays it was impossible to imagine that anyone could write such a thing in 1945: the Jack of Diamonds school and patriotism. In those days, however, the reputation of the movement had grown by leaps and bounds, and the Moscow Arts Council had allotted him a studio in an abandoned garret on a little side street on the Arbat. After obtaining canvases and brushes, Sandro had transformed the musty hole into the cozy nest of the flourishing bohemian painter: it had a huge, semioval window with a view of the rooftops of Moscow; a spiral staircase to a balcony; a fireplace; shelves filled with books, albums, old steam irons, copper bowls, teapots, and samovars. On the floors, which he had sanded with his own hands, he had put down two old carpets from Tbilisi; from somewhere he had got himself a "pile of wood that still sounds good," that is, an antique baby grand piano, which "sounded good" only in the imagination, since it was missing two thirds of its strings and most of the keys stuck. Someday, when it was restored, of course, it would create that atmosphere peculiar to Moscow artistic evenings, the most important decoration of which, and the most constant, would undoubtedly be the poetess Nina Gradov.

"Well, then, 'gallant fighter and patriot with powerful impressions of your recent martial past,' " said Nina when she visited the completed "Pevzner pad," "you might say that this is your final victory. I'm never leaving here again!"

So Nina took to living in two flats, one on Bolshoi Gnezdnikovsky Street and one on the Arbat. Happily, the distance between the two was not great. The growing Yolka quickly got used to the situation and had nothing against it. She liked the painter and called him simply "Sandro," without the bourgeois addition of "Uncle." For that matter, she often called her mother "Nina," as though she were one of her girlfriends.

Sandro pleaded with his beloved to "make their relationship legal and decent," but she played dumb every time he brought up the subject, asking him what he meant—after all, she tried every time she was in bed with him to make their relationship as decent she could.

In a word, everything was going wonderfully well in the life of the "divine dauber" as Nina sometimes called him, until the ideological whirlwind of the late 1940s blew through. Following the arrest of the members of the Jewish Anti-Fascist Committee, Jew-baiting edicts began to make their way down from on high to artistic organizations. In January 1949, the Party published a directive entitled "On the Repertoire of Drama Theaters and their Improvement." An unpatriotic group of theater critics was unmasked, a group consisting specifically of Yuzovsky, Gurevich, Varshavsky, Yutkevich, and Nathan Altman, who were trying to discredit positive phenomena in Soviet theater and from aesthetic, un-Marxist, and cosmopolitan positions were attacking outstanding contemporary dramatists, namely Aleksei Surov, Anatoly Sofronov, Boris Romashev, and Aleksandr Korneichuk, while trying to promote the ideologically alien plays of Aleksandr Galich (Ginzburg) and other Jewish authors who use Russian pen names, kowtowing before the bourgeois West. A mighty "anti-cosmopolitan" campaign was mounted by the Soviet people, and indignant letters from milkmaids, metallurgists, and fishermen demanding that "every last one of the cosmopolitans be unmasked" poured into the editorial offices of the national media. Within the artists' organizations, there were endless plenums and general meetings at which the speakers hysterically demanded "the revealing of the parentheses" that enabled the cosmopolitans to hide behind Russian pseudonyms. The writers, of course, were particularly diligent in their efforts, but the artists didn't want to lag behind.

Sandro's turn did not come right away. The gendarmes had obviously been tripped up by his Georgian given name, which concealed his Jewish surname. Friendship between the peoples of the USSR had to be guarded by whatever means necessary, and it was clearly thanks to this postulate that Sandro was able for a time to "play the fool," as Nina acidly put it.

One day, however, the eye of the secretary of the Moscow Arts Council, a certain wormlike art critic named Kemyanov, searched him out in a hall that was overcrowded and sweating from fear, and announced that the time had come to seriously bring up the question of the last holdouts of the decadent Jack of Diamonds and Donkey's Tail groups, and in particular the artist Alexander Solomonovich Pevzner. What was he presenting to Soviet man on his own canvases? A rehash of the decadent poetics of Marc Chagall, Alexandra Exster, El Lissitzky, and Nathan Altman. The Russian people, with their lofty realistic traditions, had no need of such teachers.

They asked for an explanation. The pale Sandro at first stammered from the speaker's platform but then regained his strength, and, had he been trying to choose the worst words possible, he could not have improved on them. In the first place, he said, I don't understand why the aesthetic principles of the Jack of Diamonds are in conflict with patriotism. In the second place, one should not lump the "Jack" and the "Tail" together, as they are implacable enemies. In the third place, both of these groups are composed of bright personalities, and it would be a good idea to speak about each artist separately. In the fourth place, Comrade Kemyanov listed only the surnames of Jewish decadent cosmopolitans just to arouse greater fear. At this point, Kemyanov slammed his fist down in anger on the dais of the presidium and glared at the speaker with eyes of fire that resembled those of a serpent much more than those of a worm . . . but for some reason Sandro went on, he did not cite a single Russian family name of such masters as, say, Natalia Goncharov, Mikhail Larionov, Vassily Kandinsky . . .

Now the representative from the Central Committee, a certain Gilichev, a man with a block of clay for a forehead and damp, plant-like suckers for lips, turned to Kemyanov with a dreary question. In reply, the latter quickly whispered something about those who had been mentioned. Gilichev interrupted the artist Pevzner, who was trying to confuse those present with long-winded reflections on some sort of "melting down" of the traditions of the revolutionary avant-garde, and asked how it was that a Soviet painter and member of an artistic organization had turned out to be so knowledgeable about the so-called work of the émigré rabble, the White Guards of art? Might there not be some sort of trick in all of these ruminations about creative "melting down"? Isn't this an attempt to introduce bourgeois scale into our steel?

Sandro came down from the platform, and the "unmaskers" immediately took his place. Several of his old friends disowned him on the spot. Someone proposed the immediate debunking of the myth that Sandro Pevzner was talented. A sleepy-eyed, perpetually tipsy bear of a sculptor even shouted that they should "reveal Pevzner's brackets," whereupon Sandro, forgetting any beating about the bush, shouted, "What sort of parentheses do you need, you moron? Take the brackets off your own stupid head!"

The drunken man roared with laughter and began to mimic a Georgian accent. No one supported him, however: everyone knew who else in Moscow spoke with a Georgian accent. Silence reigned, and in this silence, already consumed by fear, Sandro Pevzner proudly left the hall. That, in any case, was how he told the story to Nina, with a sharp, dismissive wave of the hand to one side and then upward: "And then I walked right out of the hall!" he said in his broad Georgian accent. In fact, he had scarcely made it to the door and then had run pell-mell down the hall in the direction of fresh air. His friend cognac came to his rescue until morning as he awaited his arrest, which, however, never came. Almost none of the leading "cosmopolitans" was arrested then: perhaps it was because the hands of the Party did not yet have them by the balls, or perhaps it was because they had decided to let the affair "marinate" for a while for future use. An animal, stomach-wrenching fear tormented them all, though. It was inhuman; it really did hit them in the stomach, right where they lived, as they say; and it was the kind of fear that causes a humiliating peristalsis in the belly, when gases begin intermingling with a dimly felt yet clear menace in the lower regions at moments of high drama. The fear was not surprising: after all, behind every line of Party criticism stood a police agent, a torturer, an executioner, a guard in the ancient cold of the camps.

All the liberals in Moscow were tongue-tied by fear. The members of Nina's circle no longer told one another jokes in which even the slightest sarcasm about ideology might be detected, however fleetingly. There was no call for even ironic mimicry. Just try to snigger after hearing some speech by that All-Union swine Anatoly Sofronov. Someone would race off straight away to report you to "the appropriate authorities." There remained only glances, which were exchanged without the slightest movement of the facial muscles. By means of these looks, with which, one would say, no one could find fault, the liberals learned to judge who was still holding out, in the sense of belonging to their set. Eyes raised ceilingward immediately said, Don't count on me anymore; soon some ugly article, some treacherous denunciation, or some vile "patriotic" short story is going to come out over my signature.

Life, nevertheless, went on, and one had to make money in order to ensure its continuation. Sandro found himself completely besieged: there was no point in even thinking about the possibility of an exhibition or an official reception for his paintings. He was happy just to be able to get a bit of hackwork: doing the layout for the wall newspaper of a collective farm in the Moscow region or receiving an order, or sometimes two, through an intermediary for a mock-up of a postage stamp dedicated to heroic Soviet artillerymen. The household's principal income came from Nina, who had managed to set herself up as a translator, working from interlinear cribs, of the leading poets of the Caucasus and Central Asia, those monstrous offspring of socialism who were creating a new culture, "national in form, socialist in content." Nina received rather handsome honoraria from these republics, one of which, despite its belated arrival, conferred upon her the title of "distinguished figure" of its culture.

These so-called translations, from a language they didn't know a word of, were the chief source of income for many poets. Even Akhmatova, pursued by Zhdanov himself, and Pasternak, who remained silent and hiding behind his shrubs in Peredelkino, did this sort of work. Just forget about everything, Nina thought sometimes, and live like Boris Leonidovich. He doesn't seem to give himself over to grief. He writes his own things "for the desk drawer" and makes a decent living with translations; they even say that he's fallen in love at sixty. He lives as though he doesn't notice what's going on around him: "Dear friends, what millennium is it outside?" Why is it that everyone is constantly thrashing me? Why can't I get away from these loathsome articles that "lay bare the parentheses," why do I go to these nightmarish meetings and remember who said what, as though one day it will be possible to ask questions when one has unclean lips?

★

After dinner, she slapped her hand down on the latest *Pravda* with forceful spite, crushed out her cigarette, and laughed out loud.

"I tell you, señors and señoritas, there's quite a bit to read in this one today!"

Everyone looked at her in surprise.

"Stop it," Sandro said calmly. He didn't want her to begin reading the wooden phrases of *Pravda* in different voices, as she often did when they were alone together. There was no need to disrupt a peaceful family meal in this way, not to mention the fact that she could pass on the virus of dangerous sarcasm to the young people here.

"What have you found there, Auntie Nina?" Boris IV asked condescendingly. He himself looked only at the back page of this newspaper, where they sometimes printed sports articles.

"Today's text deserves everyone's attention," Nina went on, refusing to quit. "Just listen to the stylistic wonders that are produced in these times!"

The article was entitled "A Depraved Book." The author, Comrade B. Pankov, told with measured anger and a tinge of Party-spirited mockery the story of how a certain Vologda writer by the name of G.

Yaffe had taken up the pen to write a book called *The Collective Farm Girl from Shleibucht* as part of a series of portraits of contemporary innovators. As his heroine he had chosen a Stalin Prize laureate, the pig herder Alexandra Yevgrafovna Luskov.

In describing this splendid farmworker, G. Yaffe says that "It is though she comes forth from the face of nature, knowing all of the characteristics of pigs, chickens, and roosters, right down to the smallest detail, analyzing every grunt and peep, by the aid of which she can even predict the weather. It is precisely this profound understanding of nature that allows Luskov to reconstruct living organisms. Thus, according to Yaffe, faith in a rooster's forecasts will lead to serious practical and scientific results. . . . The writer is clearly not without scabrous intent when he characterizes this innovator as "a farmer's wife," "a guardian," "a zealous trustee"; what sort of terms are these, where do they come from? He debases the language of the people, using far-fetched proverbs like "I don't like to walk backwards on my heels."

. . . Yaffe crudely distorts the endeavors of a deputy, saying that all Luskov does is struggle against injustice. Life in the Soviet countryside and the achievements of the innovators are presented in an erroneous form. . . . Some, he writes, have arrived at utterly fantastic (?) results. Fortunately, these achievements found expressions in live, numbered piglets. Otherwise, the story about them would undoubtedly (?) seem like one of the stories of Baron von Münchhausen. . . . And how do you like these pearls, reader? "Sows often give birth to creatures that have no sooner looked at the world than they decide 'Bah, life's not worth living!' "

This is the kind of stupidity that quasi literature leads to!

And can you not see the insulting smirk in lines like this, for example: "We need to hold to a Michurin line in all our gardening, down to the roots." It is incomprehensible why K. Gulyaev, editor in chief of Vologda Publishers, was so careless with such ridicule of the experience of the most progressive people in our country. Books about the progressive Stalin Five-Year Plans should extol the inspired labor of the builders of communism.

When she finished reading, Nina was already breathless from laughter. "Well, how about that?" she asked those around the table.

"How about that Yaffe, isn't he Gogol? And Pankin, isn't he Belinsky? Why, Comrades, this is nothing less than a new 'Belinsky's letter to Gogol'! I don't think I'm mistaken in calling this one of the fundamental texts of Russian culture!"

She was savoring her caustic *bon mot:* a new "Belinsky's letter to Gogol." Again and again she looked at those around her to see if they got the joke. Mama cautiously, very cautiously, smiled. Papa smiled more freely, but with what looked like a slight shaking of his head, as if to say "your tongue is your enemy." Yolka burst out laughing: they had just studied "Belinsky's letter to Gogol" at school, so it was not impossible that it reminded her of something that had nothing to do with Mama's escapades. Boris IV smiled as well, chewing on a bit of a meat pie as he did so: he had been taught in the secret services not to laugh at the State, and a newspaper, after all, was "the sharpest weapon of the Party." The housekeeper nodded her head in an inadequate gesture of grief. Sandro, while beaming at Nina's comparison, thought it wisest to say nothing. In short "the people were silent." And tomorrow I'll take this issue to the translators' section and read it again there, thought Nina, knowing full well that she would never do so: she wasn't crazy, after all!

The silence was interrupted by Agasha: "Why do you always have to smoke like a chimney?" she asked Nina severely, reaching for the cigarette in the other's mouth. Unable to reach it, she turned to Yolka. "And you, why do you always swallow everything without chewing, like a seagull? Take a lesson from Babochka here, see how well he chews. He'll be a tiger."

At this point, everyone broke into laughter—loudly, marvelously—and the tension was broken. "By the way, your highnesses, I have a surprise for you," Boris IV said to his grandparents. "I trust, Boris III, most august sovereign, that you will not fall off your chair when you learn that your lackadaisical offspring has finally decided to go to medical school!"

It had not been for nothing that he had made a joke about the chair. It had been a long time since the seventy-four-year-old surgeon had experienced an emotion as strong as that of happiness. Do my ears deceive me? Do my eyes deceive me? Do my hands deceive me? Boris Nikitovich walked around his grandson, then took him by his powerful shoulders and looked into his steely eyes. Can it be that the heir to the Gradov dynasty of Russian doctors sits before me? Babochka, my dear, I'm sure that you'll make a good doctor! After everything that it has been your lot to live through, you'll be a splendid physician and clinical scientist.

The evening concluded on a note of Chopin, as in the good old days. Mary Vakhtangovna improvised on the theme from the Second Concerto in F Minor; today it came out major! Her loyal knight, who had never been unfaithful to her in his life (in contrast to her, a sinner, who had cheated on him once at the time of the brief Georgian renaissance), stood, as he had in the old days, with his elbows propped up on the piano and nodded with profound understanding. He knew that this performance was not only in honor of Bobka-Babochka but in his honor as well, as a sign of gratitude for the courage he had displayed. Just that morning Boris Nikitovich had turned down an offer by the Party bureau of the academy to promote him to vice president. He had alluded, it was true, to his age and the state of his health, but everyone understood perfectly well that the conscience of a Russian doctor would not permit him to occupy the post of a banished "rootless cosmopolitan," the Academician Lurie.

★

After the concert, Boris, who had decided to stay the night with his grandparents, went off to walk his aunt, his cousin, and Sandro "maybe husband, maybe friend" Pevzner to the streetcar stop. All four of them smoked steadily as they walked along the tree-lined path. No, the author has not made a mistake, dear readers, you who are familiar with the puritanical standards for young schoolgirls that reigned at the end of the forties and the beginning of the fifties: Yolka got away with smoking from time to time—though not, of course, in the presence of her grandparents—and it always brought her to a state of quiet exaltation. "What prompted you all of a sudden to follow 'the noble path,' Boris?" Nina asked.

Her nephew shrugged. "What else did you want me to do? Of course I thought about the Moscow Aviation Institute, but those representatives—well, you understand who I mean—let me know quite clearly that I had no chance. Just tell that to anyone, and they won't believe it. The son of a twice-decorated hero, a marshal of the USSR, and almost a hero in his own right. . . . You know, I was nominated for 'Hero,' but then they changed it to a 'Red Banner.' And now I have no way of getting into the really prestigious schools. It's a lot of crap. One uncle, you see, is an 'enemy of the people,' and, most important of all, Mama is in the USA, married to a Yankee imperialist. That's enough to tip the scales. So I have to keep my head down. What was there for me to do? I have to get an education! The only way to do it is to be taken under Grandpa's wing. By the way, he promised that maybe even this year I could take the entrance examinations late, as a returning soldier. Why not become a doctor, when you come right down to it? There is, after all, this dynasty, the tradition. I'll race for the "Medic" team. . . .

He was still talking, shrugging his shoulders, grinning, and tossing away and lighting one cigarette after another when Nina suddenly took him firmly by the arm, hung on it lightly, and looked into his eyes. "Tell me, Borya . . . do you miss her? Would you like to see her?"

Why am I doing this? she wondered. Writer's curiosity taken to the limits of cruelty . . .

Boris walked a few strides further with his aunt on his arm, yet she already felt the extremity hardening in enmity. He jerked his arm away, went on ahead slightly, then suddenly turned his splendid features, burning with youthful intensity, toward them.

"You . . . you . . ." It was clear that he felt like a drowning man looking for straws to clutch at and, finally finding some, smirked haughtily. "I hope you understand that if I wanted to see her, I would do it just like that!" He snapped his fingers over his right ear. What a strange gesture, Nina thought. But then, God knows what he went through in Poland!

"What have you got in mind, Borka?" asked the horrified Yolka. "Crossing the border?"

He shrugged. "Why not?"

The girl threw up her hands, which flashed white in the darkness. "But it's impossible, Borka! Across the Soviet frontier? What are you saying?"

Satisfied that his flash of childish desperation seemed to have passed unnoticed, Boris IV grinned. "Nothing in particular. In theory, there's nothing easier. . . . You'll have to excuse me, Nina, Yolka, and Sandro, but you don't seem to understand what kind of man I am and the work that I had to do during the war and for three years after."

By then they had stopped beneath a streetlight and formed a small circle. Boris was looking at Nina with an inscrutable smile.

Oh, what a brother I've got, thought an enraptured Yolka.

I believe I do understand what kind of work he did during the war and in the three years that followed, thought Sandro. These murderers. . . . He resolutely crossed out the frightful word and replaced it with "cutthroats," as though that made it at least a bit better. . . . He had had occasion to see those fellows: from time to time they would fly back from the enemy's rear to receive instructions at front headquarters.

Nina was suddenly pierced by a thought: why, he's only a child who's lost his mama, long ago. After that night in 1937, she never came back to him. He's just an orphan, his grandmother's Babochka. She threw his arms around his neck, embraced him, and whispered into his ear, "I beg you, Borka, dear, don't ever say anything about this again, not even to us! Don't you realize what you're making jokes about? For the sake of everything holy, for the sake of all the Gradovs, you have to stop even thinking about crossing the border!"

He was dumbfounded. What are all these impassioned prayers? Does that mean she takes it all seriously, that Auntie Nina still doesn't understand the jokes of guys like me?

"Calm down, Auntie Nina. . . . Take it easy, now, I'm just a kid making a joke." He stroked her back and suddenly felt something entirely inappropriate for a nephew to feel toward his forty-two-year-old aunt. He quickly moved away. Damned Freudian theories, he thought. The lighting of a cigarette came to his rescue. "By the way, Comrades, I should add that I haven't the slightest desire to see my little mother. Let her—"

The two large, electrically lit boxes that were streetcar 18 approached. Two hooligans with eight-panel caps with the brims cut down jumped off. The household of Pevzner the artist got on, Borya pulled the cord, and the bell jangled. The boxes of light moved off into the blackness with the three cherished heads in the second one.

Boris crushed out his cigarette with his heel and immediately lit another. The two toughs were standing by a closed kiosk and looking in his direction. Do these two characters want to have a word? It would be good to have a chat with them right about now. A left to the liver for one of them, a right to the teeth for the other. He'll go flying straight into that fence. Don't take any shit from anyone! He walked up to them and stared intently at their faces. Both of them averted their eyes fearfully. One of them sniffed.

☆

Lyuda Sorokin, a student at a hairdressing college, had been sitting trembling for at least three hours in a mansion on Kachalov Street, waiting for she didn't know what. But what could a girl in such cozy, luxuriant surroundings have to fear? A huge pile carpet covers half the drawing room floor. A drawing room—there's no other name for it—with soft, unobtrusive lights dimmed by ornate lampshades. Three lush roses—one red, one pink, one cream—stand in three narrow crystal vases. Two more magnificent carpets, not new, it must be said, hang on the wall. They've obviously seen some use. One of them shows a scene of some Moors in a fortress, the other depicts sea monsters. A third wall contains a library of leather-bound books. A fourth is draped with material of the highest quality, silk decorated with tassels, on the other side of which is a high window. Peek through a part in the silken curtains, and there's a soldier walking back and forth on guard outside. What else did Lyuda Sorokin notice in the course of those three hours? In one corner stood a marble figure of a female nude with rather the same figure as Lyuda herself, when she could see it in the mirror at the Danilovsky Baths on the way to the wash hall. Just the day before Lyuda had been in the bathhouse, with her mother and one of their neighbors, and had scrubbed all of her private parts. The marble girl covered her most important spot with the remnants of her clothes, but she had a depraved smile on her face. Lyuda's lips were quivering: she did not know what awaited her in the drawing room, what charges would be brought against her. There were three beautiful mirrors here like those at the Danilovsky Baths, in carved frames. One was to the left of the bed, one to the right, and one, which was rather more interesting, was directly over the bed. So the bed looked like what the senior hairdresser, Isaac Israelevich, would have called "a work of art." You couldn't even call this bed a bed, since the entire nine-square-meter room that the Sorokins occupied in the far-off Zamoskvorechie district didn't come close to it in area. It had a headboard with—my heavens!—two interwoven swans carved into it, but no footboard. The bed was very low, eighteen inches or so off the floor; you couldn't hide beneath it. On the whole, it wasn't a bed, then, but rather what Alexandre Dumas Père called a loge in *La Reine Margot*. That's it, a loge, spread with yet another carpet bearing a pattern of intertwining flowers and, in addition, velvet cushions scattered about. It seems like . . . Lyuda looked around and then touched the surface with her hand: the small, taut area was resilient. What are they going to do with me here? Are they really going to have me copulate with a male organ, as they say at school? But the general who invited me was so handsome, seemed so reliable. Oh, I hope they're not going to have me shot!

A mature lady in a lace apron and a cap of the same material on her head came in. She brought in a tray—my heavens!—with delightful fruits and three kinds of chocolates, a pair of silver tongs in each box. "Dear lady, where am I?" Lyuda asked.

The woman smiled without a trace of warmth. "You're a guest of the government, miss. Do try some of these things, they're very tasty."

Lyuda ate a piece of chocolate. Oh, how delicious, the kind of thing that you taste once in your life: a chocolate-covered walnut! Well, the government doesn't shoot people, after all, that is, it doesn't do the job itself. And there's probably not going to be any copulating, either; otherwise things wouldn't look so impressive, somehow. Suddenly, music began to play, and at the symphony's first sounds, which made Lyuda tremble all over again, she realized she was not going to get out of there on her own. And now, finally, after three hours, an old man wearing a theatrical dressing gown hung with tassels, like on the curtains, arrived. On his head was a skullcap, and on his fleshy nose spectacles without earpieces, a "penis-nay," or something like that. Lyuda jumped to her feet and stood as straight as the young lady in marble, though she herself was fully dressed.

"Good evening," said the old man politely. He appeared not to be Russian. "What's your name?"

"Lyuda," the young hairdressing student managed to blurt out. "Lyuda Sorokin."

"Pleased to meet you, Comrade Lyuda." He extended his hand. He seemed to have heard only "Lyuda" and to have no use for the "Sorokin." "And I'm Lavrenty Pavlovich."

The rather pleasant-sounding name reached the ears of the fear-stricken Lyuda as something ferocious. What was the name—Vavery Salovich?

"There's nothing to be worried about, Comrade Lyuda," said Vavery Salovich. "We're going to have dinner now." He sat down in a leather armchair next to Lyuda and pushed a button on an elaborately decorated table. Almost immediately, the woman of a short while before, together with a military man, rolled in a table on wheels; Lyuda hadn't even known there were such things. All of the dishes on the table were covered with silver lids, except for a crystal bowl containing a mound of caviar. Lyuda was familiar with this particular edible from the cultural excursions to the Young Spectators' Theater, when they treated themselves to sandwiches during the intermission. What was hardly familiar to her at all, however, was the bucket on the table, from which protruded the neck of a bottle. Two other bottles had made the trip on their own, that is, without buckets. Everything was spread out on the artistic table before Lyuda and Vavery Salovich. After that, the servants wheeled away the means of transport. Vavery Salovich smiled like a kindly grandfather and showed Lyuda how to put her napkin on her lap.

"Do you like Beethoven?" he asked.

"Oh, my," Lyuda exhaled.

"Let's start with the caviar, then," he advised, then added sternly, "You have to eat three tablespoons straight away. It's very healthy." Maybe he's some sort of government doctor, thought Lyuda. Is he going to give me a physical?

"How wonderfully you sup upon this silvery caviar, Comrade Lyuda," Vavery Salovich said with a smile. "Your lips are like cherries. And probably just as sweet, eh?" His booming laugh briefly drowned out the music. No, doctors don't laugh that way. "And now we must have a sip of this connoisseur's wine." With his own hand Vavery Salovich filled a crystal goblet with a deep red, translucent liquid.

"But I don't drink, Comrade," she muttered. He beamed with kindness. "That doesn't matter. The time has come for you to drink a good wine. How old are you? Eighteen? Almost? Ho, ho, again these RSFSR laws! Well, drink it down, to the bottom!"

Lyuda took a swallow, then another, and then another—well, you just can't put this wine down. Suddenly she laughed with the warble of a nightingale. "Vavery Salovich, you're a doctor, right?" I feel like I'm bobbing on waves. The whole table is swaying gently on the water. The most pleasant waves are rocking the whole room back and forth. Vavery Salovich has the right word for it, it's our "boudoir."

"Do you like our boudoir, Lyudochka?"

We're rolling together with the furniture of the whole boudoir, and that's why the plates don't fall. But why are you getting so close to me? If you want to examine me, that's fine, but why are you dragging me? They're pulling me out of the boudoir, dragging me someplace. Vavery Salovich, help me! I'm a guest of the government, after all! Vavery Salovich, don't pull on me that way—you should be helping me to get out of this, Vavery Salovich. Oh, it's funny, you turned out to be not very reliable after all, Isaac Israelevich . . .

Beria dragged the drooping girl across to the ottoman and began to undress her. Her cherry lips were babbling as if she were still a total child, and from time to time she squealed like a young pig. What dreadful undergarments they wear in this city. They're enough to make the desire to fuck her disappear. A homemade polka-dot slip, pink flannel panties, a nightmare. . . . It's good that girls at least shorten them, cutting them off above the elastic, which does the Devil's own work of deforming their thighs. It's an outrage, we show no concern for youth. In the first place, we need to provide for the distribution of ladies' underwear. He removed her panties and then put them to his nose. Not a bad smell, musty, maybe a bit sour, a little scent of shit along the seam, but that's normal with this sort of underwear. The desire was growing again quickly. Now I've got to undress her entirely and forget about social problems. After all, don't I have the right to a few small pleasures? I carry such a burden!

He stripped Lyuda naked and saw that she was first-class material. He played with her breasts, taking her nipples into his mouth, raised her girlish legs, and began to enter her. Right now is when she'll start yelling . . . no, she's just smiling in blissful detachment, murmuring some Jewish name—can't get away from them even here! No, these days, as you can see, you won't find a virgin in Moscow!

Now Beria realized that he was in his best form, one big blissful, uncontrolled libido. Now I'll fuck her for half an hour without stopping. It's even a pity she's only semiconscious, otherwise she could appreciate it. These powders from the pharmacological labs are a bit too strong. He removed his dressing gown and saw reflected in the mirror a scene that was at once enchanting and scandalous: a lousy old man with a sagging, hairy potbelly fucking a young shepherd girl. The spectacle in the upper mirror was even more breathtaking: an acorn-like bald spot, a wrinkled neck, a fleshy back, along which hairy atavisms ran from the lower region to the shoulder blades. The porous, rosy pork of the rhythmically moving buttocks could be seen as well. From beneath all of this property there sprawled out to the sides the legs and arms of a girl, whose cloudy eyes and moaning mouth were glimpsed here and there from behind his shoulders: what poetry! It's too bad only that it's not possible to simultaneously light up and observe the principal units of this combat action. We still haven't made that advance in technology.

Beria dragged Lyuda Sorokin back and forth across the vast ottoman. Now and again, for variety, he would turn the girl over on her stomach, shove a cushion beneath her pubic area, and bend her legs into the desired configuration: here's the ideal partner, a hot-blooded doll!

She was bleeding slightly from her vagina. Hasn't been worked on enough. This Isaac Israelevich still hasn't broken the girl in. Never mind—in the not too distant future we'll have the ideal vagina here at our disposal! To make his triumph even more complete, Beria began to pinch Lyuda Sorokin's stomach in order to make her cry. She didn't make him wait, bursting into tears through the haze of MGB pharmacology. What a beauty, *sheni deda movtkhani,* a scoundrel from the Caucasus fucking a weeping Russian child.

And now, finally, the moment had come for what Beria, Lavrenty Pavlovich, named by N. S. Khrushchev at the July plenum of the Central Committee four years later as an "insolent and impudent enemy of the USSR," always dreamed of in the dungeons and corners of his ill-lit soul. All overriding considerations or external motives for his insatiable lust vanished. Forgetting about his own all-powerful villainy and all the other mythology which he had invented for himself and that always worked him up into a state of filthy excitement—I'm a Mingrel, a mountaineer from northern Georgia—I can screw any Russian woman, can turn any one of them into a whore, a slave, a trophy, I can shoot or pardon, torture someone or give them a fine apartment and French underwear, or turn right around and trample everyone into the permafrost—forgetting all of that, he suddenly felt himself nothing more than a man, hot and passionate, in love with the universe, which had spread its legs wide open to him, in the form of Woman, with a capital "W," Comrades.

If there's anyone who understands this, it's Pyotr Sharia, thought Beria, coming to peace with himself next to the girl muttering unconsciously wiping his still warm shoot with her polka-dot slip. It's a good thing I rescued him from the claws of that Bolshevik bumpkin. Found all kinds of treason there, you see—pessimistic poetry dedicated to his young son dying of tuberculosis. He imagined that he heard the shrieks of his lawfully wedded wife somewhere in the depths of the mansion. She's demanding to be admitted to the boudoir. But if I give the order to let her in, she'll get frightened and run upstairs to hide. She'll wait for me to tie her to a birch tree in the garden and to beat her with a Nogai whip. The proud Princess Gigechkori, *Chuchkhiani chatlakhi!* Who told you that the number two man in the government has to be under the heel of a frigid woman?

Sharia understands this. I can be open with him. He's a poet and a pessimist, the same kind of son of a bitch as I am, he's not afraid of me. Nugzar is no friend, he fears me. There's no more life in him, there's nothing living in him but the fear of Beria. I can't open myself up to him, but Sharia I can tell all about my screwing around and about my wife, I can forget about politics. If I invite the two of them right now to come for a nightcap and to fuck this little dove, Nugzar won't want to. He'll come, that *khle,* of course, but only out of fear. Sharia will come, but only if he wants to. And if he doesn't want to, he won't. A poet, a Party adventurist—he's completely unafraid of me.

I'm surrounded by shit. When the time comes, I'll clear all the shit away. I need to surround myself with real comrades when the time comes. With real men, poets, not Bolsheviks. I'll drive all this rabble out of the Politburo. The people have been tormented long enough. The numbskull Molotov, the cretin Voroshilov, the plowhorse Kaganovich, Nikita the swine Khrushchev—to the scrap heap with the lot of them. Zhorka Malenkov, Zhorka Malenkov . . . I'll sweep him away too. He'll never last in Beria's new society. As soon as the time comes, I'll begin a *perestroika* of our whole society from the ground up. Communism can wait. We'll disband the collective farms. Drastically reduce the number of camps. There can't possibly be such a high percentage of enemies in the country. It could all have a bad effect on the future. What is the most important thing that needs to be done? The transfer of power from the Bolshevik rabble to the iron secret police agents, my guys. Bit by bit, we'll root out all the Central Committee spies from the government organization—the Kobulov brothers can handle that. It can't be done all at once: there will be howls about "bourgeois revanchism." To begin with, we'll fence the Party into the backyard. Let them worry about their cadres and propaganda, they won't get near affairs of state. If they start to put up a fight, we'll organize the trial of the head swine and accuse them of . . . well, of espionage in the service of the English Crown. No doubt about it, they'll all confess. Abakumov could get a donkey to confess it was a cow. I can just picture Nikita confessing. It will be interesting to see that, I would never refuse myself such a pleasure. That whole pack of fools isn't worth a damn, we'll grind them down into gulag dust.

Beria covered the girl, who was snoring in a deep slumber, with his dressing gown, then rolled over to the edge of the ottoman and stood up on his spindly legs: must lose weight. Let's examine just what communism is. A little while ago when we were having a drink at Mikoyan's place (we won't purge that Armenian—he's capable and cynical, figured out everything long ago), I asked Nikita, So, what's your idea of communism, Sergeyevich? Well, what would a peasant from Kursk say? There'll be lots of beef and lard, he says. Many sectors of our agriculture have been sadly neglected, he says. What good is communism, he says, if there aren't lots of hotcakes and butter? And this is the future for a great country? The USSR has to be rich and chic, and if that's not communism, you can feed it to the dogs.

Three small lamps continued to burn in the boudoir, pouring a deep creamy light over the carpets. The violated girl trembled beneath the dressing gown, revealing a straw-colored tuft of hair. Beria poured himself a glass of wine from a *different* bottle. When he had downed it, he lit a long Cuban cigar. This is Paradise, satisfaction by night of one's erotic and aesthetic desires, the development of my cherished secret plans. We can't get along without the West, of course. We have to show the West right away that they can do business with us. We'll make significant concessions to them. For one thing, we'll give back East Germany—what a pile of shit, what the hell did we ever create a monster like that for, anyway? As for Ulbricht and his band, off to Kolyma with them! A united Germany would have to be a peace-loving, neutral country. The long-range goal is to play Europe off against America, just to balance things out. With America, it'll be business, business, business! We'll open the doors to the big corporations. There's your "Cold War," Mr. Churchill! What sort of absurdity is that, *batono?* If there is a war, then it ought to be a hot one, like fucking. A cold war is just masturbation.

Of course I'll make peace with Tito. I'll go down to visit him in Brioni, see how he's getting on. Mediterranean leaders should respect each other.

When the time comes, we'll have to sort out our nationalities policy, of course. The bumpkins who run things here have chopped down quite a few trees. The backbone of many a nation has been rooted out, in the western Ukraine, in Lithuania, in my beloved Mingrelia. We'll have to carefully choose people from among those who survived to help us with such a great *perestroika.* I need people with whom I can talk in an unspoken language or, better yet, who can understand only a glance. When the time comes, we'll often have to say one thing and then do another. . . .

Suddenly, in the corner of the boudoir, the most important telephone in the country rang, as if warning the marshal "Enough daydreaming, the moment hasn't come yet." The muted double signal aroused Beria even in a deep sleep. The boss! He had taken to sitting in his office late at night. Clearly his owl was hunting him down in the Kremlin once again. No, the time has not yet come. "Yes, Comrade Stalin!"

Just then, Lyuda Sorokin flashed white like a dolphin on the divan and muttered: "Isaac Israelevich, Vavery Salovich . . ." Beria started and covered her cherry lips with his hand.

"What have you got there, Lavrenty?" Stalin asked.

"One of my staff," he replied.

Stalin cleared his throat.

"If you're not sleeping, come on over here. I've got an idea."

The Press

Enver Hoxha, *Zëri i Popullit:*
Tito is nothing but the plucked parrot of American imperialism!

Ilya Ehrenburg, *Pravda:*
A coed in Penza is sitting over a small volume of Radishchev. Her heart beats faster from his noble words. What is Standard Oil to her, and what does she care about the speeches of Dulles and Churchill? . . . Now the American swindlers want to trample the gardens of Normandy. . . . They fear the Russians because the Russians want peace.

Time (February 28, 1949)

Anna Louise Strong on the Soviet collective farmers:
One hundred million of the world's most backward peasants almost overnight [swung] into ultramodern farming . . . Their increased income [was] translatable into silk dresses, perfumes, musical instruments.

The Kremlin on Anna Louise Strong:
The notorious agent and American journalist, A. L. Strong . . . was arrested by organs of state security on February 14, 1949. Miss Strong is accused of espionage and subversive activities against the Soviet Union . . .

Time (February 28, 1949):
This week Moscow announced that Anna Louise Strong had been deported from Russia. As with all her other idols and deities, disciple Strong had lost the Communist god whom she had served so well.

Nikolai Gribachov, *Pravda:*

> Yes, again in the Senate and Congress,
>   they make up their lying attacks,
> The newspapers lie, and the page
>   of the book, as do the airwaves.
> But time rushes on,
>   there's no turning back—
> The world is now different,
>   and so is the age.
> We see the game they are playing.

Elie Caesar, poet, island of Martinique:

With the name of Stalin, the working people of the world will win the struggle for peace!

I. Stalin:

Competition is the Communist method of building socialism.

Time (April 4, 1949):

The most tragic visitor of the week was Russia's famed composer Dmitri Shostakovich. He came to New York to attend the Cultural and Scientific Conference for World Peace. A symbol of the harshness of the police state, he spoke like a Communist politician and acted as though he were impelled by hidden clockwork rather than the mind which had composed resounding music.

Time:

Among the sponsors of the New York Peace Congress are such well-known figures of the Left as playwright Arthur Miller, novelist Norman Mailer, and composer Aaron Copland.

The boss of the Soviet delegation is Alexander Fadeev, ruddy-cheeked and squinty-eyed, the political leader of Soviet writers and an MGB functionary.

Time (February 14, 1949):

Two Soviet aviators have flown a stolen Russian plane to Linz, Austria, and taken refuge with U.S. forces there.

Culture and Life:

Our theaters must become places where all things progressive are cultivated. . . . However, at the F. G. Volkov Yaroslavsky Dramatic Theater, the country's oldest, the resolution of the Central Committee "On the Repertoire of Dramatic Theaters and Measures for its Implementation" is not always put into practice. . . . Harmful plays of no ideological content are staged, including even *The Canvas Briefcase* by M. Zoshchenko; and a play such as *Taimyr Is Calling You* by A. Galich (Ginzburg) has no place on the stage of the theater named for Volkov. . . .

Artistic manager Stepanov-Kolosov and director Toptygin have come under the influence of the yes-men of the bourgeois cosmopolitans exposed in the Central Committee's resolution "On the Unpatriotic Group of Theater Critics."

Literary Gazette:

The toilers of the Soviet Union demand the unmasking once and for all of the cosmopolitan critics Yuzovsky, Gurevich, Altman, Varshavsky, Kholodov, Boyadzhiev, and their ilk.

The New York Times (August 20, 1949):

The regional military court in Wroclaw, Poland, sentenced a scrap metal collector to death yesterday for stealing copper wire.

Time (July 18, 1949):

A report received by U.S. military intelligence in Germany says that Cardinal Mindszenty is in a "state of delirium" as a result of drugging and mistreatment, and that he has been taken from prison to a hospital for the insane.

Time:

Colonel V. Kotko in the newspaper *Moscow Evening News* exposes the un-Marxist approach to the question of tipping. "At the barbershop," he writes, "a little man with a brush shakes hair from you that you don't really have and then looks at you expectantly. At the theater they offer you opera glasses, and in answer to the question 'How much do they cost,' they say 'Whatever you want to give.' The social relationships have made these humiliating practices repulsive."

Time (August 29, 1949):

Soviet newspapers charged these atrocities to the personal account of Yugoslav Minister of the Interior Aleksandr Ranković, who spent part of 1946 in Moscow learning his business from Soviet secret police boss Lavrenty Beria.

Boris Polevoi, "Yankees in Rome," *Pravda:*

On the street you see a fat boor from across the sea in enormous boots. He is masticating his chewing gum and dragging a local girl along by the hand. . . . The enslaving Marshall Plan is being sold to the Italians by the insolent advertisements of American firms. . . . Here and there you see a picture of a shameless woman with a Coca-Cola. And that in the country of fresh lemonade and orangeade!

I. Anisimov, *Literary Gazette,* **on the occasion of the Goethe Jubilee:**

Understanding such a complex, multifaceted, and contradictory phenomenon as the life and work of Goethe has proved to be beyond the abilities of bourgeois thinking. Only Communist thinking was able to show the full scope of Goethe's work.

"For a Militant Journal of Philosophy," *Pravda:*

In the article "Cosmopolitanism—The Ideology of the Imperialist Bourgeoisie," an excessive amount of space is devoted to various sorts of rubbish, among them the stillborn writings of the reactionary bourgeois professors Milyukov, Yashchenko, and Gershenzon—writings that give off a stench of decaying corpses that can be smelled a mile off.

V. Ozerov, "Raise the Ideological and Artistic Level of the Journal *Zvezda,"* *Pravda:*

Profoundly detrimental is Yury German's novella "Lieutenant Colonel, Medical Corps." Progressive Soviet people are depicted as spineless and frail, burdened with tiresome psychological self-excavation. The main character, Dr. Levin, is an empty, cantankerous old man, falsely put forward by the author as a bold experimenter.

Literary Gazette:

Le Monde has printed an article by a certain André Pierrat. He maintains that the works of Pushkin are supposedly impoverished when they are translated into the crude languages of the Buryats, Komis, Yakuts, and Chuvashes. A group of Yakut writers exposes the Fascist scribbler and his bosses. This obscurantist, who plays with aesthetics, obviously hasn't heard of the world-renowned thirteen-volume dictionary of the Yakut language prepared by Academician Pekarsky. Responding with immeasurable contempt for the sallies of André Pierrat, we send warm greetings to the working people of France.

Time:

Six months have passed since Vyacheslav Molotov was dismissed from his post as Minister of Foreign Affairs, and though he continues to hold the office of Deputy Prime Minister, his cannonball head has not yet graced a single official photo.

"Trial of a Betrayer of the Hungarian people" (report from the courtroom), *The Washington Post:*

The number two man in the hierarchy of the Hungarian Communist Party, László Rajk, has confessed before the peoples' court in Budapest that he was a spy successively for the dictator Horthy, Hitler's Gestapo, and American intelligence.

Boris Polevoi, *Pravda:*

Their lordships the scribblers of Belgrade are trying in vain: the secret levers of the conspiracy were in the hands of Allen Dulles and Aleksandr Ranković. . . . Radio Belgrade continues to babble incoherently about the "intrigues of the Cominform." The court listens to an indifferent monotone recounting the story of monstrous betrayals and murders, both planned and already committed.

Pravda:

To the great leader and teacher Iosif Vissarionovich Stalin from the Moldavian people. Our dear father, teacher, and guide!

Maurice Thorez, *L'Humanité:*

By their campaign of slander against the Soviet Union, the reactionaries would like to make the people forget the simple fact that socialism is peace and capitalism is war.

Nepszabadsag UPI:

The counsel for the defense at the Budapest trial said of his client, Lieutenant General Derde Palfy, "I have to defend this man even though I find him repugnant."

Time:

It fell to the lot of Mrs. Thelma Dial, an attractive Negro woman, housewife and wife of a musician, to announce the verdict concerning the twelve accused (four men and eight women), the bosses of the American Communist Party: each of the accused was found guilty of conspiring to incite the forcible overthrow of the government of the United States.

The longest trial in the history of the United States has come to an end. It was presided over by Judge Harold Medina, a heavyset man with an elegant mustache and large, sad eyebrows. It went on for nine months. The defense called thirty-five witnesses, the prosecution fifteen. The testimony amounted to 5,000,000 words. The cost of the trial to the defense was $250,000, and $1,000,000 to the government. It was established that the accused desired, at the appropriate moment, to paralyze the economy, to forcibly overthrow the government, and to establish a dictatorship of the proletariat. The orders to follow this course of action came directly from Moscow.

Pravda:

The harsh legal reprisals carried out against the Communists went on for nine months. The jury had been thoroughly infiltrated by the FBI. Among the witnesses called were thirteen spies, agents provocateurs, renegades, and sellouts. Judge Medina has become a symbol of the savage persecution of Communists and all progressive forces in America.

The Kukryniks brothers, cartoonists, *Pravda:*

"Judge Medina is a stick striking the American people."

Pravda:

Millions of acres in the United States have been brought to a state of utter exhaustion by the capitalist method of agriculture. By putting Stalinist plans into action, the peasants of the collective farms have fully mastered the forces of nature in the interests of creating an abundance of produce and building communism.

Pravda:

The impressions of a Soviet sailor, electrical mechanic Zadorozhny, of New York . . . "no customers in the stores . . . well-dressed people begging pennies to be able to eat. . . . Three strapping youths beating up a Negro. . . . Everywhere we went our boat was greeted with shouts of 'Long live Stalin!' "

Valentin Kataev, *Literary Gazette:*

Pavlenko's novel *The Sun of the Steppe* is a warm, energetic, optimistic tale of the great works of the little people of the Soviet Union.

Time:

On Moscow screens, they are showing five films that are simply called "foreign" with no indication of their source. Among them are *Last Round* and *The School of Hatred,* about the Irish uprising against England. These films are in fact products of the Goebbels propaganda ministry and were intended to incite anti-British and anti-American feelings.

Life:

No small number of rumors is making the rounds in Moscow concerning Lieutenant General Vassily Stalin, son of the Soviet dictator. According to one of them, Vassily Stalin was once piloting an airplane, aboard which, in addition to himself, were a certain woman and a child. Over the fields of Belorussia, Vassily Stalin jumped from the plane with a parachute.

The New York Times:

372 refugees from the USSR have reached Sweden in a craft designed to carry no more than fifty passengers. Among them were Poles, Estonians, Belorussians, and Latvians.

The New York Times:

Eleven of the convicted bosses of the American Communist Party appeared in court to hear their sentences. Ten of them received five years and a $10,000 fine for incitement to forcibly overthrow the United States government. The eleventh, the holder of the wartime Distinguished Service Cross, received only three years.

Time:

It was established at the meeting of the Cominform that Marshal Tito, leader of Yugoslavia, is a Titoist.

Life:

The delighted Muscovites all had their eyes fixed on the heavens when the huge four-engine bomber flew over Red Square with its fighter escort. The next day, jaws dropped all over town when it was announced in the newspapers and on the radio that the airplane had been piloted by Air Parade Commander General Vassily Iosifovich Stalin. Most of the citizenry had been unaware that the father of all the peoples had a son.

Vassily in his turn has two children by his second wife, the daughter of Marshal Timoshenko. He has distinguished himself by his irascibility, his drinking, and his inclination to settle an argument with his fists.

Yekaterina Shevelyova, "Daughter of the Fatherland," *Pravda:*
> "Soviet Woman" is my name,
> proud is my stance!

Yury Zhukov (from Paris), "The Poison Merchants," *Pravda:*

The Truman government wants to implant American ways throughout "Marshallized" Europe. Paris is overrun with Hollywood stars in uniform. . . . Chasing after large sums of dollars, Marlene Dietrich played in an anti-Soviet hatchet job that proved to be a resounding flop on the French screens. . . . In the film *The Scandalous Woman from Berlin,* the writer's satire on American mores is on target, but the movie also constitutes a cynical and insolent slander against the Soviet Army.

Jan Drda, *Rudé Právo:*

I love the Soviet Union! I saw with my own eyes how Pablo Neruda, Emi Sao, and many young women kissed its soil. We live in the epoch of Comrade Stalin!

Pravda:

The serpent is wriggling. In Sofia, the trial of Traicho Kostov has begun.

Alexei Surkov, *Pravda:*

> With Stalin, the dream has entered our home.
> Like the song of the morning still young . . .

Leonid Leonov, *Pravda:*

In the time that Stalin has been with us, every secret dream of the Soviet people has become a reality.

Jambul, *Pravda:*

If Stalin is with us, then truth is with us.

In *Pravda:*

"The Father of the Toilers of the World" by Sholokhov; "The Moving Spirit Behind Construction" by F. Gladkov; "Our Stalin" by A. Perventsev; "The Hope, Light, and Conscience of the World" by M. Isakovsky.

SECOND INTERMISSION
Suckecows! Step this way!

Professor Gordiner's cat loved to stand on one leg—but not simply on one leg, forgetting about his other three extremities, rather he loved to pirouette on one leg like the ballerina Lepeshinsky. He also loved to put his front paws on a windowsill and observe the goings-on on the other side of the street, on the corner of the side street, on the rooftops of the low houses and the tops of the high cornices, and in those moments he would raise a leg, now the left, now the right, to his belly, and come to resemble those people who are sometimes seized by the desire to stand on one leg.

It's not by accident that I named him Velimir, after all, thought Professor Gordiner. Sitting in a deep armchair next to the radiator and waiting to be arrested, wrapped in a heavy plaid camel's hair blanket, he regarded the cat, which was regarding the objective world. He was remembering the man in whose honor he had named the plump, feisty kitten that had been given to him as a present by his lover Oksana seven years before. It may have been silly, but there was something in its meowing that reminded him of Khlebnikov's joyous transsense poetry. Thus had the cat's name been born. The real Velimir, of course, would not have been offended; on the contrary, he would have been flattered by the fact that the cat, once grown, had acquired the Khlebnikovian manner of standing on one foot—on one paw, that is.

Bronislav Gordiner had once belonged to the Centrifuge of Poetry Futurist group and consequently had met Khlebnikov on more than one occasion. The latter was several years older than he was; he was the mythical figure of the poet-vagabond, the wordsmith, the enumerator of history. The young critic revered him, though by virtue of his belonging to the group that he did he was not supposed to show reverence. Rather, he was supposed to poke fun at the founder of Heleya and one of the leading Cubo-Futurists, who brazenly presumed to hold the rights to the entire movement.

Khlebnikov, it must be said, was very little occupied by group politics, just as he was little occupied by the young critics genuflecting before him. In the heat of a stormy discussion, anyplace, at a *soirée* at the home of the Sinyakov sisters, or in a crowd at the Sukharevsky Tower, he could suddenly freeze, wind one leg around the other, and with the expression of an utter idiot on his face mutter something through his puffy lips beneath his constantly restless nose. At such times, the atmosphere around the poet seemed suddenly to clear entirely: he's creating, don't bother him!

Oh, what a great life everyone had then, all those half-starved artists at the gallery openings! The dizzying sensation of belonging to a new era, of being the creators of a new culture! All that was long since over. First everyone had stopped laughing, then they had stopped smiling, and finally they had stopped meeting, leaving the group—in other words, they had dismantled their associations entirely by their departure *en masse*. After that had come the years when they tried to forget about groups, when the friendships that had been formed in those sinful years were not something one particularly liked to advertise, and if a famous name resurfaced in some inappropriate place, the former group member would only mutter, "Oh, him," and immediately shunt the train of the discussion back onto the main line. Khlebnikov, suffering from recurring bouts of typhus, undernourishment, and, most important, Persian dope, had died in 1922. The Centrifuge of Poetry, whose task it had been, in the conception of its theoreticians Sergei Bobrov and Ivan Aksyonov, to make the cream of verbal craftsmanship rise to the surface, went awry and stirred up the sediment on the bottom. They were better off, those who had gotten out in time, like Ivan; what would he do now with his "Elizabethans," with his "Picasso"? We're pathetic, those who are left: Sergei, me, Nikolai, even Boris. . . . This is how it's been, decade after decade, sitting in a cold sweat, waiting to be arrested, not poking our noses out, Velimir, curling ourselves up into little balls like your mice, dashing off tidy little well-intentioned reviews, making miles worth of literal translations rhyme: we're a sorry bunch, Velimir. I know what you'd say now. . . .

"*Vremyshi-kamyshi! Zharbog, zharbog!*" the cat responded in proto-Slavic gibberish.

"That's the way it's done," Gordiner said. "It's not for nothing that I named you Velimir."

Velimir leapt back from the window, and it even seemed to Gordiner that before the cat jumped up onto his knees, it did a pirouette on one paw. Fidgeting about, settling itself in on the knees of the dear Bronislav, digging into his blanket and his velvet trousers with its barbed paws, butting into his belly with its round head, the cat meowed: "*Pin', oin', pin', tararakhnul zenziver. O, lebedivo! O, ozari!*"

They say that cats love not their masters but their territory, thought the recently unmasked cosmopolitan-critic. That may be, that may be, but it's still clear that Velimir loves me more than the room. That is, the thing that he loves most in this room is me. He prefers me even to the sofa. He never stops following me around, licks my heels when I'm copulating with Oksana. It's entirely possible that he sees in me not a man, but his territory, a place that suits him so well. A place that groans, mutters, curses, smokes, farts, pisses in a bucket when he can't be bothered to go to the communal toilet, makes squeaking noises with a pen and rustles pages. Only his fascination with the wide-open spaces on the other side of the window competes with his attachment to me, only the poetry of the feline cosmos. . . .

"Well, what did you behold today in your expanses across the ocean, Velimir?" The cat looked down at him conspiratorially and, making sure that there were no dirty tricks afoot, sang out in a state of excitement:

Siyayushchaya vol'za zhelaemykh resnits
i laskovaya dol'za laskayushchikh desnits.
Chezory golubye i nravy svoenraviya.

O, pravo! Moya moroleva, na ozere sinem—morol'.
Nichtrusy—tuda! Gde plachet zorol' . . .

"Now that's going a little too far," muttered Gordiner. "We all deceive ourselves, Velimir, my friend. Our world is just a pitiful conspiracy of culture."

He remembered how, in this same room in 1934, they had discussed this subject with Ivan Aksyonov, but Aksyonov had sat not on Gordiner's knees, of course, but on the bear hide that had not yet been worn through. If only they could hang some new wallpaper and blow away the odor of misanthropic bachelorhood!

The usual dreary Soviet form of the expectation of being arrested, which extends over many years, had recently changed in Professor Gordiner into a sensation that had produced a few spasms in his intestines. His name had appeared a few times on lists with other names that were not pleasing to a Russian ear, all of his articles for journals had been rejected, and he had been purged from the faculty of the Lunacharsky Theatrical Arts Institute, where he had taught a course on Shakespeare. Though none of the unmitigated cosmopolitans had been locked up, there appeared more and more often in the press demands by the toilers that these scoundrels be exposed to the last man, which meant that the final "parentheses" were about to fall away.

All this was embellished with monstrous irony. Against a background of endless demands to "reveal the brackets," Gordiner revealed himself to be a paradoxical eccentric of literature and fate. The fact is that within his parentheses was hidden the most magnificently harmonious, non-Jewish, Belorussian name imaginable: Pupko. In the long-ago years of Futurism, the young critic Bronislav Pupko had decided he'd never get ahead in the avant-garde with a family name like that and had chosen himself a pseudonym in which, it seemed to him, one could hear a Slavic arrow flying over a German stronghold. Literary circles had soon got used to the name, and he himself had become so accustomed to it that he had even forgotten about the "Pupko" of his origins and had received a passport at the beginning of the 1930s in the name of Gordiner. Who would have thought then that one day he would have to answer for such carelessness, that such ineradicable Jewishness would stick to his gray sideburns and piebald whiskers along with the pseudonym? What was to be done now? To get up on stage, to beat his breast and cry out, "I'm Pupko, I'm Pupko"? No, he would not fall so low! Renouncing Gordiner would be tantamount to renouncing his whole life, to crossing out his place in literature, to spitting on his creative legacy! No, let them come and take Gordiner if they wish, but Pupko is not going to run away. It would be a shameful thing to go back to the Komsomol!

"You must get away," he said to Velimir. "When they turn up, I'll open the window, and you'll jump out and get away by the rooftops. You know where Oksana lives, go to her alone or with your *moroleva queeney*. Don't give yourself up to them!"

"*Proum, praum, preum, noum, veum, poym, zaum,*" the cat answered.

Toward evening, Oksana arrived and began to raise her skirt as soon as she crossed the threshold. Their affair had been going on for many years now, and, as they told each other as well as themselves, it filled their prose corridors with romance. Naturally, Oksana had at one time been one of Gordiner's students in his Shakespeare course, at which time it had turned out that neither of them could talk about Macbeth and the earth's "bubbles" without exhilaration. Over the years she had turned from a girl with her nose high in the air into a stately woman with a bridge of metal and ceramic gleaming faintly between her still splendid lips. There was always a hint of something melancholy and majestic in her face, and during their assignations Gordiner used all his powers to make that enraptured young girl from the Shakespeare lectures of the old days peep through, if only for a moment, the fatigue that was characteristic of Moscow women. Their meetings, however, became more and more businesslike, as though they were calculated down to the minute. Oksana's family was a burden to her—she had a husband who was a functionary in the Ministry of Heavy Industry and three children. She was convinced that the middle child, Tamara, had been conceived in this very room, right on the worn bearskin rug.

At the end of their meetings, Gordiner would often think of the Ego-Futurist Igor Severyanin and begin to whine:

> You will not return to me even for Tamara's sake,
> For her sake, tiny as a rabbit, our little offspring.
> Now you have a dacha and lobster on your plate,
> Now you are protected by the raven's wing.

Laughing, gathering her undergarments and constantly sneaking a look at her watch, Oksana objected, "Lobster? What a hope! We live on 'Mikoyan cutlets,' for your information!"

Even now, barely across the threshold, having thrown off her soiled boots and unbuttoned her skirt, she was already casting sidelong glances at her watch. Loneliness is the lot of the cosmopolitan critic, Gordiner thought, rising from his armchair with a wry smile. The cat, meanwhile, continued to describe socially sophisticated circles around the rapidly undressing Oksana and then headed decisively for the window. Recently, he had sharply reduced his participation in the "filling of the corridors of romanticism," that is, licking Papa's heels. Oksana's visits had begun irritating him, because the woman refused to move in with them.

"*Galagala gegege! Grakakhata grororo!*" he demanded.

Gordiner opened the transom window. "Return to the darkness!" Velimir sprang out onto the cornice, then down onto the roof below and made his way toward the chimney, keeping his swaying tail perpendicular in the manner of a sultanate guardsman's sword. Among other things, he was the flag officer of the local fleet. The rays of the setting sun shone through the dense fluff of his tail, outlining precisely the powerful pivot at the heart of it.

. . . When they had filled the corridors with romance, Oksana and

Bronislav lay in each other's arms for a while. The professor calmed his beloved's inner tumult by applying a light pressure to her shoulder blades. "Stop looking at your watch!"

She stroked his head, gently pinching the old organ that still worked like a charm. "Yes, yes, you're right, Bronya, we won't look at this strange mechanism." She sighed. "Yesterday *he* was looking for cigarettes, went into my handbag, and found the key to your apartment. Naturally, he made a scene. How many times does that make now? It's almost unbearable!"

Gordiner said nothing. After announcements of this kind he would usually make a blustering demand that she leave the bothersome Mr. Heavy Industry immediately so that they could begin a new, romantic life together, without any hypocrisy and distressing scenes. This time, however, he remained silent. "Why don't you say anything?" she asked. Even though she knew she would never leave her husband for him, she wanted him to pester her about it anyway.

"I'm not saying anything because I don't have anything to offer. They're probably going to come for me soon. Yesterday at a Party meeting of the critics' section, they again demanded a full unmasking. Look after the cat, Oksana, don't let him die."

The cat, meanwhile, was dashing along the ridges of the rooftops. The last rays of the sunset were striking the open transom windows, they intoxicated and blinded him just as they had once upon a time in a long-ago life, in the flux of the mouth of the Volga; through the reeds, the patches of remaining sunlight struck blind and inebriated the little boy who was racing along behind his papa the ornithologist, dragging a Kalmyk canoe and a brood of ring-tailed birds. What happiness then, and what happiness now! Forward, forward, on young, or at least not yet old, muscles, the terrible reinforced concrete radio diagram of the narcotic night in Santalovo, where he died, still lay ahead . . . or was it already behind? Maybe it didn't exist at all, even though it is present . . . but the most important thing is these spots of light, this flight of love. The most important thing is to announce to his favorite walking place, that is, to Papa, to Bronislav Grigorievich Gordiner, formerly Pupko, that he will not be arrested!

Where had Velimir the cat gotten that from? Had he listened in on some high-frequency line? Had there occurred some sort of shift in the airwaves that cats are able to catch but is inaccessible to people? In any case, he had suddenly had a revelation, and he knew that all their fears were over: Papa is going to survive! Now, Hurry! Hurry! How to convey this crucial piece of news to Gordiner? Will he understand the universal language, inherited from the ontological depths? Oksana was weeping. It was only today that she had realized Gordiner was doomed. She was sobbing not only from grief but also from shame, for she knew she would not stay with him even today, that he had been ever so slightly a burden to her for some time, because, in spite of all of their noble suffering and modest, though vain, attempts at self-sacrifice, there still appeared constantly in her treasonous thoughts a clerk, fifteen years younger than herself, at the All-Russian Theatrical Society library who had been letting her know for some time that he would not be averse to a fling. Gordiner was no comfort to her.

Suddenly, just outside the window, the cat with fire in its eyes tempestuously reared up to its full height, its hackles raised. It drummed its front paws on the glass, demanding to be let in. There's one who will never be a traitor, thought Gordiner, hastening to the window.

Leaping into the room, its tail high in the air, the cat ran in several different directions and then between the legs of Papa and his lover. Loudly and triumphantly, he tried to impart the news to them:

> Lili egi, lyap, lyap, bem.
> Libibi niraro
> Sinoano tsitsirits.
> Khyu khmapa, khir zen', chench'
> Zhuri kaka sin sonega.
> Khakhotiri ess ese.
> Yunchi, enchi, uk!
> Yunchi, enchi, pipoka.
> Klyam! Klyam! Eps!

"What's gotten into him?" Oksana asked in fright. "Has he been sucking down too much tincture of valerian somewhere or gotten a sniff of arsenic?"

The professor suddenly had an illuminating thought. "Why, don't you understand? Velimir has found out somewhere that they're not going to arrest me! Isn't that right, Velimir?"

The ecstatic cat executed a pirouette on one leg.

> *Iverni vyverni,*
> *Umnyi igren'!*
> *Kucheri tucheri,*
> *Mucheri nocheri,*
> *Tocheri tucheri, vecheri ocheri.*
> *Chetkami chutkimi*
> *Pali zari.*
> *Iverni vyverni,*
> *Umnyi igren'!*

Oksana looked on with excruciating incomprehension. Her elderly lover, who had always made her feel somewhat uncomfortable because of his age (even though she had not noticed that lately people on the street had ceased to see any disparity between them during their infrequent strolls together), now stood on one leg in the middle of the room, balancing himself with his arms and muttering, "Even though there's no objective beauty in it, it still has rhythm, and that's something. Well, then, let it go on a while longer, this cultural conspiracy, let the game be played out. . . ."

Chapter 4

THE BLIZZARD
OF 1951

The winters at the beginning of the 1950s were exceptionally severe, a fact that would subsequently give indignant Stalinists the chance to growl, "In those days, everything was strong, uncompromising, there was order everywhere—even the winters stood out by their vigor, real Russian winters, not this mush we get nowadays!"

And in fact, the climate did indeed turn noticeably mushy after Stalin. In 1956, for example, winter was very slow to arrive in Saint Petersburg, that is, in what was then known as Lenin's city. When a flotilla of British ships led by the aircraft carrier HMS *Triumph* entered the Neva, it was as though it had brought the warm current of the Gulf Stream, that progenitor of Atlantic democracy, along with it. There was even a minor flood, which provided a romantic embellishment to one of the nights of our youth. Naturally, the superficial hypothesis that all of our liberalization depended upon something like solar explosions or sunspots suggested itself, or that the slightest variations in energy currents had an effect on one's state of mind and, consequently, on the political situation. Those who wish to develop this idea I refer to the beginning of the preceding volume, that is, to the place where Lev Tolstoy's conception of history with its "millions of arbitrary acts" is debated.

On the other hand, if one lingers on the hypothesis of "mass acts of arbitrariness," it is possible to rise above history's gravitational field and to suppose that a change in the state of millions of minds is able to disperse some kinds of astral clouds, which, in turn, influence the climate.

Be that as it may, on the January night with which we are concerned at present, the thought of liberalization of the climate and a softening of the political line would not have entered the mind of anyone in Moscow. The evil-tempered blizzard emanating from the Kremlin and following the lines of a circular topography seemed eternal. It goes without saying that Boris IV Gradov did not devote his time to philosophy or historiosophy. Catching up on his sleep after taking an exam on bones in the dissecting theater and driving from his mind nauseating thoughts about an exam on tendons, he had decided for that evening, and perhaps for the whole next day as well, to squeeze the studious bore out of himself and to return to his essence—to youth, motorbikes, and alcohol, that is.

Coming down in the elevator from the fifth floor, he was wondering whether or not he would even be able to get the Horch started. The temperature was already −29 degrees Celsius, sometimes falling in a gust of icy wind to −40. There was no garage, and the Horch was parked outside, across from the back door of Russian Wines. There it is now—transformed into a giant Third Reich tomb. Well, what the hell, we'll see who's better. In motorcycle and auto circles, it was considered a sign of superior class to pay no heed to the weather: an engine always starts! All sorts of "supplemental rations" were added to the oil: airplane lubricants left over at the polar airfields from the Lend-Lease days of the war and smuggled by grandiose and secret channels from the Special Operations Garage were valued the most highly. Other motorcyclists who were particularly renowned, fanatics, and those who had made a study of their craft preferred to prepare their own mixtures, the formulae of which, naturally, they kept to themselves.

Boris IV, alas, was not one of the latter. The institute took up too much of his time, along with the sports club, restaurants and "huts," as parties with various combustibles and girls were called then. The fanatics and "professors," particularly one elderly apostle of the internal combustion engine with the nickname "Pistonevich," often kidded him, "Boris, you have a rare mechanical gift. Why did you go in for medicine, why are you simply wasting your time?" Sometimes when he had a hangover, Boris would make his way to Pistonevich's garage, where he would spend an entire day like a sinner doing penance in a church. It's funny, Boris thought, but there's something holy about these people who are obsessed by cars; in any case, they have a certain isolation from this vile world—or so it seems, at least.

"This vile world" sometimes presented itself to the twenty-four-year-old Gradov as an enchanted fairy tale, only later to go beyond the limits of even "vileness" and to come crashing down in a moldering dungheap. Perhaps the problem lay not even in his drinking bouts but in his general postwar, postservice hangover, which made him feel useless, unrewarded, profoundly and irreversibly wrung out. "If you can't find anything fresher, then call me 'the squeezed lemon,' " he would sometimes say to his partner in the "slow-tempo dance," the currently accepted name for the tango, bestowed as part of the struggle against harmful foreign culture. Girls rolled their eyes and opened their mouths slightly in delight. Borya Gradov was known in the party circles of the capital as a mysterious, romantic, and disenchanted figure: a modern-day Pechorin! The dissecting theater of the First Moscow Medical Institute was firmly anchored among the symptoms of his hangover. He would never have thought that he, who had buried so many comrades cut to pieces by bullets and shell fragments, and who had himself riddled and impaled a fair number of bodies with a bayonet, would find himself driven into such a state of sordid melancholy by the formaldehyde-soaked remains from which he had had to learn anatomy. "I'm coming into some sort of monstrous paradox," he complained to his grandfather. "The war, with its countless deaths, seems to me the high point of my life. Anatomy classes, vats of formaldehyde, the preparation of cadavers—it's even drearier than death, man's final impasse. . . . Did that ever happen to you, Grandpa?"

"No, that never happened," the old man replied firmly. "I remember perfectly how inspired I felt in my first year of medical school. My first steps in the universe of the human organism, my future service to people . . ." He laid on his grandson's shoulder a hand that, though strewn with age spots, was still fully serviceable for surgery. He looked into the empty, slightly alarming eyes of the retired commander. "Perhaps we were both mistaken, Babochka? Maybe you should quit?"

"No, I can hold out a bit longer," replied his grandson and avoided any further discussion, feeling a dreadful awkwardness. Grandfather obviously thinks that if I have such an aversion to anatomy, I'll never make a good doctor, while I, in saying "I'll hold out a bit longer," show myself up as a complete horse's ass, like some bumpkin who has memorized only one principle since the age of fifteen: "I'm a man of direct action, and I'm not in the habit of pulling back in the face of trouble." This was something he had learned long ago—from Sasha Sheremetiev. . . . Mother would get so angry then, suspecting us of plotting something . . . Mother . . . where is she? . . . She's turned into some sort of evil spirit. . . . All that's left of her in this house is insult and oblivion. . . . "Well, now, Herr Horch, are we going to start or not?" he said, addressing his words to the immense snowdrift that seemed to have begun to petrify. Ruslanka the truck driver bolted from a shop and ran to his van. As soon as he spotted Boris, he changed course and went up to him, sinking up to his boot tops in the drift that had been swept aside from under an arch. "Hi there, Grad! Want to warm 'er up a bit?" Boris was already a popular figure with the truck drivers on Gorky Street and with the police as well. The cops on the beat usually touched the brims of their caps as the Horch raced by, and some would approach him when he was at a traffic light to shake his hand: "I spent the whole war at the Reserve Front under your dad, saw him with my own eyes three times. He was an eagle, your pop, the best commander!"

He and Ruslanka liberated the limousine from its ice-bound captivity with snow shovels. Over the last frigid week, the car had been reduced to the state of a woolly mammoth excavated from the permafrost. "Let's stick a fire under her ass," Ruslanka proposed. "Then we'll get 'er started with a jump from my truck." A man of uncommon efficiency—this driver for Russian Wines! In a flash he had produced a sheet of roofing metal, on which he laid some oil-soaked rags and started a fire, which he then shoved under the crankcase. The same fire of oily rags warmed up the locks and allowed the men to tear open a frozen door. Boris climbed in like a diver entering a sunken submarine. The leather seat was burning through the seat of his SS-issue leather trousers, which he had taken as booty after a skirmish on the outskirts of Breslau. It would be ridiculous, of course, even to try to get the engine started with the key. Even if it does have a tank battery, it's still dead. You won't get the oil flowing even with the fires of hell. Backing off, though, wasn't allowed once you'd begun: the engine always starts! Meanwhile, Ruslan was trying to drive his truck up closer, maneuvering it through the drifts. Boris pumped the accelerator, turned the steering wheel to the right and to the left, then finally turned the key in the ignition. Strange as it may seem, the sound that followed did not seem hopeless to him. The spark had obviously made the jump, and the engine turned over two or three times. He tossed the hand crank out of the window and asked Ruslan to turn it. For ten minutes they tried to make one of the revolutions catch, but nothing came of it. Boris wanted to give up, so as not to exhaust the battery, and simply to count on the jump start. Just then, however, the Horch roared like Guderian's entire army heading for a breach in the lines and then, as soon as Boris let off on the gas, began to run evenly and steadily at a slow idle. What a miracle! What was the deciding factor in the end? German technology, Pistonevich's "moonshine," or the enthusiasm of the two young Muscovites? "You and I are whales, Ruslanka!" Boris exclaimed, using a Moscow student expression he had picked up recently. "You'll get a half liter from me!"

"I'll take you at your word!" the truck driver replied merrily. "Wait for me at your place, Grad!" All the young men of their set dreamed of visiting the flat of the enigmatic marshal, in whose honor a memorial plaque with an engraved profile of the hero had already been attached to the façade of the building. Now the Horch was showing energy, heating up, small chunks of ice sliding off the windshield. Inside, the leather upholstery was thawing out, and the radio was playing a selection of arias from the opera *Cossack Across the Danube*. Boris went back upstairs, washed his grease-smeared hands, changed into a dark blue suit with wide, drooping shoulders, parted his dark red hair with a comb, and applied a dab of brilliantine. Then he donned a light black tight-fitting topcoat and a tricolor scarf: *Liberté, Egalité, Fraternité*. No hat for tonight. Moscow dandies are a fearless lot.

For a solid hour, through swirling snow that sometimes covered everything with a broad canopy only to be whipped into spirals like tornadoes, he drove along the Garden Ring with a single aim: to warm up and revive his luxuriant "baby." Then he returned to Gorky Street and came to a stop next to a heavy door above which hung one of the city's few illuminated signs, a cone-shaped glass with multicolored viscous layers and the words "Cocktail Hall" entwined around its base like the snakes of a caduceus. In addition, a small lit-up stick protruded from the glass, which meant that here was a place where they don't guzzle the striped drinks all in one go, but rather sip them elegantly through a straw. This was the most intriguing of all of the Moscow high-life spots of the early 1950s. Its very existence under such a sign was in itself a mystery during the struggle against foreign influences, particularly those that were Anglo-American. Even words like "fox-trot" had been outlawed, and yet here, in the heart of the capital of socialism, across the street at an angle from the Central Telegraph and Post Office, a sign reading "Cocktail Hall" glowed with discreet effrontery; a sign that was no better than those reading "Jazz" and "Music Hall," which had been done away with and which perhaps even surpassed them as a trademark of capitalist decay. Some Moscow wags proposed that if the place wasn't going to be closed in disgrace, then it should at least be given the name of a working-class dive, say "Booze Hut," where no one would worry particularly about layers in different colors or about straws. Time passed, however, and the "Cocktail Hall" continued to exist quietly on Gorky Street, greatly intriguing the average Muscovite as well as visitors to the city. It was even said that F. Coragesson Strawberry, the American correspondent for United Dispatch, would stop off there on his way home after sending off his anti-Soviet slanders from the Central Telegraph and Post Office.

This establishment was exactly fifty seconds' walk from Boris's building, and it goes without saying that he had become a regular. Many times he had severely, with even a slight scowl, circumvented the line and banged on the oaken door that looked like it belonged to a prosecutor's office. The unpleasant and unassailably Soviet features of the doorman—his narrow eye and broad jowls—appeared through a chink. When he saw the visitor's face, though, his face immediately lost all of its inaccessibility: "Boris Nikitovich!" The clientele, of course, did not object: if they let this comrade in, then it must be because they have to. In fact, the customers could be divided into two groups: the chance passers-by, among them sometimes even a student who had decided to blow his entire monthly stipend in one night, and the "regulars," who were known by sight, if not by name. The latter, of course, were for the most part leading figures in art and literature, sports stars, and the children of the top Party brass, "Americanized" young people who called Gorky Street "Brod-vay" or, even better, "Peshkov Street." Naturally, they didn't have to wait in line.

A semicircular bar gleamed at the entrance like a multitiered altar. Behind the counter, the priestly functions were carried out by Valencia Maksimovna, the senior bartender, and her two young assistants, Goga and Seryoga, who everyone said were captains in the secret police. These two were pouring the ingredients of cocktails into mixers and churning them up. Valencia Maksimovna, who with her halo of hydrogen peroxide–blond hair looked like Peter the Great's daughter Elizaveta, merely took orders. It was only for carefully selected personalities that she deigned to do any of the preparation with her own royal hands.

"What can we do for you this evening, Borenka?" she asked the young man in a tone that was at once serious and well-intentioned.

"A 'battering ram,' " said Boris, taking a seat on a high stool. Giving her head a faint reproachful shake, Valencia Maximovna went over to the multicolored pyramid that was her domain. The room was crowded but not entirely packed, and here and there among the tables and velvet alcoves there were a few free chairs. Nearly everyone there was a regular. It was a cozy, cheerful get-together, and one would have been hard pressed even to imagine that on the other side of the door the "general public" was waiting in line in gusts of snow. A small orchestra was playing in the loft. Its repertoire, of course, was also subject to strict ideological control, but the musicians had figured out a way to play even "A Maple Lived on the Edge of a Grove" so that it sounded like jazz.

Valencia Maximovna set a large wine glass with a gleaming, bubbly, many-colored liquid before Boris.

"You shouldn't start with a 'battering ram,' Borenka. Have a 'champagne cobbler' instead," she said in a manner that brooked no objections.

"Hmph." Boris shrugged. "It looks like you still take me for a kid around here, is that it? Well, you're probably right, Valencia Maximovna." A burst of laughter from one of the velvet niches in the walls reached the bar. Someone was gesticulating to Boris. "Tie up over here, sir!" They were writers and artists, a constellation of prizewinners. The field was ruled (this was a new expression popularized by the light touch of Vadim Sinyavsky, who announced football matches on the radio—to "rule the field") by the composer Nikita Bogoslovsky, who had written the song "Dark Night," which was second in popularity only to "Clouds in Blue," by Boris's Aunt Nina.

"Not long ago in Moscow, respected comrades, a remarkable discovery was made . . ." "Respected comrades" on his lips, moving above a polka-dot bow tie, sounded like "ladies and gentlemen." "Please direct your attention to this ordinary postcard . . ." With these words, he drew from his pocket a snapshot of a couple copulating in an obscene position. "A most ordinary product . . . who among us is not familiar with this sort of article? . . . In a word, an elementary bit of porn . . ." Bogoslovsky tossed the picture onto the middle of the table with the same careless manner with which he spoke. Everyone around him was laughing at his nonchalance—an ordinary pornographic article, you see, and in the most puritanical country of strict proletarian morals at that. Everyone was laughing loudly, but Boris, to his surprise, noticed that some, the writers Valentin Kataev and Konstantin Simonov in particular, were exchanging meaningful glances. "Now, just take any newspaper," Bogoslovsky went on. "Take anyone you want! This daily, for example." He reached into his briefcase and pulled out a copy of *Pravda,* which he unfolded next to the photograph. It didn't matter much that the "just any newspaper" turned out to be the war trumpet of the Central Committee of the Soviet Communist Party, which was put every morning onto the desk of not just anyone, but of the Leader himself! The laughter began to die down somewhat at this point, and the company's attention returned to their drinks. Noticing this, Bogoslavsky screwed up his surprisingly fresh, round face into an expression of amazement for comic effect. "No, no, comrades, there's nothing counterrevolutionary about it! It's just a surprising distortion of human logic, that's all. The fact is that this snapshot could be the illustration of any headline of any newspaper. Want to make a wager on it? Be my guest! Go ahead,

Sasha, read the headlines, and I'll show the picture," he said, shoving the newspaper in the direction of Alexander Galich, the author of the comedy *Taimyr Is Calling You,* which had recently been harshly criticized. Galich was a young man with a high forehead, whose neatly trimmed mustache and elegance clashed with the celebrated mustaches of six-time Stalin Prize winner Kostya Simonov. "Begging your pardon," he replied, turning away from the newspaper, "but read it yourself!"

"No, there's no interest in it that way." Bogoslovsky surveyed those present with his eyes. "There has to be someone else reading. Ruben Nikolaevich, maybe you'll do it, being a master of reading aloud? Misha, how about you? Ah, there's Seryozha Mikhalkov now, he'll read for us!"

"S-s-start without me!" said the gangling Mikhalkov, composer of the USSR anthem. He resembled a woodpecker as he passed by on his way to the toilets.

"Come on, then, I'll read," said Boris IV Gradov. "Ha, ha, ha!" cried Bogoslovsky. "Here's the student reading—out of the mouths of babes, and all that . . ."

Kataev, whom Boris wound up next to, muttered faintly, "What do you need that for?"

" 'New Fit of Madness in Camp of Warmongers,' " Boris read.

"If you please!" Bogoslovsky exclaimed, holding up the photo of the couple.

" 'Ties Between Science and Practice Grow Stronger,' " Boris read.

"You couldn't ask for anything better!" called out Bogoslovsky.

The photograph did, in fact, provide an excellent illustration of the indivisibility of science and practice.

" 'Folk Tales of the Latvian People.' "

"And here's an illustration for them!"

" 'District Animal Breeding Exhibition.' "

"Comrades, comrades!"

" 'Preparation of National Leadership Cadres.' "

"Well, isn't it brilliant?"

" 'Moldavia Answers the Call . . .' "

At this point, Boris, who was by now quite worked up, was interrupted by Simonov.

"That's enough, guys! We all could bust our guts laughing like this."

"Who thought this up, by the way?" Kataev asked, mopping his brow with a silk handkerchief.

"No idea," replied Bogoslovsky. He gathered up the photo and the newspaper and walked away satisfied.

Everyone suddenly began to talk about the war. In those days, people knew how to make a joke, everyone appreciated a good laugh. Quite a paradox, isn't it? The soldiers in the trenches had more of a sense of humor than we do now in peacetime.

Boris, it must be admitted, was extremely flattered by his easy admission into this circle of older, and quite famous, men of Moscow, even though he was of interest to them only because he was Marshal Gradov's son. Many of them, particularly Simonov, had made his father's acquaintance at the front during the war. "Your father, young fellow, was a hell of a nice guy and a great soldier," the six-time Stalin Prize winner had said with his well-known French "r," considered a speech impediment in Russian, when the actor Druzhinnikov, almost plastered at the time, introduced young Gradov to the group. They had all dismounted their stools in haste, lifted themselves out of their velvet chairs, and surrounded Boris. It can't be—Marshal Gradov's son? Let me shake your hand, old man! Your father was a hell of a nice guy and a great soldier! What, Kostya already said that? No, I said it myself! In the Hemingway style. Well, of course, in the Hemingway style. Yes, Nikita and I . . . I wrote a piece on him for *The Little Star*, don't you remember? "Marshal Gradov's Rucksack," it was called. He'd probably be minister of defense by now. I remember flying in his plane to the Königsberg sector. He had some great fellows on his staff, like Koka Shershavy, and Major Slabopetukhovsky in charge of the rear . . . we played some cards there and, well . . . Nikita, Nikita . . . another week and you would have lived to see victory . . . a real man . . . irreproachable bravery . . . philosopher of war, and a practitioner, too. . . . Someone's flabby paw took Boris by the shoulder, and a damp mouth whispered directly into his ear: "And I knew your mama, Borenka. . . . Oh, what a woman she was . . ." Borenka whirled around, threw aside the flabby paw, and could barely restrain himself from punching the speaker's wet mouth. Someone pulled the lover of intimate revelations away. Have you lost your mind, you drunken fool? What a thing to tell the guy—you call that reminiscing? Everyone in the company quickly came to understand that you could talk about anything you wanted with the marshal's son, just don't bring up his mother.

In the course of conversation, it was mentioned in passing that Boris had seen action himself.

"How did you manage that, old man?" asked Kataev in surprise. "Maybe you were what they call a 'son of the regiment'?"

Everyone laughed. The respected master of the Southern School had won his own Stalin Prize five years before for his story "Son of the Regiment."

Boris grinned. He knew it was not a question of age; it was simply that they were all sure that a marshal's son hadn't had to get his ration of lice in the trenches.

"I was never in a normal regiment," he said. "We were a select unit no larger than a company."

"All the same, old man, your company must have been part of some regiment, no?" asked someone who had just sat down—someone who did not have the right to sit down in such company and certainly not to use a fashionable term of address like 'old man.'

Boris peered at him intently, noticing nothing but the man's small yellow eyes.

"No, our company was not part of a regiment, 'old man,' " he said.

The prizewinners smiled in appreciation at Gradov's sarcasm. Boris went on in the same vein, though he realized straightaway that he was overdoing things a bit.

"I'm sorry, but I can't say any more about it, old man."

Simonov poured out what was already the third bottle of cognac into the glasses. Who else could order drinks like the fine Ararat, if not a six-time prizewinner?

"By the way, boys, an interesting crowd has just entered our establishment," he said. "Don't look now, but three Americans have taken a table over there beneath the balcony."

"W-w-wh-what? Th-three Americans? How?" Mikhalkov stammered excitedly, and immediately directed his eyes, which resembled the lenses of two movie cameras, in the direction indicated.

"Two of them I know personally," said Simonov. "The one my age is F. Coragesson Strawberry. He's no coward, that one—speaks good

Russian, sailed on the Murmansk convoys, flew into Leningrad during the siege. The second one, boys, the big man ... that's right, chaps, that old man there ... he's a big anti-Soviet SOB, the celebrated Townsend Reston. Just open any newspaper—" Everyone giggled, recalling Nikita Bogoslovsky's "invention." "—and you'll see right away how our newspapers fuck over the parasite for slander and disinformation. The third must be someone from the embassy, I don't recognize him."

To see three ruddy-cheeked Americans popping out of a Moscow blizzard in the winter of 1951 was comparable to seeing men from Mars. Mikhail Svetlov, who had been on the point of falling asleep in his chair, shuddered. "Maybe they're not Americans but Martians?"

Borya Gradov went up to the bar and asked Valencia Maximovna for a ten-ruble cigar. When he had lit it, he went back to the table, surrounding himself with something approximating a smoke screen. A great idea—to observe the enemy through a screen of cigar smoke! They can't see me, of course—to them, I'm just a shaggy cloud instead of a face—but I can see them with their bald spots, glasses, school and wedding rings, fat fountain pens sticking out of the pockets of their thick herringbone jackets (why not toothbrushes?), with their gold watches and leather cigarette cases. . . . I wonder why the hell all three of them are looking at me, if I'm just a shaggy cloud of smoke instead of a face? There they are, their fake smiles, there's the "face of the enemy" for you, as our friend Simonov put in the report in verse that he filed from Canada ... "Stalingrad, Russia, and Stalin, the first three ranks are silent."

He returned to his table and consulted the author of the lines he had remembered about the struggle for peace: "See here, old man, you said you know two of those three personally. So why don't you go say hello?"

"You don't understand, old boy, why I don't go over and say hello?" replied Simonov with raised eyebrows. "They understand why I don't greet them, and they don't say hello to me either. They're displaying excellent political tact."

"Well, I'm going to go say hello to them myself, then," said Boris, catching even himself by surprise. Just like that, he was going to beat a path across the hall with a ship's cannon between his teeth to make the acquaintance of the warmongers.

"You won't do that!" Kataev objected, in a surprising falsetto. "As the elder of this table, I advise you not to do it!"

"I'm very sorry, but there's no way for me not to do it," Boris said, getting up. "As a 'man of direct action,' I can't not do it."

The orchestra had struck up "I'll Give You a Little Red Rose." Through the balustrade of the balcony one could see the bass player, wearing thick glasses and already balding even though quite young, a fleeting, mysterious smile on his thick lips, plucking nimbly at the strings with his frankfurterlike fingers. Kataev had said of him one day that he was a talented writer named Yury . . . Yury . . . well, it doesn't matter. . . . Boris was heading for the Americans. Just then, two attractive girls darted out of the powder room and, as they passed by, said, "Isn't that Boris Gradov, the great athlete, in person?" The Americans, naturally, and the international situation, which was becoming more and more complicated with each passing day, were entirely forgotten.

For the rest of the night, Boris would consign many other fundamental problems of the mid–twentieth century to oblivion. Finding himself in the company of people his age, in a muddle of students from a variety of institutes—FOR-LANG, PHIS-TECH, INT-REL, AVIA (the winter holidays had just begun, and the students were on the prowl)—Boris IV immediately became one of the two chief actors in the discussion of a vital issue. The question was put provocatively: Who will get drunker, someone who knocks back an entire half liter of Moscow Special vodka all at one go or someone who takes the same quantity in shot glasses spread out over half an hour? As a "man of direct action," Boris, naturally, came out in favor of the first variant: better either to swig it right out of the bottle or take it in two big glasses. His opponent was a heavyset lad, the Moscow State University champion in Greco-Roman wrestling. He was called "Pop," which would lead one to suppose that his family name was Popov. On the arm of his chair sat an enchanting young thing in a sweater emblazoned with two arctic deer. It was to this very girl, Natasha, that the advantages of direct action over foot dragging, of the motorcycle over a lump of fat, would now be shown. Right now you're all going to see how GRU commandos hold their liquor, especially when fortified with advanced medical knowledge, that is, when they're experts in normal anatomy. Let all these pigeons look on and learn, all of these Mama's and Papa's boys from the top of the class who can afford to go to Riga to order a new pair of three-buckle boots, the cream of our youth with their impeccable biographical data. . . . Take it easy, he said to himself almost aloud, whatever you do, don't become an animal. They're good people—Natasha is going to leave with me, and Pop the wrestler, a great guy, will lie on the floor like a carcass.

He filled a narrow glass to the brim and downed it in one gulp without even tasting the vodka. Meanwhile, Pop, a clever customer, had finished his small glass in one wave of his hand and laid hold of a piece of salmon the size of a hundred-ruble note. They hadn't agreed to anything about zakuski, but to hell with it. As he was pouring himself out another 250-gram glass—just what the doctor ordered!—a lush wave of drunkenness suddenly hit him. In an instant, he regained his concentration and didn't spill a drop. The wave receded, and the vodka passed. He turned the bottle upside down, symbolically shaking out the last few drops—the procedure in his reconnaissance unit. There was a roar of applause. The plebeians of Moscow, eager for bread and circuses. I thank you anyway, my good people. "Have a bite to eat, Grad!" Natasha cried. "Otherwise you won't be able to do anything!" "Don't worry about me, Natasha!" he replied with a dazzling grin like the hero of the film *Waterloo Bridge*. "Just look after yourself!" With a precise guardsman's step, as though he were on parade, on his way to the Mausoleum to toss the standard of the Totenkopf Division at Generalissimo Stalin's feet, he strode over to the bar to get a new cigar, along the way taking a cut-glass tumbler containing a "lighthouse," a drink of an emerald-chartreuse shade with an egg yolk in it, from the hand of Señora Valencia. This he swallowed in one gulp as well. "Hey, Pop, I'll give you a head start!" Everyone in this place must be staring at me, seeing how fabulous I look up here at the bar with a cigar, knocking back a lighthouse. Or maybe it's just the opposite—no one is looking at me, worthless shit that I am. What the hell did I get involved in this stupid argument for? I'm not eighteen years old anymore, I'm not Mama's little boy. No, no, I'm not Mama's little boy—I'll be anyone else you like, but not that. Maybe Grandma's grandson or Auntie's nephew, but there's no way, absolutely no way—and I swear it by the Polish People's Republic, that I'm not Mama's little boy.

The writers, meanwhile, had left the bar. A heavy figure in a sheepskin coat with a beaver collar and a boyar hat was standing there. Someone else, perhaps a celebrity, perhaps someone who had just joined the fun—by this point, one couldn't tell the difference—threw an arm around Boris's shoulder of steel. "We're off to the Gypsy Theater—want to come? There's a banquet there tonight, we're going to sing until dawn. It's a great thing to drown your grief with a Gypsy song during a snowstorm!"

I should go with them, thought Boris, turning in his hands the glass that had contained the lighthouse—imagine that, singing during a blizzard! Too bad I'm not a Gypsy, I'd tell them all to go fuck themselves and go Gypsy myself! No, now you're getting carried away, we'll go by another path! Who said that? To whom? Was it Gogol to Belinsky, or the other way around? No, no, it was Lenin who said it, our own Vladimir Iliich, talking to the czar. Fingers hooked in the armholes of his vest, with a faint smirk . . . no, my good man, we'll go by another path. We know where we're going tonight. The idea suddenly crystallized over Boris's right ear, a beautiful, liquid crystal. Now he knew how that night would end. We know where we're going, and to whom we're finally going to show that we're not Mama's boys—maybe we're SOBs, but by God, we're not Mama's boys.

Suddenly all of the sounds of the bar cut through over his left ear in the form of a different crystal: the sound of chairs knocking together and drunken laughter; the *boom-boom-boom* of a contrabass, that hope of Russian prose, resounded; the voice of Valencia Maximovna: "Close the door, Gavrilych, you're going to give us all a cold!"; someone next to her was laughing in a non-Russian accent; bang, someone smashed a wine glass; time to set sail out of here, otherwise they'll be wiping up the floor with you.

He went back to the table, where an experiment was under way. The wrestler, after regurgitating a bit, was still going through shot glasses. His bottle was only half empty. "I lost," said Boris and tossed his bet on the table, three hundred-ruble notes with a picture of the Kremlin, the Moscow River, and a small steamship on the water.

"Where are you off to, Grad?" Natasha blurted out in near desperation. This very Borya Grad, and not Pop, the champion in Greco-

Roman wrestling, must have been for her the embodiment of a prince.

"I'm drunk as a skunk," said Boris by way of an excuse. "And Mama's waiting up for me at home."

He walked crisply to the exit, following the diagonal panels of the parquet floor, and didn't stumble once. Behind him, Pop slipped from his chair onto the floor, muttering senselessly, "Ha, ha, drank Gradov under the table, ha, ha." The champion's training regimen left quite a bit to be desired, as they say.

The Horch was still in the same place, it hadn't gone anywhere. Everything was all right. Visibility was zero. The precipitation was in the form of witches' locks and tails rather than snow. If this is peacetime, why complain about war? Let's get her started up with a half revolution. The tank heart of Russia in the iron guts of Germany! We won't even scrape the snow off, we'll take off like a humpback whale. Traffic police, how do you do! Marshal Gradov's son is rushing to an amorous encounter with a certain singing prostitute.

★

He didn't have far to go: two blocks down Gorky Street, a left turn into Okhotny Ryad, then right up to the entrance of the Moscow Hotel. There, every night, in the huge restaurant on the third floor, his dream Vera Gorda sang.

Many times Boris had said to himself: you should just forget this bitch. It's all lies, all fake—she probably isn't even that young if you get a look at her in the light of day. Then again, he said, correcting himself, you don't need to see her in the light of day. She's the dream of your drunken nights, a night bird from a lullaby, the embodiment of both whoring and tenderness. Many times, he had seen a dangerous argument break out among the drunken men in the audience near the end of her set—who's going to take Gorda home? Sometimes she vanished or left escorted by the musicians; sometimes she would wait for the outcome of the dispute and then, as if challenging the winners, would leave accompanied by some of her companions, often Georgians. At moments like those, Boris seethed with jealousy: How dare those goats lay a hand on this creature destined for me by the hand of fate itself? What was he thinking, "lay a hand on her"? They're probably going to drag her off, get her drunk, and use her! Next time, I won't let anybody take her away. I'll kick their asses and take her home in the Horch. It'll be more interesting for her, too, with a guy like me instead of all of these filthy bastards. The "next time," however, came, and again, like a little boy, he watched the tall woman in the tight-fitting black dress, intimately bending over the microphone, standing just a bit off to one side and allowing a leg in a silk stocking to peek out ever so slightly from the long slit in her outfit. Her deep voice stirred something distant, almost forgotten, something of the child in the depths of the former commando:

> Here beneath foreign skies
> Like an unwelcome guest
> I listen to the cries
> Of the westward-flying cranes.

Any number of times he had gotten drunk when he came to see and hear her, and any number of times he had sensed the preposterous inaccessibility of this, from all appearances, most accessible of beings.

Time to say "to hell with it all," he had said to himself a few months ago, and he had been fairly successful in sending to the Devil all these oppressive and dissolute feelings that were sucking the life out of him, all the more since his life in Moscow was becoming ever more intense: medical school, sports, motorcycles, the girls who followed the athletes, drinking bouts with the men . . . for months at a time he didn't set foot in the hotel that was so close. Then suddenly it was as if a great whitecapped wave emerged from the murky seas to wash him up right at the foot of the restaurant stage, where Vera Gorda stood in the spotlight, raising her bare arms to her golden locks and seemingly carrying the rhythm of the big band by her voice alone.

> The camels lie silent in the sands,
> And in this deserted land,
> The slow night knows no end . . .

Her repertoire consisted entirely of songs that were more or less banned, which one would never hear for any reason on the radio or at concerts: rhythm and blues and tangos, with a strong note of Russo-Gypsy romanticism—in a word, the most perfect example of "restaurant rubbish," and in those years restaurants, though they still existed, were considered pagan temples of sin, leftovers from capitalism.

In the circles of restaurant habitués—people who were no example for the young to follow—it was said of Vera Gorda, "Did you hear the way Gorda sang Aivazyan's 'Caravan'? It's really something, you know!"

☆

The Horch moved toward its intended destination with one of its windows down. Boris did not notice it and became quite covered with frost and snow. He even remembered a few lines from Blok: "The snow whirls about, an age rushes by in a moment, a blessed shore appears in a dream . . ." In spite of his mind's bent for things motorized, he was not averse to picking up a volume of poetry from his mother's collection, which stood on the shelf amid all the junk in the apartment. *Over there,* she had probably forgotten Russian poetry. What does she need Russian poetry for now? He didn't notice how he had suddenly sobered up and become timid. I don't need to go there. Why should I go there and make a fool of myself? Even if I approach her, what will I say? Excuse me, Vera, but I want you. That's absolutely unthinkable—from me to her. Any one of these fatcats could say that to her and it would be normal. For me, though, it would be anything but. Monstrous. Unimaginable. With young girls these things happen naturally, almost casually, but for some reason this whore seems totally inaccessible.

It was almost midnight. Must get home, howl in loneliness, and then switch off. He had already driven around the center of Moscow twice: the gigantic hotel, the Stereo-Kino movie theater, still showing its one and only film, *License Plate 22-12,* then the Grand Hotel, then the Moscow again. . . . His drunkenness had passed, leaving him with only shame at having played the dashing hussar in the Cocktail Hall: in the end, the only thing I'll manage to do is to have everyone take me for a fop. Hell, I drove myself into a trap tonight, the blizzard must have frozen my brain. In the end, the MGB is going to haul me in for running around. I've got to put a stop to this once and for all!

At the entrance, there were only two Pobedas—taxis with their engines running. There was not even the usual queue for them in sight. The doorman yawned behind the half-frozen glass portals. Inside, in the vestibule, some drunk was making a racket. Two waiters, a bull-dog and a marmoset, were going through his pockets: he had had quite a go at the buffet, this Mr. Moneybags, but he had forgotten to pay. Usually, the rumble of the orchestra could be heard from here, but now all was silent. Boris left his overcoat with the doorman, who, of course, knew him. He had also served under the colors of Boris IV's legendary father on the Reserve Front. Boris mounted the steps to the hall at a run. The orchestra was obviously on a break, the stage empty except for a few instruments left behind: a grand piano with the lid raised, a small mound of drums, the weighty question marks of the saxophones. Good for bourgeois caterwauling and not much else. Not long ago, *Culture and Life* had declared saxophone playing to be the worst kind of hooliganism.

Boris made his way among the tables, trying to find a place with a view of the stage. By this hour, everyone was drunk to one degree or another. Salads lay in ruins, smeared everywhere. Cigarette butts jutted up from the most unexpected places—from an orange, for example. Many mouths were open, displaying teeth of pure gold. In some places there was too much wine, in others not enough. Supported on either side, a staggering man was being led out. Another took off under his own power, weaving, holding a hand over his mouth until he could make it to the toilet with his festive revelation. On the whole, however, the atmosphere seemed to have glassed over, a condition caused in all probability by the half-hour absence of the band. At one A.M., of course, everyone wanted to move, to press against each other, swaying "in an intoxicated trance"—a favorite phrase of the writers of the era when they described the decadence of foreign countries. Suddenly someone called his name. The Army Club racer Seva Zemlyanikin was waving to him from behind a pillar. "Hi, Bob! Listen, come over to our table. Here's one of my mates from school, a test pilot, out for a good time. He just brought a wagonload of money back from the Far East."

Figuring that from there the stage would be so close that it would be as if he were holding it in his hand, Boris walked behind the column and immediately saw Vera Gorda sitting at the far end of the large table with an air force captain. The latter whispered something in her ear, and she smiled. There, in a dark corner, with a wine-colored curtain in the background, behind a collection of empty, half-empty, and unopened bottles, some three paces away, as though she had suddenly stepped out of a movie screen, was Vera. She sat, her bare right elbow on the table, her left hand holding a long cigarette alongside her ear, her eyes haughtily half closed and her red mouth half open as though she were already in bed with this creep of a test pilot, whose hand, hidden beneath the tablecloth, had probably already started making its way between her knees some time ago.

There were no fewer than ten other people sitting around the table, but Boris noticed exactly none of them and didn't even hear the words addressed to him. He shook someone's hand, then someone else's, without taking his eyes off Gorda, greedily fixing all the details in his mind: the dangerously half-torn strap of her stage dress, her large permanent-waved curls, her earrings, her bracelet, a small mole on her temple.

She moved away from the flier slightly and smiled at the newcomer, dousing him with waves from her warm, deep blue eyes. He was pierced by the sensation, which immediately left him, that he had experienced this moment once before in his life.

"I'm sorry, I wasn't listening. What's your name again?" she asked.

"Boris Gradov." He said it as though he expected her to contradict him.

"Boris Gradov, not a bad-sounding name," she said, as if she were speaking to a little boy. "And I'm Vera, in case you weren't listening."

"I was listening," he said.

"Let's have a drink!" the pilot shouted, pouring champagne and vodka into the same glass, creating a drink, popular in those days, called "northern lights."

"Edka is stuck on Gorda," Seva Zemlyanikin said to Borya. "When he heard 'In a Dusty Pack of Old Letters,' he went into a nosedive, and now he's ready to give everything he's got for just one night."

"What if he is?" said Boris and then wheeled around to face the test pilot. "Just what is it you test, Edward, if it's not a state secret? Big planes or small ones?" With a tipsy grin, the pilot wagged a warning finger at Boris, even though it was unlikely the young man was in focus for him.

"As a matter of fact, it's just that, a big secret, young man. A small plane that's a big secret." He inclined his head, clearly struggling with an excess of alcohol, and then, triumphant, beamed cheerfully and spat out the most gargantuan state secret imaginable. "I'm trying out this plane, friends and Verochka. Where, you ask? Just between us, in Korea. It's not easy work we're doing out there, Verochka and the rest of you. You're pulling the trigger with one hand and stretching your eyes with the other so that you have the squint of a Korean, that's what it's all about."

In this way, the filthy slander of the imperialist press to the effect that Soviet fliers were fighting on the side of the Democratic People's Republic of Korea received unexpected confirmation. No one present, even in the state they were in, wanted to touch the subject; only Gorda laughed and covered the swaggering flier's mouth with her hand. Borya suddenly felt a certain sympathy for the drunken fool: he's one of us, on secret assignment; he's fighting the Americans, and his nerves can't take it.

Onstage, the grand piano came to life. Vera rose to her feet and peered past the column. "Well, time for me to work." There were still no musicians to be seen on the stage, only a pianist playing "Saint Louis Blues" at a slow tempo. The flier started to get up to accompany his guest, but his hand slipped from the table and he nearly fell over. Borya slid past the chairs, took the singer under the arm, and led her toward the stage. "A professional job, Bob!" Seva Zemlyanikin chuckled behind him.

"Let's dance," Boris proposed.

"Why not?" She laid a hand on his shoulder.

They began to dance to the soft piano music, she half singing, half humming something in English to herself. Then she asked, "Who are you? I noticed you quite some time ago."

Spinning her around in the dance, his body grazed her breasts and hips. In high heels, she was almost the same height as he. Her back was damp, and the perspiration added a touch to her fragrance that was nothing short of devastating. "I—I—" he muttered. "I'm an intelligence officer in the reserves, a top-ranked motorcycle rider, and besides that—besides that, you know, I'm Marshal Gradov's son. . . . I have an empty five-room flat on Gorky Street—plus a Horch car, and all of that . . ."

She pressed herself to him for a moment. "What are you trembling for, kid? Don't worry, I'll come with you." The musicians in the band were already returning and taking their seats. The pianist continued

playing with a wink at Gorda. By now Boris could not get another
word out. Finally, the conductor, looking like an old baboon in a
starched white shirtfront, announced, "Respected comrades, the stage
orchestra of the Moscow Restaurant will now begin the final set of its
program."

"Wait downstairs in the hotel lobby after the show," Vera whispered.

The lights went down again, the colored glass sphere began to spin
beneath the ceiling, and many-colored flashes of light poured down
upon the crowd of dancers that quickly gathered. Boris did not go
back to the pilot's table but flopped down on a chair closer to the
stage. Gorda was standing at the back of the stage, chatting gaily with
the piano player—maybe about him, about that very same "crazy
kid" whom she had been dancing with while the pianist played "Saint
Louis Blues."

Then the spotlight ushered her forward, and, pressing the microphone almost to her lips, she began to sing, maintaining the slow,
swaying rhythm with her shoulders and knees:

> One day, the bad weather will pass
> And happy days will come back at last,
> And we will ride this road to the end,
> When they come again,
> When they come again.

Oh yes, she was singing for him now, only for him; certainly not
for that filthy rich captain who had such a hard time squeezing the
trigger when he had to stretch his eyes to look like a Korean; certainly
not for her well-off longtime Georgian admirers, who were applaud-
ing her so loudly now, banging with their rings; not for any of the
stuffed faces in the crowd; only for Borya Gradov, whom she had
promised to go home with, having called him what he had longed so
painfully to hear: "kid"!

A waiter approached. Boris ordered a bottle of Gurdzhani wine
and a plate of cheese. Looking around, he saw that he was sitting in a
group of young men, none of whom was paying any attention to him
or his dream. The conversation revolved around sex, naturally. One
of them, an enormous, self-assured thirty-year-old, was telling the

story of how he had suffered for an entire evening with some tart because he couldn't find a "pad" where he could "drop the piston." Everyone else was listening with rapt attention. Just my luck, Petka wasn't home, they were playing cards at Gachik's place, and Semichastny had his aunt and her daughter staying over. We dragged ourselves around the whole night, hugging each other to keep warm. It was freezing, goddammit, and my balls were about to crack from the strain. You couldn't do it standing next to the fence. Finally, she says, grab a cab, Nikolai, let's go to my place. "The tart" was obviously well known in this group. One of them, with false teeth, said, "She lives in Sokolniki." Another one of them, a fellow with glasses, confirmed it: "That's right, in Sokolniki." A third man, bearded, only guffawed. The storyteller went on, "That's exactly right, in Sokolniki, in a dilapidated hut. You open her door, and there's a pit full of water right behind it. She's quite a hot number, but she lives in conditions like that. It's a tiny little room with only enough space for an oversized cot, and her granny's lying on it, shivering under a rag of a blanket. Then I realized that their hot-water radiator had burst because of the cold. 'Come on!' she yells at Grandma. 'Get out of here!' She chucks the old woman on the floor and pulls me down on top of her. Well, comrades, at that point, I forgot about the way things are done in the world's works of literature. I pulled her panties off, drove my rod in, and went at it full speed. All smiles and sin, you bet! The cot was short, my legs were too long, and my feet were jammed up against the wall, magnifying the energy coefficient, the bitch is howling, blowing bubbles, Granny is crying in the corner: 'Quel Cauchemar!'

"Why are you telling this story?" Boris suddenly asked loudly. Everyone turned in his direction as though they had only just noticed him. The one with the beard breathed out a "Ha!" and a smile deep in his whiskers froze in place.

"What business is it of yours?" asked the handsome raconteur, whose name was Nikolai, as he turned to Boris.

"It's just disgusting, that's all," replied Boris, still louder and with a resounding ring in his voice. Again a sensation of rapidly increasing speed arose within him. "A girl in desperation took you to her dump of a place, humiliated her grandmother, who might be all she has in the world, because of you, and you call her 'a bitch' and say she was 'howling and blowing bubbles'!"

Several of the men immediately raised a fuss: "Here's a loser with a big mouth. . . . Just look at this fashion-following piece of shit. . . . Did anyone invite you to come listen? . . . You're sitting here with your Gurdzhani and your cheese, just keep your trap shut, you snot-nosed brat!" All of them were very angry, with the sole exception of the one with the beard, who only laughed in a deep, unnatural bass voice with an expression on his face that was familiar for some reason. "There's something in what he says, brothers . . . oh, yes, there's something there—it's just like something Dostoevsky might have described!"

Gradov faced this chorus calmly, drinking another glass of wine and nibbling at the cheese.

"Excuse me for happening to overhear your conversation, gentlemen, but I still stick to my position, and if I knew the girl whom you're talking about in this way, the whole conversation would have taken a different turn!"

This new act of insolence, even worse than the one before, nearly made them choke. The hero of the group banged a hand the size of a shovel down on the table.

"What, don't you understand, guys? Our comrade here is asking for it. He walks around this place, looking for some adventure for his ass, he's asking for it."

"If he's asking for it, he's going to get it," said False Teeth. "We'll wait for you outside," he said to Boris.

This is all I need, thought Boris. Instead of a date with Gorda, I've gotten myself into a bar brawl. He picked up the remains of the bottle and went back to Seva Zemlyanikin's table.

"Where's Vera?" shouted the flier when he saw him. "What have you done with my love, you bastard?"

"What's with you? Can't you see where Vera is?" Boris shouted back. "She's up on stage singing. Can't you see, can't you hear? Or did you go blind and deaf in Korea?"

"What is this, the whole evening is screwed up!" Seva Zemlyanikin exclaimed in a hurt voice. "They forgot how to hold their booze in the army!"

When the show, after several requests from "our guests from sunny Uzbekistan, sunny Moldavia, and sunny Anywhere, USSR," was finally over and the light on stage had been turned off, Boris left the hall and ran down to the lobby. People who had been promised rooms for the next day were sleeping in armchairs. The doors opened, and ferocious gusts burst in from the street. Drunken voices rang out all over: people "explaining themselves" to each other insistently; someone, naturally, was shouting that no one had respect for him.

They were waiting for Boris in the lobby. A group of about five or six had formed around the group hero, who turned out to be six feet six at the very least. Everything has fallen apart again, and someone else is going to take Vera home. Maybe even this Goliath with his "rod" will take her off after he's stomped on my throat with his size thirteens. Maybe this time they won't be playing cards at Gachik's. Off we go! Just walk by quickly as if you don't notice him. The band is leaving by that door beneath the stairs over there, and Vera should be showing up in about ten minutes. Then, like a whirlwind, he'd have to make off with her in the Horch!

"Listen, boys, my advice to you is not to mess with Boris," the one with the beard was persuading the others. "The man is an expert in unarmed self-defense!"

"Get lost, Sanya!" the powerful Nikolai said to him. "If you don't want to get involved, don't. Everybody knows you've got a good reason. Maybe even two good reasons. Hey, you!" he then shouted to the "adventure seeker," who pretended to be strolling by them calmly. "Hey, Boris, I'm talking to you!"

Gradov froze in his tracks. "How the hell do you know my name?"

Nikolai smirked. "The world turns on gossip. Come closer!"

He took a step forward, and Boris took a step forward. At that very moment, Vera Gorda swooped through the door of the performers' entrance, wearing a fur coat thrown over her stage dress.

"Here I am, Boris!"

Gradov rushed to her, took her by the hand, and spirited the beauty across the huge lobby in the direction of the faithful Horch, which, as gossip had it, had been driven at one time by an SS swine named Oskar Dirlewanger. Given the advantage of their strategic deployment, it would have been easy for Nikolai and his band to stop the lovers, and they would undoubtedly have done so were it not for the traitor in their ranks. The bearded fellow, Sanya, jumped out and met his friends, who were rushing forward, with two tremendous blows: a right jab to Nikolai's stomach and a left uppercut to False Teeth's cheek. Both of them staggered, the one bent over in a question mark and the other bent back in the opposite direction. This gave Boris the opportunity to escape. Astounded, he looked back at the one with the beard, but without slowing down. Vera rushed along as well, laughing, holding her flying hair with one hand. It seemed to her, of course, that another battle was taking place in her honor, something which had happened quite a few times before. In fact, she wasn't far off: from the far corner of the lobby, Edward "the Stalinist falcon" was bearing down on them. Out of habit, a habit that he had acquired flying jets over the Korean Peninsula, he was squeezing an imaginary trigger with one hand and stretching the skin around his eyes with the other so that he really did look quite Asian. Now Boris had to adopt a tactic that had been worked out, and worked out well, in the time of struggle for the establishment of socialism in fraternal Poland— that is to say, throwing the captain over his hip, thereby becoming an unwilling accomplice of American imperialism for just a second. After that, he took off with the singer, as though he were jumping out of a Douglas, into the howling storm.

Well, start, you SS piece of crap! The old jalopy, which had been involved in a fair amount of dirty business before and which was now mixed up in this not particularly glorious affair, did not let him down; it roared to life like a column of tanks rushing to breach the lines and take Dunkirk. The hands of insulted men tore at the doors, the mugs of guys who hadn't said their last word slid along the side windows. All of a sudden, one dear and piercingly recognized, even though bearded, mug of a face plastered itself against the glass—his comrade in arms Alexander Sheremetiev! What a night! "Sashka, I'm still in the same place—you know!" Boris roared through a chink in the windshield. The bearded face nodded. The windshield wipers cleared away the snow so he could see Nikolai standing in front of the car in a heroic Mayakovsky-like pose: "I sing for my fatherland, for my republic!" "Permission to run him down?" Boris asked with a wicked grin.

"Under no circumstances! Put 'er in reverse, Commander!" Vera Gorda laughed.

"Thanks for the option," growled the retired commando. Turning around in the middle of Okhotny Ryad, transformed by the blizzard into a Russian field that the peasant rebel Pugachov himself might have stood on, the Horch headed for Gorky Street. In a moment, it was out of the sight of the unruly crowd, with Nikolai the Giant surviving in order to make another appearance later in this novel.

★

All the movements that followed, both of the flesh and of the spirit—and the latter were present in force, even though there are some critics who will say that there was nothing spiritual about it, that it was only animal sex; they were there, these movements of the spirit, though in an unbelievably confused heap that no one would ever be able to untangle—would be remembered later by Boris as a continuation of the same storm, but in a hot version.

By the time they were in the elevator, he had already lost the ability to answer Vera Gorda's questions. Entering the apartment, he took her firmly by the hand and, without saying a word, pulled her across the entrance hall, the dining room, and the study, straight to his parents' bedroom. "My God, what an apartment!" she muttered. "Who would ever imagine such an apartment?" In the bedroom, not even turning on a night-light—the snow-covered streetlights were throwing shadows of the storm through the windows—he laid her down, still in her fur coat, on the wide Pavlov bed so lovingly obtained by Mama at an antiques shop. He began pulling her silken undergarments from beneath her long skirt, got them caught on something and tore them, then drew them out like a garland of fragments. Then the thing that had filled him with such an overwhelming thirst for so long opened up before him. She moaned, stroking his head and murmuring, "Borenka, Borenka, my little boy!" He felt as though his brains were completely scrambled by these endearments, and he was barely able to restrain himself from saying the fateful word. Then she stopped calling him by any name at all and only shrieked over and over again, more wildly each time, until she suddenly said through a shudder of contemptuous semiconsciousness, "You fucked the hell out of me and never even kissed me, you disgusting prick! Don't I exist for you except as a cunt?" He realized that this was just the moment when she would have to say something dirty, and he smeared his mouth across her hot lips, those same lips that whispered crass, mind-dulling lyrics into a microphone. Her long nails digging into the back of his neck, Vera Gorda was writhing as though she were trying to tear herself

loose and run away, and he immediately became one with her convulsions, seeming to plead to her with each new stroke. When that
moment, too, had passed, he felt a momentary shame: What makes
me any better than that Nikolai? He immediately chased the thought
away, though: Can you really compare this to that nasty piece of
work? They were lying next to one another now without touching,
still wearing their shoes and outer clothes.

"How old are you, Boris?" she asked.

"Twenty-four," he replied.

"My God!" she sighed.

"What about you, Vera?"

"Thirty-five." She laughed. "Does that scare you?"

"I wouldn't want you any younger," he muttered.

"Is that so? That's interesting." She began to raise herself from the
bed, dangled her legs, and then stood up. "Oh no, you tore everything
off me, all my expensive lingerie . . ."

He drew a pack of broken cigarettes from his pocket, found a
fragment that looked usable, and lit a match. "Over there in the
wardrobe," he said, "there's plenty of good underwear, and your size,
too, I think . . ."

He gave a start, afraid that he'd said too much, that now she would
begin to ask who left it, and why . . . Gorda, saying nothing, however,
turned on the night-light, opened up the wardrobe, fingered some of
Mama's lingerie and gave a whistle: "Not bad!" She looked at him
with a mixture of amusement and gaiety. He laughed joyfully: how
easy it would be with her!

She looked at herself in the mirror, still in her stage dress with its
lap crumpled and frayed. "Well, well," she said, whistling again. "A
violated thirty-five-year-old singer."

She went to the telephone, dialed a number, and said simply, "I
won't be home tonight." Then she put the receiver down.

"Who were you calling?" Boris asked and was immediately
ashamed of the question. She hasn't asked me anything yet, and here
I am already prying into her personal life.

"What difference does it make?" she answered with a touch of sadness. "I was calling my husband."

Her saying "my husband" made him want to pull her right back
down onto the bed. He watched with delight as she moved about the

room, taking off her fur coat, slithering out of her silvery dress like a snake. "I imagine your bath works?" she asked suddenly in a strange tone that was at once both teasing and humiliated.

"Why not? Of course it does," Boris said in surprise. "Down to the end of that corridor, and take a right. Sorry the place is such a dump, Vera, but I live by myself and my biker friends are always hanging around."

"Doesn't matter, doesn't matter!" she shouted buoyantly and clattered off on her high heels, hitching up her torn garter belt, directly to the bathroom.

While she was splashing in the tub, he made the bed. Fortunately, he managed to find clean sheets. He undressed, got under the covers in expectation, and then fell asleep. He was awakened by a most pleasurable sensation. The naked Gorda was kneeling between his legs and licking his manhood. She took it entirely into her mouth, sucked it, and then began licking it again, all the while regarding Boris with large, innocent eyes. Then she moved up closer to him and, with remarkable agility, introduced him into herself and mounted him like a high-society woman used to galloping on purebred stallions. Bending forward, she offered "Boris the kid" her breasts with their pointed nipples. Borenka began to suck one breast while fondling the other and then, remembering fairness, sucked the slightly offended second member of the pair while stroking and lightly pinching the first.

"Now, Borya, my boy, let's get some sleep," Gorda said after the steady trot that had ended as a mad steeplechase was over. She trustingly laid her head on his shoulder, her right arm and leg embracing him, and fell asleep, a whistling sound coming from her nostrils. Blissfully stretching out in her warm and tender embrace, he too fell asleep or, perhaps more accurately, dissolved—was this Nirvana?—until he and all of his members woke up again.

"Here he goes again," she muttered sleepily. "That's enough, Borya, save your strength. . . . What are you doing? . . . Well, all right, do what you want, just don't wake me, I'm tired. . . . What else do you want? My ass in the air, right? . . . Be my guest. . . . Do it as much as you want, Borya, just save yourself a little for the morning . . ." He went back to sleep and was again awakened by the exhortation "Save your strength, Borya!" How had she managed to find the very words he was dying to hear?

Finally they decoupled, but half an hour later he leapt out of bed and unconsciously rushed to the cupboard to pull a commando's toy called a Parabellum, engraved with his name, from beneath a pile of sheets. The doorbell was ringing and ringing. The clock said ten minutes to five. Vera, snoring contentedly, did not even stir, only muttered something incoherent. The first thing that came into Boris's head was: Has Sashka Sheremetiev brought that mob here with him? I'll scare them off with my gun, no fooling around! He tied his dressing gown and then ran to the door barefoot. Meanwhile, the bell had stopped ringing. He looked through the peephole. The tiles of the staircase landing shone dimly beneath the dull ceiling. No one. Cautiously, pistol in hand, he opened the door. Emptiness and dead silence except for the faint howling of the storm in the ventilation shafts. A large paper bag stuffed with something stood by the door. It was standing there, this strange sack, not lying, as one might expect an ordinary bag to do. It was standing on its hindquarters, that is, on its flat, fleshy bottom. That bag isn't one of ours. Russia couldn't produce a bag like that. It will take Russia at least another hundred years to make such a sack with noncollapsible two-ply walls of thick brown paper, with a flat bottom, with blue tie strings.

He took the bag into the dining room, set it on the table, and undid the blue strings. The first thing that he took out was warm and soft. It was two sweaters wrapped together—one was dark red, the other dark blue. Each had an identical label, bearing only one word: "Cashmere." Then two warm, closely woven shirts appeared, one with a large green check pattern, the other brown. Two pairs of leather gloves. A watch on a metal bracelet. A device he had never seen before, which was later identified as an electric razor. Then wool socks in red, light blue, and yellow. Fringed moccasins and fur-lined boots. A white winter union suit. Finally, the last thing in the bag, pressed down at the very bottom—it was difficult to believe that such things actually existed—was a leather pilot's jacket lined with sheep's wool, with big and small pockets everywhere, gleaming with zippers, with a chain for hanging and a large leather patch depicting a Flying Fortress and stating, so there could be no confusion, "Bomber jacket, large."

Oh hell, oh hell, I can't understand any of this—I've had too much to drink, I'm too tired. . . . What is this, what are these things, who are they supposed to be for, what sort of . . . Suddenly, a thought took shape in his mind with terrifying clarity: What sort of provocation is this? Drenched with sweat, fingers trembling, he began unzipping zippers and frisking pockets. He found nothing. He looked into the now empty bag—there was still something there: a large, glossy picture showing a Western city on a late winter afternoon, lights already on in the windows, the sun setting early, a frozen pond with men, women, and children in nineteenth-century clothes skating on it, and, of course, dogs frolicking artlessly and unself-consciously among them. On the reverse was a silver ribbon added to the paper, bulging outward and bearing the words "Merry Christmas and Happy New Year!" and beneath that in a round, childlike hand—her writing— "My boy, how I love you!"

She sent this gift to me, her son, for the New Year just passed, and someone, stealthily, in the dead of night, like a commando, delivers it. An American, maybe one of those Americans who were sitting in the Cocktail Hall, or maybe a different American in some *secret* business. Has she lost her mind? Her boy, whom she loves so much, could be chased off to Kolyma for such a present. A secret delivery in the night from hostile, spying, aggressive America: a *contact*! No, you don't even get off with Kolyma for things like that, they just shoot you in a cellar. So long as she has the satisfaction of knowing that she sent me a gift at New Year's, she doesn't care if the world comes to an end. Maybe in the bucolic cities and around those Connecticut ponds she has forgotten the place where she did a four-year term only to be spirited away by her Shevchuk? He hurled the priceless flight jacket into a corner in a rage. This sharp movement immediately summoned up a whole train of opposing thoughts: Since when did I become a coward? As I recall, I learned in Poland not to be afraid, neither of a submachine gun nor of a bayonet, and here I am afraid of a gift from my mother? From my own dear mother, who is in no way to blame for the fact that the world around her has gone off its head, fragmenting and dispersing her family? Better to take a look at how lovingly all of this was put together, one piece after another. Everything is first rate and, most important of all, warm, as if it were her very own heat she wanted to send to me in this bag, a bundle of her own warmth. I'm going to wear all of it, and I'll wear the jacket with pride. If there are any questions, I'll answer: my mother sent it to me from America!

He went over to the window, drew back the shutters, and saw that the snowstorm was over and that the skies were striving to clear themselves. In the dark lilac light, long white clouds were swimming in the shapes of ancient boats and at the pace of a symphonic *bravura allegro*. Suddenly he felt choked with happiness. All you have to do is want it, and you'll swim away in the company of those spots of white in the dark lilac skies.

"Borenka, where have you gone?" came the voice of stage singer Vera Gorda from the bedroom.

Chapter 5

———— ☆ ————

TALK ABOUT
TURNAROUNDS!

A little over a month after the snowstorm just described, we find our-selves in a period of permanent blue skies, with flashes of sunshine, a frigid, immobile sky, when the ice-covered bowl of the capital's Dy-namo Stadium seemed to reign supreme over the city. There was no end to the frost, and dry snow, flaking off surfaces, crunched beneath one's feet. The cold had killed the microbes in the air by freezing them, aspirin sat on the shelves at the pharmacies, and the people on the street, at least those we see here at the Dynamo, displayed healthy Russian faces accustomed to the winter. Everyone realized that it had fallen to their lot to live now—the "thaw" was still five years away and *perestroika* thirty-five—and if you managed to both survive the war and not end up in jail, it was possible to live to the full in the dry, microbe-free air of the late Stalinist era and even to take some plea-sure in life, in particular by gawking at the training sessions for the upcoming competitions in motorcycle racing on ice.

A few connoisseurs, as well as, of course, a few career layabouts and pensioners from government departments dealing with internal affairs and with sports, watched from the stands as the motorcycles on snow tires roared by below them like wild boars in the spring, negotiating turns and throwing up a fanlike spray of ice dust.

"So Cheremiskin has switched from Arda to NSU?"

"They say Gringaut never goes out on the ice anymore."

"What do you mean 'never goes out on the ice'? I saw him putting the snow spikes on the tires of his IZh-350 myself."

"Who's that over there, the fast one?"

"That's Borya . . . Gradov, I think. He took second place in cross-country in Moscow over the summer, and now he's trying ice as well."

"Does he have decent numbers?"

"Ninety and some from a standstill, 125.45 from on the move."

"Not bad!"

All of the expert riders training on the Dynamo ice-racing ring were working with their own coaches, and Boris, too, had his personal trainer, who timed him on each segment of the course and tossed him quick tips. The trainer was very polite, addressing his protégé in a formal, even elegant fashion: "What the hell are you doing, Mr. Gradov, you asshole, why didn't you give it gas on the turn like I said?"

With a happy reddened face sprinkled with ice dust, Boris slowly drove up to the rough figure in a fleece-lined watchman's coat and galoshes over his felt boots. "Sorry, Sashka, I didn't turn it on in time. Let's take it from the top." He did not let show, of course, that he found the seriousness with which Sheremetiev took his new job a bit comical. The former boxer was still a complete amateur when it came to motorcycles.

★

Their friendship had been reestablished shortly after the night of the snowstorm. One fine morning, Boris, having mastered his biochemistry lesson with gritted teeth, went to answer a ring of the bell and saw at the door a young man in a navy jacket with a clean and intelligent, if somewhat angular, face. It was as though he had never had a beard. It turned out that he had shaved it off right after the fracas in the lobby of the Hotel Moscow. "When I saw you, sir, you SOB, I looked at myself in the mirror and realized what a disgusting state I'd fallen into. I shaved off the beard and stopped hanging around in beer joints, even turned down invitations to restaurants."

A meeting like this, however, after six and a half years, called for a restaurant celebration. The friends went to Yesenin's Place, as the Muscovites then called the arched cellar beneath the Lubyanka Passage. You couldn't ask for a better place to tell sad tales. They would refill your beer glass without being asked. Weakened moral fiber can always be supported by a triple shot glass of vodka.

Here is the history of the last six and a half years in the life of Alexander Sheremetiev, which he told in lapidary fashion. His shattered leg had been amputated soon after his evacuation from Warsaw. They had managed to save the knee joint, however, which meant that the leg was still alive, as it were. "With much pomp and circumstance, the secret hero—they put me in for Hero of the Soviet Union then—was given an American prosthesis, an amazing, permanent thing. Just look—you can touch it, don't be afraid—a gift of B'nai B'rith, the Jewish society." Getting used to it quickly, Alexander had even begun to contemplate a return to the ring. All he would have to do was to put on some weight in order to get into a category where there was less movement. "Well, it was a joke, of course. I had a bigger problem—I was a drunk! I stuck like glue to the commanding officers and asked them not to write me off as an invalid. The war is still on, I can still be of use, not to mention in peacetime. You know, Borka, you can say what you like about the GRU, but they try to take care of their own, especially cutthroats like us. They sent me to the military interpreters' school in the Far East to make me a specialist in American English. Well, of course that perked me up right away, I had enough fantasies in my head to keep forty barracks full of prisoners happy: international espionage, hotels in the Caribbean, an American with a slight limp, the life of the party, a swimmer and a diver who was in reality a Soviet spy, and so on in that vein; you'll permit me to remind you that, in spite of all of our experiences in Poland, we were only eighteen then. In short, I tried to outdo everyone in the school in everything, except on the obstacle course, naturally. And damn it to hell, I did it. My English was fairly good even before, as you remember, and after a year in that school, where we were forbidden to speak Russian even in the bathhouse, I was already speaking like a Yank, could even imitate the accents—southern, Texas, Brooklyn Jewish. In shooting, as you remember, I wasn't the worst of the bunch in our outfit, and back here, to compensate for my injury, I became the absolute and undisputed champion. Everyone was especially surprised by my swimming. I swam in the bay in between the blocks of ice, quite often with a pack of walruses. I could lie on the bottom and descend into a sort of half-alive state, allowing the current to drag my inferior body slowly along in order to come up noisily right beneath the guard tower. The political officer, by the way, was quite concerned by these amphibious capabilities of mine. 'One mustn't exaggerate the lack of concern on the part of a potential enemy,' he would often say to me, meaning that the object of our energies—the American imperialism that has installed itself on the islands of Japan—might one day draw me into its net.

"To make a long story short, at the end of the two-year course, I expected, not without justification, either to be sent abroad as an 'illegal' or at the very least, to be assigned as a top secret consultant to the general staff. And suddenly everything went right over a cliff, or right up a deep asshole, my friend.

"This was preceded by a certain romantic interlude which I'm not going to tell you about just now. Well, I'm not going to tell you everything. Later I will, but not now. Because I simply don't want to tell the story at the moment. I know, Borya, you bastard, that you want to hear romantic stories more than anything in the world and to tell about your own romantic adventures in return, because you're such a lucky man in love right now, the conqueror of Vera Gorda, but maybe that's why I don't want to tell you anything about this love affair right now. No, no, it's not that at all. There's a more important reason: I just want to spend some time with you, and if I tell you the story of my dreadful little 'romantic'—in quotation marks—story, I'll have to leave you right away. Whenever I bring that 'love affair' back up from memory, I don't want to see anyone for three days. Well, I see you're quite intrigued, you walrus prick—yes that's right, a walrus. You guessed right, I know what I'm talking about, and I see there's nothing else you want to hear about. Okay—if you want to hear about it so badly, order us up another bottle and a plate of ham and pickles.

"To give you the short version, I crossed the path of some three-star bastard and paid for it. And instead of Caribbean hotels in the colonial style, they tossed me onto Iturup Island, the asshole of the universe, so far from anywhere that a dead horse washing up on the beach there is considered an event of significance for the whole Pacific. There was a station out there for tracking American airplanes, and I had to work twelve-hour shifts on radio intercept duty, that is, eavesdropping on chatter between pilots and their bases and among themselves. As you can probably guess, you don't have to have spent two years combing through Oxford dictionaries, reading Shakespeare and modern American writers to do this kind of work. The vocabulary of the cockpit consists of no more than three hundred entries, as they call them, including all possible obscene variations. Contemplating the waves washing up on the island for three months turns into a kind of delirium that won't leave you alone. Your colleagues with their drinking and their games of dominoes start to drive you bonkers, and then our famous penchant for making everything a secret just makes you want to scream."

"By the way, Sashka," Boris interrupted at this point. "You understand, of course, that by telling all of this at Yesenin's Place, you're violating our famous principle of 'making everything a secret' in a major way?"

"To hell with it!" Sheremetiev flared. "Secrecy is making us all paranoid!"

"You young people want anything else?" the manager asked from behind his paunch. He was supposed to see to it that no secrets were divulged, as it should be in a place so close to the headquarters of the "armed guard of the Party."

"Well, no—just think about it, Arianych," Sheremetiev said to him indignantly. "They send us an English catalogue of the minerals that are found in our country to be translated in a few days, and half the text is inked out. Who is this sort of thing a secret from, I ask you?"

The manager, resting his potbelly on the edge of the table, listened, nodded, and said, "I'll bring you some chanakh now, Sasha, you need to eat something," and then walked away.

Boris laughed. "I see you can do pretty much as you like here."

"You know, this den reminds me of a London pub somewhere in Chelsea," Alexander said seriously.

Boris laughed even more loudly.

"So, little Sasha, that means you've been somewhere else besides Iturup? Somewhere in Chelsea, you say?"

Sheremetiev's expression turned gloomy, and he dangled a lock of his black hair in his yellow beer. "I haven't been anywhere, and I never will. I committed suicide on Iturup."

"A catalogue of mineral resources is one thing, Sasha," Boris said, "but a radio intercept station is quite another. You should take more care about that subject."

Sheremetiev unbuttoned his jacket and raised his cheap sweater. On his left side, just below the heart, was a dark blue hole.

Adrianych set two pots of the thick mutton soup called chanakh on the table. "Go ahead, go ahead, guys—eat, or you'll get plastered!"

After swallowing several spoonfuls of the liquid, which had been peppered to the point of blazing, Boris said, "Well, go ahead, you SOB, tell me about your suicide."

Sheremetiev continued his tale. "This base of ours on Iturup, like ninety percent of everything else, was what the French call a *secret de Polichinelle*—in other words, a secret to no one. Do you really think that the Yankees flying by in their Fortresses stuffed with electronic gear didn't know who was monitoring their airwaves? They had probably already photographed everything, right down to the last tin of sardines. Several times we even saw them photographing us. An enormous plane makes a low-altitude run with no signal lights, probably taking pictures with an infrared camera. These events were much more interesting than the dead horse, but talking about them was strictly forbidden. We had to pretend no one was photographing us. In short, I realized that I had to say good-bye to the armed forces and to my whole past, with all of our childish notions of 'direct action.' I filed a request for discharge on the grounds that 'the condition of my shortened right lower extremity was worsening' and made a request to continue my education. After a month, the answer came back: inadvisable to accept for discharge. So I filed another report, and again after a month: inadvisable to accept. So the months went by. You say that you went through that too, Borka, in Poznań, but at least in Poznań you could pay visits to the tarts, while on Iturup the only imaginable female partner around would be a sympathetic guard dog. The human population of the island didn't allow for the slightest erotic notion. The only thing there was plenty of was drink. We went so far as to drain the fluid from our gyroscopes, even though the bastards in command weren't stingy about supplying us with vodka. It's as if they were saying: just become drunks quietly, lads, and forget about your education.

"The worst thing of all, Borka, was the feeling of being totally abandoned, of being of no use to anyone. Except for those replies to my reports, I received no mail at all, neither from my mother, nor from—well, from my 'romantic story.' Later on it turned out that my mother had been writing nonstop, but that in our system her letters went directly to that three-star swine whose jaw I broke later on . . . yes, I broke his jaw with one direct punch and a second hook . . . weak, it was, feeble and frail, cracked straight away in two places, all of headquarters heard it . . . but that's later—everything in the proper order. . . . It turns out, Boris Nikitovich, that when you don't get any letters, it can be a lovely evening—when the weather is fine, no precipitation of any sort, the huge sea stretching out before you . . . it's possible to sign a receipt for your weapon, supposedly for target practice, which wasn't forbidden, then to go down to the beach, load up on almost two-hundred-proof alcohol, cry, feel sorry for yourself, imagine that you're Pechorin or Childe Harold, like those Russian romantics in provincial garrisons, and then to stick the barrel under your ribs and fire. The result was, fortunately—or maybe it just made me a laughingstock—that the bullet passed within two inches of my heart. To this day I enjoy torturing myself: maybe I was just bluffing there on the out-of-the-way coast of Iturup, maybe I knew I was sticking the barrel in a place where it wouldn't be fatal. Was it all just the bravado of a provincial officer? I don't know the answer to that.

"After the operation and an investigation, they finally reassigned me to the reserves. My file contained the remarkable phrase 'emotionally unstable.' Whenever anyone asks me to explain it, I answer, 'I'm just touchy.' I went back to the school, supposedly to pick up my books but really to have a look at my 'love story,' who had been strangely silent all that time. Then I found out she no longer existed. No she hadn't gone anywhere, she was just no more. I'm sorry, I can't talk about it now. Let me just say that that was the very day I broke Colonel Maslyukov's jaw and wound up in the stockade. They were a long time in adjudicating my case, because some contradictory opinions came up. Some decent guys told the court how it really was: assault and battery of a senior officer while in a rage motivated by jealousy, which gets you a stiff term. But the swine in the court, of whom there were more than enough, with Maslyukov's help rigged up a case of 'complicity in espionage,' and for that, as you understand, Iturup's Lord Byron could earn a bullet in the back of the head.

"Okay, okay, sometime I'll tell you more of the details, but right now there's just one thing I want you to know: I escaped from that hell only because of my friendship with you. Strange as it may seem, it's true. Marshal Rotmistrov came to the sector on an inspection tour, and my angel managed to suggest to him that he take a run out to the stockade. Who was the angel? What strange questions you're asking, Borka. By 'angel,' I mean my guardian angel, that's all. There, in the stockade, a decent sort in the administration managed to slip the marshal my file: well, he says, here's a hero, lost a leg behind enemy lines but stayed in the service. What we have here is another classic Soviet novel: *The Story of a Real Man*. This was also the doings of my angel. The marshal had me come and see him, and we talked for two hours. It happened that he had heard about our landing in Warsaw and had even known Grozdev—Volk Dremuchy, you remember—personally. Then all of a sudden he asked, 'And did you know Borya Gradov out there?' As it turned out, he and your father had been good friends, and he had a great deal of respect for your grandfather, had been a guest at Silver Forest any number of times. That's why all of Maslyukov's intrigues didn't do him any good. I wouldn't even be surprised if the swine had serious troubles; then again, lowlife like that knows how to wriggle out of any situation. There's one situation he won't squirm out of, though, and that's if I ever get my hands on him again. To make a long story short, they closed my case, gave me a medical discharge, and here it is a year now that I've been leading a miserable existence in Moscow, dragging my burden like a bargeman hauling a load of shit. That's the way it is, Borka. I'm drifting along without a rudder and without sails. I don't count my kopecks, but they certainly count me; the bastards squeezed every last drop out of me and ground me down to a few holes. . . . I'm as full of holes as a Swiss cheese, but I'm without tears . . . old buddy.

I declare in the presence of my angel: don't expect any tears from me—I swear by the armored forces of Marshal Rotmistrov!"

Borya Gradov, motor god and fortunate possessor of the most voluptuous mistress in Moscow, clapped a hand to his shoulder: "Sashka, damn you, if our 'direct action' has fallen through, so be it— we'll hit them in the flank! No one can stop us! And no one will condemn us! Marshal Rotmistrov did it more than once, and then my father came down on them with the whole army! In the flank, friend! As Kostya Simonov wrote, 'As long as we live, we'll stay in the saddle / The major said it in every battle!' We'll take on your Maslyukov together and hang his nuts around his neck! Do you remember that gentle waltz: 'Look around us, all is quiet, but the badger's still awake / Hung his nuts 'round his neck and dances jigs around the lake!' "

In this way, exchanging these sorts of monologues, the two friends left Yesenin's Place, climbed back up into the microbe-free air of frosty socialism, and went down Teatralny Passage toward the monument to Ivan Fyodorov, Russia's first printer, to lay at his feet a quarter liter they had picked up *just in case*.

★

Alexander Sheremetiev, as they say, had "left the army with a wolf's ticket," that is, had been kicked out and, unlike our Babochka, with no money. There was no possible way for him to continue his education. His mother, of course, would not support a healthy invalid. He would have to find a job and pick up some money on the side as well. The latter would be easier than the former: he could give English lessons or do technical translations, but he needed official employment to satisfy the police. After all, he couldn't just limp around playing the role of invalid with accordion: "I was a battalion scout, give what you can, brothers and sisters . . ." Moscow was squeamishly and haughtily ridding itself of such types in those years. In the end, after no small number of ordeals (he even suspected that, in spite of the intercession of the powerful marshal, he was still being tailed by some operatives from the Far East), he found himself official employment in the translation department of the Lenin Library, which Muscovites in everyday usage called the "Leninka," introducing a spirit of frivolous rebellion into the triumphant-sounding name. There, in the end-less reading halls, in the corridors, and particularly in the smoking lounge, Sheremetiev made the acquaintance of the outstanding people of his generation, and those a bit older, who spent their free time there in various secret institutes reading philosophical literature. They argued at length about the past, about Russia's historical destiny, about the Russian character, about the character of man in general. They exchanged old editions of Dostoevsky and Freud. High schools and universities, after all, leave many gaps in the education of a young man. If you want to become a thinking person, you can't avoid being an autodidact, and if you work in the "Leninka" and gradually become your own man, you gain access to classified materials. In the end, an intellectual body of thought took shape among these readers, and they began to meet to exchange opinions in one another's apartments or, when the weather was warm, on the Istra or the Klyazma, on fishing trips or around a campfire with a bottle. They called themselves the "Dostoevsky Circle," but only among themselves.

Strange as it may seem, it was precisely upon the members of this circle that first-class athlete Borya Gradov had stumbled that memorable night of the snowstorm. He had taken them for ordinary thugs from the gutter, when in fact they had gathered at the Moscow to toast the major prize won by their comrade Nikolai, an aerodynamics engineer. Of course, at two in the morning, everyone had been completely smashed. Nikolai's story about his adventures in Sokolniki, however, was not just boasting or jeering. He had begun to share his recent experience with his friends because it seemed to him that there was something decidedly "Dostoevskyan" about the situation. This was how the misunderstanding had occurred: instead of recognizing Boris Gradov as a man of considerable intellectual potential, they had taken him for a *stilyaga*, a fashion freak, who was "asking for it."

In explaining all of this to his old friend, Alexander Sheremetiev said at one point that, in his opinion, it would be entirely possible for Boris to become a member of the Dostoevsky Circle and even to become friends with that very same Nikolai, who, had acquired the nickname "Giant" as early as his school days in the Zubovsky Square district.

Why not? Boris thought. It's entirely possible these characters are terrific guys. In those days, he was ready to embrace the whole world. Wearing his stunning American jacket, he would stroll down Gorky Street, or along Nevsky Prospekt in Leningrad, where he went fairly often in a two-berth compartment of the *Red Arrow* train with his beauty, Vera Gorda. Everything was coming up roses for him; even the medical school exams no longer weighed on him. He began training on ice more and more to prepare for the forthcoming end of winter competitions. He put his heart into his efforts especially when Vera came to the stadium and applauded him with her fur mittens. He was drinking less, as well, because the main incentive to get drunk—to be insolent with, to seduce, and then to stick it to that demi-monde beauty of a songstress—had vanished. This femme fatale had been transformed into the most gentle, devoted creature anyone could ask for. Exhilaration filled him, and he became somewhat afraid: Aren't the skies a bit too cloudless? Isn't nature going to be offended?

On the other hand, the clouds would sometimes show up, twisted into pangs of jealousy: What if she suddenly decides to give herself to someone else, just like that, the way she did with me, wherever the mood strikes her—in an elevator, in a train, on a staircase? It's no problem for her. She would immediately sense the gathering of these clouds and would sit on his lap, whispering tickling admonishments into his ear: Stop hanging around in the restaurant standing guard! Can't you see I'm in love with you like a cat, that I can't even think about anyone else? There was never anyone else before you. No, I'm not lying, it's just the way I feel—everything in my memory has simply been wiped out.

Nevertheless, he would go to meet her at the hotel at the end of her set. The regulars immediately caught on to the fact that Gorda had changed, had taken up with "the kid," and they didn't bother her anymore. That still left the nuts who were just passing through, though: all kinds of polar explorers, fliers, sailors, factory directors from the Caucasian republics, and Party functionaries, with whom Boris had to get rough sometimes, even though Vera became angry, saying she could quite easily deal with those idiots herself.

He wanted her to move in with him and to bring her things with her. Even though she was already spending most of her time at Gorky Street, she refused to bring her things. Sometimes, most often on a Sunday, she would disappear, going somewhere in a taxi, and not let

Boris start the Horch to take her. He realized that in the "pre-Gradov era" she had been living in two places. She had an abandoned husband someplace: "He's such a pathetic creature—just pathetic, I tell you!" And there was a favorite aunt, the older sister of her now dead mother, who lived in a dump of a communal apartment: "Refined, charming and defenseless, the whole family ended up in Kolyma." The aunt seemed to be the chief object of Vera's concern.

Somewhere in the depths of Moscow lived her father as well, but he was a demimythical creature, an eccentric old bachelor, a former Futurist, and now a professor of English who specialized in Shakespeare. It turned out that Gorda's stage name had not just come to her from out of the blue but had been derived from her father's real family name of Gordiner. It sounds Jewish, but we're not Jews, Vera would repeat insistently, just Polish nobility. All things considered, her father almost refused to acknowledge his only daughter Vera because of some old quarrels with her tubercular mother, and during her visits, which were very rare—no more than once a year—he was curt and distant. His intelligent cat, Velimir, distinguished himself by his exceptional haughtiness in his dealings with her.

"You see, Babochka, you find a substitute for your Mama Veronika in me," she said to him one day quite casually, "but no one can make up for my father, because I never had one." Boris gasped for breath. First of all, how had she learned his childhood nickname, which meant "butterfly"? It was a bit ridiculous, and frankly, for an intelligence officer and first-class athlete, off the mark. And second of all, it turned out that the secret that was the deepest under his skin, and which he had hardly ever admitted even to himself, was in fact no secret to her at all. Well yes, that was how it was: the very first time he had seen her, he had been struck by her resemblance to his mother. Maybe now in her Connecticut, she had finally aged—she was already forty-seven, after all—but he remembered her only as the young, stunningly beautiful Veronika. That was why on that first night with Gorda he had barely been able to restrain himself from crying out "Mama, Mama!"

Vera had even seen his mother once, as it turned out. Yes, yes, it was at the end of 1945. She was already singing at the Savoy then, and there was a banquet for the American allies. She had sung in English from *Serenade* and *George from Dinky Jazz*. It was even possible she had seen Babochka's stepfather. In any case, there had been a tall, no longer young colonel with whom his mother had danced all evening, a real gentleman. As for Veronica . . . oh, there was a woman . . . what class . . . how I dreamed back then about one day becoming like that famous Marshal Gradov's wife, of marrying an American! Thank God I didn't marry one, or I wouldn't have met you, my little Babochka!

Then she began to laugh loudly and slyly in order to provoke him into going on the attack again, and, it must be said, these provocations never went unanswered.

One day, however, she arrived looking sad and, striking up a conversation about his mother, tried to show by her every expression that it was no time for pouring out hidden feelings and no time for sensuality. "You have to be careful, Boris," she said. "You have to be on your guard every moment. They're watching you very closely. It's no secret to you, of course, that almost all of the musicians, and the whole hotel staff, are required to report to these, well, comrades with certain functions. And of course they have their own questions that they ask. Well, you know how all that goes. As for me, you know, I have a special relationship with them, you might say, because one day I got myself into quite a scrape, with jail hanging over my head. They helped me out of it, I guess, and now they consider me one of their own. . . . Now Borya, don't look at me like that. I'm thirty-five, I've spent my whole life in restaurants and with musicians—you didn't think that it was our Soviet martyr-virgin Zoya Kosmodemyansky you were dragging into your bed, did you? So don't turn away, look at me. Tell me: What kind of agent do you think I am? I always confuse everything for them, I bring them nonsense, and they take me seriously. And now yesterday, these three with faces like paving stones showed up. 'We,' they said . . . turn up the volume on the radio, please . . . 'we want,' they said, 'to have a word with you about your new friend.'"

"What, then who were your old friends?"

"Oh, Borya, don't be like that—there was no one. I told you, young man, that there was no one before you, no one in my life except you. 'On the whole,' they said, 'we have no objection to your new romance' . . . they have no objection, Boris—how do you like that? They talked it all over and had no objection . . . 'Boris Gradov,' they said, 'the son of a marshal of the USSR who was twice awarded the decoration of Hero of the Soviet Union, a fighting officer himself, an intelligence agent, one of our people . . .' "

"I was never one of theirs!" Boris interjected. "We had our own organization!"

"Yes, I know, I know, but I wasn't going to have an argument about that with them. So I just raised my eyebrows like a stupid doll. 'However,' they said, 'right now we need some additional information about him in connection with his complicated family situation, as well as in connection with some strange behavior on his part. Take this for example,' they said, 'we have information that he took part in telling anti-Soviet jokes in the Cocktail Hall. Have you heard anything about that? He was on good terms with the American journalists. . . . Such matters do not do honor to one of the top athletes in the USSR. Now, according to our latest information, he has struck up a friendship with a man of extremely dubious reputation, a certain Alexander Sheremetiev. Given that his mother is now in the USA and, what's more, married to the notorious Mister Taliaferro, who is now publishing one anti-Soviet article after another for the American propaganda machine, your friend should conduct himself a bit more cautiously, keep more to the straight and narrow.' Well, right away, I began to sing like a nightingale: what a patriot you are and how much you love our Iosif Vissarionovich—and not without reason, right? After all, he did lead us to victory. And how much contempt you have for American imperialism, while I was trembling from fear myself, as if at any minute they were going to ask me about the gift that came in the night. No, they didn't ask and asked very few questions on the whole; it even seemed to me that they simply wanted to get at you through me, to give you a serious warning . . ."

"And so you have," Boris said cheerlessly. "And so you have," he repeated in a sad voice that had a sharp edge to it and then felt momentarily nauseated.

She nestled close to him and whispered into his ear, "Darling, if you only knew how afraid of them I am! When I see them in the restaurant, I have to grab the microphone to keep from falling over. But everyone's afraid of them, it's impossible not to be. You're afraid of them too, admit it!"

"I'm not afraid," he whispered in reply directly into her inner ear, that is, into the orifice surrounded by the rings of the outer ear, ringed with hoops, her tender earlobe counterweighted with little pendants, counterbalanced in their turn by the earring that was a diamond abstraction. What a strange organ, the human ear, Boris thought for some reason. We find beauty in it, though, when it belongs to a woman. We decorate it with an earring. For the first time, they snuggled up to each other not to make love but so that a certain large inhuman ear would not hear them.

"What are you thinking about?" she asked.

"The ear," he answered. "It has such a strange form. I don't understand why I like it so much."

"Did you know that the earlobe doesn't age?" Vera asked, removing her clip-on earrings. "The whole body declines, loses its form, but the earlobe stays as young as ever." It was in her nature to forget about any unpleasantness as quickly as possible, in particular, about her contact with the "organs." She quickly and briskly removed the earrings, turning to Boris so he could undo the buttons down her back. "Soon I'll be old and shriveled, but you'll still love my earlobe."

The things they talk about, these idiots, thought Sergeant Polukhariev at his listening post that had recently been set up in the attic of the marshal's building. His ears were ringing from the operetta *Mademoiselle Nitouche*, through which he couldn't hear a damned thing, when suddenly, for some unknown reason, the rusty apparatus that had gone through the war began to transmit the loving whispers at deafening volume. Why are they talking bullshit? the sergeant grumbled to himself. You'd think they couldn't fuck without it.

I'm not afraid of them, Boris thought more and more often. I should be afraid. In the end they'll put me in jail. I'll escape right away, it won't be a difficult job. They shoot when you run, but I risked my life so many times in four years of service, why should I be afraid of a simple little thing like a bullet? Now, torture is another matter. I'm not sure I'm not afraid of being tortured. They prepared us psychologically to stand up to torture, but I'm still not sure it doesn't scare me. They showed us how to conduct an "active interrogation." I didn't have to "actively interrogate" anyone myself, thank God, but remember this: I saw, after all, how Smuglyany Grozdev, and Zubov interrogated the captured "Captain Balanciaga," wanting to know his real name. No, I'm not sure I could psychologically stand up to torture.

What am I getting myself so worked up for? Why have I begun waking up in the middle of the night next to this beautiful woman and, instead of making love to her, lying there thinking about them? Why didn't it ever occur to me before that she was mixed up with them? I live my life as though they don't exist, but they do, they're everywhere. They've even soiled my love, though she hasn't done anything. How can you accuse her when you're covered from head to toe in it yourself, hunter from the Polish woods? They probably crawl under every beautiful woman in Moscow on any pretext, because a beautiful woman can always be used as bait. They've gnawed away everything around them like rats. . . .

Well, now I've rolled right into outright anti-Soviet thinking, another minute and I'll start hissing "I hate the Red swine," like my adoptive cousin Mitya Sapunov. There's a paradox for you: he hated the Chekists and the Communists, yet he died for the Motherland; a simple little paradox for our mad age. It was difficult to believe Aunt Nina when she said she had seen Mitka's face in the column of traitors they were executing in the ravine. Most likely it was just her imagination: it often happens in war that you see familiar faces nearby. In the end, the differences between people aren't that great. You can see that especially when you look at corpses. Maybe to creatures from outer space it looks like we all have one face. There are no beautiful people and ugly people. Vera Gorda or Auntie Klasha, who works in the coat-check room, they're all one and the same. Poor Mitka, how terrible his short life was! I was lucky—at least I didn't have to see what he and my parents went through. Grandmother Mary and Grandfather Bo managed to guard the Silver Forest fortress through all that bedlam. That was the only place where *they* weren't around. Wait a minute, what do you mean they weren't there? Have you forgotten the night when they came to take your mother away and you looked on like an idiot as they put their seal on the door? Well, maybe *they* did show up sometimes, but they were never able to take up residence, because there was Mary's Chopin, Grandpa's books, Agasha's meat pies, and they couldn't stand all that. If they can't wreck something right away or replace it with something false, they vanish.

That's what you have to do—live as though *they* don't exist, create an environment in which *they* can't breathe. Live with an appetite, with passion, make love to Vera Gorda until she hurts, race motorcycles at top speed, master medicine, be friends with that confounded one-legged superman, go against all their warnings, dance to jazz, drink vodka to the point where everything is fun, not till it makes you sick! When all is said and done, things are shaping up here in Russia. After all, we have none other than Stalin, a personality of exceptional parameters, at our head. I'm not afraid of *them*, then!

Having convinced himself that living fearlessly was the only way to live, Boris did in fact try not to be afraid. He constantly found himself, however, trying too insistently not to be afraid, trying too hard not to think about *them*. In actual fact, he was almost never afraid, but in a large group he almost always, unconsciously, reckoned who might be the informer and how the information about the conduct of Boris Nikitovich Gradov would look in his file.

Meeting with Sasha Sheremetiev and his friends the Dostoevskyans, including "Nikolai the Giant," who turned out to be a decent guy after all and a good volleyball player, though with a little bit too much of a sense of his male irresistibility, Boris eagerly joined in the discussions about the genius of Russia, who in those years was being cast out of school curricula and pulled from library shelves as a "writer shot through with reactionary pessimism and mysticism, incompatible with the morality of socialist society." Nevertheless, meeting with them and joining in, Boris more than once caught himself thinking that he did not approve of the game his friends were playing of belonging to a freethinking organization. We meet the same way everyone meets these days, around a bottle of something, with a bit of fish and a few cucumbers—why call ourselves the Dostoevsky Circle, then? Why give *them* the chance to cook up some poisonous stew out of it?

There you have it, if you please, this is just what I was trying to prove! One day Sasha showed up and said he'd been fired from his job. Boris pounded his palm with his fist. "That's it, the game's up for your Dostoevsky Circle!"

"What has the Dostoevsky Circle got to do with it?" Sheremetiev asked coldly. Boris suddenly realized that he had come off badly in front of his friend by indicating that, even though he attended the meetings, he still had some reservations about the club.

"With everything the way it is, Sasha, I have sometimes thought there was some risk in this. The 'Dostoevsky Circle,'" he mumbled. "Any idiot could hang the label of 'underground organization' on it . . ."

Sheremetiev nervously limped around the room. He had begun to grow a beard again, and now, with two weeks' worth of bristles on his cheeks, he resembled the famous mug shot of the young revolutionary Soso Dzhugashvili. "Risk?" He guffawed. "Well, of course there's a risk. Not a bad word at all, by the way, 'risk'!"

It turned out that Sasha's firing from the library had been connected only indirectly with the Dostoevsky Circle. What had happened was that, using his administrative position, he had checked out the book *The East, Russia, and Slavdom* by the reactionary philosopher Konstantin Leontiev from the special archives. It was not the first time, of course, that he had made use of the sympathies of the girls who worked in the archives, who in fact saw "the Byronic type" in the limping young athlete and who "simply died" when Alexander kissed their hands in his best Polish manner. Usually, a book would disappear from the archives for a week, during which time a secretary he knew would type it out in three copies, which would then make their way to the club. It would never occur to anyone to want to get hold of the work of some "reactionary" forgotten by everyone on the face of the earth. Then, all of a sudden, an inspection had been carried out by the Central Committee, or maybe some other agency. A dangerous misalignment of the spines on the shelves was discovered, the catalogues were checked, an "extraordinary action" was initiated, the girls were called in, and under duress they admitted that Sasha Sheremetiev had taken one "to flip through at bedtime." So it had all ended with the expulsion from Paradise and with an accompanying report that would keep him from finding work, even in Hell, and that, you understand, promised unpleasant dealings with the police.

"Damn," said Boris, and he also began to pace around the room, but on a different diagonal. At that moment, Vera, wearing a long, tasseled, bright blue dressing gown that Veronika had left behind, came in with a steaming casserole full of sausages. Cutting along the hypotenuse, Boris went along the short side to the buffet and took out a decanter filled with some liquid.

I'll be damned if I'll drink with him, thought Sheremetiev. And why did I tell him all this here, practically in the presence of this aristocratic tart with her tassels?

For the first time he felt a sort of social hatred toward his old friend. Why did everything always go so well for him—a flat you could get lost in, an Academician for a grandfather, two legs intact, a prick with a good steady job?

"Sasha, I've got an idea," said Boris, leaping forward suddenly. "I'll give you a job—be my personal trainer!"

He quickly laid out his very simple and quite brilliant plan before the dumbfounded Sheremetiev. He was the only motorcycle ace in the Medic sports club. They treated him like a movie star. The winter races on ice were coming up, and his sports club had its first chance at a medal. "I need a trainer, and Medic doesn't have one. Suddenly I happen to find a brilliant driving coach who lost his leg on the job and has a huge amount of experience. A certain Alexander Sheremetiev. Practically, Alexander Sheremetiev is the only chance the miserable Medic team has. The council will be absolutely delighted to sign a contract with you and to pay you a salary you could only dream about in your 'repository of knowledge'—twelve hundred rubles, plus tickets for food during competitions."

They looked at each other for a moment and then, without a word, rushed to the crystal decanter to drink to the underlying text, as it were. This hidden message was quite clear to the two of them: it didn't matter whether Sasha found work with the Medic team or not. The important thing was that the offer had been made, which meant that their friendship was still intact and that Borka Gradov still understood not only the ugliness, but also the beauty, of the word "risk"!

Medic hired Sheremetiev as soon as its champion recommended him, and so now in March 1951, Gradov the master's personal trainer was checking his rider's time and had even gotten so much into the role that he dished out his advice in a stern voice.

★

Meanwhile, Boris Gradov, doing laps around the icy stadium, was the object of attention of more than just the all-knowing layabouts and veterans. He was also observed by two men who were clearly on the job, two air force colonels wearing improbably high fur hats that made them look more like cavalrymen from the Caucasus than modern aviators. It seemed as though the pair had come to the stadium for no other reason than to see Boris. They were standing on the packed snow in the second tier beneath a huge banner reading "To great Stalin and the Communist Party of our Motherland, our victories in sport!" One of them was intently studying Boris through binoculars—his face, the way he sat on his machine, his movements, and his motorcycle—while the other was minding a stopwatch, making calculations, and writing them in a small notebook.

"Well, what do you think?" one colonel asked the other when Gradov had finished his training session, handed his motorcycle over to his trainer, and gone to the dressing room.

"Completely," was the laconic reply.

Fifteen minutes later, Boris emerged from the dressing room. Over his high-collared sweater—the sort that would later be known as a "Beatles sweater" but in those days was called a "diver"—he wore the American bomber jacket known throughout Moscow. The two officers in the colonels' hats were smoking in the long, wide passage leading beneath the stands. At the sight of Boris, both of them immediately crushed out their cigarettes underfoot. It made him laugh—it was like a scene out of the film *The Roaring Twenties*.

"What do you guys want?" he asked.

"Hi there, champ!" said one of the colonels. "We're here about your soul."

"It's not for sale," Boris rejoined.

"What did you say?" the second colonel asked.

"We're from the Air Force Sports Club," said the first, laying a restraining hand on the large, padded chest of the second.

"To your health, fellas?" Boris replied, using a phrase that was the signature of the currently popular master of ceremonies, Tarapunka.

"Let's cut to the chase," said the first colonel. "In my opinion, Boris, it's high time for an athlete of your caliber to be leaving the sorry Medic team and joining our first-class Air Force squad."

"What are you talking about, Colonel?" Boris asked with a smile.

"I'm a student at the First Moscow Medical Institute, so my place is with Medic. Besides, I gave the army four years of my life, and that's enough for me and for the army."

"Who does he think he's talking to?" asked the second colonel.

"Just wait a minute, now, Skachkov." Again, the first colonel held back the second and then turned his full attention to the promising motorcyclist. "Perhaps you haven't fully understood me, Comrade Gradov. Athletes don't turn down such propositions these days. Do you know who the boss of our club is?" Boris shrugged.

"Who doesn't know that? Vasya Stalin."

"Exactly!" the first colonel exclaimed enthusiastically.

"Commander of the Air Defense Forces of the Moscow Military District Lieutenant General Vasily Iosifovich Stalin! No one understands sports any better. We already have the lead in many disciplines, and in the future we'll have no equal!"

The second colonel thrust his whole chest forward.

"Just have a look at what you'll get from us right away, Boris. The rank of captain, a salary plus an athletic scholarship, plus bonuses after your appearances. Free tailoring from our atelier," he added with a strong wink of one of his fleshy eyelids. "We have the best designers working for us! Trips to the Crimea and the Caucasus—again I say, all expenses paid! That's right away, and in the future, your own—I say again, your own—two-room flat with all conveniences!"

"All right, all right," said Boris, backing away under the pressure. "You can't be serious, comrades."

The first colonel took him by the arm.

"Wait, Boris Nikitovich. I want to tell you that having one's material needs taken care of is important, but it's not the thing that matters most. What matters is that it's only on our team that you'll be able to fully develop your talent as a motorcyclist."

"Excuse me, but I'm in a hurry. Give me a call at A15-5026," said Boris in order to get away. But at that moment, a babble of many voices and the noise of footsteps poured into the tunnel. The space was filled by a dense crowd of people approaching at an unhurried pace. Some men among them were noticeably taller than the rest because they were advancing along the concrete on skates, wearing the full battle gear of hockey players and equipped with their principal weapons, their sticks. When they had come closer, Boris recognized the new Air Force hockey team, still led by the legendary Vsevolod Bobrov. Two months before, the rest of the squad had been wiped out in a plane crash near Sverdlovsk, but Bobrov, whose luck had attained the status of a myth in Moscow, had managed to be out on the town with a girl and had arrived too late for the fatal flight.

Speaking of girls, there were at least as many of them in the crowd as there were hockey players. One could not tell if they had been inherited from the team that had perished or if they were a new bunch. In any case, they looked utterly typical: fashionably dressed sports groupies, quick-eyed and rosy-cheeked like nesting dolls in tight-waisted fur coats and fur-covered boots called "Romanians."

In addition, another entire class of people moved along with the crowd: coaches, masseurs, sports photographers, and journalists, a few officers in air force uniforms, with a short, broad-shouldered young man with a sharply outlined jaw and pouches beneath his eyes at their head. Like Boris, he was wearing a pilot's jacket, only one of slightly poorer quality and without any signs of distinction. This was Vassily Stalin. Known throughout Moscow for the scandals he had been mixed up in, he was what we nowadays would call a playboy.

Noticing the colonels in the company of Boris, he stopped, and called out in a voice of command: "Skvortsov, Skachkov, what are you doing, you motherfuckers?"

Boris eyed the all-powerful "Vasya" curiously. The latter's temples gleamed like dark copper, as did those of Boris himself. He's half Georgian and I'm a quarter Georgian, thought Boris. Of course, like everyone in Moscow who had anything to do with sports, he knew about the incredible activity the "prince of the blood" carried on to create his own sporting stable under the banner of the Air Force Club.

Not long before, at the main post office, Boris had met a young swimmer whom he had gotten to know in Tallinn, the Estonian Jew Grisha Gold. Waiting for a connection for a telephone call home to go through, Grisha was ambling about the hall wearing the full uniform of an air force lieutenant. "What are you doing here, where did you come from?" Boris asked. Grisha swore him to secrecy and then told him his curious story. The previous year he had been the Baltic states' champion in the 100- and 200-meter butterfly. He was on the Dynamo team, that is, the one under the aegis of the "organs." Suddenly one day, two air force colonels had come up to him in the street. It turned out that they had flown up from Moscow specially to seek his soul. They had begun to sing siren songs about moving to Moscow, to Central Air Force Club. A powerfully built young man, Grisha was from a bourgeois background, and he could not imagine moving to barbaric Moscow from his little Hanseatic town, where "elementary politeness" was still maintained. The next day, the two colonels— maybe the very same Skvortsov and Skachkov—along with two sergeants had pulled the polite Grisha off the street, stuffed him into a Pobeda sedan, and taken him to an airfield. As soon as they were in the airplane, they had read to him the order from the military commander of Estonia mobilizing him for service in the Red Army and announcing his immediate transfer to the Sixth Intercept Division. In Moscow, they had taken him to a room, and the first thing Grisha had seen hanging on the wall was an air force lieutenant's uniform just his size. Then they had handed him a packet of money and the training schedule for the water polo team. Why water polo when I'm a pure swimmer? Grisha had asked in amazement. That's how it has to be, they explained to him, and so he had begun to play water polo. There wasn't a proper coach there to begin with, and the same two colonels still ran everything. If, say, we were losing after the first period to the Kharkov Avant-Garde team, the colonels would order: we're changing tactics. Attack will turn into defense, and defense into attack. What are you talking about? the players would object. That doesn't make any sense at all. They would roar at them: Shut up! Carry out the order! If suddenly the team began winning competitions, the players had suits made for them in record time and were treated to a banquet in a restaurant with girls. If we "got the shit kicked out of us" (Grisha did not seem to quite grasp the full meaning of the expression in a language that was not his own), then they sent us to the airfield to clear the runway with snow shovels.

One day Grisha had been snatched away again, this time by MVD agents. We have orders for you to return immediately to the original Dynamo team. It was signed by the minister himself. Grisha didn't have time to realize how he had ended up training with Dynamo again, but when Vasya learned of it, he arranged an "extraordinary event"—smashed in a few faces around headquarters and sent a

Dodge bristling with automatic weapons from his office after Grisha. Thus, once again he was attached to the steely cohorts of modern aviation.

"From the looks of you, Grisha, I wouldn't say you remind me of a slave laborer."

"Pardon?" Gold asked.

"I said, you look perfectly happy."

"We're going to Sochi for some training matches tomorrow, you understand, and I has a woman there who has a strong interest in for this Gold." When Grisha got excited, he could confuse his Russian grammar, but that didn't keep his gangling, muscular shoulders from propelling him through the water with a dynamic energy that was as constant as it was enviable. Remembering this story now, Boris thought: they won't run that number on me, I'm not turning myself into a racehorse for anyone. The first colonel was standing at attention with his palm just beneath his hat. "Permission to report, Comrade Commander? We were just making the acquaintance of champion motorcycle racer Boris Gradov, and at the moment we're discussing his future."

Vasya turned toward Boris and squinted. "Ah, Gradov . . . yes, I remember. I like the way you ride, Boris."

The hockey players, girls, journalists, and officers came closer. Boris heard whispers going through the crowd: "Gradov . . . Borya Gradov . . . yes, *that* Gradov . . . Grad—" The blue-eyed, rosy-cheeked ones did not conceal their delight: "Oh, girls, what a guy!" The round-faced celebrity Seva Bobrov nudged him with an elbow and whispered, "Go on, Borya, full speed ahead!" The hockey players smiled and knocked their skates and sticks together. It was clear that everyone already considered him "one of ours" and that they were pleased with the fact that someone known in Moscow not only for his successes in sport but for his *savoir-vivre* would be joining their young, tough gang. Suddenly, he himself had the feeling that it wouldn't be so bad to join this new band whose *ataman* was none other than the son of the Great Leader. Maybe that's just what I need. Even if it is the military, it's a special detachment. *They* won't be able to find a way into it. Stalin the Younger suddenly took Boris by the sleeve and whistled. "Say, boys, look at this guy's jacket! It's a genuine American pilot's hide!" Boris grinned and pulled the zipper all the way down.

"Want to trade, Vassily Iosifovich?"

Stalin the Younger could not hold back a guffaw.

"There's a guy for you! Well, why not, let's trade!"

Both doffed their jackets simultaneously and exchanged them.

"A good deal!" Vassily laughed.

Boris smiled. "For me, too."

Everyone around them laughed, too. Everything had turned out fine, relaxed, they were among friends. Two guys who simply "swapped without looking," and one of them just happened to be the son of the Leader, their mighty chief Vasya. No, this Borka Gradov will suit us just fine—looks like the regiment has another member!

"Do you want to see our new squad in a workout?" Vassily asked.

Boris looked at his watch and made his excuses. "I'd like that very much, Vassily Iosifovich, but I can't now. I'm in a big hurry."

Everyone liked this, including, it seemed, the chief. In addition to his remarkable youthful nonchalance, this Borya Gradov displayed a healthy independence, didn't squirm like a whore under a client. Anyone else would have dropped everything when invited by the son of the Leader, but this one tactfully refuses because he's in a hurry; indeed, anyone can see he's in a hurry. Maybe he has a date.

"All right, see you soon!" Stalin the Younger slapped Boris on the back and headed off to the ice rink. Everyone followed after him, all slapping Boris on the back in their turn as they passed: "See you around!" Two of the most resourceful among the girls managed to kiss the motorcyclist's taut, frosty cheeks.

Left alone with Colonels Skvortsov and Skachkov, Boris said:

"Well, it looks like I'm joining the Soviet Air Force, but only on one condition: that you take my personal trainer, Hero of the Great Patriotic War Alexander Sheremetiev, along with me."

"No problem!" Skachkov beamed.

Boris ran for the tunnel exit, where his trainer with the motorcycle could be seen against the sunny snow.

Talk about turnaround, Boris thought as he rode along. So now the Dostoevsky Club is going to merge with the Air Force team!

Chapter 6

———————☆———————

THE
"IVAN AND A HALF"
CODEX

Captain Sterlyadev of the MVD medical service, entering the disinfection barracks of Quarantine IAP, NECD (Independent Administration Point, Northeastern Corrective Labor Camps), immediately saw no fewer than thirty naked backs, and, correspondingly, no less than sixty naked buttocks. Moaning as though he were suffering from toothache, he examined these dreadful exteriors for a minute or two—fresh boils, boils with a first-degree pus-filled infection, boils encapsulated and ossified, traces of boils that had been cut away—crude jobs, naturally, performed in isolated camps by the light of a kerosene lamp—one snip, two snips, dig it up and dab it dry; all possible variations on rashes, including some that were clearly syphilitic in origin; a gentlemanly collection of scars from knives, bayonets, and safety razors, even a certain number that were surgical, most of them being a consequence of the last war. There was even one, a beneficiary of a skin graft, with a pod drooping beneath his shoulder blades. The overall state of his skin was a medical mess, although in a literary and artistic sense quite solid and a demonstration of how to create a masterpiece of epidermal art. Everything was there on his back, all of the near classics: the cat and mouse, the dagger and the snake, the eagle and the maiden, the bottle and the deck of cards, so that there was no room left on his chest or stomach for such banalities. All of this is not even to mention the pirate brig armed with cannon in the shape of penises or a woman's legs spread apart to reveal an anatomically correct rendition of the flower to be found therein and with an inscription in place of the pubic hair reading "The Gaits of Hapiness," or the following jingle: "The Crimea in spring / Smells like a rose / Life's no hard thing / So hold your nose / Over here you're fucked by cold / There's nothing but pines / And cops on the road."

There were skins that were pale, yellow, black, blue, and red, while the overall condition of the fatty cellulose beneath the skin was satisfactory. Then he went into his so-called office, separated from the general chaos by a sorry bit of screen.

Captain Sterlyadev, still young though rapidly losing his disheveled hair despite his youth, had already been working in Kolyma for three years and during the entire three years had never stopped reproaching himself for going after the "big money" and signing a contract with the MVD to work in this depressing place, where there was so little sun that one could not get one's vitamins—and you thus began to lose your hair in rapid and disorderly fashion—and where someone might come at you with a knife at any minute.

Particularly if you worked in the disinfection barracks of "Karantinka," a huge transit camp on the northern edge of Magadan, where the worst elements of the thieves' world were dug in, including, according to highly reliable sources, "Ivan and a Half." Here they could cut you to pieces just like that, without even so much as an "excuse me." They could even, pardon me for saying so, "lose" a captain of the medical service in a poker game.

At operations meetings, the officers were warned that a final battle between the "bitches" and the "monks" was not out of the question. A network of agents was reporting that both sides were pulling forces into "Karantinka" from all over the country and arming themselves— that is, sharpening up and stockpiling all sorts of pikes and lances on the campgrounds.

And in conditions like this we're supposed to guarantee the steady flow of personnel to the mines. You just try to guarantee it when every thief thinks he's the boss, goes on sick call with the same nonchalance with which someone on the outside might go to a drugstore for a bottle of aspirin. And if you don't let him out of work, he looks at you like a wolf, a real beast from the taiga with a pitiless, evil-smelling maw.

The workforce consisted almost exclusively of "politicals," though even the political prisoners weren't the same as they had been in the 1930s. The percentage of intellectuals had decreased sharply. Now they were bringing in more peasants from the western regions, prisoners of war and anti-Soviet partisans who regarded the machine guns in the guard towers with great interest and firsthand knowledge. No, no, something's not quite right in this country, Dr. Sterlyadev suddenly began whispering aloud, as though it were a secret from himself. Something is going on in the country, the camps are too widespread, there could be a general explosion at any minute that no number of guards would be able to deal with.

It must have been the idea of the Devil to throw me into this system with my qualifications as a clinical physician, someone who was noticed by Professor Vovsi himself. As he said about my handling of the case of patient Flegonov, born in 1888 and suffering from a complicated liver and duodenal disease, "You, young man, have all of the qualifications to become a serious clinical physician." You didn't have to fall behind your colleagues. After all, you kept up with Dod Tyshler, who, they say, has already defended his doctoral dissertation, has a steady job as chief surgeon in the Gradsky Third State Hospital, is happy with his divine Milka Zaitsev, and has no signs of rapid and disorderly loss of hair. In Moscow, one's supply of vitamins is still ensured. It's all been for her, Yevdokia and her uncontrollable passion for buffets and sideboards, tables and chairs of mahogany and Karelian birch. All this, after all, was only to make more money for her unending purchases of antiques; this was what had prompted him to join the MVD and go to Kolyma. So you'll amass all these goods and sit in the middle of it all wearing a velvet dress, childless Yevdokia Sterlyadev. There's the greatest happiness, a painting by Kustodiev!

Such were the irritated thoughts of the infirmary physician while the team whose backsides he had examined earlier took a scalding hot shower—the zeks were not allowed to adjust the temperature.

After the wash, a sergeant came in and barked with natural ferocity, "Single file!"

The zeks took their time lining up, fixing the noncom with unfriendly stares. He was supposed to lead them along the corridor to Captain Sterlyadev's examination room, and then, before they had time to realize what was happening, issue them quilted jackets and cotton-padded trousers for the trip further north, up the line. Instead, however, the sergeant was confused. A young man with broad shoulders, well-developed chest and arms, a lean stomach, and a good prick the color of dark suede was looking straight at him with bright, pitiless eyes. The noncom was about to give the order: "Face right! Forward—march!" but when he opened his mouth he froze beneath the glance of the authoritarian thug, whose last name, as he recalled, was Zaprudnev.

"Come over here, Zhuriev," the zek said to the sergeant, crossing his arms over his chest, where, in contrast to the rest of the aborigines, there was only the tattoo of a butterfly and a whore's head above the left nipple. No, it's not a whore's head but a baby Lenin with curls, the defender of all the toiling peasants. Zaprudnev had probably had the image put over his heart to make it less attractive for the executioner's bullet. The sergeant approached and leaned his ear toward the zek, concealing his eyes.

"You go tell the doc that 'Ivan and a Half' has given our squad orders not to head north," Zaprudnev announced clearly and distinctly so that it was easy to understand.

The sergeant went cold all over, because he immediately realized the man was serious. The sergeant felt a sudden tenseness in his rectum, because no one used the name of "Ivan and a Half" in the zone in jest, and anyone who tried to make a joke of it or use it in vain immediately found himself with a good hole in his vital organs.

Still feeling a cold tautness in his ass, the sergeant stole away to the duty officer. The team was officially called "Cleanup Duty," and now, after a pleasant, albeit too hot, shower, they usually put on their street clothes instead of moving off into the areas for prisoners awaiting transport.

"Comrade Captain," Sergeant Zhuriev panted into Sterlyadev's ear, his breath smelling of poorly digested potatoes, "a zek just told me on behalf of 'Ivan and a Half' that Cleanup Duty isn't going to the mines."

Sterlyadev's delicate constitution was shaken by panic. It was the first time he had been on the receiving end of an order from "Ivan and a Half," the Stalin of the camps.

"All right, Zhuriev, you didn't tell me anything and I didn't hear it. Let them go," Sterlyadev muttered, wiping his sweat, brow, fore— What was it, the brow on his sweat?

Meanwhile, there was no need to let them go: they had wandered off on their own throughout the vast expanse of the zone. One had gone to the quartermaster's, another to the Cultural Section, another to the Education Section, one to the stoker's barracks, another to the mess hall, one to the tailor's, another to the shoe depot: there was no shortage of business at the large Quarantine camp, and everywhere the men held hushed conversations, extorted, intimidated, and gave orders, because the Cleanup Duty crew was the very backbone of the militant "monks," subordinate only to the most mysterious one of all, "Ivan and a Half," whom, it must be confessed, none of them had ever seen with his own eyes.

Foma (that was the unaccustomed name that Mama and Papa had given him in the cold Nizhegorodsky Region twenty-nine years earlier) Zaprudnev headed for the tool storage shed to revive his energies after the bath. He had the most authority among the men because the orders of "Ivan and a Half" to Cleanup Duty passed through him. In the tool shed, a large barracks that had been transformed by stacks of crates into a sort of Cretan labyrinth, Zaprudnev and three other authoritarians sat in comfort on old automobile seats. Some apprentice thieves, who by a long since forgotten etymology were referred to as "sixers" in the camps, brought them an impressive bottle of distilled alcohol, and a reliable lad from the "socially dangerous elements" stood guard. They didn't have to worry, they could relax and unwind around the engineers' campfire.

But it was business, business, business. "Rest is something we only dream about," a line from the Russian Symbolist poet Alexander Blok descended upon the foggy consciousness of Foma Zaprudnev. Some guys came to say that a thug had been brought in with the last bunch of prisoners and that despite warnings he continued to go about his dirty business, that is, dragging an underage kid named Anantsev into the barracks and putting him on the "chocolate conveyor." Intelligence also had it that the disobedient ass fancier had just been transferred from Ekibastuz, which meant in all probability that he belonged to the "bitches," who were quietly gathering in Magadan for the "final decisive battle."

"All right, haul him in here," Foma Zaprudnev ordered. The "sixers" used their knees to butt behind the crates a preposterous figure wearing a woman's coat that was in rags but boasted a fine pair of fur boots. The figure was hobbling, stooped over like death itself, trying to cover his head with the sleeves of his stevedore's tunic, and it seemed that he was sobbing hysterically, or was cackling at any rate. When he raised his head and had a look at the determined face of Foma Zaprudnev, he let out a "shriek of horror," as one might write in a novel.

Witnesses to the scene maintain that a silent grimace flitted mouse-like across the severe features of Foma Zaprudnev at the sight of the long-nosed, rodentlike physiognomy in which the pupils of the eyes were suspended like two caramel creams with the centers sucked out. It seemed as though the men knew one another, but neither of them let it show, given that the "bitch" pederast was wailing something incoherent, while Foma rose sharply to his feet and presented, as usual, a pensive figure with his arms crossed over his chest.

"Well, what're we gonna do with him?" asked one of the members of Cleanup Duty.

"Let's not make a mess here," said another. "We'll take him on down to the garbage dump."

Both of them looked at the preoccupied Foma. The garbage dump was where those who did not obey the "Ivan and a Half" codex turned up, and the pederast knew it.

"Have pity on me, guys! I'm still young! I've got a wife and kids on the mainland, and my parents are still living!" he said, squirming on his knees. "I went through the whole war—the things I saw . . . comrade, come on, you know me!" he squealed like a pig at Zaprudnev's back.

"You, you crotch louse, you got a warning from the Man himself!" said one of the Cleanup Duty-ers. "He himself ordered you not to touch anyone underage!"

"So what if I did? You're going to do it because of some lousy kid?

He had an experienced asshole, this little kid of yours. Listen, guys, I can get a first-class blow job for every man here if you want!"

The doomed fool didn't know that it was difficult to entice Cleanup Duty with such blandishments, since they had excellent contacts with the women's zone.

"Enough of this," someone said. "Come on, off to the dump with him!"

"Why aren't you saying anything, Foma?" another one asked him.

Zaprudnev turned around with a smile. "Because I want to play, boys!" he said in the Rostov accent that was so dear to him. It was known that Fomochka Zaprudnev had attended a good school of crime in Rostov-on-Don after its liberation from the German-Fascist bandits.

Everyone froze in his tracks, and the doomed pederast's lollipop eyes bugged out. "Whaddaya mean, you 'want to play,' Foma?" asked Cleanup Duty.

"Pay attention, citizen zeks," Foma Zaprudnev began his speech. "Stretch your imagination a bit, and picture us not in the tool shed of the Karantinka transit camp but in the Cretan labyrinth, well known throughout the Mediterranean basin . . ."

It was a mystery to all of Fomka's henchmen where he had acquired these literary turns of phrase that made them feel as if they were in the theater.

"Let's say we introduce a captured slave," said Zaprudnev, giving the pederast a kick with his powerful leg that sent him sprawling behind a pile of crates. And behind him, boys, comes none other than the Minotaur." With these words, he drew from an inner pocket a blade nearly a foot long.

Behind the boxes, the ugly fur hat of the pederast could be seen. He was trying desperately to find some gap and to escape from the tool shed, to his "bitches," to "sing" to the guard on duty, and to beg to be sent up the line, even though it was impossible to say what he was counting on there. Foma, unsheathing his knife, went into the labyrinth. He roared with laughter: "Hey, I'm the man-bull, the Minotaur! Citizens, they say our hero Theseus has shown up in the labyrinth? Curious, very curious!"

He suddenly raced to the right, to the left, then back to the right. The pederast stopped squirming and was seen to bend over, while

Foma's head also vanished, hidden from view. The remaining participants, assuming the roles of guests of King Minos, took their places on the car seats, sipping chifir and awaiting the cry of the slaughter victim. No one contradicted Foma Zaprudnev. If he wants to play, let him play. Say what you will, he's the right hand of "Ivan and a Half," the only one on the team to have met the hero of all of barbed-wire Russia.

In fact, Foma Zaprudnev was in no mood for games, for playing bulls and minotaurs. The meeting with the pederast—no one knew what else to call him now—had shaken him to his core, which had seemed to be hardened in crime. All things considered, he didn't even know what to do now: should he send the spirit of the past, neatly monogrammed with a shiv, to Charon (that's the one, the boatman; *The Myths of Ancient Greece* was this prisoner's favorite book), or should he have mercy in the name of . . . in the name of something I can't even give a name to . . . surely not in the name of friendship. . . . Hunched over and holding the sharp end of the knife down, he wove among the stacks, waiting, listening for footsteps, and then began zigzagging again, until a four-by-six wrench came hurtling toward his head. At the last second, he managed to get a hand in the way, and the deflected wrench so that it just grazed his cheek. The next moment, he was crushing the pederast's wheezing throat with his knee and wanting to finish him off—his hand holding the knife was already raised—when all of a sudden his former name—"Mitya . . . Mitya"—escaped from the wheezing throat and struck him with something unimaginably far away and dear to him, like the bleating of his goat named "Sister" in his childhood on the farm.

"Mitya, Mitya," sobbed Gosha Krutkin. "It can't be, it can't be you! Why, I saw you fall into the pit in a hail of bullets myself, near Kharitonovka. I was on the burial detail, we covered up the bodies ourselves. If it's you, Mitya, you won't kill me! My dear boy, Mitya, is that you?"

It had been seven years since anyone had called him "Mitya." He had changed his name and his ID so many times that he had lost count, yet he always returned to the name that belonged to the peasant boy whom, following the advice of a crow by the wayside, he had strangled: Fom Zaprudnev, native of Arzamas in the Nizhegorodsky Region. Whenever the investigators were torturing him to get him to tell them his real name, he held out stoically, not breaking down until the last minute, when he spat into their ugly snouts, "All right, you stupid cops, write down 'Zaprudnev'—that's me, Foma Iliich Zaprudnev."

Sometimes in those rare moments when he freed himself from the criminal world, he thought, "I got screwed up back there at Kharitonovka. Damn, why is it I remember that boy not as my victim, but as a good comrade?"

The fellows of the thieves' bands who had known "Fomka" as a man of decisive cruelty could not possibly have imagined, of course, that he indulged in this sort of melancholy at night, to the point where he even had to wipe his eyes with a towel as he recalled the scraps of a human life: certain faces, snatches of Chopin, the welcoming bark of a huge dog, hot pies with viziga. . . . And yet all those things were in his mind frequently, until they were quietly and politely crowded out by the most terrible day of his life when, for the first time, he killed a man who had done nothing to him. There he is, a soldier marching along the scorched earth, his boots splashing in the April puddles as he gaily whistled "Clouds in Blue." It was like a scene from a concert at the front. The only thing that didn't fit into the picture was the stinking corpse he couldn't forget . . . then later, as we were smoking together, using up all eleven cigarettes left in the pack . . . but why am I speaking in the plural? . . . After all, Fomochka Zaprudnev was just lying there, in the pink of health, as peacefully as you please, sleeping like a babe, not smoking at all, until you took away with pleasure everything he had.

"What are you talking about, 'Mit, Mit'?" He shook the captured "bitch," his old friend and betrayer Goshka Krutkin, fiercely. "Remember forever that my name is Fomka from Rostov, and you'll come running when I call." Kicking with the toe of his boot the body before him trembling with happiness—Goshka realized right away that he was to be pardoned!—he moved off to one side.

"You're going to be our man among the 'bitches' now, understand?" he grinned. "A soldier on the invisible front, right?"

"Yes, yes, Mit . . . oh, sorry—Fomka!" Krutkin was shaking as he had in the old days in the Dawn Battalion.

"And what do they call you now?" Zaprudnev asked. "What's your name, you pathetic ass chaser?"

Krutkin flopped about with a movement like a female seal and whispered quickly, "Vova Zhelyabov, from Sverdlovsk . . ."

"Well, see here, Vova Zhelyabov, you're not just going to sit around in this camp twiddling your thumbs and chasing little boys anymore—by the way, if I find out you're at it again, there'll be no mercy! Now you're going to carry out the orders of Cleanup Duty and—" He pulled the donkey-like ear of his old comrade in arms up and half whispered, half spat straight down the shaft: "—and of 'Ivan and a Half'!"

Several minutes later, Fomka from Rostov brought the enslaved but unharmed "bitch" to his somewhat disappointed colleagues.

"One more spy in the enemy camp won't hurt," he explained laconically. No more questions were asked.

★

It was already evening when Zaprudnev emerged from the toolshed and headed for the boiler room at a rapid pace. The thin crescent of a moon over the wavelike wastes promised a big yield of silver. According to his calculations, it was when the small planet was in this cycle that they would knock over the savings bank in nearby Yakutia. The boiler room had to service both the men's and women's zones, so it was situated with one side facing the land of Hercules and Theseus and the other, the magical land of nymphs and amazons. This remarkable location could not, of course, have escaped the notice of Fomka of Rostov and his team. A simple zek risked his life even to go near the low, windowless concrete building, while Cleanup Duty almost without interruption used the structure's warm nooks for even warmer encounters with their female counterparts.

That evening Foma Zaprudnev was expected by his steady girlfriend—meaning that he had been with her for nearly three weeks—a professional thief from Leningrad named Marinka Schmidt. Their first meeting had been a blind date, but they had taken to each other so well that all either of them dreamed about now was the next time they could lie together naked beneath the scorching pipes. "You and I, Marinka, are like baby kangaroos in their mother's pouch in here," Zaprudnev whispered to her one day, and soon "kangaroo" came back to haunt him: everyone in the zones who was in the know began to call the boiler room "the kangaroo."

Strange as it may seem, Marinka turned out to be quite pure, in the sense that Fomka hadn't caught any frolicking little insects from her, much less the fabled "pale spirochete," the Snow White of Kolyma. "How is it, Madame Schmidt, that you're not so much a prostitute as a finishing school girl?" Fomochka asked her one day.

"Because I played around more with girls before I met you, Citizen Rostovite," she laughed. "Nothing but filth comes from you men, while on our island there's nothing but palm trees and little birds." The "Rostovite," with his three cured cases of "the archbishop's head cold," had to have some reverence before this tender, monastic body. This irritated him. Moreover, from time to time now he would catch her looking at him lovingly. This irritated him even more. Coming into the boiler room that evening, Foma called to the duty man, "Petro, listen here—let up a little on the steam, otherwise Marinka and me are going to be roasted like chickens."

He crawled down a manhole headfirst and soon found himself in a pleasant little cell with a cot, a bedside locker, and a dim electric lamp suspended from an asbestos-wrapped pipe. Marinka was waiting for him on the cot, wearing only lace panties and a bra. Where had she found underwear like that? Russian women, you know, are just one big mystery.

Not one to stand on ceremony, Zaprudnev yanked off Marukha's chic underpants and got down to business. While he was working away, he thought a great deal about the band's financial affairs, about means of transportation in case of an unexpected turn of events, about the possibility that they might meet their end in Yakutia. He was so deep in thought that when Marinka came with a shriek, he even asked her in surprise, "What's the matter with you?"

After sex, they usually played a bit, tickling and pinching each other and giggling. "Then we'd be normal people, Marinka, just young specialists volunteering to build up the Far North . . . then we could . . . ha, ha . . . make our lives differently."

"Oh, Fomochka, I want so much to go to the theater with you!"

"That's no big deal—you want me to take you out of the zone?"

"Oh, take me, take me out of the zone, Rostovite! They say a first-rate musical is on at the House of Culture: *Eleven Unknowns* by Nikita Bogoslovsky, and our zeks are in it!"

Suddenly becoming gloomy, Marinka Schmidt From-the-Five-Corners, as she sometimes called herself, turned her light green eyes to Fomochka. "And I've also decided to have a child by you, Citizen Zaprudnev." The Rostovite was in the habit of answering unexpected dirty punches like that by sending his mighty right fist forward. Marinka flew into the burning hot wall, shrieked, and bristled, like a real undomesticated Kolyma cat. "Bastard, bastard!"

Foma Zaprudnev, that is, Mitya Sapunov, recovered from the unexpected event and stretched out the palm of his left hand to stroke her. Marinka clamped down her teeth and nearly took his fingers off. "Have you lost your fucking marbles, Marukha?" he yelled. "You want to bring another slave into the world for *them*? One more slave?"

"I want to have a thief!" Marinka wailed. "It's none of your business! I'm not asking you to be the papa! All I need from you, you rotten fucker, is your cock!"

Fomka-Mitya was already backing out of the manhole. He wanted to block his ears with wax like Odysseus so he wouldn't hear his beloved Marukha's howls. The fool, the idiot—whom did she choose to have a child by? A killer and lowlife! What sort of world would she bring this wondrous baby boy or tender little girl into—this world of Bolsheviks?

After a long time he was still shaking, sitting in a corner behind a boiler and puffing on a cigarette. Finally, when he had calmed down, he went to the duty man's room and changed into ordinary street clothes that one might wear on the outside, put on his castor coat and a neat, leather-topped cap with fur flaps. In this civilized outfit, looking for all the world like a young specialist and volunteer for the Far North, he calmly and without a hitch crossed the checkpoint and left the zone: most of the guards at Karantinka had been "greased," you only had to be sure to look out for anyone who wasn't in on it.

It was less than three miles from the camp to the city, not a great distance, yet a Diamond truck, one of those American iron mammoths, turned up now, advancing slowly. All the same, it moved faster than a man. Mitya hopped up onto the platform of a trailer it was dragging, found a handhold, and in this position rocked along with a cigarette in his mouth for all of twenty minutes, until the "auto-train" rolled into the capital of the Kolyma region. An immense sunset was spreading out over the low volcanic hills, early stars were shining with a green light that was the shade of the lovely Marukha's eyes, while chains of streetlamps and dots of light in private homes went on in the darkening valley. Too bad I didn't go to Italy back then, in 1943. I could have gone by way of forests and ravines, in stages by night. I shouldn't have gone over to the Dnepr partisans, but quietly, and with a purpose—with Goshka, that piece of shit—made my way toward Italy. Of course Goshka would have been caught by the Hungarians along the way and been strung up by the balls, but I would have made it to Italy and gone over to the side of the Atlantic Allies. Well, there's no point in replaying that scenario, it's just too bad. Still, I really didn't want to turn into an evil creature back then!

In the city, the "gold-shoulder-boarded riffraff," as Mitya called them, were parading along streets with their women, who were in furs. "Valentina, my dear, did you arrive from the mainland a while ago?" "Ah, we had such a marvelous time at the resort in Sochi!" Somewhere in the middle of this aristocracy, he thought, your own brothers are floating around. They're former zeks, meaning they have the status of slaves, despised and debauched. But with the cockiness of a civilian, Mitya paid no attention to the crowd. He went into the grocery store, bought a block of cheese, and crammed it into his suitcase: it's not bad to have the luxury of cheese in the zone. He went into the drugstore and bought a half-dozen vials of Pantocrine for the boys in Cleanup Duty, who were of the opinion that Pantocrine made you able to get it up so far you could hang a bucket on it. Mitya himself had no need for the alcoholic drink extracted from the horns of the northern elk—you could hang weights on his tool if you wanted, especially when he was with Marinka Schmidt. Then he casually popped by the savings bank and withdrew twenty-five thousand rubles from an account in the name of Georgy Mikhailovich Shapovalov. On the mainland they might refuse to hand over such a sum right away, and even then they would call the police for an identity check on the depositor, but in Magadan where one was paid two, three, sometimes even four salaries, the withdrawal of a chunk like that was a normal affair. This was, in fact, the main object of this evening's stroll: the guards at Karantinka not only had to be kept in fear, but also be "greased" regularly.

Two hours remained before the evening guard shift came on. There was time to go to the movie theater to see the first half of the captured

German film *The Girl of My Dreams*. Goshka and I saw that movie when we were in Germany. Back there, Marika Rëkk, the female lead, had jumped out of a barrel full of water—naked—but here, of course, the barrel scene had been cut, so that Soviet Man wouldn't lick his chops at the sight of a real live body. At least you could see shots of the German Alps before you had to come back to reality.

Right now, fifteen minutes before the show starts, you can cross Soviet Street, to look at *their* windows at number 14.

Soviet Street was empty. In the absence of any great snowfall, the board sidewalks had been blackened with the cinders the city produced and had already begun to look a bit like frosting, as they would in the spring. The lousy dim streetlights were suspended against the sky, today of a color that one rarely saw, like Italian oranges. A patrol of two guards and an officer went by. They looked carefully at Mitya but didn't stop. Magadan, as a solid Soviet town, the pearl of the Far North, seemingly didn't provide for an ID check of every citizen strolling along with a small suitcase in his hand. If they had asked, though, Georgy Mikhailovich Shapovalov could have presented all sorts of proof of his loyalty, from his passport to his snub-nosed revolver.

Those two windows at number 14 were dark. Mitya went around the two-story building that was entirely fit to be inhabited, painted in the color Magadanites like so well, "the body of a frightened nymph." Here and there in windows, large braided lampshades were shining. String bags with perishables were hanging from transom windows. From our window—he grinned wryly: "our!"—a leggy chicken was suspended. So she'd bought her Jewish chicken and a French roll. . . . More than once he had gone up to this house at twilight and, hiding behind a transformer shed on the other side of the street, had watched the windows of the flat of his adoptive parents, Cecilia Naumovna Rosenbloom and Kirill Borisovich Gradov. At first they had had a lamp with a bare bulb, and then, as people do, had added a wide lampshade with silk tassels. Sometimes their heads appeared at the window. One day he saw them shouting at each other and waving their hands: probably arguing, as they had in the old days, about theoretical questions of the world revolution. Another time, his thief's eye had caught them in a prolonged kiss, at the end of which the lights in the flat had gone out. Showing his false teeth in a grin several times, he shook his head: Can they really be doing it right now, those old, sick people?

☆

Some six months had passed since the day when, wearing his Georgy Mikhailovich Shapovalov suit, he had run into "Aunt Celia" nose to nose at the main intersection of Magadan, the corner of Stalin Prospekt and the Kolyma Highway. He probably would not have noticed his father: there were thousands of half zeks drifting around in the area. Cecilia, however, was impossible not to spot in the crowd, dragging herself along in her usual disheveled state, a button of her coat attached to the buttonhole of her sweater, her scarf trailing in the slush, her carrot-colored lipstick not quite lined up with the edges of her mouth, a profusion of freckles, a mop of half-curled gray hair, and an internal monologue entirely audible to the outside world: "Excuse me, excuse me . . . here's the information . . . the cubic capacity . . . stay within the framework . . . socialist morality. . . ." Thus his Jewish "little mama," the shame and the pity of his adolescence, had materialized from the swaying crowd. Mitya froze in his tracks. Sliding an unseeing glance over him, Cecilia had walked on by.

He trailed her for the rest of the evening. She made her litigious rounds at the Far North Administration office and to the city Soviet, then stood in line for evaporated milk, then tramped by the radio repair shop, from which his father, now bowlegged, suddenly appeared carrying an enormous radio that seemed to be homemade. Mitya could see that the man's aging face was beaming with happiness. It was obvious that this sort of life was very much to his liking: swaggering around with a huge radio set in his arms like a grandfather clock, seeing that his wife was waiting for him on the street. . . . So they're both alive then, still together, only they don't have me: I perished without a trace. Fomochka from Rostov, who made all of Karantinka tremble in fear, was racked by convulsive sobs.

☆

Mitya, of course, had no way of knowing that just a week before this sighting, his adoptive father had been released from the Magadan prison, called the "House of Vaskov." No more than six months after their reunion, Kirill and Cecilia had their "Paradise," a dilapidated shack on the outskirts of Magadan. In the city, former politicals were being arrested again at an unhurried pace. Discussing the latest arrest, intellectuals who knew one another came to the conclusion that the campaign was being carried out in alphabetical order: Antonov, Astafiev, Averbukh, Bartok, Baturina, Berseneva, Blank. . . . "Yesterday they took away Zhenya Ginzburg," Stepan Kalistratov said one day, "so it'll soon be your turn, Comrade Citizen Gradov. Celia, make him up a bundle with the *Short Course in the History of the Bolshevik Party* in it. There's still a few letters left before they get to me, so we can stroll around."

The camps had almost cured the Imaginist poet of his passion for alcohol, but on the other hand he had acquired a predilection for certain powders and tablets, which, he maintained, gave him an exceptionally optimistic and humorous outlook on real life.

"Stop talking nonsense, Stepan," Cecilia said immediately, attacking him. "What do you mean, arrest in alphabetical order? What sort of rubbish is that? This gallows humor with regard to the laws of a great country is misplaced, to say the least! You can pay for your tongue if you want, but Kirill and I will have nothing to do with it!"

They really did live with the strange sensation that now, after their reunion, everything would be all right: living conditions, provisions, the cultural level of the population, the international situation, even the climate. Kirill managed to find a job as a stoker in the boiler room of the city hospital and thus to tear himself loose from the world of the camps and the boorish guards. Cecilia almost immediately succeeded in having her name put on the list of instructors at the House of Political Enlightenment and began to nourish the local populace with theoretical analyses of the collapse of the world imperialist system against the background of the growing struggle of peoples for peace and socialism in the conditions of the rapidly approaching final triumph. The leadership of the Far North Administration of the MVD of the USSR, very happy at the arrival of the civilian theoretician, thanks to whom the squares on the schedule plan for political enlightenment were promptly checked and filed, promised Comrade Rosenbloom a nice room at number 14 Soviet Street, which would soon be free because it was presently occupied by a lady with inoperable lung cancer.

For the time being, the walls seemed to breath in unison with them.

When Kirill went off into a corner by himself to whisper prayers at his Franciscan altar, Cecilia would noisily flip through the pages of *Anti-Dühring* or *Imperialism and Empirical Criticism,* exclaiming "How deep!" or "Kirill, just listen to this: the so-called 'crisis in physics' is only an expression of the fallacies of idealism in the interpretation of the latest stage in scientific development." Quite often after these "sitting bouts" they would have a row, during which, when they came together in the center of the room—there was nowhere else for them to go—either this or that head would be singed by the electric lightbulb.

"Why, it's been known since the time of Democritus, from the time of Epicurus, that no one created matter!" Cecilia shouted. "The world is knowable—from beginning to end!"

Holding up his hands, Kirill would cushion the shock of her heavy breasts, which breathed furious Party fire as they advanced. "Who knows that, Celia, my dear? How can that be known? What does that mean, 'no one created'? Tell me what 'the beginning' is. And what's 'the end'? And if you're helpless before these questions, then how can you say that we 'know the world'?"

The duels would go on for hours to the accompaniment of the howl of the hopeless Kolyma wind and the sound of shrieking in the corridor, while, as the reader will undoubtedly have noticed, Cecilia fenced with exclamation marks and Kirill parried with question marks.

"Hey, Naumovna, Borisych, enough of your hullabaloo, come get some cabbage soup!" Mordyokha Bochkovaya, a visitor at the chronic venereal clinic, would yell from the other side of the partition.

In the "Paradise" where they were living, the women in the communal kitchen seized one another by the hair almost every night and tried to throw anything they could find with sharp edges into the pot, while children, some with syphilitic lesions or tubercular sores, who were sustained only by their destructive instincts, ran along the decaying corridor day after day. At the same time, at the far end, next to the toilets, lived the angel of creation, an old man from Odessa, Uncle Vanya Xronopolous—not even a ten-year sentence had been able to knock his eagerness to create a masterpiece out of him: sometimes it would be a violin of marvelous appearance out of surplus drawers, sometimes a small cigarette case that was also a music box that played the "Vienna Waltz." Most of his efforts, however, were expended on phonographs, radio receivers, and radiolas. It was from him that Kirill had the radio the size of a house that we saw him carrying out of the repair shop several pages back. We need the repair shop to remind ourselves of the fact that while Kirill was sitting in jail once again, the Magadan Office of State Security was rolling along through the alphabet and even raked up the letter "X." Its far-off position in the Russian alphabet, however, for a long time enabled Uncle Vanya to go on turning his screwdriver, sawing with his saw, soldering a lamp—in other words, enjoying life in "Paradise" under the protection of Xronos.

In buying this "Uncle Vanya Xronopolous" brand tube radio receiver, Kirill had never imagined in his wildest dreams that one day from the homemade rig, amid the crackle of electric discharges, a Russian Orthodox prayer would break through and then grow stronger. It turned out there was a radio station directed at listeners in the Soviet Union called "Voice of America," and on the airwaves of this very radio station run by the imperialists, a priest from San Francisco read Russian prayers.

Strangely enough, the hostile radio station concealed in the ridiculous box did not occasion any objections on the part of Cecilia Naumovna. On the contrary, she would now rather frequently come out with a growled, "Well, turn it on!" and, hearing the slick summons, "Listen to the Voice of America, listen to the voice of free radio!" would smirk with affected mockery: "Free!" and then be unable to tear herself away from the news summary.

When Kirill was picked up directly from the city hospital and taken for interrogation to the house occupied by State Security, which looked as though it had once been a noble mansion, he was sure the radio would appear among the accusations. However, it seemed as though the KGB had not even heard about the powerful rig. Monotonously and indifferently, they repeated the accusation from 1937 point by point: participation in a counterrevolutionary Trotskyite-Bukharinite organization in the trade union movement, attempt to discredit the policies of the Soviet government by means of dragging harmful ideas into the press, and so on. "But I already did ten years for that," Kirill objected weakly. "Don't be too clever, Gradov," the investigators said to him. "Come on, sign it again—you know what'll happen if you don't sign right away." They obviously did not want to have to thrash him: anyone could see they had no appetite for this wiry, humble, wrinkled stoker whose little remaining hair had gone gray. To this argument he had no objections, not even weak ones, and he signed again. Here I am coming back to my nature, he thought calmly. My nature isn't to sit in a warm hovel with my wife, and not to stuff myself with Moscow sweets, but to wander around in a penal colony, to stand in line for watery soup, to have my mouth swell up from scurvy. Lord, give me strength!

Cecilia Naumovna was shaken by the second arrest of her husband, perhaps no less than by the first. "Why, why?" she would whisper in the night, clutching her bosom in desperation. Whom am I asking that question of, she thought. If it's *them* (it was the first time she had thought of the government of the working people in these terms: *them*), then at least this time, unlike in '37, there's some reason for it, even if it's a slim one: he has become a religious type, after all, listens to foreign radio stations. . . . I ask questions not of *them*, but of something nocturnal, silent, all-knowing. . . .

We've got to smash that damned radio, drag it out to the scrap heap, she would think, enraged, in the morning. She had already raised a hammer over Xronopolous's contraption but then right away had embraced the accursed thing and covered it with her tears: after all, it was together, together that my darling and I would sit in the evenings as the wind howled outside and listen to those strange un-Soviet voices that seemed to come from some unreal world!

So I'm not going to throw it out—on the contrary, I'm going to listen to it the way I used to with my Kirill! As she had before, she went to the prison gates, again with sacks and bags, with the difference this time that the queues were not as long as they had been at Lefortovo prison and packages for delivery were accepted without any red tape. And again she wrote letters, no longer to the Control Commission of the Central Committee (it would be absurd somehow to petition the Central Committee on behalf of a "religious type"), but to the Far North Administration, to the MVD, and to Comrade Abakumov, minister of State Security.

One day in Magadan's department store, she saw Styopka Kalistratov standing in line for tea. In expectation of being arrested, he had begun to wear elegant outfits that astonished the locals: a soft hat, a coat with a caracul fleece collar, a scarf thrown over one shoulder, a walking stick—in other words, exactly the same getup he had once worn in a celebrated photograph with Mariengof, Esenin, Shershenevich, and Kusikov. Cecelia rushed at him and pounded his elegant, herringbone-covered back with her fists. "You, Styopka, you brought this on us! You and your talk about arrests in alphabetical order!"

He turned around, the epitome of worldly graciousness, in a wonderful mood: the proper combination of codeine and papaverine! "Countess Cecilia, lovelier than a lily!" He took her by the arm and whispered excitedly, "They've started to get out!"

"What are you talking about? Who?" she gasped.

"Our people! Several people whose names begin with 'A' have gotten out, some 'B's too . . . and today, something sensational—they let out Zhenya Ginzburg. . . . So don't lose heart, Cecile, they'll open the Bastille!"

The dissipated poet, curiously enough, turned out to be right again. Five months had not passed since the day Kirill was put in jail when bored KGB agents, with their pseudoleonine yawns, released him with a document stating that he, like all the other "alphabeters," was to reside in perpetual exile within a five-mile radius of the city of Magadan.

After that, strange as it may seem, everything settled down. The Gradov-Rosenbloom pair even discovered a certain feeling of stability: "perpetual exile," at least that's some kind of status! Cecelia even felt a sort of satisfaction. It was somehow more respectable to say "my husband the exile" rather than "my husband the former prisoner." After all, Vladimir Iliich Lenin had been in exile in the village of Shushenskoe, and even the Great Leader of the Peoples, Iosif Vissarionovich Stalin, had been sent to the Turukhan region, from which, in the manner of "Ivan and a Half," he had daringly escaped. Kirill was taken back at his old job, Cecilia got a pay rise. The room at 14 Soviet Street soon became free, and now began a quiet enchanting, if not actually idyllic, period of their lives—moving to a new flat in which there lived only two other families, where sounds that were not too loud almost didn't go through the walls—such as, for example, the melodious snoring of Ksaveria Olympievna, ticket seller at the House of Culture, and where they even had their own burner on the gas stove. The only limitation was a rotation for use of the warm places of convenience.

☆

It was to this very house that Foma Zaprudnev the "Rostovite," the terror of the Karantinka camp, had gotten into the habit of coming. He was in fact Dmitry Sapunov, one of a litter of kulak wolves, found, or caught, twenty-one years before by the young collectivization activists Gradov and Rosenbloom. What am I to them, anyway? wondered Mitya, squatting down in the style of the camps behind the transformer shed, furtively exhaling the smoke of his cigarette into his sleeve—they never even think about me anymore. An adopted son is just another distant relative. It was just some noble impulse they once had. The kid died in the war and that's the end of it, right, Dad? Right, Cecilia, mother of mine? . . .

As usual, he began to feel very sorry for himself and thought that maybe this was the main reason he permitted himself these short vigils behind the transformer shed, at the end of the earth, beneath the windows of his adoptive parents: pity, weakness, and snot are all mixed together with a tear just before the wolf man that I am spits it all out and rears up on his hind legs again.

He came out from behind the shed and walked away from the house right down the middle of the street, as other inhabitants of Magadan often did at night, since there was little passenger car traffic in those years in that region. Beneath one of the lights at the top of the street, where the overly long arm of the statue of Lenin was visible through the gates to the park like a raised semaphore flag, two comical short figures carrying string bags appeared. He realized immediately that it was them, his parents. He leapt to one side, over a ditch, and pressed himself against the wall behind the projecting ledge of a building. Kirill and Cecilia were slowly coming nearer, passing from a lit spot into darkness and then reappearing in the light. Their voices could already be heard. They were engaged in a philosophical discussion, as usual: positivist thinking fighting obscurantism. Cecilia said hotly, "You know, Kirill, you look at the world like an illiterate peasant! It's as though you slept through the whole Enlightenment!"

Kirill, getting on his high horse, said, "Your so-called Enlightenment, Cecilia, has nothing to do with what I'm talking about! Enlightenment and faith exist in different spheres! In different spheres, you understand!"

"Your logic is deserting you! You see nothing but dead ends!" Cecilia retorted hotly.

"These aren't just dead ends! They're signs of our limitations! They say, after all, that one cannot embrace what is limitless!" said Kirill from up on his high horse.

Cecilia's furor reached the point of chaotic churning. "How about a hug for your wife, Kirill Borisovich?"

Kirill impulsively hugged his large-breasted wife as if to keep himself from simply flying away. Mitya, by the way, was right: they rarely thought about him, but not because he wasn't their own son. Too caught up in each other, they never remembered anyone else.

At that moment, Mitya, giving in to an incomprehensible something, an uncontrollable urge, came out of his hiding place and asked in a changed, hoarse voice, "Hey, comrades, got a light?"

The married couple gave a start.

"What do you want?" Cecilia cried sharply, seemingly protecting Kirill with one shoulder.

"No problem, comrade," Kirill said, moving his spouse out of the way. He produced a box of matches from his pocket, struck one of them, and, cupping his hand around it, extended it to the passerby. The wind was blowing between his fingers, yet Mitya managed to light his cigarette. The match went out, but he did not immediately take his eyes off the callused palms. The moment lasted long enough so that in one red, flickering instant, he was able to see, probably for the last time, the lines of his father's destiny.

THIRD INTERMISSION

The Press

Time:

The 26-story building which is going up in Moscow on Smolensk Square would look quite ordinary in Manhattan, but for Europe, it is a colossus.

. . . Magnificent subway stations built on Moscow's underground ring.

. . . Before soccer games at the Dynamo Stadium, gleaming cars belonging for the most part to the Communist elite arrive together.

Time (March 20, 1950):

Western diplomats at Kremlin dinners have been struck by Malenkov's grim reserve and aloofness. Obese, agate-eyed, sallow and waxy-faced, Malenkov exuded a vague menace. "If I knew I had to be tortured," said a former Western envoy to Moscow last week, "and if I were picking people from the Politburo to do the torturing, the last one I would pick would be Malenkov."

Time (March 20, 1950):

Most striking was the complete disappearance of N. A. Voznesensky. It was as if Voznesensky had never been. For example, a recently published popular Soviet history book omits his name from a wartime list of Politburo members. George Orwell's "Ministry of Truth," which rewrote history to suit the doctrine of Nineteen Eight-Four, was not more thorough than the erasers of Voznesensky.

Pravda:

The stream of greetings of congratulations on his seventieth birthday continues to flow in for Comrade I. V. Stalin. The toilers send their Leader heartfelt wishes for good health and long life.

Izvestiya:

Units of the People's Army of Korea in close cooperation with units of Chinese people's volunteers sank an enemy destroyer which was shelling the area around Wonsan. Many peaceful inhabitants were killed.

Soviet Sports:

At the annual Tallinn motorcycle competitions, first place in the 750cc class went to V. Kulakov of the Air Force Sports Club.

Pravda:

Mohammed Mossadegh, head of the Iranian government, called for a continuation of an anti-imperialist "holy war for oil."

Yury Zhukov (Paris):

At the annual Fête de l'Humanité in the Bois de Vincennes, hundreds of white doves were released. Workers chanted, "Fascism shall not prevail! Peace will triumph over war!"

Time (March 27, 1950):

In 1936 the Nazi Propaganda Ministry endorsed the old German nationalist policy of *Sprachreinigung* (language purification). *Radio* was changed to *Rundfunk*, *Telefon* to *Fernsprecher*, *Automobil* to *Kraftwagen*. The *Relativitätstheorie* of famed refugee from Nazidom, Albert Einstein, became *Bezüglichkeitsanschauungsgesetz* (relativity perception law). Last week in Moscow, Communist Mother Russia trod briskly down the trail blazed by Herr Goebbels. The Soviet Academy of Sciences decided to thoroughly Russianize the Russian language.

Time (December 4, 1950):

Controversy has arisen around the philological system established by the late Nikolai Marr, who advocated one universal language, not necessarily Russian, for world communism. It only remained to be seen which way the Marxian doctrinal ax would fall. A bomb soon appeared in the form of an 8,000-word blockbuster in *Pravda* from Stalin himself, demolishing the "false" foundations of the Marr theory and setting everybody straight.

"Raise the Level of Soviet Cinematic Art!," *Pravda:*

Everyone in the Soviet film industry remembers the words of Comrade Stalin: "Endowed with exceptional possibilities for influencing the masses on a spiritual level, the cinema helps the working class and its Party to bring up the laboring masses in the spirit of socialism, to organize them in the struggle for socialism, to raise their level of culture and their readiness for political combat."

Pravda:

Volume 8 of the works of V. I. Lenin in the Uzbek language has just appeared.

Culture and Life:

A Bulgarian film studio has just finished shooting a new film entitled *Glory to Stalin!* The film depicts the boundless love of the Bulgarian people for the standard-bearer of peace in the world, Comrade Stalin.

I. Bolshakov, Minister for Film of the USSR:

The creative lapses and failures of some filmmakers have occurred above all because they are forgetting the decrees of the Party in matters of literature and art. This is particularly telling in the production of such mediocre pictures as the pseudoscientific film *A Man Follows a Trail.*

Townsend Reston, *National and English Review:*

Russia may be strong militarily, and ready to launch a blitzkrieg on the German pattern, but I do not believe she could again—and this time without Lend-Lease aid—mount anything like a sustained offensive war.

. . . The conditions under which most urban Russians live is worse than anything I have seen, even in the worst spots of Dublin or of Naples.

. . . How then are we to release the present intolerable tension in Europe? To rearm goes without saying. Equally important, but less obvious, we must strengthen the Iron Curtain.

. . . Whenever some special creative ability is vital to Russia, as in the fields of science and war, it is imported from the West. Of the four Russian types of car, two are Packards. The atom bomb and the MiG fighter came from the West. The creative energy of an entire people has waned under the influence of bolshevism.

. . . If Russia is cut off from the West she will, although her people work harder than ours, fall slowly so far behind that war, in perhaps only one generation, will become inevitable.

The Russians will not think the worse of us for this treatment, nor be more likely to resort to war, since nothing can make them more hostile to us than they are at present.

Scanteia:

Comrade Georgi-Dezh called for the unmasking of the Forish-Patroshkan band, agents of American and Yugoslavian intelligence.

Pravda:

We must train cadres in a spirit of implacable hostility to shortcomings!

"A Word on Song," *Pravda:*

The Soviet people have become accustomed to living under the banner "A song helps us to build and to live." Recently, pure and heartfelt songs have been written to the words of "Oh, My Dear Fog" and "Katyusha.". . . A. Surkov displays a great talent for composing songs: "On the Military Road," "Black Clouds Are Spreading.". . . Everyone remembers the Lebedev-Kumach composition "Song About the Motherland," "Along the Valleys and Hills" by S. Alymov, and M. Svetlov's song "Kakhovka.". . .

In this domain, however, quite a few hacks are at work. One wants to ask some composers if they have given any thought to the rhymed rubbish which they are setting to music. . . . In this connection, one cannot help but recall the empty, jarring lyrics of Y. Ziskind, Mass and Chervinsky, Dykhovichny and Slobodsky. . . . S. Fogelson is a disgrace to the poetic tradition of Nekrasov.

Time (December 3, 1951):

Air Force Chief of Staff Hoyt S. Vandenberg: "Our control of the air in northwest Korea, although by no means lost, is not as firm as it was.

"Above 25,000 ft., a MiG can outrun and outclimb the F-86."

Time:

An unusual picture of Stalin has appeared in the West. Official photographs of him are usually retouched with care. In the picture, taken at the Bolshoi Theater, the aging dictator looks gray and tired. Sitting by him with inscrutable faces are two "Politburocrats," Lavrenty

Beria, age 52, and Georgy Malenkov, age 49, both potential heirs to the throne.

Time (August 6, 1951):

Ivan Bunin, poet, novelist and aristocrat, is one of the last of these echoes of the old Russia. He is 80, almost bedridden with asthma, and he lives out his last years of exile in a Paris flat, half-forgotten by the world since he received the Nobel Prize for Literature in 1933.

Leonid Leonov:

The peoples uphold the cause of peace. . . . I. V. Stalin teaches the peoples: "A broad campaign for the preservation of peace as a means of exposing the criminal machinations of the warmongers is now of the highest importance.

. . . "They don't wait for peace, they fight for it!" This winged phrase has found a response in the hearts of millions.

Pravda:

A Soviet film festival took place in Iran, playing to packed houses. It showed clearly the role of Comrade I. V. Stalin in all spheres of Soviet life. . . . Meanwhile, the festival of American cinematic poison played to empty theaters.

TASS:

The new passenger steamer *Iosif Stalin* has begun to cruise the Dniepr.

. . . We must restore the independence and sovereignty of France, Comrade Jacques Duclos declared in his address.

. . . For the tireless raising of the ideological level of Party enlightenment!

Time (September 17, 1951):

Would the Soviet delegate to the San Francisco conference like to see a map of Russia? "I'd be delighted," said Gromyko.

Unfolding the map, Missouri's congressman O. K. Armstrong helpfully explained: "It happens to contain an accurate portrayal of every slave labor camp in the Soviet Union." Said Gromyko later: "It would be interesting to know what capitalist slave is the author of this map."

. . . Communist Russia's slave labor population exceeds 14 million; of these more than 1,600,000 can expect to die this year.

Time (November 19, 1951):

In the red and gold theater of Paris's Palais De Chaillot, Russia laughed a laugh that was heard around the world.

"I could hardly sleep all last night," Soviet Foreign Minister Andrei Vyshinsky told the U.N. General assembly. "I could not sleep because I kept laughing."

Vyshinsky laughed along as he gave Russia's answer to the West's disarmament proposals.

Newsweek:

In the course of their well-surveyed stroll through Moscow, Ambassador George Kennan and his personal guest, the journalist Townsend Reston, came upon posters proclaiming Soviet Armed Forces Day. They showed Soviet fighter planes shooting down American aircraft. Upon his return home, Kennan sent an angry letter to the Ministry of Foreign Affairs. In response, he received the next day an invitation to the parade of the Soviet Air Force. Kennan refused the invitation. The French and British ambassadors also boycotted the parade in a gesture of solidarity, but, being practical people, all three sent their military attachés. Reston was at the parade as well.

L'Humanité:

Spectators boycotted the showing of an anti-Soviet film cooked up by the Americans to a screenplay by the not unknown reactionary Jean-Paul Sartre. . . . French films should call for peace!

Pravda:

The peoples of the Soviet Union and progressive humanity are marking the fiftieth anniversary of the Stalinist newspaper *Brdzola*— the Struggle. . . . The verses that have been printed in its pages will never be erased from memory:

> "Brdzola," be a clarion call!
> Disperse the gloomy dark of night!
> Raise up the workers, all in thrall
> To the lowly restore might!

Pravda:

In England, five leading dancers of the Belgrade–Zagreb ballet have announced their refusal to return to Yugoslavia because they have no opportunity there to freely exercise their creative talents.

Pravda:

Units of the People's Liberation Army of China have entered Lhasa, the capital of Tibet, in an atmosphere of support from the local populace. The Tibetans greeted the troops with sincere pleasure and joy. It was the first time in their history the Tibetan people had seen such an army, one that brings genuine freedom to working people.

FOURTH INTERMISSION

Hannibal's Thoughts

In the course of acquainting the readers of our saga not only with the human characters of Moscow but also with representatives of the city's fauna, we have finally come to the elephant. If you please: in the capital of our Motherland there lived an African elephant *(Loxodonta africana)* named Hannibal in a stall quite comfortable even by modern standards. The reader, already accustomed to our astral incarnations, would be within his rights to suppose that the author, with the aid of this name, African in origin and noteworthy in Russian history, intended to disturb the "Sun of Our Poetry," Alexander Sergeyevich Pushkin. The author, however, desiring to avoid any misunderstandings, however slight, is obliged to state right away that he is talking about the "Moon of our Poetry," in the sense that the celestial nature of Alexander Nikolaevich Radishchev, the descendent of Tatar chieftains and a most enlightened gentlemen for his epoch—that is, Catherine the Great's eighteenth century—had taken up residence this time in a five-ton body with long tusks and ears the size of wigwams.

The elephant's age was 102 years, of which he had spent fifteen in Moscow, with the exception of two years spent in Kuibyshev after being evacuated during the war. He was a great favorite of Generalissimo I. V. Stalin. As early as the 1930s, when the Great Leader of the laboring masses had not yet even thought about taking the title of generalissimo, Stalin used to turn up as if by chance at Hannibal's stall, take a seat on a folding chair, and for a long time stare at the rhythmically swaying trunk of the most powerful animal on dry land. Someone is comparing me to an elephant in a china shop, thought the Leader. No, that's an inappropriate comparison.

At the beginning of the 1950s, when Stalin had converted entirely to a nocturnal existence, his meetings with Hannibal, strange as it may seem, increased in frequency. In the middle of the night, he would crawl out from beneath his green lamp and call for his five-car equipage. His retinue would already know where they were going—to see Hannibal!

During those fifteen years in Moscow and Kuibyshev, the elephant usually dreamed at night of chewing sugar cane on the edge of a plantation in Kenya. Munch, munch, the molars worked. Plop, plop, half-liter drops of saliva fell from his trunk. At the sight of the pensive figure of the generalissimo, the visions of sugar cane clouded over, and from the bottomless astral depths Radishchev's hatred for tyrants emerged.

My soul is burdened, the elephant would remember at night, I'm suffering and I'm tired. By flickering candlelight the features of the Urania discussion circle would appear, and Klopstock's hexameters would slowly issue forth.

The elephant turned, raised his left ear, and looked askance at Stalin. Maybe you're one of ours? Stand up, tyrant, show your secret Masonic sign, which will cover a multitude of sins. Maybe your intentions are lofty even though your power is base?

Stalin did not receive the signals, discovered no spiritual connections. Here she is, Catherine the Great . . . only, like a saving drug, the long waves of a vast shallow lake flowed through the elephant's consciousness, along with dawn, the sugary top of a mountain, an elephant calf butting its round head against his belly, the pink pallet of his mate trumpeting at dawn . . . and again a powdered, haughty creature swims to the surface of his thoughts out of oblivion, that creature revered Voltaire in flattering letters while she put her own Voltaires to the knout. She throws a fragrant powder into the eyes of Europe. Monsieur Diderot himself is in the court library, while, outside the court, she smashes the printing press of a modest customs officer.

Does that mean that we Tatar-Russians are forbidden to be more clever than the Diderots, *gnädige Frau*? Slowly, the ideas of compassion and retribution as a manifestation of human nature slithered through the elephantine brain like an old melody. Oh, Catherine, you who trembled before the Masons, and your orders were like Major Bochum's stick, which brought grief to someone's cosmically distant childhood.

Stalin carefully observed the agitations of the elephant moving slowly over the surface of its hide. The most powerful animal on dry land and not a predator, he thought. The most powerful animal. He stood up and went over to the board on which was written the number of buckets of potatoes the elephant was allegedly capable of eating. "Increase the ration!" he ordered tersely, after which he returned to the fortress of all the peoples.

One day in the late spring of 1952, however, at 3:30 in the morning, Hannibal left his stall, trod across the enclosure, and without any effort—thank God, he had learned by watching during his fifteen years minus two—opened the gates with his trunk, went out onto the street, and began his "Journey from Presnya to the Kremlin," which went on for exactly one hour. The closer he got, the more he realized he was going to the right address: it was right there behind the crenellated wall that the monster lay, enormous and hydralike.

An annoyed General Vlasik was forced to interrupt his caviar-and-sturgeon dinner, which was turning into breakfast. Stalin raised his head from beneath the green lamp. What a pleasure it is to work while all 190 million sleep—and then they interrupt you. What a pleasure it is to take the Leninist whip to Academician Marr, who has run off in his pseudoscientific mental gymnastics, and now they come and report that "the most powerful animal on dry land" has arrived.

"Where's the elephant?" he asked.

Hannibal was waiting for Stalin on a square within the Kremlin. "Morning is greeting us with freshness," the words of a popular song, came to Stalin's mind. "The river greets us with a cool wind." Proud, bloodred flags crackled as they fluttered in the predawn sky.

"Well, what can we do for you?" the generalissimo with the head of a scientist, in the uniform of an ordinary soldier, asked drily.

Hannibal the elephant addressed his old acquaintance with the entire front part of his body, that is, not only with his most expressive organ, which took the form of a curving finger, but also with the faintly quivering strata of his ears and even with the advancing columns that were his legs, and even with the profoundly concealed "Lenin Lights," that is to say, his eyes. Some of the elements of the rear section of his body participated in this address—for example, his tail—but the hindmost columns stood firm and unmoving, as if removing any possible doubt that the address would be heard.

"Repent before it's too late, old friend!" the elephant said with its whole body. "Have a look at me—I've been repentant for seventy years now about having once crushed a jackal pup with one of my hind legs; but I've noticed that you, brother, never repent of anything. Do it before it's too late; otherwise you'll die unrepentant!"

"I don't understand you," Stalin replied. The early morning had suddenly lost all of its attraction for him. The elephant made it into the Kremlin—does that mean I can no longer rely on the guards? That beast of an owl no longer fears the daylight, and it hovers over my shoulder—so even Professor Gradov is a shit of a doctor? The guards, however, trying to make up for things, had formed a circle around Hannibal and rolled out a 75mm antitank gun.

He doesn't understand, thought Hannibal, again with a long and extended feeling of alarm like the one an entire jungle grove feels when a tiger appears in it. He raised his trunk and trumpeted some of his faraway Radishchevian sorrow. Well, now do you understand?

"Lead him away," Stalin said with a frown, but no one moved forward.

"Get rid of him," the Leader corrected himself squeamishly, and then the cannon roared.

Thus perished "the most powerful animal on dry land," and his thoughts, which had gathered together after the shot into a tight ball, dispersed again and went spinning out of the fortress and off into freedom.

Chapter 7

———————☆———————

ARCHI-MEDICUS

In the spring of 1952, mushroom spies once again appeared in the manure that had been spread around the Gradov home in Silver Forest the previous year. The oily head of one of them was constantly inserting itself into the gaps of the dilapidated fence. Two others, their little hats cocked at rakish angles on their morel faces, strolled the tree-lined walk unconcealed. From time to time a dark blue Pobeda limousine would stop on the corner by the telephone booth in which three more earthy thugs could be seen.

What variety of mushroom people is this? wondered Boris Nikitovich. They appear on the surface and thrust out their existence without any justification whatever. They appear in God's creation in order to become MGB spies! Then again, even these people can get sick, and then they join the noble tribe of patients. Falling ill, even these unthinking, poisonous mushrooms become people again. People who are suffering. People who must be cured. Perhaps it's only then that they justify their existence, taking part in the most humane of all processes: disease and treatment.

Indeed, the "appropriate authorities" never shortchanged the Gradov nest of its rightful share of attention. The telephone, in all probability, was constantly bugged, and the local constables, no doubt, starting with "Junior Commander" Slabopetukhovsky, had received special instructions to keep an eye on things. Sometimes there appeared at the door unusual, even strange meter readers and fire inspectors. It was the third time the house had been besieged in this way: there was 1925, immediately after the operation on Commissar Frunze, 1937, after the arrest of Gradov's sons, and now.

The first two times, I wasn't afraid of anything, the old surgeon recalled. In 1925 I might not have noticed the men tailing me if Mary hadn't said anything. Indeed, what was there to fear, what tortures, when the worst was already being played out inside me, in my soul? I felt as though I had betrayed myself, that I had disgraced my whole kind, the entire Russian medical profession. And in 1937 I wasn't afraid because I had been prepared to accept punishment for 1925. At any rate I convinced myself I wasn't afraid. All things considered, I was ready. In principle, they couldn't have thought up anything worse than taking away the guiltless. They always unconsciously—it's obvious that it's unconscious and obvious that it is only by the strength of their infernal nature—find a way to humiliate by the strongest, most irreparable means. The most striking thing was that both times, instead of my arrest and ruin, they began to shower me with decorations, honors, titles, and pay raises. Here again, there was clearly an unconscious logic at work. In spite of everything, they obviously sensed some concealed fault in me, a lack of, say, chivalrous qualities. Perhaps they were not mistaken. Obviously, fear of them had always lived within me, otherwise I would not have given in to panic that time on Red Square when I shamefully fled from a foreigner. And that purge of Stalin's intestine! What rotten, shitty meaning was contained in that top secret procedure? Still, all I did was my duty as a doctor. What should I expect now, when such mysterious and ominous events are taking place in the medical circles of the Kremlin? Professor Goettinger was arrested and vanished somewhere, and consequently it's very likely that Professor Truvsi has also been arrested; Professor Scheidemann was been driven from his department and is awaiting arrest. . . . What does it mean, and why have all the victims been Jews? If it has something to do with the liquidation of the Jewish Anti-

Fascist Committee and with the disappearance of dozens, if not hundreds, of Jewish intellectuals, doesn't that mean that they're trying to attach medicine, too, to the "anticosmopolitan," anti-Semitic campaign?

But that doesn't concern me—I'm not a Jew, after all, he thought, and immediately felt himself tremble from shame. It's a pity I'm not a Jew. I'd like to be a Jew so as to avoid any ambiguity. To these devils, any Russian intellectual must be a Jew because he's . . . alien!

I can't end my life purging their dirty, cannibal innards, thought the unhappy Boris Nikitovich Gradov, professor, Academician, and cavalier of numerous Soviet orders. I beg you, you bastards, take me and have me shot! All my grandsons have already grown up, they'll fight their way through somehow, they'll survive. I don't want to live alongside you anymore!

Thoughts of this sort sometimes came to him on sleepless nights. One night he knocked at the entrance to Agasha's room, from behind the door of which came a narrow shaft of light. "Agasha, my dear, don't be afraid—it's me, Bo!" On the other side of the door there was a commotion, almost a panic-stricken murmur, a rushing back and forth. Finally, the door opened a crack, and an old lady, her hair in braids like the tails of two mice, appeared. Wearing a long flannel nightgown and glasses on her nose, she stood trembling in the doorway.

"What's happened, Boryushka?" He patted her on the head. "Let me come in, my dear!"

In the forty-five years Agasha had lived in this house, it was the first time Boryushka, forever loved, had come to her room. Oh, our sins are a burden, yet in our younger years, when we were full of the juices of life, we used to dream about this sort of thing! The quiet squeak in the night, and Borya will come in to caress me, to fondle me, even to hurt me a bit, and then the three of us will love one another even more—Borya, Maryushka, Agashenka. . . . I can't count the number of times I've sinned in my dreams . . .

He came in and sat down on a rickety Viennese chair. Quivering, she sat down on the edge of the bed.

"Agashenka, my dear," he said, "you read the Bible, don't you? Where is the story of the Beast?"

She immediately felt calmer and nodded gravely. "It's in the Revelation of Saint John, Boryushka."

Boris Nikitovich coughed. "Won't you give me your Bible to look at, Agashenka? I need to—well . . . for my work, you know, I'm almost writing literature . . ." She felt ill at ease, seeing how awkward this was for him. Immediately, she produced the desired object from beneath a pillow on the bed. That means she was reading the Bible when I knocked, thought Boris Nikitovich. In other words, she reads at night, in order not to disturb the professor in his positivist thinking.

Positivist thinking is the purest sort of return to the primitive, Boris Nikitovich said to himself as he left Agasha's room and walked along the loudly squeaking floorboards of the hallway with the Bible underneath his arm. It's time to relay this floor, and it's time, too, to have the fence repaired, so that those mushroomlike thugs can't look through the cracks anymore. How little positivist thinking understands man, how little it tries to understand! What sort of strange model of the world is it that dialectical materialism offers us? Why, it's nothing but a ghost of the primitive past, if not actually the Devil making a fool of us with a hidden smile. It's the same thing as making a likeness of Archi-medes out of cardboard and then saying that this is the real Archi-medes.

A year earlier, his granddaughter Yolka had given him a thick-pawed German shepherd puppy for his seventy-fifth birthday.

"Here you are, Grandpa—in memory of Pythagoras. His name, if you please, is Archi-medes!" she explained with a burst of laughter. "Only you have to spell the name of this Archi-medes with a hyphen, because he's none other that Archi-medicus, like you, my dear grandpa!"

Naturally, everyone was immediately taken with the heir of Pythagoras. Mary added, "If it's not actually Pythy who's come back to us . . ." Agasha, of course, immediately changed the proud name to "Archipushka." Barely having begun to grow, Archi-medes immediately singled out the head of the family and began to follow Papa Boris everywhere. He stopped moving only when the old professor sat or lay down or left the house. Now, having became a huge, handsome one-year-old, the half-asleep Archi-medes nonetheless accompanied the sleepless old man along the squeaking parquet floor and sat down next to him beside the armchair in the living room, in the same way Pythagoras had once done. Well, he really does look like a reincarnation—it's just a pity that a new fifty-year-old professor in the prime of life isn't sitting in my place, not yet crushed by the operation on Commissar Frunze. He opened the Revelation of Saint John and immediately found the passage about the Beast:

". . . and they worshipped the Beast, saying, Who is like unto the Beast? Who is able to make war with him? And there was given unto him a mouth speaking great things and blasphemies . . .

". . . and power was given him over all kindreds, and tongues, and nations.

"And all that dwell upon the earth shall worship him . . ."

Boris Nikitovich read and reread Chapter 13 of Revelations and thought about the secret that was concealed here, and about whether or not all these secrets and prophecies could be applied to what was happening in the twentieth century—after all, the first Beast is followed by a second, his direct descendant, who defiles those "that dwell upon the earth, saying that they should make an image to the Beast . . ." In youth, in the prime of life, and in maturity, Boris Nikitovich, when he had paid any attention to these secrets at all, had done so with a smile. With a good-natured smile, it must be said, but with a condescending smile nonetheless, which was natural before these poetic liberties. Now, however, it was as though a bottomless cosmos had suddenly opened up beneath him with all the horror of unrecognized mysteries. . . . "Here is wisdom. Let him that hath understanding count the number of the Beast: for it is the number of a man; and his number is six hundred threescore and six."

How can I make sense of this with my head stuffed with Darwinism and materialism? What sort of terrible signs and preordained events are these? The only thing that is clear is that our age has come under the power of the Beast and false prophecies. All of this replacing Christian values with the "new values" is in essence nothing other than false prophecy and the Devil's mockery. Even the very cross, the symbol of the Christian faith, has been replaced by caricatures, turned, twisted, and bent, the Nazi swastika and our beetle of a hammer and sickle. Everything has been replaced—the state, politics, economics, art, and science, even the most humane of all sciences—and the sense of all of these acts of replacing is contained only in that replacement itself, in that mocking leer addressed to us from the dead cosmos. . . .

One spring morning, when the rays of the sun were breaking through the veil of fog, the thuggish mushroom spies disappeared, but Boris Nikitovich had scarcely had time to notice it before the telephone rang. A certain Tsarengoi Vardisanovich—a powerful figure, one supposed—was calling from the Fourth Directorate of the Ministry of Health.

"This evening, at six o'clock, Boris Nikitovich, a car will come for you. You will have an important task to perform for the State."

"Can you be more precise, Tsarengoi Vardisanovich? I need to prepare myself, after all."

"No, I can't give you any details right now. Everything will be made clear to you as you work. All I can say is that this is a highly important task for the State. Try to get some rest and be fresh at six this evening."

Is it really to Him again, to the embodiment of the Beast? After 1937, Gradov had not seen Stalin again, though word had reached him more than once that the leader had not forgotten his savior-purger. Even more, the name of "Gradov" had become a sort of talisman, a medical court of last appeal, as it were: any of those Truvsi-Vovsis, Goettinger-Ettingers can disappear, but Gradov will remain—there's one who will never let me down!

★

He was not mistaken: the car, a new-model ZIS with blinding white-wall tires, took him to Stalin but not to the place where he had once performed his holy rite over the priceless body, not to the "near dacha" at Matveevskaya, but directly to the Kremlin.

This time, the Leader was not moaning in a semicomatose state; on the contrary, he personally opened the oaken door and walked on his own two feet into the antechamber where Professor Gradov was waiting for him amid the fine carpets and leather-covered furniture. They shook hands and then sat down in facing chairs. He's aged a great deal, thought Gradov, looking at the graying hair and at the face with its pouches and drooping skin. The photographs of him don't tell the truth. "We're not getting any younger," Stalin said with a smile, answering the other man's thoughts.

"I'm much older than you, Comrade Stalin," Gradov said.

"Only by four years, Comrade Gradov," the Leader replied, again with a smile, a most good-natured one. The fingers of his right, healthy hand were trembling slightly; he's nervous, Gradov thought.

"How may I be of use to you, Comrade Stalin?"

Stalin coughed into a handkerchief. It was the stagnant bronchitis of a career smoker. "I want you to give me a full physical examination, Professor Gradov."

"But I'm not an internist, Comrade Stalin."

If any one of the millions under the leadership of this man had looked at the Great Leader at that moment, he would not have found a trace of threatening, hypnotic power. Stalin did not like, and even feared, doctors: it always seemed to him that once you started having dealings with them, you just kept on rolling unstoppably to the end; there was simply no room in his mind for the concept of what that end might be. What sort of nonsense is that, "to the end"? To the end of the cause, perhaps, to the end of communism? Given his dislike for the Kremlin medical staff, he had, ever since the 1930s, maintained a final barrier, a last resort: Professor Gradov. The name embodied for him something more essential than "progressive Soviet medicine." And now, for several reasons, he had to call upon this last resort and, consequently, to rely on him, having no forces left in reserve. For the first time in many years, Stalin felt a strange dependence on another human being, and this drove him to distraction. We, however, the professional revolutionaries—this was how little Svetlana had once perfectly described her father, filling in the space under "Father" on a biographical data form with "Professional revolutionary"—we the professional revolutionaries are not entitled to ordinary human weaknesses. Wasn't it Trotsky who had put it so well: "A revolutionary is the megaphone of the ages." No, it couldn't have been him; Trotsky couldn't have said anything good, he was an accomplice of Hitler and Churchill . . . no . . . who is it in front of me? . . . Oh, yes, Dr. Gradov, Professor Gradov, doctor by God's mercy . . . no, mustn't say things like that. . . .

It did not escape Gradov that Stalin was strangely perplexed for several moments, but then he said in his usual weighty tones, "I consider, Professor Gradov, that you are first and foremost a physician . . . hm . . . by calling. . . . You are a prominent scholar, an opinion which is confirmed by your book *Pain and Anesthesia.*"

Boris Nikitovich was stunned. "You're familiar with that book, Comrade Stalin?"

"Yes, I read it," Stalin replied with natural modesty and not without pleasure. To catch an interlocutor unawares with an unexpected bit of knowledge was always pleasant.

Now Professor Gradov began to worry. "But that's a book for specialists, it's purely medical and biological and even deals with biochemistry in many places. The general reader could hardly—"

I'm getting things wrong, thought Gradov, and he became even more worried. Stalin smiled, extended a hand, and lightly touched the professor's knee.

"Obviously, I didn't dig into the medical subtleties, but it was possible even for me, the 'general reader,' to follow its overall humanist orientation. Man and pain—this is perhaps the fundamental question of civilization. I wouldn't be surprised if you were to win a Stalin Prize, first class, for this work. Although I must admit that it seemed to me that you sounded some pessimistic notes here and there, but we won't talk about that."

What a type. "Type," that was just the word that came into Gradov's mind as he thought about the man with whom he was speaking. He catches notes of pessimism even in a medical text. Our conversation is starting strangely. It's obvious that things could go either way here—I could win a prize or lose my head. Somehow the thought put him more at ease, even made him cheerful.

"So, Iosif Vissarionovich, you wish me to reach a conclusion about your overall state of health. Will you permit me to ask first of all how you feel?"

What a strange character, thought Stalin, he didn't even thank me for my high opinion of his book. It's as though he doesn't understand that the pessimistic notes in his book could make him a target. Then again, this is Professor Gradov we're talking about, not some Ettinger or Vovsi, but a real doctor . . . a doctor by vocation. . . . With him, I'll have to leave the political aspects of my state of health aside. . . .

"On the whole, I feel perfectly—" he said. Then he frowned. How to put it: perfectly normal? Then why did I call for him? "—perfectly capable of working," he went on. "However, I've reached a ripe age, and the comrades of the Politburo . . ."

"I beg your pardon, Iosif Vissarionovich," Gradov put in gently when Stalin paused, "but as a doctor, the opinions of the members of the Politburo don't interest me right now, but rather your feelings, as my patient for the day. Do you have any complaints?"

He had the impression that Stalin at that moment was looking in annoyance at the embellished oak panels of the walls of the receiving room. Hasn't this Gradov noticed that I'm afraid of eavesdroppers? thought Stalin.

"What are your first name and patronymic?" He asked the professor for the formal form of address, surprising even himself.

Gradov shuddered: he read *Pain and Anesthesia,* and he doesn't remember my name. "My name is Boris Nikitovich."

"Good," nodded Stalin. "It's less awkward to address one another in this way, Boris . . ."

"Nikitovich," Gradov prompted once again.

"I have complaints, Boris Nikitovich, of course. I find I tire more easily. I'm very irritable sometimes. I have a cough and pains in my chest, arms, and legs. I feel dizzy on occasion. My stomach doesn't always function exactly the way it should. My urine acts up, shall we say . . . that's how things stand, Boris Nikitovich, a little of this and a little of that. . . . You know that people in my part of the country live to be a hundred." At that moment, it seemed to Gradov as though Stalin had raised his voice. "They go along quietly and live to be a hundred. They have complaints, but they live." He smiled as he said this, obviously remembering someone "in my part of the country," on the Sakartvelo plateau.

"Well, let's get to work, Iosif Vissarionovich," said Gradov. "I'll begin with a few personal questions—do a case history, as we say— and an examination, and then, as you'll understand, we'll need equipment and assistants."

"Equipment, assistants . . ." Stalin muttered discontentedly. Clearly he had pictured his meeting with Professor Gradov somewhat differently.

"Well, of course, Iosif Vissarionovich, how else can we do it? Without X rays, an EKG, and laboratory data, I can't reach any conclusions. In this connection, I would suggest to you that we move over to Granovsky Hospital."

"There won't be any Granovsky!" Stalin interrupted. "Everything can be done in the Kremlin." Turning in his chair, he pushed a button on a desk. Two men in white smocks entered the room almost immediately. It turned out that an entire medical team from the Fourth Directorate lived next door, at his disposal.

"Oh, well, perfect—that's even more convenient," Gradov said.

He shook hands with the men who had come in and asked them as the first matter to bring him the history . . . he had been about to say "history of the illness" but corrected himself in time: "the history of Comrade Stalin's checkups." The doctors eyed their monstrous patient timidly like rabbits.

"Bring it," Stalin growled. He was feeling more and more out of sorts. So, in the end, Professor Gradov can't get along without all these medical rituals either.

The "history of the examinations of Comrade Stalin" turned out to be a thin folder tied shut with two attached ribbons. Opening it, Boris Nikitovich immediately saw the joint conclusion of Professors Goettinger and Truvsi, the two recently disappeared stars in the therapeutic firmament: "Hypertonic illness, arteriosclerosis, coronary insufficiency, emphysema, profound bronchitis, evidence of pulmonary insufficiency, suspicion of sclerotic urinary alteration in conjunction with chronic pyelonephritis . . ." Well, that's quite a bouquet! "Diagnosis awaits confirmation following a battery of clinical tests." The words were written in Truvsi's hand, which was well known to Boris Nikitovich. Maybe this diagnosis was why they had vanished? Maybe a "mysterious disappearance" awaits me here, as well?

He asked Stalin to remove his tunic. The historic one, of course, favored and comfortable, in which perhaps the first Stalin Five-Year Plan had been born, was a bit threadbare at the cuffs now.

Everything here belongs to history: the jacket, the flannel underpants, the riding breeches with their suspenders, not to mention the kidskin boots. The strong smell of the old man's sweat probably won't go down in history: the Leader is obviously so preoccupied with affairs of state that he forgets to bathe. Perhaps he has some idiosyncrasy about baths, imagines that Charlotte Corday will fly into the room when he's in the middle of his ablutions? Jokes of this sort are out of place in a medical examination, Professor Gradov, even if they are only fleeting swallows amid your reflections, serious as the clouds over Russia. Above all, you have a patient in front of you. He began to go over the Leader's flaccid body.

"You don't take any exercise, Comrade Stalin?"

"Ha, ha . . . who do you think I am, Voroshilov?"

He felt his glands, including those in the groin, for which he asked Stalin to lower his breeches, revealing a long, flaccid penis. They say the entire older generation of the leadership was long and limp in that particular member. Boris Nikitovich was very interested by the blood vessels in the Leader's extremities. His hypothesis was confirmed: his legs just below the knees and the calves were disfigured by bluish swellings and puffy hematomas. Spreading varicose veins, obliterating endoarteriosis. . . .

"Do your legs feel numb, Iosif Vissarionovich?"

"Sometimes. Doesn't that happen to you, Professor Gradov?"

Has he forgotten my name again, or is he annoyed? The aging Bolsheviks, obviously, were in a rage against their physicians. Stalin had a clear case of iatrophobia—he hated doctors because they destroyed his myth of greatness.

He tapped Stalin sharply on the back in the area of the kidneys, using his grandfather's method: the base of the palm, first on one side, then on the other. The kidneys are diseased, the left one more than the right. Now you'll have to lie on your back, Iosif Vissarionovich. Let's press everything with these fingers—still sensitive, even if they are seventy-six years old. Each one of them has fifty-five years of medical practice in it, which means they have 550 years of practicing medicine in them altogether! We'll press the flabby stomach, sound the internal organs even through the fat that has built up on the Leader over the years of our glory—no matter how much you despise a man, when he becomes a patient you can't help but feel a certain sympathy for him. Here are the duodenum, the pancreas—a momentary reaction of pain. The liver, of course, is enlarged and compressed, lumpy, it could even be something very bad, though at his age everything flows sluggishly, at a reduced rate; these organs of his have nothing to do with anything, they're just the same as those of all human beings. Neither collectivization nor the purges of 1937 can be felt in this flaccid paunch.

It's just ordinary sad human fate: gas, peristalsis, heartburn, the taste of lead in the mouth . . . no, no, not when they shoot you in the mouth, but when the kidneys are no longer fulfilling their cleansing function.

Let's proceed now to percussion and auscultation. The same unfortunate Truvsi—we used to play remarkable chess together after dinner at the House of Scientists—said to me on more than one occasion that the surgeon hadn't killed the internist in me. My God, we're hearing and tapping out all sorts of things in the chest cavity of the Father of the Peoples! Wheezes, both dry and moist, exudate in the lower regions of the pleura, deep tones in the upper lungs, an enlarged heart, arrhythmia, noises. How he still manages to move around with this alleycat serenade inside him. . . . And in addition to everything else, a solid decapitated hypertonia of threateningly small amplitude.

Stalin liked Professor Gradov less and less and forgot his name and patronymic again. He's asking unseemly questions. One mustn't ask such questions of the most important person in so-called humanity, even if he is your patient. You can feel in his hands that he doesn't like me, they aren't shaking at all, like most people's. What have I done to him, though? I took his son from a prison camp and made him a marshal of the Soviet Union, was that bad? In response to a request from his comrades in arms I let his widow, known throughout Moscow as a whore, go to the kingdom of capitalism. For the sake of humanism they let him have some of the finest women. Maybe he's angry with me because of his second son, the Trotskyite? All of a sudden, he remembered clearly Poskryobyshev's report on Marshal Gradov's letter in defense of his brother and how the resolution had been formulated: "Sentence remains in force." It was impossible to pardon a Trotskyite then: it could have set a bad precedent, with a political resonance. That was it: resonance and precedent.

"And how is your son Kirill Borisovich Gradov?" Stalin suddenly asked.

The professor was preoccupied at that moment with listening to the aorta, and it seemed to him for an instant that it was in fact through this blood-carrying vessel, clearly filled with plates of cholesterol, or from a fast-flowing Kolyma River, that his son's name reached his ears. He remembered a name! Does he really remember everything, even with his sclerosis?

"Very well, thank you, Iosif Vissarionovich. He's in internal exile, and in good health. He's working—"

"If you have any requests to make with regard to your son, just ask, Boris Borisovich," said Stalin with a proud glance out the window, on the other side of which the flag of State power, which never faded under any circumstances, and which was the hope of peace-loving peoples of the world, rippled optimistically in the spring breeze? He says "thank you," but that doesn't mean at all that he's my friend. He learned something unpleasant from those clever Jews. These professors have no historical gratitude. We saved them from the Black Hundreds and from Hitler, and they still look at us as they would at a naked body, as they would at a scientific aid for their theories. A professional revolutionary, however, is a man of a different caliber, as Trotsky said. No, Trotsky didn't say anything. Lev had too high an opinion of himself, and he said nothing good. If he had been more modest, a phenomenon as outrageous as Trotskyism would never have come to be. Now it's too late to talk about that. We didn't eradicate it in time, and now it's spread to the entire body, to turn into these ugly diagnoses. Professor Gradov could turn out to be an unwilling accomplice of international Trotskyism. I would never have expected that from you, old friend! *Genatsvale!* I often imagined that after all these drones had been driven out of the Kremlin, Professor Gradov, the age-old savior, would come, the one who already once cleared the excess lead out of my system and forged a path into the Alazan valley or, to put it in men's language, helped me to take a shit, and did his small bit in the struggle for happiness everywhere; and now he comes, forehead high, eyes bright, hands warm. Carefully and gently, tactfully, he carries out the examination, after which he says: "Stalin, old pal, you're as healthy as the whole USSR, and you shouldn't pay any attention to what all these Truvsi-Vovsis and Goettinger-Ettingers tell you." Instead of that, he feels every vein, listens to every cell as though he were trying to decide what I'm dying of. What he's really thinking is that I will die unrepentant. A strange desire, no better than anti-Soviet espionage. After all, he was summoned to deny and not to confirm, doesn't he understand that? A strange sort of deafness . . . must read his book *Pain and Anesthesia* again, maybe a lot of things will become clear then. Maybe I, the great Stalin, as everyone around me here is shouting, am already doomed, and now

I'm all alone again as I was in my school days, with no help and no repentance? "Relieve me of my sins, your Holiness," the patient said faintly in Georgian. No, that's the wrong thing to say, the wrong thing to turn to. . . .

"Did you say something, Comrade Stalin?" Gradov asked.

Stalin emerged from his profound daydream and smirked.

"No, no, you just put me to sleep a bit with your examination, Professor."

"Well, the examination is finished," said the doctor with professional vigor. "And now, Iosif Vissarionovich, the medical staff and I are going to take an electrocardiogram, do an X ray of your thorax and a blood and urine analysis. After that I will need an hour or two to analyze all the data."

"So after the analysis, I can go back to work?" the Leader asked.

"No work today, Iosif Vissarionovich, if possible. The best thing to do would be to relax, read something light, or go to a movie."

"Today you're the boss in the Kremlin." The somber joke was made in a tone that was somehow not joking at all but rather foreboding. Gradov, without replying to this sally—when you have a doctor come, you submit yourself to him, even when you're the king dragon of your country—opened the door to the adjoining room and said loudly, "I'd like a gown for Comrade Stalin! What kind of gown? A warm one would be best!"

The personnel began to bustle about with no apparent purpose.

"Idiots," Stalin said wearily.

Gradov shrugged. Their mutual dissatisfaction with the incompetence of the personnel somehow took the hard edge off of their dealings with each other. Suddenly, one of those wonders that happen in the Kremlin happened: the gown appeared. Only it was not really a dressing gown at all; the general agitation and horror had produced a long, heavy, crimson robe that reached almost to the floor. It did not lower the dignity of the general secretary in any way whatsoever, however; on the contrary, it even raised it. Long garments increase the dignity of a chief; why not return to them?

Together with Stalin, who was led by two lackeys in white, Professor Gradov walked down a corridor of the Kremlin to the treatment room of the infirmary. A whole other crowd of flunkies in white kept themselves at a respectful distance to the rear.

The whole business took some three hours, and then Stalin and Gradov found themselves alone again.

"I have the impression, Iosif Vissarionovich," Gradov began in a kindly but not ingratiating tone—indeed, it was perhaps a bit too far short of ingratiating to be good form—"that the state of your health gives cause for serious concern. In addition to treatment by medications, the list of which I have prepared, I would propose for a sick man like yourself—" At the words "a sick man like yourself," Stalin looked at him like a dying tiger. "—I would recommend measures more serious than medication—namely, a completely new way of life. Your two most serious troubles, Comrade Stalin—that is, I mean your two chief concerns—are colossal hypertension and an excessive level in your body of a substance called cholesterol. Unfortunately, at the moment no medical technology in the world can do an angiogram of the blood vessels with the required precision, but I am afraid that in your case the vessels are distorted because of cholesterol. There are, however, means of reducing this confounded cholesterol, which is ruining your arteries. First of all, you must stop smoking, immediately and for good. Second, you must radically change your diet: you have to avoid animal fat and concentrate on fruits and vegetables. A third important factor is exercise. Under the direction of a special doctor, you should begin daily physical exercise, light at first, and begin a more serious regimen later on. As far as your hypertension goes, you must do everything you can to reduce the strain on your nerves in your daily routine. In other words, you must no longer work the way you are working now. In principle, you should not be allowed to work at all, Iosif Vissarionovich."

"Do you understand what you're saying, Professor Gradov?" Stalin asked, interrupting him and looking at the physician as though it were he who was presenting Gradov with an unfavorable diagnosis, rather than the other way around. "Do you understand what that would mean, for me to stop working?"

Gradov stood up under his stare coolly and calmly. He had already made up his mind. You don't scare me anymore. I'm seventy-six years old, and I'm not going to lose a bit of my dignity. Maybe I'll even manage to raise it a bit. Why should you have any at all at the age of seventy-six? Just think about it, Generalissimo, I need that.

"Whether or not I understand what it means in a political sense has no importance at the moment. I was called here as a doctor, and I will not hold anything back when I announce a medical conclusion, Comrade Stalin."

"That's odd," Stalin intoned, barely able to rein in his anger and disappointment; his guardian symbol named "Professor Gradov" had fallen, vanished, and before him sat a cold and composed (!) man who was almost an enemy. "Odd that the conclusion of an old Russian doctor coincides with the opinion of those two, Goettinger and Truvsi."

"Professors Goettinger and Truvsi, Comrade Stalin, are leading specialists in the domain of cardiovascular ailments, and I regret greatly that I am unable to consult with them now."

Gradov looked with great attention at Stalin's face in which something of the young bandit he had been would suddenly appear from time to time in the course of their conversation. Did he know that the professors had vanished? Had it really been on his direct orders that they had disappeared? It was difficult to read anything on that face except terrible and repugnant power.

Stalin suddenly stood up and strode to the far end of the study, where he stood for some time with his back to Gradov, beneath the painting by Brodsky depicting Lenin sitting amid the folds of furniture covers that resembled the sort of blanket one could use to cover an elephant.

"I don't like the fact that you're studying my facial expressions, Professor Gradov," he said without turning around. "Tell me, what is your opinion of Professor Vinogradov?" he asked, in a momentary flash of humor stressing the "vino."

"Of Vladimir Nikitovich?" Gradov suddenly remembered, inappropriately, that the chairman of the Department of Elective Therapy of the First Med had recently been tagged with the nickname *Kutso*— short-tailed. He was a stutterer, and a speech therapist had recommended to him that when he had a crisis he should repeat the word *kutso* over and over again as a form of self-hypnosis, which he did successfully at lectures, to the great delight of his students.

"Vladimir Nikitovich Vinogradov is an outstanding doctor, a great therapist of our time."

"I won't keep you any longer, Professor Gradov," said Stalin and immediately left the office.

Well, that's it. Boris Nikitovich threw himself back into his chair and closed his eyes. Will I see my home again today? It was definitely subject to question. The expression of unlimited love in the eyes of Archi-medes flashed through his mind. Without saying it in so many words, I showed them I'm not afraid of them any more. They're not likely to forgive such a demonstration. He sat there for several minutes with his eyes closed. No one came for him. Two cleaners rolled a heavy unit into the room—it was a vacuum cleaner. Then Gradov stood up and headed for the door. The sentries in the corridor followed him with the indifferent eyes of human surveillance machines but made not the slightest attempt to stop him or escort him.

In the lower hall, the duty officer silently showed him to a line of chairs at the other end of the room and then took up the telephone receiver and reported something into it under his breath.

Gradov sat in the empty hall for at least half an hour. Following the method he had worked out for himself, he tried not to think about anything and not to change his position in the chair, and thereby to calm the trembling and dizziness that were wearing him down. He used something similar to Vinogradov's method for overcoming stuttering, only, instead of saying *kutso,* he repeated in his mind a random sequence of sounds: "bom, mom, brom, grom, from, som, kom, flom . . ." In this way he could protect himself from external influences and at the same remain present in the world, with the same status as, say, a lily pond.

Suddenly they called him: the car had come. What had come? Where? Why? For whom? Finally it came to him: the car has come for me to take me out of the Kremlin. There was only the chauffeur in the car, who indicated that Professor Gradov should sit in the back. They drove out of the Kremlin through the Borovitsky Gate and for some reason stopped by Manège Square. Two men in black suits got into the backseat from either side of the car, squeezing Professor Gradov slightly and giving off an odor of equine sweat. "Take your hat off!" one of them ordered.

"I beg your pardon?" asked the professor, turning to him.

"Take your hat off, you old fucker!" barked the second and, not waiting for the professor to comply, ripped the hat from the man's head and tossed it onto the front seat. Then they tied an opaque blindfold tightly over the professor's eyes. The car started forward and then moved on for some length of time. The slow phrases of the two men hung suspended like spiders above the swaying lily pond. "Well, what's with him?" "Nothing's with him." "And what's with her?" "What about her?" In addition to seizing Professor Gradov, they clearly also had their own agenda.

The car came to a stop, and the professor's blindfold was removed. He was in the middle of a courtyard that was dimly lit and revealed nothing about itself. They took him into a building and then up in an elevator. The doors opened onto a network of rooms, each one of which was furnished in a nondescript fashion. In one of the rooms, a short, round man with a face that revealed nothing came toward the professor. The tunic with a general's insignia did tell him something, however.

"So they brought this shit," he crowed by way of greeting to the new arrivals. "Throw him over there!" He indicated a couch.

They took the professor beneath the arms and literally threw him onto the couch, causing Boris Nikitovich's hair, which, though entirely gray, had not thinned, to fall down over his eyes.

The general lit a long cigarette, came closer, and put one leg up on a bolster of the couch.

"So, you yes-man for Yids, are you going to confess, or we going to have to beat the truth out of you?"

"Excuse me, but what sort of a way is that to address me?" The Professor raised his voice angrily. "Don't you know that I'm a lieutenant general in the medical corps of the Soviet Army? I outrank you, Comrade Major General!"

The round little general, who looked like a bookkeeper in a building manager's office, listened to this tirade with interest and even nodded, after which he asked, "Tell me, do you want to shit or piss? Come on, let's take a walk down to the john before we have our little talk, otherwise you're going to make a mess right here, in a clean spot."

He suddenly seized Professor Gradov by the shirt and tie, pulled him to himself, and breathed an odor of partially regurgitated vinaigrette from the day before in his face.

"Now, you bastard, I'm going to make you howl in a way Truvsi and Goettinger never did! We'll shove all your medals right up your ass!" Without even realizing what he was doing, Boris Nikitovich in reply seized the general by the padded tits of his tunic and shook him with such force that the latter's eyes, perhaps from amazement or perhaps from the shaking itself, bugged out, while his head bobbed back and forth like a rooster's. Boris pushed the disgusting general away and fell back onto the couch. How is it I'm still alive? he wondered calmly, as if he were on the outside looking in. Where does the body find such unexpected reserves? Something unknown, other than adrenaline, is at work here, obviously.

The general, clearly shaken in a figurative as well as a literal sense, was trying to catch a button that the professor had torn off and that was now rolling along the floor. In all probability, it had been a very long time since the "organs" of state security had received such an affront. The button rolled between the legs of a chair, until it finally came to rest, star facing ceilingward, in the northeast corner. Ryumin—that was his name—picked up the button and put it in his pocket. Well, what am I going to do with this fucking professor? he wondered. The order to beat him has not yet been given, his instructions were only to intimidate. Should I take the initiative myself? Even in my present position it would be risky. Abakumov was higher than me, and look how he ended up.

He stood with his back to the professor and picked up the telephone, without, however, lifting the lever to make the connection.

"Send me Prokhezov and Poputkin! Someone needs to be made to see reason!"

Probably the same ones who brought me in, thought Boris Nikitovich. Or maybe they're different ones. There's no shortage of Prokhezovs and Poputkins in this place. They won't make me howl, though. Yells, shrieks, moans, sobs—these are natural, unconscious reactions to pain. To disconnect one's conscious mind from the expectation of new pain and plug it in to something else, that's the task. Let this be my last experiment.

The door opened. Instead of the expected gorillas, a man in a raincoat and hat entered—Lavrenty Pavlovich Beria in person. He removed his hat, shook some raindrops from it—how had the all-powerful deputy chairman of the Council of Ministers managed to get caught in the rain? Had he really come on foot, or had he been standing beneath a lamppost, daydreaming? He tossed the coat into

Ryumin's hands and, seemingly taking no notice of Professor Gradov, asked, "What's going on here?"

"Well, Lavrenty Pavlovich, this—this professor here doesn't want to have a chat with us," Ryumin began to complain in the tone of a little boy whose feelings had been hurt. " 'I outrank you,' he says, 'stand at attention' . . ."

"That won't do, Boris Nikitovich," Beria said in the kindest of tones, now turning to Gradov. "The Party teaches us to think democratically, to have comradely relations with those beneath us in rank. In addition, this major general, you see—" He pointed at Ryumin with his thumb. "—occupies the post of Deputy Minister of State Security at the present time."

Ryumin froze: What does that mean, "at the present time"? Am I going to be taken off right behind Abakumov? Have they decided to close the file on the "Jewish Case"?

"This man threatened me in the filthiest language," Boris Nikitovich declared. The words of this sentence seemed disconnected to him, suspended in the air and distorted into shapelessness.

"And who was it who tore off my button?" Ryumin suddenly shouted foolishly. Beria looked at him intently, and he immediately had the feeling that this shout might have been the biggest mistake of his life.

"Now, now, friends, are we going to start arguing about 'who started first'? Mikhail Dmitrievich, could you leave us alone for a bit? I have to have a confidential chat with the professor."

His receding chin trembling, Ryumin picked up a folder from the table and went out. Beria looked him up and down—Mishka's off to the bar to refill his tank with cognac—and then pulled a chair up to the sofa and sat down opposite Boris Nikitovich.

"Has it been for a long time now that you dislike Soviet rule, Boris Nikitovich?" he asked in a friendly voice.

"Lavrenty Pavlovich, why do you apply these methods?" Gradov replied in irritation. "I'm seventy-six years old, my life is over . . . you should take all of that into account, after all!"

"Why do you say 'methods'?" responded Beria in a tone that implied that his nobler instincts had been insulted. "I just thought a man of your ancestry and upbringing might possibly dislike Soviet rule. It's purely theoretical, right? That happens sometimes, Boris Nikitovich. A man can faithfully serve the Soviet government, while in reality he doesn't like it. Man is more complex than some think," he said with a look at the door. "It was no secret to us, for example, that your son, even though twice decorated with the medal of Hero of the Soviet Union, didn't like the Soviet government. That is, he didn't always dislike it—sometimes, of course, he did. You know, some prefer blondes, but sometimes they take a fancy to brunettes, even though, when all is said and done, they prefer blondes."

No, this professor doesn't get the joke, thought Beria. You talk to him in a friendly way, and he doesn't even smile. What a wet blanket!

"Let's get down to the heart of the matter, Lavrenty Pavlovich. On what grounds was I detained and brought here?"

"Do you mean they didn't explain?" asked a surprised Beria. "That's very strange. They should have told you at the Kremlin that I wanted to see you. I'll look into why they didn't explain it to you. We in the government, you understand, are very concerned about your conclusion regarding the state of Comrade Stalin's health. Tell me, do you really think he shouldn't work, or is it just your emotional state about, let's say, the general situation?"

"You can think anything you please about me, Comrade Beria," said Professor Gradov with a severity that surprised even himself, he then even defiantly slapped himself on the knee. "I'm in your hands, but I'm not afraid of anything. And you know perfectly well that I'm a doctor, above all a doctor! Nothing is more sacred to me than that calling."

An interesting man, thought Beria. He's not afraid of us. That's odd. That says something. It's too bad that he's so old. If only he were a bit younger! After all, he's not an entirely ordinary man. . . .

"Boris Nikitovich, my dear friend, it's precisely with a doctor that I want to talk!" implored Beria. "How could it be otherwise? You are a great doctor, your services during the war, you understand, were colossal; and every Cheka operative ought to read your book *Pain and Anesthesia*: we're in a dangerous field of work, after all. Comrade Stalin believes in you as though you were his father, and that's why—" At this point, it was as though Beria waved a dark fan in front of his face and emerged from behind it a different person: his glossy jowls had turned to stone and his eyes were blinding. "—that's why we're so worried by your conclusion. To recommend to Stalin, a man who literally is the standard-bearer of peace, to retire is, in my opinion, too bold and too insolent a declaration, Professor Gradov. This isn't some Churchill you're dealing with, after all. We the leadership are horrified. What will the people say?"

These slowly uttered words were more terrible than the hooligan shoutings of Ryumin. Boris Nikitovich, however, remained so cool and calm that he surprised himself.

"I beg your pardon, Comrade Beria, but you don't quite understand the 'doctor-patient relationship.' When I examine Comrade Stalin, he is no more or less than any Ivan or Boris. As far as the political side of the case is concerned, I am perfectly aware of its importance, but I cannot advise my patient to race to his doom."

"He is already . . . doomed?" Beria asked slowly, as though he had taken a strange cat into his hands.

Boris Nikitovich smiled. "I think you understand, Comrade Beria, that every man is doomed. And Stalin, contrary to popular opinion, is a mortal man."

How he talks! thought Beria, and how he carries himself! It's a shame he's too old, and yet . . .

"The state of his health is reaching the critical stage," Gradov continued. "That does not mean at all, however, that he's going to die soon. He can come out of the crisis if he goes on medication and changes his way of living entirely. A diet, physical exercise, and staying entirely away from emotional, psychological, and intellectual burdens—that is, work—for, say, a year. That's all there is to it, it's as simple as boiling a turnip."

Silence reigned for several seconds. Boris Nikitovich's face was blank. No point in putting on a mask, everything's clear, everything has been said. And so that everything will be clearer still, let him notice my contempt. He grinned.

"As for the people, well . . . in the present conditions, the people might not notice the absence of their Leader . . ."

A most interesting man! Beria almost blurted out. Leaving the professor sitting on the high-backed sofa, he walked away to the window. Once there, he flicked his lighter and with relish lit up a sweet-smelling American cigarette. KGB "residents" unfailingly brought him stocks of Chesterfields from abroad.

"And yet you were not always such a steadfast, unbending doctor, Boris Nikitovich," he said slyly from his place at the window, even wagging a threatening finger at the proud man. "I was just going through your file, and I saw something written by our comrades quite some time ago."

Professor Gradov stood up sharply.

"Sit down!" Beria barked.

"I won't!" the professor shouted in reply. What's happening to me? he thought. "Why should I sit down? Issue a warrant and then have me arrested!"

Later on, he tried to analyze his so improbable behavior in the lair of the KGB, and as he tried, in keeping with intelligent habit, to humble himself after all, Gradov decided that in those minutes he must have unconsciously sensed that Beria liked his independence and, consequently, his bravery—but it wasn't bravery at all, but rather something like the stubbornness of a star pupil.

Beria smiled and said in the kindest of tones, "Listen, you old dog prick . . . if this information leaks out anywhere, you goddamned piece of shit, if you tell anyone about our meeting or our conversation, I'll hand you over, giblets and all, to Mishka Ryumin, and you'll swallow your pride along with your guts and your nuts, you pile of goat shit, just like your Jew friends Goettinger and Truvsi swallowed theirs. We'll skin you alive, you asshole, literally!"

He donned his hat and coat and wiped his glasses with his scarf. A kindly smile still flickered on his lips, which had a strange habit of sometimes pressing themselves together and turning his mouth into something like a shark's maw and then opening again like some massive carnivorous blossom.

A most strange man for the Bolshevik government, Boris Nikitovich thought suddenly with perfect calm. He's less like a Bolshevik than almost anything else. There's something Italian about him; he seems like a bandit from abroad. He hasn't even learned to curse properly in Russian. So what's the most frightening secret: Stalin's health or his interest in it?

"We're practically related after all, Boris Nikitovich!" Beria suddenly laughed in his friendliest manner. "Your wife Mary Vakhtangovna is my countrywoman, and it's true, you know, that all Georgians are related to one another in one way or another, even the

Mingrels and the Kartlians have intermarried. Go have a look in our chronicle *Kartlis Tskhovreba* and you'll probably find family ties between the Berias and the Gudiashvilis. No need to shake like that! We're all people, and your wife's nephew Nugzar Lamadze is my closest assistant. You see . . . ha, ha, ha . . . ha, ha, ha . . . that the world is narrow!"

"Yes, it's a small world," Gradov replied by way of correction as well as confirmation.

Beria came up to him and took him by the shoulders in a half embrace. "Come on, I'll take you to your car. Don't be afraid. I'm pleased with your devotion to the Hippocratic oath, you understand . . ."

☆

Now, at the end of his life, there was a cloying aroma around the house of *Nicotiana alata* in the night air, following the rain. The pines, his sisters for life, gently and evenly rustled in the undying wind, at once the youngest and oldest inhabitants of all the nooks and crannies of the earth. In an illuminated window passed the silhouette of his old companion, the only woman I ever loved—well, unless you count a few nurses during official trips. . . . Her spine hasn't become bent, her hair is still in a heavy gray braid and still proudly floats over her breasts, which I once caressed with such rapture, and the left one of which was deformed by a recent operation.

Let's now savor every moment in the old family home, the smell of *Nicotiana alata* and the wind, and look tenderly upon my old ladylove: have I been let back out into life for long? Why doesn't the puppy bark, sensing my presence? No, he's no guard dog. He gets the same affection from my women that the one before him did.

I'll pluck one of these white flowers, bury my long since ossified nose in it, and go up the front stairs, enjoying every step of the way. I'll raise my hand in order to enjoy the sound of the knock on the door of my own home. Archi-medes is barking. Finally! It's me, Archie, your master, Archi-medicus Boris. You see, they've let me out to live a little longer.

Chapter 8

———————— ☆ ————————

"YOU KNOW,
I KNOW YOU!"

"How about it, Grad?" "How'd you do, Grad?" "Hey guys, Grad just passed therapy!" "What'd you get? An 'A'? I don't believe it!" "Come on, Grad, show us your 'A'!" "It's on the up-and-up, guys, Grad's got an 'A' in his grade book!" "Way to go, Borenka, congratulations. We're so glad you sat the exams with us and that you got an 'excellent'!" "You're so famous, you know!" "And so handsome!" "And you have such style!" "Listen, Grad, who was your examiner, Tareev or Vovsi?"

Boris IV Gradov, third-year student at the First Moscow Medical Institute, was also the All-Union motocross champion in the 350cc class, a recognized first-rate athlete and a member of the Air Force Sports Club. "Borya Grad," a young man who was a celebrity in Moscow, removed the abbreviated, short-sleeved white gown from his athletic shoulders with pleasure. At last, the exams were over! And the most exciting thing of all was that there was nothing to make up! "I can't believe you managed to blow through it all in one session, Grad," said one of the students who came up to him, a young man nicknamed "Plus," a boxer at the top of his class who was one of the few students in his class whom Boris treated more or less as an equal.

"A simple Soviet man can move mountains," Boris explained.

All around him, girls were chirping and twenty-year-old young men were speaking in deeper voices that occasionally broke into falsettos. Grad viewed all of this joy, which seemed to him like the frolicking of young calves, with condescension. They're green, these people, just young pods. The young people of the postwar period are suffering from a colossal case of arrested development. One hundred percent virgins, lagging behind in sexual development. One day, when they were looking at one another over their shoulders while a professor was kneading the stomach of a patient, a female student named Dudkin had pressed herself up close to Boris. This girl, with her magnificent figure, should have taken her place at the head of Moscow's trendsetters long ago. Instead, she was trembling at this instinctive contact. In order to encourage Dudkin (who was one of the class Komsomol organizers), he had put his hand on her bottom and even begun inching downward toward the ends of the curves. The girl had practically passed out, for Christ's sake! Had to give her Zelinin drops in a small glass. Ever since then, she's been trying not to notice me, and if I suddenly catch her eye I can read "Tatyana's letter" in her look. It's enough to make you laugh yourself sick.

And here's Komsomol organizer Dudkin now, coming in his direction. Right at the one who devours baby birds. "Borya, are you going to celebrate the end of the year with us?"

He embraced her around the shoulders as if she were one of the guys.

"You know, Eleonora, I'd be happy to, but I'm leaving with the team for the Caucasus in two days."

Her caramel-colored lips trembled touchingly.

"In two days . . . but it's the day after tomorrow that we . . . well, forget it, I was just asking . . . we're just taking up a collection, and—"

"How much are you asking from everyone?" He was already pulling bills from his pocket.

Eleanora Dudkin's eyes sparkled happily. "Fifty rubles."

"Isn't that too much?" he asked, a patronizing note in his voice.

"You don't think the guys will have too much to drink?" He thrust a hundred into the pocket of her lab coat.

"Don't try to teach me how to live, fellow!" she said with slightly out-of-place chic.

It was a line from *The Twelve Chairs*. A copy of the semiforbidden book, a prewar edition with *The Golden Calf* in the same volume, had been making the rounds of the department, and many students now spoke in almost nothing but quotes from the once famous but now almost inaccessible satire by Ilf and Petrov. So that meant that even Dudkin, the top student, had now discovered the lexicon of Ellochka the Cannibal, a satirical character in the novel, just to show Boris Gradov, the hero of her dreams, that she was no slouch and that even if she was at the head of the class she was no "nerd," and that if he'd chip in for the party at Sasha Shabada's a pleasant surprise might await him. It wasn't hard to imagine what this gathering of greenhorns would be like: everyone quoting Ilf and Petrov, a phonograph playing a few records from before the war, and "jazz on bones"—that is, Nat "King" Cole and Peggy Lee copied onto X-ray film—and, of course, dances with the lights off, that is, with a little friendly squeezing.

In theory, I guess maybe Sashka Sheremetiev and I would have been the same kind of children when we were twenty if we hadn't ended up in the commandos, where they did such a god-awful efficient job of teaching us to kill. It was absurd after those years to try to begin all over again, just to blend into the herd of calves, to study the accepted wisdom in order to practice healing when you've already been a specialist in killing for some time, to make virgins like Eleonora Dudkin tremble after sexual training at the Air Force Club. And it was just as absurd to speak in quotations from *The Golden Calf* or to take part in fifty-ruble class parties.

That year, when the courses in internal diseases and general surgery had begun, Boris IV had begun for the first time to see some sense in his studies. For the first time he saw before him not an abstraction but a suffering human body, which needed help and which it was indeed sometimes possible to help. Now the call of the Gradov genes has been awakened, he laughed to himself. It demanded the continuation of the interrupted dynasty. His grandfather Boris III, who had clearly not expected Babochka with his motorcycles to make it into the second year of his studies, had been flattered beyond words when one day during Sunday lunch at Silver Forest his grandson had deigned to ask a question having to do with the treasured domain.

All the same, to be able to take off the white lab coat and throw it in a corner until September was the height of bliss! In two days, an enormous band of motorcycles and service personnel would race off to Tbilisi, the site of that year's All-Union competitions. Several days of riding would be enough to shake the constant alcoholic fog of Moscow from his brain. And then there was Georgia, his ancient motherland, where he had never been . . .

He had been near it, though. The races the previous year had been in Sochi. Sochi, that's almost Georgia. A magical kingdom. The sparkling sea. The Primorskaya Hotel in the "joyful thirties" style on the high bluff above the sea, where the Air Force Club had an entire floor to itself. Something unpleasant surfaced in his memory at the word "Sochi." What was it? Oh, yes, those girls! There's no point in pretending, none of this "oh, yes" business—the supermen of the Air Force had acted despicably toward those girls and their lads.

☆

They were sitting at dinner in a restaurant when the band appeared, six young men with their girlfriends, who immediately became the center of attention. At the time they were a new phenomenon in Soviet society—*stilyagi*. The newspapers were now full of articles about *stilyagi*. Cartoons lampooning them, depicting the *stilyagi* with a long mane and a rooster's comb in an enormous checkered jacket and narrow trousers, sporting a necktie with a monkey design on it and wearing driving shoes with thick rubber soles, appeared everywhere. People quickly learned to whistle in derision at these decaying bourgeois Americanized *stilyagi* and sometimes even applied physical methods of educating them. Maybe this was why the *stilyagi* preferred to show up in groups, so that people would give in to these pedagogical inclinations less often.

The group of a dozen that came into the Primorskaya that night were *stilyagi* of the highest grade; that is, they had little in common with the caricatures of the cartoons. Everything about them had a *stilyagi* bent to it, without being overdone, and perhaps even done with some taste. The Air Force athletes had such tastes themselves, so none of them thought, "Let's have a go at the *stilyagi*!" The girls with them were knockouts, that's why they were the center of attention. They all seemed to be slender and short-haired, with well-applied eye makeup.

"That crowd showed up this morning in three Pobedas," said Chukasov, the hurdler.

"Those cars are their daddies' Pobedas," Gavrilov the swimming coach put in, remembering the cartoon in *Krokodil* that had roused such a fuss, railing at the ungrateful children of prominent parents. It had hit home, it seemed, with many of the readers. Boris even had the feeling that he had met two or three of the lads in the group in a Moscow restaurant. Someone said that these were the sons of the prizewinners out for a good time while Pop was home writing a symphony or papers on metallurgy. Everyone laughed, after which they stopped looking at the young folks and got wrapped up in talking sports. Everything would have gone peacefully if the boss, Vassily Iosifovich, hadn't shown up . . . well, and also if the band hadn't started to heat things up by playing "Gulf Stream" at a racy pace.

Vaska was already thoroughly drunk, and mean. Everyone in the club knew that when he was in this state he started to look for "adventures," to pick a fight over nothing at all and then give someone a punch in the face. One day, however, he had gone too far. Four jet pilots whom he had insulted had waited for the omnipotent son at the hangar that night, thrown a coat over his head, and taught him a good lesson. The next morning the entire division had formed up by their aircraft, expecting to go before a firing squad. To Vaska's credit, however, he had given no sign that anything had even happened to him the night before. He had only moaned a bit, holding on to his sides where he had been beaten and swearing a bit more than usual.

He had not profited by the lesson, though. As soon as he had a bottle of cognac in him, he immediately set off in search of new adventures. Thus, he went right up to the edge of the athletes' table, leaned on it with his fists in the manner of an ataman, and surveyed the young men with ill-tempered eyes. "What the hell are you doing sitting here chewing on your chops, you cocksuckers?" he asked, and then ordered fifteen bottles of cognac from the waiters, who had appeared immediately. The trainers, as usual, were unhappy about this: on the one hand, Vassily Iosifovich gets his boys drunk, and on the other he demands the best results from them. Let's have an understanding, Comrade Lieutenant General: it's one or the other, sports or boozing. But it didn't matter to him; all arguments were useless.

Gradually, as the levels of the fifteen bottles went down, the athletes began to pay more attention to the semicircular hall of the Primorskaya restaurant, outside the windows of which cypress trees swayed as the moon, ever the inspiration of youth, floated by. There was a fat little Jew with red hair and a large baritone saxophone. He and the drummer together were speeding up the tempo of "Gulf Stream." The new arrivals began stomping out a dance to the rhythm, pulling their dates around the floor, tossing them so that their skirts went up in the air, and all with terribly serious, if not dramatic, expressions, as though they were throwing down the gauntlet before the existing order of things.

"Come on, Air Force, let's take their broads away from them!" Vassily Iosifovich said suddenly. "Why are girls like that sitting with those clowns instead of with real men? I tell you, justice ought to be reestablished." Chuckling, the fellows went to invite the girls to dance, simply pushing aside the men who were already dancing with them. Boris IV Gradov, the hereditary Moscow intellectual, joined in with the rest.

Later he would ask himself more than once: What happened to me in those years, why did I sell out to Vaska Stalin's team for peanuts? Maybe he had caught a whiff of the extraterritoriality, of the feeling of belonging to the "musketeers of the king," who defied even the all-powerful MGB and its Dynamo? It must have been some sort of unconscious attempt to revive the spirit of his old saboteur squad, subordinate to nobody except the High Command. One way or another, he was one of the closest cohorts of the Communist "prince of the blood" for two years. He had been the one, in leather from head to toe, to take the ladylove who had been Vaska's since the man's school days, the wife of a famous playwright, away on his own roaring motorcycle. It had been none other than he who had wrested Dynamo's brand-new Belorussian discus thrower away from them. He had been the one who had taken part in Vaska's idiotic practical joke when they had taken a drunk who had passed out at the foot of the Pushkin monument in Moscow and flown him by jet to Kiev, where they had deposited him at the foot of the statue of Bogdan Khmelnitsky and watched, greatly amused, from a distance when he woke up and did not recognize his surroundings. And how many other drunken, mean, unfair, and mocking escapades that made them feel like supermen had they pulled off during those years! Was I born with these inclinations to act like a swine, or did I acquire them during the war years? It was many years later that Boris would ask himself such questions; in the early summer of 1952 he had not yet begun to ask them and only tried to shake off the unpleasant recollections of events connected with the Sochi resort.

Three of the six *stilyagi* turned out to be experts at unarmed self-defense, and one of those three, at the height of the brawl, used a trick Borya Grad had never seen and that laid him out: a kick just below the jaw with the heel of one of his "shit stompers." He had never been knocked out before, even in Poland. He felt himself floating for a few moments to the unceasing din of "Gulf Stream," trying to determine from where in the undergrowth the machine gun was firing, that is, where he should throw a grenade. . . . His opponent, however, was unable to take advantage of this moment. The next second, his own jaw took a blow from Gradov's fist, and he flew over the table and landed out on the balcony, breaking bottles and scattering food everywhere as he went. Boris and another member of the Air Force team—soccer halfback Kravetz, to be exact—rushed at him, but the lad would not give himself up to the enemy. Instead, he leapt up onto the railing, somehow ripping his shirt in the process, then gave a tragic wail and plunged downward, into a flower bed. "Did you hurt yourself?" Boris shouted from above, but the guy was already racing down a tree-lined path in the direction of the water with the militia hot on his heels.

The battle did not last long. The powerful group of athletes did not give the *stilyagi* much of a chance. They dragged the girls off to their rooms. The last thing Boris remembered as he was pulling a blond, blue-eyed, slightly round-shouldered girl out of the heap of infuriated lads was Vassily Iosifovich's hysterical laughter. "What a night, what a night!" exulted the offspring.

In the corridor, the girl was swearing violently, brandishing a lit cigarette and trying to burn Boris's cheek. She had already had quite a few drinks even before the battle had started. In the dark room, she threw the cigarette into the washbasin, burst out laughing, then began to sob, hammering the wall with her fists. Then she turned to Boris. "Well, are you going to screw me, you creep?"

"Don't be a fool," Boris said with a grimace. "What do you take me for, a soldier in an occupying army? If you don't want to, then take off. Just wait until the guys have all scattered."

He lay down on the bed and began to stare at the ceiling, along which were swimming the reflections of the lights of the police squad cars. A few crazed howls could still be heard from the restaurant. As usually happens in drunken brawls, by the end no one remembered who had started it and for what reason; everyone just wanted to fight. The voice of the red-haired saxophone player reached them, singing of rain clouds, hurricanes . . . and love. Then the musician began blowing into his curved horn. He obviously loved his work. The girl quietly sat down on the edge of the bed and began to unbutton Boris's shirt.

The most remarkable thing of all happened the next morning. Boris was in the dining room when three of the *stilyagi* from the night before approached him.

"Good morning," they said.

"Good morning," a surprised Boris replied. He looked around to see what chair he could grab to defend himself with.

"Quite a night last night, wasn't it?" the *stilyagi* asked.

"You mean you're not mad?" Boris asked.

"No, we're not mad. You did it with our chicks, and we did it with yours."

"What do you mean?" Boris asked in astonishment.

The *stilyagi* were only too eager to explain: "Well, when Vasya gave the order to the cops to let us go, we came back here again, and three of your chickies from the swimming team were sitting around a bowl of sour cream. So we picked them up and took them out of there, thanks awfully. When you come down to it, it was quite a memorable evening, Borya Grad! Right, Borya Grad?"

★

As he went down the stairs of the department building, Boris was recalling the faces of the three. Beaten, daubed with iodine, swollen, trembling with servility, the faces of three puppies. What had happened to the gift that yesterday's Childe Harolds had for artistic gloom? They force their friendship on you and then dream up some nonsense about chicks. We're even, they say. They should have smashed a bottle over my head then and there instead of telling lies about sour cream. They're afraid to make enemies of Vasya Stalin's Air Force Club, and so they play up to me and then spin yarns in some dive about how they went whoring with Borya Grad in Sochi. . . .

Bolshaya Pirogovsky Street was flooded with sunshine and outlined by the angular shadows of buildings, as in a Futurist drawing. A smell of young greenery was in the air. As Agasha says, "The forests all come out for Whitsunday." At night, the nightingales sing here. Eleonora Dudkin the dreamer is here to listen to them. The idea suddenly struck him that this street was, in fact, none other than the one that led directly to Novodevichy Cemetery and that along it, obviously, had passed the funeral procession with his father's remains. After a direct hit from an antitank shell, there must not have been much left. At the head of the crowd, a mother in elegant mourning. The American allies, of course, had been marching alongside our bigwigs. "O, woman, you have not yet worn down the heels on which you trudged behind the coffin. . . ." We're all shit: the *stilyagi* from the Primorsky, the Air Force squad, the insolent band—everyone. No one I know, and I'm the worst of the lot, is worth even one of the tires on the old Horch, even if it did serve the SS.

The Horch was waiting for him with morose fidelity at the corner of the side street. Boris put on his sunglasses (an object of particular envy on the part of the Moscow *stilyagi*, something pulled from the bottom of the American paper bag that had come that stormy night) and then took them off right away because he saw a tall officer approaching him at a rapid pace. He was suddenly hit by an unfamiliar and untimely feeling that life was speeding up madly, rather like the sensation you get when you turn the accelerator handle on a GK-1 motorcycle until it refuses to go any further, and the speedometer is already reading over one hundred, and you're afraid the carburetor is going to suck in a piece of the gravel roadway, so you turn off the ignition to keep the engine from overheating, but the motorcycle keeps on accelerating, and for a minute you think it's never going to stop picking up speed and that you're totally helpless.

The colonel was coming toward him. In keeping with the habit he had picked up in the service, Boris looked at his shoulder boards first and only then at the man's face. The insignia of an artilleryman. Gray at the temples, a graying, neatly clipped mustache. Semicircular pouches beneath the eyes, the lithe frame already beginning to acquire the weight that comes with age. The army jacket, unfortunately, only served to emphasize his spare tire.

Colonel Vuinovich (yes, that's him, the very same—my mother's lover!) carried a thick leather folder under his arm. "Boris, they told me which car was yours, and I waited for you here. Do you recognize me?"

"No, I don't."

"I'm Vadim Georgievich Vuinovich. You saw me fairly often when you were a child, but the last time we met was in your flat on Gorky Street in 1944."

"Oh, right! Yes, now I remember you."

"Well, then, hello!" said Vuinovich, extending his hand.

"Hello, indeed!"

Vuinovich, taken aback, squinted at him: Why is he so cold? He didn't pull his outstretched hand back, however, but laid it on the young man's shoulder.

"Listen, Boris, I need to have a private conversation with you. It's urgent."

He was visibly excited. He drew the folder from beneath his arm and began, a bit absurdly, to weigh it on his palm. Now it was Boris's turn to squint, ironically and with hostility.

"What's up, are you going to hand over some artillery secrets to me?"

Vuinovich laughed. "Nothing of the sort. It's much more serious than that. Come on, let's go someplace where there are fewer people walking by, and not as many cars. The Lenin Hills, say."

In the car they were silent. Looking from the corner of his eye, Boris twice caught the colonel's gaze, full of love and sadness. He doesn't have a bad face, this Vuinovich, he thought, surprising himself.

"One of a kind, this car," said Vuinovich. "I used to see them at the front, but not often."

Boris nodded. "It's SS." He was silent for a moment and then, to embellish the story, added, "I seized it in action."

The cupolas of Novodevichy Convent drifted by on their right. They drove across the bridge and soon came to the observation platform built over the floodplain of the Moscow river, over the entire "capital of happiness."

Boris drove on a bit further and parked the car next to a church that, though darkened and disused, was still beautiful, a living representation of the first half of the nineteenth century; just as, in a certain way, Colonel Vuinovich embodied the Russian officer class of the nineteenth century. It was as though some erstwhile rake and duelist had arrived from his run-down estate, a former "superfluous man," no longer very useful even to literature.

They went up to the balustrade. As they walked, Vuinovich was speaking. "Whether you trust me or not, Boris, is your business, but perhaps you know I've been a friend of your parents all my life . . . and you've probably figured out that all my life I've adored your mother."

Boris looked at Vuinovich. The latter, not returning the glance, continued: "I now command a division in the artillery, and we're stationed in Potsdam, near Berlin. You can believe it or not, as you wish, but I had the opportunity there to get in contact with your mother. An old friend of mine from the front, an American officer, arranged it. He was a technical instructor in our unit, teaching us how to use American equipment. He and I ran into each other quite by chance on the street in Berlin a few months ago. It is very dangerous, of course, but things were worse at the front—you know that just as well as I do. In a word, Borya . . . well, the fact of the matter is that I saw your mother just a week ago."

"No!" Boris suddenly cried desperately and clapped his hand over his mouth, as though he were afraid that some impermissible revelation about his childhood might escape.

"She flew from America especially to see me, that is, in order to send greetings through me to you. . . . We met in the Western Sector, in a small, dark beer hall. Our entire conversation took no more than twenty minutes. You have to understand that Berlin is simply crawling with spies, agents from all sides, and all sorts of unpleasant things can happen at any time."

"Tell me the details, Vadim Georgievich," Boris said, already calm. His hands were still shaking, though, when he pulled out a Ducat and lit up.

Vuinovich nodded. "His name is Bruce, this friend of mine, which means he's practically your namesake. In fact, we called him "Boris" at the front. He arranged everything perfectly, and out of purely philanthropic considerations, as far as I could tell. He was waiting for me in a car at the place we had agreed on on the other side of the American border control—they call it 'Checkpoint Charlie.' If someone had followed me from the checkpoint . . . it's strange, you know, how a Soviet colonel can just walk into the West, even though I gave the impression of concentrating fully on business, as though I were on an assignment from the Allied Control Commission. Nevertheless, Bruce and I immediately shook off any possible tail. He had brought a huge coat and a hat. Granted, my Soviet boots were sticking out from beneath the coat, but the streets were dark, so no one paid any particular attention. When he had left me in the beer hall with its wood shavings on the floor, Bruce went to bring Veronika. He was beaming, by the way, this Bruce Lovett—it was obvious that he was imagining himself as the hero of some adventure film. Strange, the twists and turns of psychology, you know: that whole day, I had been terribly nervous, gulping down tablets, and now, all of a sudden, in that bar, I was perfectly calm, savoring a glass of excellent beer, the old, warm overcoat, the sound of the jazz coming from a radio behind the bar. I remember being quite touched as I watched two cocker spaniel puppies playing in the wood chips on the floor. I was sick of the army, I guess, and I was weakened by the illusion of a different life. . . .

"When they appeared, I recognized her right away. She was wearing a raincoat with a belt, and her head was covered with a dark scarf. It was quite cold in Berlin that day, and this whole masquerade of ours seemed quite natural. She came toward me immediately and then took off her scarf. It had been eight years since we had last met—"

"How did she look?" Boris broke in. They were now leaning against the balustrade above the huge city in which he had spent the stormy days of his youth and which for him in those few minutes had simply ceased to exist.

"You know, she'll be forty-nine soon," Vuinovich said slowly. "She hasn't changed much, but she has another kind of beauty now. She asked me to give this to you." He unbuttoned the top buttons of his jacket and from an inside pocket drew out a color photo—not painted or touched up, but a real color photograph, taken on Kodak film.

Everything that came from over there, from the West, always seemed to be from another planet, and now, on a petal of one of these flowers from Mars, on a Kodak color picture, he saw the two dearest and warmest faces from his own world: Mama and Verulka.

The photo showed a group of sweetly smiling people on a bright green, well-manicured lawn with an old white clapboard house in the background: his mother, wearing wide white slacks of light material, her waist as narrow and her chest as high as ever; her husband, tall and lean, with his well-shaped equine face; Verulka, a charming little American girl wearing cowboy pants, hanging on to her new papa's shoulder; and one other person, an elderly man, his jacket over one shoulder, a pipe in his hand, and wearing an expression of ironic good-naturedness.

"Who's this?" Boris asked.

Vuinovich laughed. "You can probably imagine that was my first question, too. She explained that he's an old friend of Taliaferro's, a famous journalist. A year or so ago he was in Moscow as a guest of Ambassador Kennan, and she sent a package with him for you, which, according to her information, you received."

Fear suddenly whistled past Boris's ears: What if he's working for them, what if this is some sort of provocation? Raising his eyes and looking at the colonel, he felt ashamed. An agent provocateur couldn't have such a human, kindly, and melancholy face. You can't put on a mask like that, it's an honest face, one that seems to embody the very ritual of parting.

"You're all she thinks about," Vuinovich continued. "She wormed all the information she could out of me about her Babochka. Unfortunately, I didn't know very much. I had heard about the medical school and read about your successes in sports. All that was new to her. One hundred percent isolation—all this time she hasn't received a single letter from the Soviet Union—"

"Grandma writes to her, though," Boris put in.

"Then they're intercepting the letters," Vuinovich said. "Veronika herself stopped writing a long time ago—she's afraid it could hurt the ones she loves."

Yet another treacherous thought occurred to Boris: Hadn't she been afraid to send a parcel via the channels of American espionage?

Vadim Georgievich, as though he had been listening in, replied to this thought on the spot: "She cursed herself for sending you that package, she said—a lot. The temptation had been too great. She would wake up in the middle of the night afraid, until she found out that everything was all right, that you had picked up the parcel yourself and that no one had seen who had brought it." He fell silent, looking off somewhere over the rooftops of Moscow, and then sighed. "That's the sort of world we live in. Most women who married Allied soldiers during the war, you know, ended up in the camps."

"If you should happen to see her again . . ." Boris said.

"Unlikely, but not entirely out of the question," Vuinovich put in quickly.

"Well, if you're able to write to her, then tell her she shouldn't worry about me. I'm not the little Babochka she used to know."

Vuinovich amicably laid a hand on his shoulder. "I can see you've become a strong lad, Borya. But—"

"Don't worry, there are no 'buts.' " Boris grinned.

It seemed, after all, that there was a bit of that same "Babochka" in him, thought the colonel.

"Tell me, Vadim Georgievich, were you my mother's lover?"

In asking this question, Boris tried to show Vuinovich that he didn't attach any particular importance to it, that it was just for information. He could not believe his eyes when the colonel became flustered, a sort of blush appeared on his cheeks, and something youthful shone through the wrinkles, gray hair, and warts.

What should I say? wondered the pained Vadim. I can't tell him, after all, how long and in what detail I dreamed about being his mother's lover or how pathetic our one and only intimate encounter was.

"No," he said. "I was never her lover, Boris. I've adored her my whole life, it's true. She was my dream in the old-fashioned sense. You know, there's not much truth in all the talk in Moscow about Veronika. In fact, she loved only one man her whole life, your father."

"Everything was so complicated in your day, Vadim," said Boris. "It seems to me that everything is simpler now."

Vuinovich was happy. He hadn't held out much hope for a pleasant conversation, but now here was "Babochka" calling him by his first name, without the patronymic, like a friend, as though he were Nikita. This boy really was very much like his father, enough to create the illusion that time was working backward.

"Let's live another ten years, Boris, and then we'll have a chat about life's complications," he said with a smile.

"Where are you staying?" Boris asked.

"You're not married yet?" asked Vadim.

"Whatever for?" Boris inquired.

"Do you have someone, though?" Vadim asked.

Boris burst out laughing. "So where are you staying? You can come to my place on Gorky Street."

"Thanks. I'd be glad to spend the night under the same roof with you, but there's no time." Vuinovich clearly took no great pleasure at having to return to his affairs. "I have a flight in four hours."

"To Germany?"

"Yes, to the GDR."

"What do you think about—" Boris began and then cut himself off.

"About what?"

"Nothing," replied Boris with a wave of his hand. He wanted to ask "will there be a war with America" but then thought that it would be inappropriate in a conversation with a colonel in the artillery, and one stationed in Germany, at that. And it's a silly question anyway. What does that mean, "war with America"?

"When someone wants to ask a question and doesn't, everything begins to bog down somehow," Vuinovich said after a minute's silence.

Boris grinned guiltily. He suddenly felt he did not want to emphasize his superiority to Vuinovich and display condescension; on the contrary, he wanted to ask some silly questions and to listen interestedly to the answers. Just then a preposterous idea popped into his head: if only, after the death of his father, his mother had married this Vadim, we could have all lived happily ever after.

"Not at all, Vadim. Don't think I'm trying to keep anything from you. It was just that a stupid question about war with America occurred to me."

Vuinovich looked at his watch and laid his bulging leather folder, obviously holding more than it was meant to, on the balustrade.

"War with America is something you and I can talk about later, unless, God forbid, one breaks out. Right now I have to hurry off, and . . . you know, I brought this folder with me just in case—I didn't know if I could trust you. . . . Well, now I see that I can. . . . I'd like you to have all this stuff. . . . These are, you might say, my most intimate archives . . . snapshots, notes, letters, poems. . . . On the whole, it's just sentimentality. . . . I have to leave this somewhere, and there's no one else besides you, Borka. . . . Well, all right, I can see I'll have to explain everything. I'm almost sure, you understand, that I'll be arrested any day now. No, no, it has nothing to do with this business in Berlin. I'm sure they don't know anything about it. It's just that I find myself in the sort of atmosphere that comes before they take you. I sense it in snatches of conversations, in the glances of the secret police operatives, in the questions at Party meetings. It's quite likely that someone in my inner circle is filing reports on my moods, and then . . . well, the case from '37 certainly hasn't gone away. . . . They remember, of course, how I carried myself at the interrogation . . . and in the camp. . . . Of course, they would have destroyed me there if it hadn't been for your father. . . . In a word, my pardon is in question, in spite of all of my decorations and my wounds. . . . There's no getting away from jail or the beggar's pouch, as one of the bits of wisdom of our mysterious people would have it. However, I can't bear the thought that those—" He broke off, then looked Boris in the eye and completed the sentence. "—those filthy rats will rummage around in my papers, in what's most dear to me, again. That's why I'm asking you to take this."

"Of course I'll take it," said Boris.

"You can read what's there, have a look at the photos, everything, with no restrictions. Maybe you'll understand your parents' generation better then."

"Sure, I'll look at them," Boris promised.

"That's great." The colonel sighed. "Now I'm going to get on that trolley and go back downtown, and from there to the airfield."

What a sad life this Vadim had, Boris thought. No triumphs. Constant and hopeless rivalry with my father, a hopeless love . . .

"Listen, Vadim, what's the point in just going back to be slaughtered?" he said. "Maybe you should fight it. Listen here, do you want me to talk with someone I know? He can really help."

A pang of worry showed itself on Vuinovich's face. "Not under any circumstances, Borka! Not a word to anyone about our meeting. Whatever will be will be, no more protection, no more games. Believe me, I'm an honest man, and this is the most important thing for me. My life is going by, and I have no ambition left. The only thing that I dream about—okay, so now I'm going to start telling you about my dreams—is to grow old quietly and to see my aging Veronika—from time to time, only. As a matter of fact, it's a dream about a dream, and no one can take it away from me, anywhere. Well, I'm off. Let me give you a farewell hug!"

They embraced. The army colonel gave off an odor of sweat and cologne. Damn it all, it's really just like saying good-bye to my parents' generation.

Vuinovich ran heavily for the trolley. Before he climbed up onto the step, he turned and waved. His jacket, stretched tightly over his back, emphasized not only the overabundance of his flesh but its flaws as well, chiefly a hollow beneath one of his shoulder blades. What the hell, I guess he really told me quite a lot. I guess he said what I had decided not even to think about.

★

The "farewell to his parents' generation" was not, as it turned out, final: there was still one more surprise waiting for Boris that day. You will agree, dear reader, that such things happen not only in novels, after all. Your days flow by like a current, one after another, containing nothing but routine, nothing but common sense (or the lack thereof), just the humdrum business of living and counting up money (or debts), when suddenly someone hits the accelerator—Boris IV, naturally enough, compared it to a motorcycle—and events began to flash by one after another, as though all they had been waiting for was a day when they could all happen at once. The reader may say that there is no comparison between reality and novels, that in life events occur spontaneously, while in a novel they occur according to the whim of the author; this is both true and untrue. The writer, of course, invents a great deal, yet once having found himself in the snare of a novel, he sometimes catches himself turning into a mere recorder of events, as it were, which are determined in a certain measure not by him but by the characters themselves. The ways of the novel are obscure and capricious at the same time. It is said that some writers, in order to bring order to this bedlam, make up file cards on which the possible actions of the characters are determined ahead of time. We, on the other hand, just ten pages ago, did not even suspect that Tasia Pyzhikov might reappear in our story—and not alone.

Passing under the arch over the entrance to his building with his rucksack containing well-read medical textbooks in one hand and Vuinovich's archives in the other, Boris spotted a woman with a pretty face who looked as though she had just arrived from the provinces, sitting on the chair of the forever absent elevator operator. The first clue that she was a provincial was provided by the frightened expression on her face with its brightly smeared lips, and it was only later one noticed her short jacket with the ruffles on the shoulders. At the sight of the young man entering the gloom of the entrance hall from the sunny world outside, the woman leapt from the chair as though she were a petitioner waiting to see a government minister when suddenly the respected comrade enters the office waiting room. Boris looked on her with surprise, in the manner of a young man brought up properly by his grandmother, even with a slight nod, as if to say, good day, gracious lady. Then he pushed the elevator button. The elevator had already arrived when he heard the agitated voice of the "gracious lady" behind him.

"Comrade, you wouldn't be Boris Nikitovich Gradov, would you?"

He looked at her and saw that she could barely catch her breath in her excitement. Her arms were folded across her chest, her lips were trembling.

"That's me," said Boris, considerably taken aback. "I'm sorry, you're—"

"I've been waiting for you all day," she muttered. The train got in at 6:50, and we came straight here—well, we got lost a bit, of course, but in the end. . . . Oh, I'm not saying the right things at all!"

"And why is it that you've—" Boris began, but she did not wait for him to finish the question. She dashed past the elevator to somewhere at the end of the entrance passage, calling out, "Nikita, where are you? Nikita, dearest, where have you gotten to now? You're breaking my heart!"

Her words flew resoundingly up the staircase. Two cats, one orange and the other dark red (a ray of light refracted through a stained-glass window seemed to color them in those hues), looked down when they heard them. All of this is a bit like a dream, thought Boris. The woman emerged from behind a pillar, the heels of her evidently home-made shoes clattering. She had a rather good figure. She was holding by the hand a boy of six or seven in a cardigan, short pants, and high socks.

"Look, Nikita, it's Uncle Borya!" the woman said. "That's him, the very same Uncle Borya. Come on now and meet him!"

The little boy hid shyly, looking with his small light gray eyes from beneath a sharply sloping forehead, his none too neatly trimmed mop of hair a dark copper shade.

As yet comprehending nothing but already sensing something having great importance for him and his family was going on, Boris opened the door of the elevator. "Come on, let's go up," he said.

"Nikita has never taken an elevator," the woman said proudly for some reason.

"Mama, I don't want to," the boy said in a hoarse voice.

Boris smiled at him. "Don't be afraid." He extended a hand to him, and in sudden eagerness the little boy gave him his small palm.

In the elevator, the woman dabbed at her eyes with a handkerchief. "Oh, what a person you are, what a man you are, Boris Nikito-vich . . ."

When he had opened the door to the apartment and let his guests in, Boris asked, "First of all, what should I call you?"

"They call me Tasia," she said. Suppressed sobs could already be heard in her voice. "Taisia Pyzhikov."

"Come in here, into the dining room, please. Sit here, make your-self at home. I've already more or less figured out who are you, but I still can't believe it." Boris pulled up a chair for himself that turned out to have a box of spark plugs on it. He laid the box on the table, once magnificent but now spotted and grease smeared, and saw a pair of leather trousers lying there in a heap as well.

"Sorry about the mess," he muttered, and thought about how quickly the place always turned into a dump. The nomadic team of racers and their Gorky Street fans left behind all sorts of things, but the most unpleasant leftovers from these get-togethers were the tins of canned fish left open and unfinished that immediately began to give off a powerful stench. And these cigarette butts, where the hell had they all come from? They had been stuck everywhere, crumpled up and as disgusting as drunks one might find beneath the garden fence, producing a stench of their own. Someone had brought a soap dish from the bathroom and filled it with the smelly rubbish. Vera Gorda, who at the beginning of their romance had so zealously set about cleaning up the "Boris stable," had lately lost some of her ardor as a result of certain circumstances in her increasingly complicated private life and dropped by less and less frequently. The apartment, as though it had only been biding its time, had immediately reverted to a garbage dump.

"My goodness, how much you look like him!" Taisia Pyzhikov exclaimed softly. She seemed to have settled down somewhat, though she continued to fold her arms over her quivering chest. As for the little boy, he clearly found the apartment to his liking. His attention was drawn particularly to a Harley-Davidson motorcycle frame, one wheel already mounted and encompassed by numerous other bits and pieces, propped up on blocks in the hallway.

Boris could not take his eyes off the boy. He looked exactly like the photos of his father as a child.

"Have you really already heard about me?" his guest asked.

"You know, Tasia, I didn't come back from Poland myself until 1948, and I didn't know a thing. My grandmother found out something from the staff officers, though. As I understand it, you're the woman with whom Father spent the war?"

She burst into tears. "Yes . . . yes . . . it was me. . . . I was what they called a FW—a field wife—back then. . . . It was even a bit humiliating . . . and we . . . I'm not lying, I swear . . . Boris Nikitovich . . . we really did love each other. . . . I didn't want anything from him but love, after all . . . only to stay by his side, to see to it that everything was clean . . . that he got good hot meals on time. . . . He was such a military leader, after all. . . . Oh, Boris Nikitovich, I've never talked about this to anyone but you. . . . Why, when the NKVD told me to go to Gradov, play the guitar for him . . . how could I have thought everything would go into a whirl like that? . . . that my whole life with him, whom I never forget, would spin around so . . . that he and I would turn out to be so close to each other. . . . I didn't ask him to marry me, you know—I understood that I was just an FW, and you wouldn't believe that I greatly respected Veronika Yevgenievna, his

lawful wedded wife. . . . It was only sometimes when I saw the photographs of you on Nikita Borisovich's desk that I cried a little. . . . So
there you have it. . . ."

"So this young man is my little brother?" asked Boris, in whose
throat a lump was beginning to form as well. His hand reached out
for a saving cigarette.

Taisia sobbed even more loudly. "That means you recognize him,
Borisochka Nikitovich, you recognize him? Who else is he to you, if
not your little brother? After all, I was in my sixth month when he was
killed. . . ."

"Come to me!" Boris said to the little boy, who immediately made
his way from the sofa and climbed up onto the man's knees. Taisia
was by now all but swimming in tears, her clumsily applied eye
makeup was running, her mouth was smeared. She tried to wipe away
all of the blue, red, and black with a silk handkerchief, her shaken face
peering out from behind its lace edges. Still a young and pretty
woman, Boris thought. Seven years have gone by since that time, so
she must be a little bit older than thirty-five. Younger than Vera
Gorda.

"What's your last name, Nikitushka?" he asked the little boy.

"We're the Pyzhikovs," he replied firmly, throwing his small arm
around the powerful neck muscles of the All-Union champion. "Is
that your motorcycle over there? Is it a toy?"

"He should have our family name," Boris said. "He's poured from
the same mold as Papa in childhood. Enough, now, Taisia Ivanova,
enough crying. Tell me what's what now, and you, little brother—"
He gave the little boy a pat on the bottom. "—go over to the motorcycle, just make sure nothing falls on your foot."

Taisia ran into the bathroom to put herself in order. Boris squirmed
as he remembered that in one corner of the bathroom a condom left
from the night before was still lying around. He watched as the little
boy bustled around the motorbike, in deep concentration on something he was muttering. An unfamiliar, warm feeling welled up within
him: now I'll have to look after my little brother, a brother so young
he could almost be my son.

Taisia returned. She appeared not to have noticed anything. In any
case, her expression was serious. Well then, what should she tell him?
The everyday life of an ordinary woman. After the marshal's death,

she had gone to stay with her sister in Krasnodar, where she had been born. She had worked in the clinic of a medical school, her experience in the Far East helped her to reestablish her qualifications quickly. She had met an interesting man there, an internist and musician by the name of Ilya Vladimirovich Polikhvatov. He had a coloratura tenor voice and sang in the opera at the Medical Workers' House of Culture. An encouraging, hopeful man, pure of heart, he had never been angry when her thoughts had turned to sad reminiscences. I respect you for your memories, Taisia, he would often say to her. And his attitude toward little Nikita was one of the utmost fairness. That year, he had divorced his wife and they had signed the marriage register. Naturally, there had arisen the question of where they were going to live: get into line for an apartment and you'll grow old waiting, you won't live to see your turn come. They could buy a little house in the suburbs, but "finance can get in the way of romance," all the more since child support payments took such a bite out of Ilya's salary. Then they had had the idea to move up north, specifically to Taimyr, where in three years they could earn the sum required. Doesn't seem like a bad idea, right? What should we do with Nikitushka, though? You can't drag a growing little boy off to the land of permafrost and polar nights! Then Taisia had remembered this flat on Gorky Street, which she had walked by in tears so many times after the war was over, already pregnant, and watched as the absolutely magnificent Veronika Yevgenievna would come out of the building. Maybe Boris Nikitovich, an All-Union champion, could find a place for Nikitushka in some boarding school, provided he would acknowledge him as his half brother, of course. She had seen Boris Nikitovich's picture in *Soviet Sports,* and he had seemed to her like a young man of substance. . . .

"That's a brilliant idea!" Boris exclaimed at the end of her story. "Really, Taisia Ivanovna, you couldn't have thought of anything better!

He jumped up and began to run around the apartment, banging the doors of cupboards, rushing to the kitchen and then back again. Though she didn't understand what he was running for, Taisia Pyzhikov realized that, once again, something had picked her up and cast her not particularly wonderful life onto the crest of a wave, even if not for long, even if for only a moment. Glory be to thee, O Lord, she thought, that I saw his picture in *Soviet Sports*. Boris, meanwhile, was still bustling about the apartment, trying to see if there was any food around. Finding almost nothing, he burst into the dining room where Taisia was sitting like a blissful child, the color back in her cheeks.

"Let's go!" he shouted. "We'll think up something for dinner! Where are your things, Taisia Ivanovna? At the Kursk Station? We'll figure out something! Where are you now, Nikitushka-Kitushka?"

He had not felt this sort of enthusiasm for a long time. What's happening to me? he wondered, looking at his excited reflection as it flashed by in the mirror. Some deep feeling of clannishness, joy that the Gradov family has been added to?

Nikita crawled out from behind a bookcase, a pair of boxing gloves hanging around his neck, and dragging one of Boris's dumbbells in his hand.

"Nikitushka-Kitushka was what my father was called when he was a child," Boris explained to the happy Taisia.

★

Well, one could imagine no greater gift for a little boy than a ride around Moscow in a big foreign car with a reserved roar! Nikita, standing tall behind the driver's back, kept yelping and casually mussing his mighty brother's hair. I could adopt him myself, thought Boris. The law permits formal adoptions of that sort. The important thing is that the kid should be a Gradov, not some Polikhvatov from the provinces. When they had retrieved her things from the baggage checkroom and stocked up at the delicatessen on Smolensky—sturgeon, salmon, caviar, ham, smoked meats, chicken, dumplings, candies and cakes, the best the flowering commerce of the capital could offer in those days—they went back to the marshal's flat. "We're going to have a feast! We're going to have a feast!" exulted little Nikita. Taisia Ivanovna was clearly in her element; her hands worked magic. It was not long before a dish of cauliflower was steaming alongside a dish of dumplings, themselves steaming in appropriate measure, and all the delicacies were arrayed in sumptuous fashion in immaculately washed dishes.

After dinner, Taisia Ivanovna turned to the master of the house, and said shyly, "Boris Nikitovich, how would it be if I get this place into order a bit? No, no, I'm not tired at all—in fact, it would be a great pleasure to tidy up this flat."

Unable to believe his eyes, Boris looked on as Taisia, who had donned a housecoat, raced zealously around the apartment, throwing her energies at the corners Vera Gorda usually called "places where no decent person would set foot."

A lucky man, this Polikhvatov the tenor and activist, thought Boris. The kitchen, the home, brushes and soap suds—all of that was clearly her calling! In the meantime, Nikita took him by the hand and led him from room to room, asking questions: What's this? And that? That's a globe, Nikita. And that big light is called a floor lamp. This is a barometer, it tells you what the weather is. This is a spare-parts drawer, my dear friend. These are pistons, and these are washers, they're serious stuff. This, my friend, as you've probably guessed, is the skeleton of a man—your big brother studied the anatomy of bones with it. These are from the animal world: the skin of a Usurian tiger. Some say it was your father who shot it, others say it was Vaskov, the chauffeur. That's an encyclopedia, Nikita, en-cy-clo-pe-di-a, put it back in its place. And now take a close look: this is a picture of mar-shal of the Soviet Union Nikita Borisovich Gradov, your father and mine. That's right, he does have a lot of medals. Well, count them yourself—how many medals? You only know up to ten? Well, then, how about if you count how many times ten there are? That's right, three times, and three foreign crosses—that makes thirty-three medals altogether. And this is a television. What's a television? Ah, you still haven't seen how a television works!

The latter object, a monstrous box with a tiny screen and a convex water lens, made an overwhelming impression on Nikita. No sooner had the ballerinas of the Bolshoi Theater with their little legs as short as the Japanese and their slightly blurry heads come through the lens than he flopped down onto the carpet and did not take his eyes off the enchanted spectacle until he fell asleep.

The sounds of energetic housecleaning continued to reach Boris for some time as he spoke on the telephone with Gringaut, then with Karol, and then with Cheremiskin. In great detail, and with the aid of the most muscular expressions in the Russian language, the motorcyclists were discussing the next day's "Caucasian haul." It was decided they would all leave the city on their own and that the rendezvous point for the caravan would be Oryol.

When he finally got off the phone, Boris was about to put out the light when Taisia Ivanovna came into the bedroom after knocking gently. She showed no signs of fatigue; on the contrary, the little lady seemed blissfully radiant.

"Well now, Boris Nikitovich, may I be so bold as to assure you that you won't recognize the public conveniences," she said in a tone of solemn triumph.

"The public conveniences?" he asked in some confusion.

She laughed. "Well, yes, this isn't a communal apartment, after all! You're sitting in this palace all by yourself! I meant the bathroom, the toilet, the kitchen, the pantry. . . . Just come and see, come on, do!" She put her little fingers around his wrist and tugged slightly. "Come and look, Borisochka Nikitovich!"

Suddenly a sweet feeling of attraction passed from his hand through the rest of his body. That was all he needed. . . . He took his hand away.

"I believe you, I believe you, Taisia Ivanovna! Anyone can see right away that you're a fine housekeeper."

She looked over the walls of the bedroom. "Of course, you can't set everything straight in one night in such a palace. If we weren't in such a hurry, Boris Nikitovich, I'd stay here for a week and really put the sparkle back into the place. You've probably read the novel *Tsushima*, haven't you? This is how the admiral used to inspect the cleanliness of the ship: he would take a snow white handkerchief from his breast pocket—" She imitated the admiral drawing out his hand-kerchief. "—and wipe it on the deck." She bent down to show how the admiral had inspected cleanliness and looked up at Boris.

Heat once again coursed through his body. That's all I need . . . no, it's not going to happen, it would be too much even for an animal like me. . . .

"Surely you're tired, Taisia Ivanovna? You must be dead tired after a day like today, eh? There's a second bed there in Nikita's room, it's quite comfortable. . . ."

"I'm not tired at all, Boris Nikitovich. I'm not the least little bit tired. I feel so much joy today, Boris Nikitovich, and I'm so grateful to you that you acknowledged Nikita and took me in. . . ." Sobs welled up in her throat again, and, seemingly so as to prevent them from bursting forth, she quickly took off the housecoat, flung it away, and stood there in only her underclothes. "I just don't know how to thank you, Borisochka-dearest-Nikitovich." She sat down on the bed with her back to him and said, "Unhook my bra, Boris Nikitovich."

A fairly long time passed before they had gone through all of the classical positions that Boris loved and uncoupled from each other.

"Now I'm tired, Boris Nikitovich," she whispered. "I can't move my arms or legs anymore. . . . Oh my, it's been a long time since I've been this tired. . . .'"

So now you've got yourself one more mama, you idiot, thought Boris in annoyance, at the same time as he tenderly stroked Taisia Ivanovna's disheveled chestnut brown hair.

"Thank you, Taisia Ivanovna, thank you for your tenderness. Now, please go into the room where Nikita is. Or would you like me to carry you in my arms?"

"I couldn't even dream of that," she murmured.

He lifted her up and carried her to the other bedroom, once a child's room, where in fact the newest Gradov child was now sleeping. Putting her head on his shoulder, she continued to mutter her gratitude. When they entered the room, Nikita suddenly sat up in bed and immediately threw his head back down onto the pillow. Boris laid Taisia Ivanovna on the second bed and covered her with a blanket. She fell asleep instantly.

It's a good thing Vera didn't show up that night with her key the way she often does, thought Boris as he returned to his room. Another dramatic scene would have broken out. For some reason she's allowed to be jealous, but I'm not supposed to ask her about anyone, especially not her husband. As a matter of fact, she told me about her husband herself, I didn't have to worm it out of her.

★

You know, he's a man who's been deeply hurt, just an overgrown child, Vera suddenly began to recount one day. His parents are in the camps—that is, his father is in a camp and his mother is in internal exile, but he invented a fictional biography so that he could graduate from the Moscow Aviation Institute, where he was studying. Now he has a classified job, you know, in a place with only a postbox instead of a name, and he trembles for fear that everything will come to light. For that matter, he's scared of everything around him, and of me, too. When we got married, it was a month before he slept with me, he was so afraid of his shortcomings. He got drunk, acted like a boor, made scenes. . . . Oh, you can't imagine how much he hurt me. Now, though, everything has gotten better; he's more of a human being, kinder in all respects. I'd wanted simply to throw him out, you see, but now I feel sorry for him somehow: he is my husband, after all. His friendship with that pal of yours, you know, "Lord Byron," exercised a positive influence on him, I mean that one-of-a-kind Sasha Sheremetiev.

"I beg your pardon?" Boris asked in amazement.

"Well, of course it's him," the star of the nightclub stage said with some embarrassment. "You know him—Nikolai Umansky, the one they still call 'the Giant.' "

After this unexpected confession, a sort of distance grew up between Boris and Vera, into which entered not only "the Giant," but Sasha Sheremetiev and all of the other members of the Dostoevsky Circle as well. It seemed to Boris that he and Vera were pushed apart not only by her warm feelings for her hapless husband but also by her indirect involvement in the Circle.

Over the past year he had been at their gatherings several times, and more than once one had sensed a certain reservation in his presence. The "Dostoevskyites" obviously didn't take him, his motorcycles, and his apartment on Gorky Street seriously. Just once did he invite the group to meet at his place (when they were reading and discussing the banned novel *The Possessed*), and the invitation had been flatly refused by everyone, even Sasha. It's not likely that they take me for an informer, but all the same they obviously don't trust me, since I'm one of the "golden boys." Well, to hell with them, thought Boris. I can get to know Dostoevsky's books without them, after all: Grandpa has a set of the collected works in the Academy edition. I can do without these "thinkers and poets" too—all they do is drink and open up cans of European whitefish in tomato sauce and then wave forks at one another!

The only thing that hurt was that he and Sasha had parted ways. He shouldn't have thought Sasha would last long as a personal trainer, given his pride, which was nothing less than Homeric. One day Sasha had said to him, "Your Air Force Club, Borka, is nothing but a dirty palace stable, and I don't want to have anything to do with it!" It turned out that he had already found a job as a security guard in a book warehouse.

"Sashka, your passion for the printed word is going to be the ruin of you one day," Boris had told his friend.

Sheremetiev had laughed loudly: "You've read the coffee grounds accurately, you son of a bitch!"

To tell the truth, Boris had never had time in his hurried life to figure out the psychology of this man, whom he had once lowered on the remains of his parachute straps from a burning building on the point of collapsing in the Old Town section of Warsaw and whom from that time he had come to consider almost his brother. The despondent pose Sasha had adopted now seemed to Boris to be a role he was playing, a modern variation on the "superfluous man," a combination of a character from Byron and Dostoevsky's "underground man." Quite a few girls simply adored him, swooning and shaking as soon as the limping figure with the black beret cocked at a rakish angle appeared on the horizon. From time to time, he would condescendingly arrange "visitation rights to his body," as he put it, but he would not consider a serious involvement, like Boris and Vera Gorda's romance, with any of his admirers: there was something in Sheremetiev that would not allow for romance.

☆

One day he disappeared from Moscow. He was gone for a month or two, and when he returned he invited Boris to come over and "belt down a few," as he put it. The first thing Boris noticed when he entered Sasha's tiny room was a human skull on the shelf among his books. Having become accustomed to such things as teaching aids in recent times, he was not surprised, but then he reflected that Sheremetiev had nothing to do with anatomy lessons. "What sort of novelty is this you've got, Mr. Sheremetiev?" he asked. They had gone back to addressing each other formally, perhaps out of inertia, perhaps out of snobbism. In order to impart a natural touch, though—or perhaps it was to be even more snobbish—they always tossed in a curse word or two: "What the fuck sort of novelty is that?"

"It's her," Sheremetiev replied, in a matter-of-fact tone, and then was silent, engrossed in removing the wire wound around the bottle's cork. A rosé wine called "Tsimliansky Bubbly" had become fashionable lately as a warmup to the basic drink, that is, vodka.

"What does that mean, Sasha, 'her'?" Boris asked. "Stop fucking around, sir, and tell the story: it's why you got me to come over, isn't it?"

There then followed a story that had a certain pathological quality to it and that was told in tones of measured indifference. It was the skull of Alexander Sheremetiev's first love, a nineteen-year-old radio operator named Rita Bure. They had loved each other like Paolo and Francesca, even though they were both at a major intelligence center near the Korean frontier. It was Rita, in fact, who had become the apple of discord between the young lieutenant and Colonel Maslyukov. The old goat had been wanking off with her with all his strength, calling her every day to come to see him and to sit on his cock. He was the one who had banished Sheremetiev to Iturup and forbidden Rita to follow him under threat of court-martial. In all probability she had given in, and the colonel had just gone on torturing her and using her for his lewd fantasies. Then something had happened between them. A fellow who had already been in Moscow and told Sheremetiev the whole story was of the opinion that Rita must have rebelled fiercely and made an attempt to free herself of the scum, who had then begun to blackmail her. One day he had gone to a Komsomol meeting and accused the girl of having relatives abroad, saying that there was a White Guard branch to her family and that she had concealed this when she filled out the biographical data forms. After that, everything had gone according to the usual pattern: a summons to Special Affairs, interrogations . . . they had been waiting only for the go-ahead from District Military Headquarters to arrest her. It had also been known at the infirmary that Rita was pregnant. In short, she had disappeared from the face of the earth; according to the official version, she had run away into the taiga and there committed suicide. Some time after, her beloved Sasha, who himself had virtually played out this far-eastern version of *Romeo and Juliet* by shooting himself in the side, seemingly on the very day she had vanished, had showed up at headquarters, and it was then that Colonel Maslyukov had turned out to have too fragile a jaw.

They say everything becomes overgrown with legends, but by "everything" they probably have just nonsense in mind. Love and crime do not become overgrown with indifferent myths. Not a day had gone by that Sasha Sheremetiev hadn't thought about Rita Bure and Colonel Maslyukov. It was as though he had known that the story wouldn't end there. Sure enough, three years later, there had appeared before him a fellow with whom he had graduated from the language school. His former classmate, who had just been discharged, had told him a version of the story, which, as it turned out, had existed three years before but which had remained unknown to Sheremetiev because everyone had been bleating like frightened goats. That's how things had turned out. . . .

"So what happened next?" asked Boris, trying to remain as cool as the storyteller. The skull, clean and lusterless, now sat on the table between an empty bottle of Tsimliansky and a nearly empty bottle of Moscow Special. The mandible was neatly bound with wire.

"Is it worth telling the rest?" Sheremetiev said, looking him in the eye.

"Whom are you going to tell it to if not to me?" Boris smirked.

"Well, all right, listen, Mr. Borka, but don't go complaining later on about how I put fear into the heart of an unspoiled Soviet sportsman. I dug my pistol out of its hiding place and headed east. From Blagoveshchensk, I made my way through the forests for a week into the forbidden zone. I saw Maslyukov in the morning, when he was taking his younger daughter to school. A positive father figure, the model paterfamilias, they'd fixed his jaw, he was puffing on cigarettes, giving lessons to his daughter. . . . On his way back from the school, I dragged him into the bushes. When he came to his senses, I said to him, 'I think you know now that I'm not kidding. Stand up and show me where you buried Rita.' To be honest, I don't know why he was so diligent about leading me to the spot; maybe he was waiting for the moment when he could run away or disarm his kidnapper. He talked a lot of patriotic stuff, appealed to my Komsomolist's conscience. We walked nearly the whole day, and then, in front of me like a mirage, amid some fallen trees, a swampy pond opened up, and beyond it a hillock with three fir trees and a deep hole facing east. And Maslyukov said, 'Here lies the spy Bure, and here I often sit, remembering what she was like.'

"The grave, Borka, or rather the pit had long ago been dug up by animals, so you don't have to think that I lost my marbles completely and began to dig like a vampire. I simply took this object that you now know so well through your studies and that is now looking at us with eyes as empty as the universe. It was in the same state it's in now, I only gave it a good wiping with my raincoat."

"What about Maslyukov?" Boris asked.

"There is no more Maslyukov," the prone Alexander muttered, his hair dangling above the ashtray. Then suddenly he sat up and slammed his fist on the table. "What do you want?" he shouted. "Was I supposed to play out some sort of scene of Christian forgiveness or shed a tear with a killer over our object of mutual passion?"

"Stop yelling!" replied Boris, slamming his own fist down on the table in his turn. "Don't you understand that you don't yell about things like this?"

The two loud blows had disrupted the harmony of the table. A dark bottle rocked back and forth and then fell down on the carpet, but it did not shatter. The clear bottle rocked as well, but it was caught in time, emptied into a glass, and then thrown onto Sheremetiev's breeding ground of a bed with a mirror at the head and a decadent portrait of Leda and the swan carved into the wood.

"I'd like to know how much truth there is in that yarn," Boris said in exasperation.

"I don't know," Sheremetiev replied with a wily squint. "Sometimes I put my hand on this skull and it seems to me that these are the very same bumps I used to touch when I was stroking her beautiful face. I'm just sure these are exactly the same bumps. . . . That means she's always with me. At least I've been able to do that, even though I was completely helpless and abandoned—to unite her dust with mine. . . ."

"Listen here, Sashka, aren't you going a bit far with this act?" Boris felt his irritation growing for some reason. "Doesn't it seem to you that you're trying to outdo all of Dostoevsky's heroes? You guys are going over the top with this Circle of yours. You know, I read not too long ago that Dostoevsky himself was sentenced to death for belonging to his circle and that they had already put the sack over his head, and times were very different then. Have you heard about that?"

"Well, what do you think?" Sheremetiev asked haughtily, with the skull in his hands. "Do you really think we didn't know about the mock execution on Semyonovsky Square? As you know, we took the Petrashevsky Circle as our point of departure and swore on that sack that we wouldn't lose our nerve."

"Aha!" Boris exclaimed. "I see this club isn't only for educating yourselves, then!"

"Go fuck yourself, Mr. Borka," Sheremetiev replied with a dismissive wave. "You still have a schoolboy's approach to reality. That's why all the guys avoid you like the plague. Your thing is racing motorcycles, not—not reading Dostoevsky."

Cursing himself for his irritation at such an inappropriate moment—whether the cause had been a strange envy for Sheremetiev or annoyance with himself for an absence of such deep and terrible hollows in his unconscious—Boris stood up and took a step towards the door. Then he suddenly laid a hand on Sheremetiev's shoulder.

"Forgive me, Sashka, for not entirely believing your story. Maybe you're right—I've developed some sort of frivolous and outrageous way of thinking that comes with being involved in sports, or some sort of insolence as a result of belonging to the Air Force Club. I wanted to ask you, however: can you remember a single instance when I lost my nerve or betrayed anyone?"

"No, I can't," came Sheremetiev's gloomy reply.

On that note they parted. Their friendship, it seemed, had been reaffirmed, yet neither of them was particularly eager to meet again.

☆

Remembering this recent conversation now, on the night before taking off for the Caucasus, Boris was wide awake. He couldn't sleep a wink. He was pacing around his bedroom listening to the faraway snoring of his dear guests, when all of a sudden his eyes fell on the bulging leather folder he had received that morning from Vuinovich, lying in a corner. He tossed it onto the bed, flopped down beside it, undid the clasps, and then instantly, unexpectedly, laid his cheek on the folder and fell asleep.

☆

The garden was shrouded in fog, but the sun was already up. "I will arise on a foggy morning, and the sun will strike me in the face"; it was just this sort of morning that Alexander Blok had had in mind. The words really were unforgettable. Mary Vakhtangovna was trimming the hedges with garden shears and attaching weighty roses to the fence. Archi-medes was sitting on the front porch, occasionally following the flight of fat bumblebees with his eyes.

Mary suddenly had the sensation that she had been trimming the hedges in this way for fifty-odd years and would perhaps continue to do so until she got to be a hundred. A woman trimming hedges and making up bundles of roses had been a favorite subject of the Impressionist painters: *un impression de la vie,* or perhaps it would be better to say *un impression de l'existence.* From far away through the sunlit fog hanging in the air and the ever-present cackling of rooks, she could hear the bells of a hansom cab. Dear Bo already coming back from his rounds? I beg your pardon, a hansom cab? It was just a trick the barometric pressure and her past life were playing. When you think about it, how are the shouts of the students at the *gymnasium,* racing on their bicycles along the tree-lined walk of Silver Forest, different from . . . I beg your pardon, what students? There are no more *gymnasia.* Now the fog is rising again, and everything is back in its place.

Beyond the fence, a car snorted to a stop. Was it Bo coming from the commissariat? My God, there are no more commissars, ministers have come back. . . . The gate opened, and a young man appeared on the walk: Nikita II, Boris III? . . . No, it's Babochka, our fourth, the one and only!

"Merichka, I've brought you a surprise!" her grandson called out. Archi-medes was on the spot right away, running in circles and jumping up onto his favorite young man, who took him by the collar. A look of surprise of the human, two-legged variety froze on the dog's face.

Meanwhile, the delicate hips of a lace maker passed through the gate; that is to say, an unknown woman who belonged to that type that was always classified as "boutique seamstresses" was approaching. She was holding by the hand . . . yes, yes, she's already bringing him up, pushing him gently, presenting a hedgehog of a little boy with a broad forehead and light gray eyes, my little boy. . . .

"Kitushka!" cried a delighted Mary Vakhtangovna, and the little boy immediately ran to her.

The sight of this picture made Archi-medes give a yelp that sounded almost indecent coming from a keen-eared watchdog whose size gave nothing away to the legendary Indus, the dog who with his master Karatsupa so vigilantly watched over the borders of the Soviet Union.

☆

"So there's your boarding school for Kitushka, Taisia Ivanovna," Boris laughed. "Believe me, you won't find a better one. And now permit me to offer my excuses. I don't have much time, because I'm leaving today for a competition in Georgia. I hope we'll see each other again, and more than once."

"You're embarrassing me, Boris Nikitovich," she said, blushing.

"I can understand my father very well now," he said, lowering his voice slightly.

"You really are embarrassing me, Boris Nikitovich," she whispered happily.

On that note they parted.

☆

He returned to Gorky Street and began—must hurry! must hurry!—to throw his things in a knapsack. The knapsacks will go in the sidecars as far as Oryol, and then they'll be loaded onto the club's bus. Any of the boys who like speed will take their place in the sidecars or on the backseat. We've got to get out of Moscow as early as possible—it's nearly another two thousand miles of road after Oryol, and what a road! Wait a minute—my classmates are waiting for me at their party this evening. Eleanora Dudkin has probably been on the verge of fainting all day. But stop! There's been quite enough of this business of women and girls, even too much. The competition is about to begin, and I'm taking a vow of celibacy!

He went into the bedroom to pick up shorts and undershirts and saw Vuinovich's leather folder on the bed. Should I take it along? No, it's impossible: the Devil only knows where it might turn up and what nosy types might start asking questions. He opened the folder, took a black package of the kind used to hold photographic paper from one of its pouches, dumped the snapshots out onto the bedspread, and immediately forgot about competitions, motorcycles, and the road, that very same road on which Alexander Pushkin had raised the dust as he tried to catch up with the expedition of Count Paskevich before they began storming the Turkish bastions.

My God, it was Veronika, a thick braid brought forward onto her chest. She couldn't be more than eighteen here, the hair on her temples taut but nevertheless slightly frizzy; it was an enchanted glance full of the expectation of a wonderful life. The photo had in all likelihood been taken even before she met her handsome young officer. Sure enough, an inscription scrawled on the back of the photo in pencil read "June 1921" Thirty-one years ago! His parents had met in the Crimea in 1922, hadn't they? I wonder how Vadim managed to get hold of this photo, Boris thought. He had probably been nonchalantly looking through the album and then, when the lady of the house wasn't looking, had pocketed it. There were other probably stolen keepsakes as well. Or maybe he had taken a picture of the beautiful girl himself? It was hard to imagine an officer with a camera in that era. Here was a photo from the Crimea: a group of holidaymakers in a small inlet, on a pebble beach, their naked bodies burned by the sun. Mother for some reason was wearing a white dress. There must have been a wind, she's holding down her skirt, though why would she want to hold it down when everyone around her was nude? What a girl she was! I wouldn't have left her alone if I'd been born in those days to another woman; that is, if I'd been the same at the moment this photo was taken as this laughing fellow stripped to the waist and wearing baggy army trousers, that is, my father.

Now, this photo Vadim must have gotten entirely on the up-and-up, because the three of them were in it. This was obviously a training ground: a tank in the preposterous design of the period was in the background as a platoon of Red Army soldiers marched by. Veronika was in the foreground, leaning back on the shoulders of the two officers Vadim and Nikita. Her hair was cut quite short here, she was trying to look like a movie star. She was always playing at being a movie star, sometimes for a joke and sometimes seriously.

Boris began to stick the photos back into the packet: if I start looking through the whole show, I won't go anywhere for days. I have to leave it all at home and go through it carefully when I get back, and maybe then I really will manage to get something out of the lessons in love gone wrong. As he was putting the packet back in, a thick notepad fell out and flew open to a lined page, where he glimpsed a verse from a poem:

> Forget her now, the moment's not yet come,
> He whispered in the hospital, a maze of cells.
> Love is not the best thing to be hung
> On a soldier's ammunition belt.

It looked like a diary. Poetry alternated with lines of writing, and dates near the end of the war flashed by. A small, triangularly folded letter with an address written on it in indelible pencil that had in fact almost faded away was attached to one of the pages with a paper clip. On the page was a notation from April 1944: "I'm writing in the air on the way to the front. What grief this unexpected and, it would seem, happy meeting has brought me! Again I failed to deliver this ill-fated letter. One more burden is lying on my heart. This greeting, more than likely the last, of that poor man—how many years has it been following me since Khabarovsk? Then again, it's undoubtedly better that the triangle be left with me than being seized at N.G.'s flat. With my experience, it is not difficult to guess how the unfortunate man managed to throw the folded letter through a grating on the prison car, having almost no hope that it would reach its destination. Nevertheless, this 'almost' turns out to be a decisive factor in such a case—he crawls on top of his comrades to the tiny window and throws it. What difference does it make, whether his hope was great or small? Hope, perhaps, cannot be measured according to the usual standards. And once again I did not deliver it, and tomorrow I will have forgotten about this letter. And this is the way it is in all things: we fight bravely, and we seem magnificent to ourselves, but as soon as the bullets stop flying, we turn out to be dogshit."

Boris took the yellowed triangle, folded from a piece of graph paper from an arithmetic exercise notebook, and turned it over in his hand repeatedly. The address was still legible: Strepetovs, 8 Ordynka Street, Apartment 8, Moscow. He looked at his watch: well, why not, a short detour—have to do at least something that's not for myself, even if it's only a small thing like this. . . .

★

The entrance hall of the yellow building, naturally, smelled of cats; the elevator, naturally, didn't work; and naturally the tiled mosaic on the floors was crumbling. A child was playing alone on the third-floor landing, building something out of whatever rubbish came to hand: fruit drop boxes, hair curlers, the remains of a small kerosene stove, rolls of film. . . . "You wouldn't be one of the Strepetovs, would you?" Boris asked. "Fifth floor," was the child's indifferent reply.

"Strepetovs: two long rings one short" said a narrow strip of paper among dozens of others like it. Boris always felt guilty when he came to a communal apartment: after all, he occupied a space that by Moscow standards would have accommodated no fewer than fifteen or twenty people. In the end, he said to himself to ease his conscience, the flat's not mine, it belongs to the ministry. They could boot me out at any moment, if they decide, say, to open a museum to the marshal there or, more likely, give it to some bigwig; why not live in it for the time being?

At first, the door opened a crack on a small chain. A hoarse woman's voice asked out of the darkness, "What's your business?"

"Good day," Boris said. "I've come to see the Strepetovs,"

"What's your business?" the voice repeated. The face, with a cigarette hanging from it, moved closer to the chain. Boris unexpectedly found eyes of a clear blue looking at him.

"No particular business," he shrugged. "I've just brought them a letter."

Obviously he was being surveyed intently. Then the chain was pulled back and the door opened. A stooped "not yet old lady" stepped to one side.

"Come in, but Maika's not home."

"I don't know who Maika is, but I have a letter for the Strepetovs. Are you Mrs. Strepetov, madam?"

"What did you say?" asked the smoker in amazement.

"I have a letter . . ."

"No, you said 'madam'?"

"Yes, that's right, I said 'madam.' "

"I know you're being ironic, young man, and yet it's a good, polite way of addressing someone."

"I'm not being ironic at all," Boris laughed. "I've just got this letter for the Strepetovs."

Several faces appeared in the doorways. A boy of about fourteen froze in his tracks and opened his mouth wide at the sight of the "motor knight" dressed entirely in leather, his leather gloves tossed over one shoulder, his goggles pushed back onto the top of his head.

"Come in, come in, comrade," said the "not yet old lady," bustling about as though she were at pains to shield Boris from curious eyes. "Maechka will be here any minute." She tugged at the boy's sleeve and said, "Don't just stand there, Marat, show the comrade through!"

Boris came into a fairly large room, partitioned off into sections by rickety walls that did not reach to the ceiling. All of the articles of furniture—chiffonnier, pier glass, round table, ottoman, bookcase, screen divider—were pushed closely against one another; everything spoke of another life, in which perhaps there had been more space. The window of this, obviously the main room—the living room, one might say—opened onto a side street. Nothing could be seen through it but a brick wall. The two bearing walls and three plywood partitions were decorated with reproductions of paintings, for the most part sailing scenes and central Russian landscapes. The well-known *Princess Tarakanov* leapt out at the observer, along with a framed and enlarged photograph of a pleasant, well-groomed young man in a light gray, clearly well-tailored suit, perhaps the author of the ill-fated letter.

"Sit down, please," said the lady of the house and paused to give the guest the chance to introduce himself.

"My name is Boris," he said.

The woman smiled contentedly. "And I'm Kaleria Ivanovna Urusova, the mother of Alexandra Tarasovna Strepetova."

The round table, covered with a worn "tablecloth" that was in fact carpeting, tilted dangerously beneath the elbow of the motorcycle racer. Marat, the adolescent with oriental features and already the beginnings of a mustache, stood in the doorway looking at the guest.

"Do you want some tea?"

"No, no thank you, Kaleria Ivanovna. I'm in a hurry. I only wanted to deliver this letter, which is many years old, and to explain to you in two words the circumstances—"

A loud squeaking sound came from behind the partition, followed by something crashing to the floor. Kaleria Ivanovna aimed a panic-stricken glance in that direction, while Marat became as tense as a Doberman pinscher preparing to spring.

"Maechka should be here any minute. If you'll be so good as to wait, Boris . . ." the lady of the house intoned with put-on politesse, without taking her eyes off of the partition.

"Grandma, can I take a look to see what's wrong with her?" Marat asked with suffering in his voice.

"Stay where you are!" Kaleria Ivanovna ordered sharply.

"Forgive me, but I seem to have come at a bad time." Boris stood up and pulled the triangle from his jacket pocket. "I'm sorry, but I don't know your Maechka—I only came to deliver this letter."

Something else came crashing down behind the partition, a window shade was shoved to the side, and a woman draped in a green velvet dressing gown, beneath which her nightshirt was visible, emerged from the tiny enclosure. There was no doubt that she was closely related to Kaleria Ivanovna: they had the same eyes and the same facial features, adjusted for the difference in age of twenty-some years. Then again . . .

"What letter?" the woman said in a ghastly voice. With a convulsive movement she stretched out a hand for the letter, her hair fell in disheveled locks, and it seemed as though some sort of witch had just entered, a Shakespearean hag.

"Alexandra! You should be sleeping!" Kaleria Ivanovna said in a strong-willed, hypnotic voice. Marat was already quietly approaching as if to lay hold of the newly arrived Alexandra.

She managed nonetheless to snatch the triangle from Boris's hands, glanced at the address, and all at once let out an utterly mad, staggering, incinerating howl that turned everything around her to ashes.

Right away a fuss was raised in the corridor. "What's going on in there? It's outrageous! Another madhouse scene!"

The door to the room flew open, and on the threshold appeared a slender young girl in a little blue dress and with a tangled mane of hair that seemed bleached by the sun, though how it could be bleached at the beginning of summer, it was hard to tell. Throwing her hair back, the girl yelled over her shoulder into the corridor, "Stop your bleating, Alla Olegovna! You should be looking after yourself!" Only after she had said this did she rush up to Alexandra, who was still howling, though with decreasing volume. "Mama, calm down. What's happened?"

Alexandra stopped shouting at the sight of her daughter and was now only racked by trembling, the sister of convulsions. Meanwhile, Kaleria Ivanovna had put a new cigarette into her mouth and was snapping her fingers as a signal that someone should give her a light. No one was paying any attention to her, however.

Boris took one more cautious step in the direction of the door.

"He's alive!" Alexandra said in a grief-stricken, whistling murmur. "Maika, look! A letter from him! Papa is alive! Well, well! No one believed me, but he's alive! Maratka!" She turned to the lad. "See that? Your papa's alive!" At these words, something like a leaping frog flashed across the boy's face.

"Alive!" Alexandra yelled, triumphantly and in the same ghastly voice as before.

This time, no answer from Alla Olegovna in the corridor followed.

"Where's the messenger?" Alexandra asked suddenly in a perfectly pleasant, composed, and mannerly voice, and turned to Boris. Ah, that must be me, "the messenger," he thought. There was nothing left to do, though, but to bow: the messenger at your service, madam. It was only following this that Maika saw "the messenger." She suddenly flushed and gaped in amazement with her blue Strepetov eyes that were an even more vivid shade than her dress. The eyes of all of the female members of the family shone with this blue color, while the boy Marat's radiated a Caucasian agate. Maika was holding her mother, who was excited to the point of madness, by the shoulders, while she herself was entirely turned, in joy and amazement, toward the "messenger." This is the sort of scene that stays with you, thought Boris, and took one more step in the direction of the door.

"This letter came into my hands quite by accident. As I understand, it's at least fifteen years old. . . ." he said.

"That means that you saw Andrei quite recently, young man?" Alexandra asked, continuing the conversation in the same mannerly tone. "You're an athlete, aren't you? You probably had quite a few interests in common—oh, the morning exercises he used to do! The weights he used to lift! I couldn't pick even one of them up off the floor!"

Maika took the letter from her hands, rapidly unfolded it and turned away, shielding her eyes with her arm. The indelible pencil, which had miraculously preserved the address, was entirely smeared on the inside.

Boris, still closer to the door, spread his hands apart in a gesture of chagrin. "I'm sorry, I didn't know. . . . It was only this morning that I found this letter in some papers . . . a friend of our family. . . . As I understand, it was tossed out of a boxcar in 1937 . . . you know, one of those specially commandeered cars . . . and then our friend . . . well, himself . . . and so I thought . . ."

"Well, let's read it now," Alexandra proclaimed with triumphant calm. "Children, Mama, everyone to the table! You too, young messenger! I wonder what Andrei writes? You know, I wouldn't say no to a glass of wine!"

Maika suddenly broke away sharply, went around the table as if it were square rather than circular, then took Boris by the hand and led him out into the corridor.

"Let's go! Let's go! She doesn't need to know any more! Thanks for the letter, and now forget about it! You know, I know you! I do, you know! When I saw you, I thought I'd go crazy! There he is!"

Alla Olegovna's face, about as attractive as a cowpie, peered out from the bathroom. Maika, her teeth and eyes flashing, pulled the motorcyclist out of the apartment that was sweating with its calamities. She's so thin, thought Boris, that you could get your hand around her waist and make your fingers touch.

"Where do you know me from?" he asked when they were on the stairs.

"I saw you at the First Moscow Medical Institute. I'm a therapeutic nurse there. As soon as I saw you, I almost cried out. "There he is!' "

"What do you mean by "There he is?' " Boris asked in confusion.

"Well, mine, that is," Maika explained.

"And what does 'Mine, that is' mean?" Boris smiled.

They were going down the stairs, and Maika was still not letting go of his leather sleeve. The owner of the sleeve, not to mention of the arm thrust in that sleeve, felt the tenacious little fingers. The foul atmosphere of the communal flat quickly dispersed.

"By that I mean the one I've been dreaming about," Maika said by way of explanation and with some irritation, as though she were speaking to an idiot. "You know, my guy."

"Just like that?" Boris looked at her askance.

"No sense beating around the bush," she laughed. "I was hanging around at First Moscow, I was shy for a while, then I came to my senses and went looking for you, but you'd already taken off on your bike. You blew down Leninsky Prospekt and then you were gone. Well, I thought, that's that, I'll never see my guy again. And all of a sudden today, Mama yells, I come running, and . . . well, well, what do you know, there he is, sitting right in the house, mine! How about that!"

"Has your mama been . . . odd like that for long?" Boris asked cautiously.

"Grandma says ever since Papa . . . well, disappeared. . . . Sometimes she's better, sometimes worse, but lately she's been getting worse. The neighbors insist that we turn her in to the asylum, but we don't want to. So I look after her, and so does Maratka—you know, my brother—and Grandma, so . . ." She abruptly broke off her account, as if to show that wasn't what she wanted to discuss at all.

Now they were at the entrance to the building. Boris looked up one last time. There, the excited face of Marat was hanging over the railing of the balcony like an orange with black hair. He must recognize me from *Soviet Sports,* Boris thought.

"What is he, Marat? Your adopted brother? Or is he your mother's?"

"No, he's my natural brother, by Mama and Papa."

"Beg your pardon, but how can he be your brother? How old is he?"

"Thirteen, almost fourteen."

"Well, that letter is fifteen years old."

"So what?"

"Well, you're a nurse, aren't you?"

"Yes, so what?"

"So, how can he be your brother without your father?"

"Well, Mama says that he is, and so does Granny."

"Of course."

"I've had enough of this. Where are we going now?"

They were already standing on the street. A strong, warm wind was blowing down Ordynka Street. Maika was holding her hair with one hand and her skirt with the other. The wind was even wreaking havoc on Boris's brilliantined coiffure.

"I don't know where you're going right now, but I'm going to the Caucasus."

"Oh, I'll go with you! Can you wait ten minutes?"

"Stop playing the fool!"

He went over to the motorcycle. The sidecar was tightly covered with a tarpaulin.

"Is that the same one?!" she cried joyously.

Boris shrugged. The situation was beginning to annoy him a bit. It's just like when some unhappy little dog latches on to you. You can't beat it off with a stick.

He sat down in the saddle, removed the antitheft bar, put the key in the ignition, and turned it. The GK-1, which he himself had fine-tuned to perfection, rumbled with restrained power.

"Good-bye, Maya. I'll come by when I get back."

"No, you won't!" she wailed in desperation. "I'm coming with you! Wait!"

But he had already taken off.

When he had gone a dozen or so yards down Ordynka Street, he looked back and saw that Maika was running after him. Her dress was clinging to her adolescent figure, her hair was flying behind her, fists were flashing. Instinctively he squeezed the accelerator and then looked back again. She was falling behind, naturally, but she wasn't slowing down; on the contrary, she seemed to be picking up speed, her fists pumping up and down more quickly. What do you know, now she's running barefoot—she's thrown away her sandals. What a stupid situation, what do I do? Just say "to hell with it" and step on the gas? In another ten seconds, she'll be out of sight. And she'll weigh on my heart, just like that triangle did for Vuinovich. What is she to me, after all? A seventeen-year-old girl, one of ten times ten thousand wandering around with their cherry still intact. . . . Well, thanks for the favor, Vadim Georgievich! Suddenly an idiotic idea came to him: once she says I'm "her guy," that means I am "her guy," that I can't just get rid of her or it would be betrayal. . . . He began to apply the brakes and looked back over his shoulder. Maika raced up, leaped forward as though she were going over the vaulting horse in a gymnastics class, landed on the backseat of the motorcycle, breathing hard, and buried her nose and lips in his back, wrapping her arms around the waist of the "Stalinist" leather jacket from which the inner lining had been removed with the coming of June. Now we'll have to stop once we're past the city limits to take the cover off the sidecar and find her some quilted coveralls. Otherwise, by the time I get to Oryol, I'll have some wasted-away chicken blue with cold instead of Maika. . . .

Chapter 9

———————☆———————

THE ANCIENT WAYS

That very day, as Boris IV Gradov was heading south with his unexpected passenger on the backseat, meetings no less unexpected were
happening in the life of his cousin Yolka Kitaigorodsky. Call it a
whim of the novelist or ascribe it to the summer heat, but let us say in
our defense that at the beginning of summer eighteen-year-old . . .
that is, almost nineteen-year-old . . . girls give off some substance that
contributes to the occurrence of unanticipated situations in a city of
millions, even in the "capital of the Worldwide Socialist Commonwealth," as it had then begun to be called. Well, what can you say?
The Commonwealth was fighting desperately for peace in the whole
world, particularly on the Korean Peninsula, and life just kept going
on, stubbornly set in its ancient ways. They wiped out all the Bergel-
sons, Markishes, Feffers, Zuskins, and Kvitkos who had infiltrated
the Jewish Anti-Fascist Committee on assignment from the Zionist organization Joint; put into jail a certain Zhemchuzhin, who just happened to be the wife of Deputy Chairman of the Council of Ministers
Molotov, who was known in the circles of the notorious and treach-

erous United Nations, its voting rigged in favor of the Americans, by the nickname "Mr. No"; and yet life continued to go along principally unchanged from those patterns that had formed in it several millennia earlier in the Mediterranean basin.

If even, as we have recently seen, in the zone of a transit camp in Magadan there were individuals inclined to imitate mythological beings, what can we expect to find in the huge mass of people not taken up in the ranks of prisoners, that is, in the population of Moscow, a great city lying on the so-called Russian shield of the earth's upper proteros? Life moves at top speed here, and in this instance goes—or rather rushes—along with a folder of music in hand and a tennis racquet beneath the arm, in the form of the previously mentioned cousin of the motorcyclist, a student of the Merzlyakov School and a promising tennis player, a member of the Moscow all-star team in the girls' category, Elena Kitaigorodsky.

★

On that day, around noon, she was playing in a quarterfinal match on a court at Army Park. She was playing without particular zest, because too much of her attention was distracted from "the great sport" by, first of all, music. She had graduated from the Merzlyakovka, and now it was time to take the exams for the Gnesin Institute, which meant going nowhere for the summer: you have to stay and study piano pieces not only by classical composers but also by tedious Soviet ones. It was her own fault for giving in to Grandma's attempt to persuade her—"Lenok, you could become a world-class pianist"—as well as her stepfather Sandro's flattery—"Elka, I'm not trying to flatter you, but my heart soars when I hear you play Mozart"—and now she was roped into this forced labor; now she couldn't even get interested in tennis.

Then there was the matter of her age. Why, this is probably my last competition in the girls' category, and I'll probably never get anywhere in the women's division. Why don't they introduce a category for spinsters? These were the thoughts of Kitaigorodsky of the Spartak Club as she dueled unenthusiastically with Lukin of the Dynamo team. Having long legs helped, though: where the stocky Lukin took two steps, Yolka needed only one. "You could become a world-class tennis player," her trainer, Parmesanov, had said to her when, not long ago, after gulping down a cognac for courage, he had undertaken in the locker room to qualify her for the women's division. She had almost exploded. Well, there was no point in blowing up. He was far from the most off-putting of them, this Tolik Parmesanov. Everybody wants to see me be a "world-class" something, but I just stay a world-class idiot with my—er—membrane intact.

This problem, that is to say, a total lack of experience in love, had become an obsession for Yolka. She would look herself over carefully in the bath and rejoice: say what you like, but there's class, world class even! But then the thought of a man would suddenly terrify her: why, it's impossible, unthinkable, even, that some Parmesanov, or another one, even if it's Apollo de Belvedere . . . no, it's unthinkable that some man's *thing* might go into me, down there!

One day she had asked her mother, "Nina, when you were my age, had you already—" Nina had looked at her daughter with a humorous expression: "Alas, alas . . ."

What a naughty mom, Yolka had thought, not to just come out and tell me how it was for her. Instead, she just teases me with her "Alas, alas . . ."

It had been awkward for Nina, too. Yolka wants me to just tell her how it's done, but I can't do it. Socialism has made us all a bunch of sanctimonious bigots. No, I should tell her what free and foolish times those were, totally opposite the puritanism that reigns nowadays, though also repulsive. How I went through the same sufferings, and how the cell decided to get me together with that blockhead Stroilo, and how I made of him the myth of the triumphant and radiant proletarian. I need to tell her all that, including the most important part, the anatomical bit. Why is it hard for me to do it? Is it really because it's "not the done thing" nowadays? Or is it because her time is coming and mine is ticking away, and there's no way to stop either one? . . . These were Nina's thoughts, but Yolka—alas, alas!—couldn't read her mother's mind.

There was only a small crowd at the Army Tennis Stadium. Who would be drawn to a noontime quarterfinal in Moscow at the end of June? Chasing the short-legged Lukin from one end of the court to the other with her powerful strokes, Yolka glanced at the dilapidated stands from time to time to see if her offended coach would show up, and then suddenly, instead of Parmesanov, she noticed another guy there, some ten years younger, that is, her own age. He was sitting with his legs crossed, his hands laced together over one knee, and was watching her with undiluted delight. His hair had a hint of the *stilyaga* style about it but fortunately had no Brioline in it. His dark blue sportcoat was thrown over his shoulder, and he looked like a young Jack London in the photo at the beginning of Volume 1 of the collected works. At that moment, Lukin unexpectedly rushed the net and slammed the ball mightily, right in front of Kitaigorodsky's nose. The sparse crowd applauded, and the fellow did the same. You bastard, are you rooting against your own girl? Walking along the net, Yolka eyed him with irritation. Infatuation and delight were written on his face with its hollow cheeks and protruding chin. He wasn't seeing the game at all, he was only watching how his girl moved; that was why he had applauded at the wrong time.

The match came to an end. For all her poor playing, Yolka had still beaten Lukin. On her way to the showers, she stopped by the stands just opposite her admirer and looked directly at him. Meeting her eyes, he looked away shyly and pretended to be looking at the scenery and that the red-faced, sweaty girl had no more interest for him than, say, that tree, or that banner reading "Long live Stalin, the best friend of Soviet athletes!" Why, he's just a boy! He'll never dare come up to talk to me on his own.

"Is anyone sitting there?" she asked, indicating a bench that was entirely empty in both directions.

"What?" he said, startled, and then looked distractedly to the right, to the left, and then behind him to see if she were speaking to someone else. There was no one there. Finally he squeezed out a silly laugh. "No, no one's sitting here."

"Save me a place," she said and then went majestically past.

In the showers, she thought, There's one who can move me from the girls' division into the women's. And he himself would join the men's division. That is, of course, if he hasn't run away by now.

Well, we have women with looks that are "world class," though what people might look like out there in the rest of the world, we don't know. In any case, we're no worse off than in the "People's Democracies," if the girls who come here as students from Poland and Czechoslovakia are anything to judge by. Her hair was wet, but it would dry in half an hour and she would begin tossing it back, driving all the boys from the provinces crazy. For some reason she was sure he wasn't from Moscow, even though he was sporting narrow trousers.

The provincial hadn't run away. On the contrary, he had saved a place for her by putting his jacket on it. She walked down the empty bench and sat down alongside him. The jacket was hurriedly withdrawn, like a seal with its tail flapping.

She wondered aloud why he didn't ask her what her name was. He said he already knew, because it was written in the program: Elena Kitaigorodsky. Well, sir, it's your turn now to introduce yourself, since you've saved a lady a place on your bench. It turned out that his name was Vasya—well, you know, Vassily. Now there's a name! What do you mean! Well, there's nothing but Valerys and Ediks around, and here's an old Russian Vassily. Well, you know, we also have one in Moscow . . . a certain Vasya. . . . He had to admit that he was fed up with his name but that Elena Kitaigorodsky had a real ring to it. The family calls me Yolka . . . and where are you from? Kazan, came the reply. Oh my, she whistled in disappointment, what a God-forsaken dump! You're wrong there, he said, flaring up, there's a very old university there, the second-ranked basketball team in the Russian Republic, and, as everyone knows, the best jazz in the Union. Jazz? In Kazan? Are you crazy? You know, you laugh as if you knew, but you don't really know. We've got Lundstrem's Shanghai jazz in Kazan. . . . Remember that movie called *Sun Valley Serenade* from the war? That's how they play! He hummed a bit through his nose and tapped his cheap-sandaled foot in time. They played not too long ago in Shanghai, in the Russian Millionaires' Club. Oh brother, what an imagination you guys in Kazan have! Yolka, you think you're turning me on, but you yourself don't know that Lundstrem is one of the ten best in the world, right up there between Harry Jims and Goody Sherman; Klen Diller, one of the great musicians called him "the East's King of Swing"! Ha, ha, ha, now you're showing off your erudition! When the Shanghaiers play down in Kazan, when they're moonlighting out of sight of their bosses, everybody goes nuts: the Muscovites, too, and even the guys from Prague, Budapest, and Warsaw are amazed, they've never heard anything like it in their lives! She laughed even more loudly and gave him a slap on the back, which made him feel as though a wave were coursing down his spine. So that means that Kazan is b-i-i-g, and Moscow is sm-a-a-l-l, right? She had re-membered this line from the film *Ivan the Terrible* which had had mil-lions of moviegoers laughing themselves silly, at just the right moment. So where do you study, Vassily? He squirmed: now she's re-ally going to be let down—if only I were at the Kazan Aviation Insti-tute or at the Kazan Kirov Chemical and Technical Institute, or at the Ulyanov-Lenin University, or . . . well, I'm a medical student. Medi-cine? Good for you! Have you studied from the Gradov manual? Next year we will, why? Because that's my grandfather. You must be kid-ding! See here, Vasya, where did you get manners like that? As if you weren't brought up in Kazan? Is that the honest-to-god truth, that Gradov is your grandfather? The honest-to-god truth—what kind of an expression is that, "the honest-to-god truth"? My mother, by the way, is the poetess Nina Gradov. Now I've really made an impression on him: the boy is obviously interested in literature. Strange, why all this boasting? Aren't your personal qualities enough without trying to impress him? And then, this well-brought-up young lady from Moscow, "from a good family" as they say, asked Vasya, whom she scarcely knew, an extremely indiscreet question: So who are your par-ents? For some reason this got his dander up and he lowered his head, glowering at her like a wolf. Well, if I've already asked an indiscreet question, I'll just have to repeat it: Who are your parents? Just office workers, he answered unwillingly and then changed the subject to sports. You did a good job of beating Lukin. I don't have much talent in the way of sports, though I'm not too bad in the high jump. The coach said: develop the natural springiness in your legs! So I guess maybe I'll give it a shot this summer. I'm heading south now, to Sochi, that's where our gang's getting together. . . . The gang has come to-gether in a rip-snortin' crowd. Never heard that expression before? Strange.

It's strange that I know all your words but that some of my words, you don't know. I like that—I can see you're not easy for a girl to fig-ure out. So who said I was? Oh, you're not an easy one at all! Have you been in Sochi before? Again, Yolka felt a certain inner awkward-ness as a result of her entirely innocent question: anyone can see that I'm just asking so that I can brag and say I've been there twice, with the meaning "You should know your place, you provincial, son of rank and file, when you're talking to an aristocrat from the Gradov

clan." What I meant was that if you haven't yet seen the sea . . . What?
A man could go off his head from the way you talk. It turned out he
had already seen the sea. You can see the biggest sea in the world in
Kazan, or at least one of the ten biggest, anyway. Vassily suddenly
began to show condescension and started blowing off a bit of Jack
London fog. It turned out he had lived by the sea. Two years he had
lived by the seashore, only it wasn't the Black Sea but another one.
That's interesting, which one? The Strait of Magellan or the Ligurian
Sea? The Sea of Okhotsk? Well, I never! And what kind of an expression is that, Elena Kitaigorodsky, "well, I never"? He had lived in Magadan for two years and in fact that was where he had graduated from
high school. Why is that so impossible? Our school out there was better than anything in Moscow, with a great gym.

But how he had gotten there, that was the curious thing. If you're
not just making all this up, how did you come to be in Magadan?
Once again, something untamed appeared in the jazz lover's face, as
though some other nature that had nothing to do with Kazan were revealing itself there. Well . . . that was . . . it's where Mama lives . . . I
went to live with her, and that was where I graduated. . . . Say, Yolka,
look over there at that fat guy playing—isn't that Nikolai Ozerov, the
famous radio announcer? However much he tries to change the subject, it's obvious he keeps doing it every time the subject of his parents
comes up. Ah, so that's it: he's one of those. . . . She looked at him
now with redoubled interest: he had turned out to be not just some
likable guy from the provinces but one of those. . . . You know,
Vasya, I can see now that they're right when they "It's a small world":
I have an uncle in Magadan, you see. . . . Yes, yes, Mama's brother
. . . he . . . he's one of those "rank and file" too. . . .

Meanwhile, the number of people in the stands had grown: the
day's most important match was under way, Ozerov playing Korbut.
The celebrated man of his time, the announcer, the distinguished master of sports and actor Nikolai Nikolaevich Ozerov, son of another
Nikolai Nikolaevich Ozerov, the singer, was evidently the fattest tennis champion in the world. For all that, moving up and down the
court with exceptional agility, he quite easily beat the lithe and muscular Korbut.

Vassily was looking at the spectators more than at the match. It
was obvious that the majority of the onlookers moved in the same cir-

cles; they were well-tanned men and women in light clothing of bright shades and canvas shoes. You wouldn't see such people in Magadan or Kazan; it's almost like being abroad. Many of them were calling out to one another and laughing. Yolka was constantly waving her hand at someone or other, as well. Well, there's a girl for you! Vassily, his experience with girls being practically nil, was charmed. She would have to make the first move and approach him. Doesn't look much like the cows at med school. What a looker, what a body, and what eyes—cheerful, laughing at the world, and even a bit sad—and the way she has of throwing her hair back. That movement of her hand alone, followed by the hair flying back, was unforgettable. Even if worse came to worst, even if she suddenly stood up and said, "See you around!" I'll never forget her. This day in the twentieth year of my life will never be forgotten.

Some older handsome type with a familiar face—must be in pictures—walked by and gave Yolka a serious look. He asked, "How's your mother?" and nodded in reply to her answer of "She's fine." The granddaughter of the author of a surgery textbook, the daughter of a famous poetess, of whom even Mama in Magadan said, "She has the gift."

Not far away, a man in a warmup suit with the sleeves rolled up was squeezed in between two athletes. He had long locks combed back and held in place by a hair net; this gave him a sleek look about the head, but at the same time he had forearms as hairy as a baboon's. He was looking cheerlessly at Kitaigorodsky. "What's with you, Parmesanov, you don't even come to say hello when your protégée is playing?" What a girl, to take that sarcastic tone with a man twice her age.

"Couldn't," the guy called Parmesanov said tragically.

"What happened? The wife and kids?" Kitaigorodsky went on mockingly.

"Stop it," Parmesanov said severely. Then he turned away and immediately looked back.

Yolka stood up and said loudly, "Let's get out of here, Vasya. No sense hanging around. Ozerov is winning."

Vassily stood up on the spot with a cheerful readiness that knew no bounds. Yes, she's got me under her orders. I'm just her slave. My will is not my own anymore. Whatever she says, I'll do, and everyone around will look and say, "Look, Yolka Kitaigorodsky has already got this Vasya under her thumb!" That's happiness!

The man called Parmesanov followed them with hostile eyes as they made their way through the spectators watching them with curiosity.

☆

On the pond in the park, well-fed drakes were swimming jauntily among slow-moving rowboats. Pieces of French rolls floated on the water like small jellyfish. A statue that resembled a tall stack of wheat but that was in fact a border guard in a sheepskin coat stood on a pedestal on the central path. It was under this reliable protection that cognac flowed on the bandstand, often mixed with champagne according to the whim of the comrades of the officer corps. Vasya reached into his trouser pocket and pulled out a solid roll of Stalinist money.

"What would you say to cognac and champagne?"

"Good idea, it'll feel like Magadan," Yolka said with delight.

"In Magadan we drink hundred-ninety-two proof spirits." He began to tell her his usual silly Kolyma drinking stories about taking a mouthful of alcohol, touching it off with a match, and then running with a mouth full of fire. It's a crazy game we played on graduation night, even managed to frighten General Tsaregradsky, the guest of honor.

While they were sitting in the stands, he had been afraid Yolka would turn out to be taller than he was, but now, to his great relief, it turned out that they were exactly even—he was maybe even an inch or so taller. "Shall we drink it all in one go?" she asked. "Are you two old enough?" asked the barmaid, who looked about as fresh as forty-year-old cream.

They gulped down their drinks, and Vasya's horizons widened all at once. "Your mama is a great poet," he said to Yolka.

"How would you know? She doesn't publish anything now except translations."

"My mother read her poems to me, she remembers them from the thirties."

"Can I whisper a question to you, Vasya? Is your mama an enemy of the people?"

"Bring up your ear. My parents were victims of Yezhov's terror, and I'm a pariah in this society."

"Don't say things like that, Vasya, you're no pariah. Parents are one thing, children are another.

"As a matter of fact, they're one and the same," he said. "The apple never falls far from the tree . . ."

"Well, let's change the subject. What other poets do you like?"

"Boris Pasternak."

"My, my, Vasya, you really surprise me. All the students these days are crazy about Sergei Smirnov, but you like Pasternak. Oh, my head is already spinning—not another drop! Where did you find Pasternak?"

"My mother can recite his poems by heart, miles of them":

> The years will pass
> And they'll play Brahms for me in the concert hall.
> I'll shudder and recall our six-hearted union,
> the swims, the strolls, the flower shrubs in the garden . . .

She picked up the poem without hesitation:

> Of beauty, fragile as a dream,
> the lofty brow, the innocent smile,
> a smile like a flood . . .

They looked at each other with a tenderness that was both unexpected and unfeigned. They touched the palms of their hands together and then immediately pulled them back, as though too much electricity had built up in them.

"You know, ducks have had the same form since the time of the dinosaurs," he said.

They were walking along the pond. Yolka was swinging her tennis bag, from which the handle of her racquet protruded.

"On the whole, Brahms doesn't do much for me" was her reply to his revelation about the ducks.

"And who is your favorite composer?"

"Vivaldi."

"I've never even heard of him," said Vassily, for the first time confessing one of his shortcomings.

"Do you want to hear a Vivaldi piece arranged for the piano? On an old instrument, that is."

"Where?"

She looked at him attentively, as if sizing him up, and then came to a decision. "At my mama's place tonight, or rather at her husband's . . . or rather her boyfriend's—he's an artist, they live in a loft. Well, anyway, I'll play . . ."

"You play the piano, too?"

"What do you mean, 'too'? You're looking at a future world-class pianist! Someday you'll hear me in a concert hall and 'melt away from melancholy'!"

His face clouded over at this declaration. It's all too much: tennis, her background, playing the piano—too much for a pariah in this society!

She must have sensed this fleeting change in his mood, because she laughed and then—ye gods!—kissed Vassily on the cheek. Well, will you come? Did you think I wouldn't? Of course I will! Where are you staying in Moscow? Nowhere. What do you mean? I slept in the train station last night, with the magazine *Culture and Life* for a pillow. You see, I was getting ready to crash in a friend's room in the dorm, but he wasn't there, and the floor lady wouldn't let me in. . . . An idea suddenly dawned on her: You'll stay at my place tonight in Bolshoi Gnezdnikovsky Street. Don't worry, I live alone. How's that, then, "alone"? Well, Mama's there sometimes, but most of the time she lives with her painter, Sandro Pevzner, at his place. For Vassily, who had spent his whole life sleeping at very close quarters with his relations on folding beds, it was difficult to imagine that a girl her age could live by herself, in a flat with a separate entrance. Another cloud crossed his brow. Maybe she's one of those "creatures of free morals," a love tigress? Sometimes at night on his folding bed, Vassily had imagined himself a tamer of such tigresses, but alas, by the light of day his triumphant spear preferred to remain in the wings. The cloud passed. You think of the damnedest things sometimes! Imagining a girl like that as a "tigress"! Listen, Yolka, are your parents divorced? The war separated them, she said sadly. My father disappeared. He was killed? Well, yes, he disappeared. He was a surgeon. As you would say, Vasya, he was a "mighty" surgeon. And that "mighty surgeon," my handsome papa, disappeared at the front, that is, he was killed. She's really not that happy at all, thought Vassily, this girl whom I've fallen so madly in love with, not so unflappable, and certainly not like the tigresses of my imagination.

They agreed that he would go to the train station for his rucksack and that in two hours she would meet him at the Mayakovsky metro station and take him back to her place in Bolshoi Gnezdnikovsky Street. After that they would head for Krivoarbatsky Lane, to a *soirée*. On what? Vassily asked. Not on what, but to where, she laughed. A *soirée* isn't a kind of streetcar, my friend from dazzling Kazan. On that note they parted at the gates of Army Park, which both of them would remember for the rest of their lives as a place of young, piercing enchantment.

★

Yolka spent the first hour of their separation in her bedroom thinking about what to wear. It was a disturbing time: the fashions were changing. More and more, there was a move from boxey shoulder pads to a so-called womanly silhouette. First of all, of course, you have to put on your narrow slit skirt, the one Mama doesn't like, and as for that jacket you've liked for the past three years, to hell with it! So now that the question of what to wear down below has been solved, let's go up above. Blouses flew from the wardrobe and landed on the bed like flags at a student festival. It was not a question of colors but of lines. Alas, none of them imparted a sufficiently modern silhouette to this particular young woman. One seemed too childish, another one somehow too mature. None of them really suited the skirt. Suddenly a brilliant idea struck her: I'll put on a simple student's checked shirt over this chic, stylish skirt. That's all there is to it—brilliant! And I'll throw a sweater over my shoulders. Vassily, you've never seen girls like this in Kazan or Magadan! Then came the problem of her hair. Should she make ringlets with curling irons and try for the latest thing, a style called "the wreath of peace"? Should she pin it all up, showing off her swanlike neck, comb it to one side, or tie it back in a ponytail? Mama had had a good idea: she'd had her hair cut short like a little boy's, got rid of these doubts once and for all, and made herself look ten years younger into the bargain. The problem of her lips was inextricably connected with that of her hair. Lipstick or not? Hair down and lip-stick . . . hmm . . . that clashes with the slit skirt. Besides, adding a checked shirt to such an ensemble would just look ridiculous. Her in-nate genius came to her rescue again: I'll put on the lipstick and plait my hair in a single braid. Brilliant! Thus, fifteen minutes before the rendezvous, an intriguing young creature appeared on Gorky Street, part student, part high-society girl. High society, demimonde . . . just like Tolik Parmesanov's favorite lines for impressing his young charge: "I want to walk through Moscow by night with a mother-of-pearl riding crop. . . ." How vulgar can you get? I have to think as lit-tle as possible about all this nonsense: what I've put on, I've put on, and being casual is indispensable to good taste. I wonder if I could write that down. Men almost without exception turned their heads when Yolka walked by. A few stopped dead in their tracks. For ex-ample, a short, limping, but for all that quite interesting man came to a stop, then shook his head, shifted his eyes devilishly, said, "As I live and breathe!" and then fell behind and to the right, waiting by a col-umn on which was posted a notice advertising a puppet show called "To the Rustle of Your Eyelashes."

Everywhere around the metro entrance there were vendors selling ice cream and meat pies. At the feet of the lady selling carbonated water lay a large, pensive dog. So far, there was no sign of Vassily in the chaotic swirl. I wonder who's waiting for whom? Then again, it isn't six yet, it's five minutes to six. If I'm going to stand around like this, guys are sure to try to flirt. I'll stand in the queue at the infor-mation booth. A bootblack, gaping at her, smeared shoe polish on his customer's white trousers. The lady at the fizzy-water stand pointed across the street to a spirits shop: "Hey, you with the paint on, go over there and ask for some alcohol to remove it!" A well-dressed man with Caucasian features suddenly detached himself from the crowd and came directly toward Yolka. With one hand he touched the brim of his hat, while with the other he displayed a small red ID case with the gold letters "MGB." "Excuse me, young lady, but a statesman of the Soviet Union would like to meet you." Instinctively she looked around and saw behind her two officers: shoulder straps, buttons, fountain pen clips, rows of decorations, a Komsomol pin . . . two for one, two for one . . .

No one in the bustling rush-hour crowd paid any particular atten-

tion to the graceful young girl getting into the fat black limousine—
no one, that is, except for three women: the fizzy-water seller, the
meat pie vendor, and the girl at the information booth. These three
ever-present Moirai of the Mayakovsky stop exchanged knowing
glances and smiles but, of course, said nothing to one another.

A minute later, Vassily appeared. He was destined to spend several
hours of fruitless waiting.

★

Meanwhile, in his studio in Krivoarbatsky Lane, Sandro Pevzner was
stretching a frame for a new canvas. Paintings in varying degrees of
completion, some drying and some unfinished, stood everywhere.
Sandro was murmuring blissfully. For several months, now, he had
been in what he called his "orangerie period." Flowers had become
his favorite subjects, his best friends, one might even say, if not the
members of his family. They were his children, bearing petals of love,
an expression of Nina's most intimate nature. Sometimes he made the
flowers their natural size, sometimes much larger than life, and sometimes he reduced them in size, as though the observer were looking at
them through the wrong end of a pair of binoculars. Now and then he
painted on a canvas the size of a postcard, sometimes on one a yard
square. But no bigger. For now, unfortunately, no bigger. He had conceived of a gigantic canvas that would be a floral apotheosis, but he
was a bit afraid to begin it; he might be misunderstood. Afraid or not,
you'll begin it anyway, Nina laughed. Perhaps you're right, my dear.
For the time being he continued to work modestly at his orangerie.
Sometimes, in a manner reminiscent of Vermeer and the so-called
lesser Dutch school, he would include every vein, every dewdrop, and
a beetle or a bee in the lushness of a bouquet. Sometimes he would create impressionistic reflections with sweeping strokes. He painted pe-
onies, chrysanthemums, roses (of course), tulips, all kinds of trifles
like buttercups and cornflowers, pansies, phallic, irresistible gladioli,
the whisper of geraniums, the embodiment of lilacs; sometimes from
a model and sometimes from memory, almost out of the night, perhaps, from things seen in dreams.

"This fellow Pevzner," said Nina as she strolled among the flowers, "is getting up to things he shouldn't. He's creating an imaginary
world of beauty, which he consciously opposes to the reality of our

society. Don't you think, Comrades, that innocent quasi-botanical exercises warrant a closer look?"

He laughed. "Stop it, my dear. Of course, it's a good imitation, but it doesn't get to the essence. With his flowers, Pevzner is in fact emphasizing the beauty of our socialist reality, the illustrious successes of our Soviet floriculture, the fundamental justice of our way of life, in which an object of beauty belongs not to the bourgeois aesthete but to the simple toiler. The artist Pevzner demonstrates that he has learned a lesson from principled Party-spirited criticism."

She took a Chekhovian pince-nez from one of the mannequin heads scattered around the studio and carefully eyed the brushwork and then the person of the artist himself with his graying whiskers. "You'll go too far, Pevzner—way too far, Solomonovich!"

And that is exactly what happened. The tiny exhibit in the House of Culture in the Proletarsky district that he managed to break into with half a dozen canvases attracted everyone's attention. People showed up to see the flowers that created in them a strange thirst that was somehow familiar, as if from another life. Even Leningraders showed up especially for the exhibit. On the steps of the House of Culture opinions were exchanged, and unkind words were heard: "impressionism," "postimpressionism," and even "symbolism." In the end, *Moscow Pravda* burst forth with an article entitled "The Dubious Orangerie," in which, among other things, the editors said that "Pevzner [printing such a jarring surname without so much as a single initial was considered quite an ominous sign] is attempting to create a superficially harmless, apparently old-fashioned and inoffensive aesthetic, which in reality undermines the basic principles of Socialist Realism. This artist's orangerie has an unpleasant smell about it."

"They practically took the words right out of your mouth, my dear!" Sandro guffawed. He toasted his "success" with a bottle of red Mukuzani. "Having created a stir in the capital of 'nonconflictual' art, having drawn dangerous, subversive flowers."

"What did you think, Pevzner Solomonovich," Nina replied, "that they don't teach us anything at the Writers' Union? Every one of us has to be ready at any moment to give a rebuke to any upstart decadents at the summons of . . . mmm . . . well, at the summons of . . . mmm . . . well, you know, at the call of our hearts!"

This bit of gallows humor took Nina back to the thirties on Bolshoi

Gnezdnikovsky Street: the notes posted in the kitchen, such as "If they come for you first, don't forget to check the gas and turn off the electricity," and all the silliness that had helped her and Savka to keep from going mad. Things had been better then, in a paradoxical way: the broom had been sweeping indiscriminately, it had been something like a natural disaster. Now, however, a loyal Party critic appealed to the "organs" and alerted them to pay attention to a "superficially harmless artist." And we're still making jokes. Hasn't our irony gone on a bit too long? Isn't it time it went the way of our youth? Yet without it, it would be the end, there would be nothing but gloom and idiocy.

So what the hell. We'll go on with our lives and make jokes, perhaps the arc of life will lead us to safety, just as it did back then, in spite of her well-known Trotskyite past. Nothing else is left except to live and draw flowers.

What are they going to do with all this stuff if they come and search the place, make an arrest, and then confiscate everything? It would be interesting to see how the KGB would describe these belongings. Sandro's recently acquired passion for painting department store mannequins would wreak havoc on the MGB's inventories and lists. The most dangerous thing, however, was not on or along the walls but in that rickety old desk in the loft at which member of the Union of Soviet Writers Nina Borisovna Gradov sometimes spent hours away from her translations from the language of the Karakalpaks. Poems and prose that will never see the light of day. Which of us is better off, the artist or the writer? That depends on what you consider the end result of the creative process: a manuscript or a book? An artist, somehow or other, sees the result of his process, a completed picture. Can one consider a manuscript a finished product if it never becomes a book?

Nina was engaged in these not terribly inspiring thoughts as she lugged her shopping bag full of wine and groceries along. The question "Which of us is better off?" translated simply into "Which of us is worse off?" It angered her to think she had lived her entire life with these savage criminals. And there was no light at the end of the tunnel. Just think, never once to have been abroad in one's life! Father and Mother, in their younger days, had always spent their holidays in Europe and had even made it to Egypt once and wandered among the pyramids! The swindlers sealed all our doors, for good. There's only one way to get out of the country—to sign on with the phony struggle for peace, that is, to sell out, all at once and from the gut, like Fadeev, Surkov, Polevoi, Simonov, and, alas, Ilya Ehrenburg. . . . To start speaking at meetings, to passionately expose Wall Street and the Pentagon, to pull the wool over the eyes of the European and American simpletons who come to this country for visits. So now you yourself could join the delegation of reliable individuals to the peace congress. A woman who isn't old yet, not bad to look at, an inspired poetess . . . just pick up that idiotic pathos and make it your own . . . you might be able to catch a few Frédéric Joliot-Curies on that hook. So that's the kind of rubbish that's going through your mind now. That's because you have to carry a heavy load around while you're wearing high heels. This "far from harmless artist" has enslaved me completely! He sits there in his tower listening to records and fooling around with his brushes and paints, while "the Woman"—that is, a being whose name in Tbilisi is always said as though it were spelled with a capital letter but who is not always invited to the table—has to lug the shopping around. I can imagine the whiskered face of my chosen one when I suddenly join the struggle for peace and go off to Valparaiso.

For some reason she had lately been thinking about the West a lot. She not infrequently recalled the closest she had ever come to the West: during an air raid in 1941, in the depths of the metro, she had found herself back to back with an American journalist with a pipe protruding from the pocket of his tweed jacket. He smelled of something purely Western, an odor that could hold out for a long time, obviously, even in the sultry bomb shelters, a mixture of good soap, good tobacco, good alcohol . . . in other words, everything good. As they were speaking, it seemed to her that she recognized the sort of cosmopolitan newspaperman who would bear some relation to what Mandelstam had in mind when he wrote: "I drink to the asters of war, to everything for which I stand accused. . . . To the melody of Savoyard pines, to the reek of petrol on the Champs-Élysées. . . . To the red-headed haughtiness of English women and quinine from distant colonies. . . ." It had seemed to her then that he would offer her some way out, some sort of dizzying flight, but soon afterwards panic had broken out in the metro, and they had lost sight of each other forever.

Veronika had been more fortunate: she had shaken off everyone and everything, including the camps and all the graves. She lives in some state over there that sounds like the name of a toy: Connecticut. Then again, what do I know about her life now? Maybe she's wailing from sadness. From missing her son or her stunning appearances on Gorky Street. Maybe she would trade everything she has in Connecticut for my garret with its artist and his not-so-"harmless" flowers? There's always a motif of misfortune running through the idea of flight. It's not without reason, after all, that they say "You can't run away from yourself."

She took the elevator up to the sixth floor, walked up another two flights of stairs, and then finally opened the door of the attic lair, which more and more often she did not want to leave, for any reason. A record was playing, of course: Bach's "Concerto for Two Violins." Sandro was sitting in a far corner with his latest flower, which could not have been made to fit into any classification whatsoever. Not long ago, he had made a triangular skylight in the ceiling, and now he loved to sit there surrounded by a triple-faceted column of light, seemingly screened off from contemptible everyday life, where women were lugging around bags full of groceries. Gumilyov's *Romantic Flowers*. Nina felt a sudden pang of jealousy toward the emerging masterpiece, a half-opened bud revealing a heart that was almost kaleidoscopic. Right now I'll go up to him, start by kissing him on the neck, let my hands wander downward, and I'll take him away from his flowers. Something strange is happening to this painter. Ever since he began this series, or this "period," if you will, his interest in nature—why, it was obvious that he was always drawing her little flower, as it were— had waned. The walls were burning with a fire that was more and more intense, while his own flames turned pale. Suddenly a thought struck her: this orangerie period had begun just at the time she had met Igor. He hadn't known anything about her liaison with the youngster, of course, and didn't know about it now—how could he? He almost never came down from his garret, no gossip could reach him. But perhaps he had sensed something, with his hands, on his skin, in his member. Maybe he had felt her "new period" and was unconsciously answering her with his flowers, that is, with a memory of a time when she had had no one but him.

Without showing the slightest sign that this thought had struck her, she put the bags down in the enclosure that served as a kitchen, and shouted across the studio, "Yolka hasn't called?"

"Not yet," he answered and came to help her with the unpacking.

"Listen, Sandro," she said without looking at him, occupying herself instead with the eggplants. "Don't you think that maybe you're going . . . a bit too far with these flowers of yours? . . ."

Now they were looking at each other. He smiled and presented his bald spot, which, in keeping with their established ritual, she caressed with a few light slaps, as if patting a child.

After seven, the guests began to arrive. It was curious that Yolka's young musician friends, Kalashnikova the flutist, for example, were the first to turn up, instead of coming late. I wonder how she knew the way here, thought Nina, looking on as the lively young woman strolled casually through the fields of Pevzner's flowers. Maybe I'm wrong in thinking Sandro leads the life of a hermit. She was pierced by a feeling of jealousy, like a fleeting attack of colic.

"Your place is marvelous, Nina Borisovna," said the flutist. "I'm so grateful to Yolka for introducing me to Alexander Solomonovich's work and for inviting me to come this evening."

Of course, she's a teacher at the conservatory, Nina reasoned. Your attack of colic seems a bit silly now, respected Nina Gradov, distinguished figure of the arts in the Adygeian ASSR. After all, we're just worn-out old folks to them. Igor doesn't count, he's a poet.

The young genius Slava Rostropovich, of whom it was said in Moscow that he was second only to, if not better than, Pablo Casals, dashed in, dragging his cello in its case. He immediately set about kissing everyone in greeting. He kissed Kalashnikova like an old friend, even though he had never seen her before. He embraced Sandro, kissing him on the cheeks, lips, nose, and forehead, and in the pauses between kisses managed to cry the word "Stunning!" which in all probability had to do with the paintings, not with the objects which he had kissed. Rushing over to the kitchen, he began to cover the poetess with kisses in her turn. "Ninochka, you look simply marvelous! You're simply a wonder of a woman! You have to come and see me sometime! Or I'll come to your place!"

"But you've already been to my place, Slava!" Nina said with a smile, trying to remember since when had they been on such familiar terms, if it wasn't only just now. "And where's Yolochka?" Rostropovich asked, jutting forward his whalelike chin and shaking his crop of blond hair while eyeing the kitchen as though Yolochka, the object of his search, might be sitting on the floor or perched beneath a chair. "Where is she, where is she, where is she? I just adore her, simply revere her. Ninka, do you want me to be perfectly honest with you? When I first saw you, I thought, Here's a woman who must come to my place, I have to play for her alone, you know, tête-à-tête—and then when I met Yolochka . . . well, you can't imagine, everything was turned upside down. She's the one, to play together with her, our eyes meeting! So where is she?"

Good old Slava, thought Nina. If the two of them were really to play together, nothing could be better.

She dialed the number at Bolshoi Gnezdnikovsky Street several times, but Yolka wasn't home. After Rostropovich there arrived Stasik Neigauz, the son of the famous Genrikh Neigauz and a pianist in his own right. Yolka's intentions now became clear. The trio was to be made up of Rostropovich, Kalashnikova, and herself. Stasik, a handsome young fellow and a trendsetter, would play a solo piece as an appetizer. And now everyone was here except for the ringleader.

Stasik sedately came over to kiss Nina's hand, asked for a shot of vodka in order to understand "what century it is outside," and told her his father might be coming with "Uncle Borya," that is, Pasternak.

The latter appeared soon afterward, but alone, and immediately sat down by the telephone. All of those present—the guests numbered no more than ten in all—looked on reverently as the living classic spoke to his beloved. As people who belonged to the same set, they were all aware, of course, that the brilliant poet, who had now been hounded out of literature, had in his life an unlawful and marvelous source of inspiration, somewhat in the manner that Ararat lies beyond the borders of Armenia. Pasternak obviously sensed that all eyes were upon him and was working the crowd a bit: he gestured with his hand a bit more artistically than was necessary, frowned a bit more and slightly more romantically than the circumstances called for, and rumbled almost inaudibly. Present among the guests was a twenty-year-old student from the Institute of Literature, a rosy-cheeked "talented novice" with a dense mop of slightly greasy hair named Igor Ostroumov, who was staring at le maître in a state approaching a trance: Is that really him, in the flesh, and we're under the same roof together?

Nina, meanwhile, was pacing around with worry and casting eloquent glances at Pasternak that said "How many times can you babble the same thing?" which he obviously either did not notice or did not understand. As soon as he was off the phone, she hastened to make another call. Still no answer at Bolshoi Gnezdnikovsky Street. Then she tried the number of Parmesanov, Yolka's tennis coach. "Listen, Tolya, you must have seen Yolka at the match, how is she?" "She's fine," replied the disgruntled Parmesanov. "She won against Lukin." "Where did she go afterward? Didn't she say anything to you?" "Why would she have said anything to me, Nina Borisovna?" Parmesanov asked almost indignantly. "She took off with some *stilyaga* . . . no, there's no danger, he was still wet behind the ears."

Well, you can't ask the police to look for a nineteen-year-old girl when she takes off with a *stilyaga* and doesn't appear at a party she organized in her own honor. Well then, comrades, shall we eat? After all, it won't do to leave so many people languishing. We'll start dinner, and then Yolka, that good-for-nothing, will arrive on the run, and we'll have the concert, right?

"No, let's play first and then eat," Stasik proposed.

"Quite right!" Slava shouted. "First we play, then we'll have a bit of dinner, and then, when Yolka comes, we'll play some more! Stasik, take a seat at the piano!"

"My goodness, friends, I really do love these Vorontsov baby grands—almost as much as my own cello." He eyed the instrument carnivorously as he pawed its black sides. He seemed to be trying to decide where to kiss it and finally settled reasonably on the keys, sounding a bass note.

"Well, it doesn't matter to me when we play," said a flutist named Shaposhnikov. "I don't drink."

They started to play and went on for no less than an hour. The old Italian strains of Vivaldi's "The Four Seasons" poured forth, sometimes soaring to the heavens of inspiration. They played freely, sometimes losing their concentration and stopping, laughing, and starting again. "It's not turning out too badly, you know—we hung that together nicely, guys. Let's do 'Primavera' one more time," Rostropovich muttered as if rising to the surface of a body of water, then lifted his face, sculpted by inspiration, to the ceiling, only to dive back into the depths again. Not having yet reached the general public, the music of the Baroque reigned supreme among conservatory students.

Yolka still did not appear, neither during the concert, nor after dinner, when Slava and Stasik began fooling around and "jammed," playing something like jazzy dance music. Nina asked Sandro with her eyes: What should we do? Sandro replied with a gesture of his hands that said: What can you do? You remember what you were like when you were nineteen?

The guests went home around midnight. Only Igor Ostroumov continued to hover around Nina, helping her to clear away the dishes and humming along with Sandro, who was walking around the studio with a glass of wine, singing Georgian songs and looking at his flowers.

"Are you getting ready to move in?" Nina quietly asked the young man. "Come on, now, take your hat and say good night!"

"So we'll see each other tomorrow, Nina Borisovna, right?" Igor asked in a scarcely audible whisper. "At the same time, right? As usual?" You old fool, she muttered to herself. Something has happened to Yolka, there's your reward for your monkey business!

When they were left alone, Nina and Sandro sat down at the long table, on which cheese and bottles of wine still remained. "I'll wait another half hour, then I'm calling the police," said Nina.

"Let's wait until morning, at least," Sandro proposed.

"You, of course, don't give a damn about my only daughter! You're cold and empty! All you want to do is paint your flowers, but they're just holes, holes, I tell you! Holes that lead to a Paradise that doesn't exist! To hell with it all, I'm taking everything and moving back to Gnezdnikovsky! I'll never set foot in this place again!"

He stared at her wide-eyed and looked so comical in his fright that she could barely keep from laughing. "Ninulya, dearest, if you leave, I'll set fire to everything! I'll organize an auto-de-fé! Without you, I don't exist! Everything I do is for you, about you, because of you! Everything will be all right, Ninulya, just don't leave me!" A damned fool Charlie Chaplin, Nina thought. He turns any drama into a comedy just by the way he looks.

She began to shake: "Don't you understand, there's absolutely no reason that she couldn't have called! Okay, so she falls in love and—

well—goes to bed with someone, but she couldn't have forgotten that we're expecting her, that this is her evening, in honor of her graduation!"

Just then the phone rang. That lousy little twit! Nina flew across the studio. I'll let her have it, then drink a whole bottle of something, one glass after another until I fall asleep. Instead of Yolka, though, she heard the thick voice of a man: "Forgive me for calling so late, Nina Borisovna . . ."

★

Half an hour before this call, Major General N. Lamadze had arrived at his office in the bureau of the deputy chairman of the Council of Ministers of the USSR, which occupied nearly a whole floor of a huge building on Okhotny Ryad. This was what he usually did whenever the "marshal" (this was what secret police agents in the know called their chief, a rather eccentric figure in a soft hat and a pince-nez) took it into his head to snatch a girl off the street. It was necessary to establish the identity of the latest "lucky winner" in order to avoid any misunderstandings and unforeseen consequences. It went without saying that the parents had to be notified, out of purely humane considerations. For these nocturnal activities alone, that dirty old toad deserves a bullet in the mouth!

Captain Gromovoi, the night duty man, reported that "the objective" was presently located where it had been delivered, that is, in the mansion on Kachalov Street. Nugzar often wondered why Lavrenty always took the girls to his family home, given the unlimited number of other possibilities. Maybe he wanted to make a fool of his wife, an offspring of the respected Gigechkori family, one more time, or maybe this was just his idea of "relaxing at home"? Captain Gromovoi went on: a student identification card from a music conservatory had been found in the objective's bag. Here are the initial data: Elena Kitaigorodsky, born 1933, student in piano. They're checking her out at the Lubyanka right now, we should have more information any minute. Just then a bell rang—undoubtedly the courier arriving. After adjusting the pistol holster on his belt, the captain went to open the door for the messenger.

This girl, whom they had tracked from Pushkin Square to Mayakovsky, had totally dumbfounded the marshal's imagination.

"She, she—" he murmured, not taking his eyes from the binoculars. "Nugzar, there she is, there's my dream!"

Nugzar just snorted. "It seems to me, Lavrenty, that she's not really your type."

Beria had chuckled and issued a lazy groan. "You know my tastes better than I do, do you? You think that only hairdressers are good enough for me, is that it? An aristocrat like that isn't for me, eh? Well, old friend, you still don't know Lavrenty Beria!" His moist lips trembled, and his nose glowed obscenely. Is he making fun, or is he serious?

Both limousines stopped in the middle of the square just across from the metro exit. "Come on, Nugzar, don't look at it as part of your job, do it as a friend! You see, she's standing in line. It's a convenient moment!"

Nugzar had a bad feeling about it all that was wearing him down. Another cheap farce is being played out, as though we were two buddies on Golovin Prospect in Tbilisi. "Somehow I don't want to, Lavrenty."

Beria suddenly clung to him and whispered into his ear, "You don't understand—we're starting an all-out war soon, and we might all get killed. This is no time to play prissy games!"

Nugzar was seething as he walked toward the metro. What sort of rot was he talking, the dirty jackal? What sort of all-out war can break out if we can't even deal with the Yanks in Korea who don't know how to fight? It's time to kill him, or . . . or at least to go to Comrade Stalin by one means or another and let him know that his closest henchman is preparing the restoration of capitalism. After he had shown the flabbergasted young woman his MGB badge and intoned the sacramental phrase, he turned and walked away, inviting his escorts to stuff her into the second limousine, which had just pulled up.

And now the report from the Lubyanka was on the desk in front of him: Elena Kitaigorodsky, born 1933, Russian nationality, birthplace Moscow, registered to live in Moscow, 11 Bolshoi Gnezdnikovsky Street, apartment #48, student at a music conservatory. Father killed at the front. Mother: Nina Gradov, born 1907, registered at the same address, member of the Union of Soviet Writers.

"What's wrong, Comrade Major General?" the duty officer exclaimed. "Should I call an ambulance?"

Nugzar tore open the clasps at the collar of his uniform jacket. Two bloodshot eyes were suddenly focused on him. Everything he had just read would have to be blotted dry so that it wouldn't all be smeared. Under no circumstances must it be allowed to merge together into one illegible mass. Breathe, he told himself. Wh-e-e-w-w. "I don't need an ambulance—pour me a cognac!" he ordered. Captain Gromovoi did not need to be told twice. After the cognac, Nugzar could think calmly and even on a higher plane: well, there it is, everything is coming to an end. Nina's daughter, the daughter of the only woman I was ever really in love with, as a human being and a young man should be, and who might even be my own daughter, I handed her over to be raped by that sick monster! Hold on, now, don't go mixing with the tribe of humanity, damn it! You're a hired killer, a thug, an expert in strong-arm tactics, you have no business falling into a faint over some human nonsense. But no, no, I'm really not like that, I'm no monster. I really loved her, and I loved Uncle Galaktion, and I love my family, save and protect me! If I tortured people, it was purely out of ideological considerations, not because of devotion to the powerful band. One way or another, it's over. To imagine Nina's daughter underneath Lavrenty . . . it's too much! "Have a car and a bodyguard brought round to entrance number four!" he ordered. He thrust the unfinished bottle of Gremi into his pocket. He gathered up all the papers from the table and put them back into the folder. Suddenly he stopped in one of the corners of the office, put his face to the wall, and stood there for a minute, waiting for a thought to come to him. Finally, one did: What am I getting ready to do? Other thoughts came rolling up behind that one: I've got to see Nina right away. She might do something rash that can't be made right. I've got to stop her. Then a few selfish considerations came to him in rapid succession. Desperate people unexpectedly manage to reach the highest levels sometimes. The incident will become public knowledge. Rumors will go around that the secret police raped the daughter of a poetess, the granddaughter of an Academician, the niece of a legendary marshal. No one would dare to talk about Him, of course—they would pass the buck down the line. There's a scapegoat, after all—me, General Lamadze, the man who approaches girls on the street. . . .

The best thing to do would be to take Elena away from Kachalov Street right now. Maybe he'll let her go?

He dialed the telephone numbers of the house that only he knew. Beria answered. "What's happened?" His voice was somber and terrible.

In his agitation, Nugzar could hardly breathe. "Lavrenty Pavlovich, I considered it my duty to report something to you. An unfortunate hitch has developed. That girl . . . she's a Gradov . . . the granddaughter of the Academician . . . well, you know . . ."

"*Dzekhneri!*" the marshal growled in Georgian. "I'm asking you, *gamakhlebulo,* what is it? Why are you, *Khle,* calling me at this time of night?"

"No instructions in the matter?" Nugzar asked. "Maybe we should take her home?" This time, Beria swore in Russian and slammed the receiver down.

Well, you found a way to shake up the all-powerful satrap with your Gradovs, didn't you? How could there be a hitch where the whim of a member of the Politburo was concerned, the deputy chairman of the Council of Ministers, the chief of the internal security forces? Infallible, untouchable, omnipotent, until some brave officer comes in one day and puts a red-hot bullet between his eyes.

Nugzar went down in the elevator and walked out onto Okhotny Ryad. Moscow was deserted. Only a few drunks were sounding off on the other side of the boulevard as wide as the Volga as they emerged from a restaurant, and taxis were rushing by like devils. Lucky drunks, lucky taxi drivers, even the driver of my lousy car is lucky, and so is the thug accompanying me. Anyone who isn't in General Lamadze's skin tonight is a lucky man!

They drove to the Arbat or, more precisely, to Krivoarbatsky, to the studio of Sandro, that bastard from Tbilisi, who had already been under surveillance for quite some time. All the same, I've got to call and warn them. People get a bit nervous when men in MGB uniforms show up in the middle of the night. He called from a telephone booth a hundred yards from the house. Like a gentleman, he said, "Excuse me, Nina Borisovna. This is Nugzar Lamadze. No, nothing terrible has happened. I have to see you. I'll be there in five minutes."

She was already standing in the doorway when they reached the top of the confounded tower. Time seems to have no effect on her, what a mystery that woman is! "Nina, I swear by the Aragva, time has no effect on you, what a mysterious woman you are!"

With eyes wide with fear, Nina looked on as he approached with his bully boy. The young *abrek* could almost no longer be seen in that huge body, which made him look more like a Levantine merchant. What had he come for? Oh God, speed up the passing of the minutes if it's nothing terrible! If the "merchant" is joking, it can't be too bad, no?

Leaving his man at the door, Nugzar walked into the studio. "Greetings to you, *gamardzhoba*, Nina! Greetings to you, Sandro, *batono!* Talk about the twists of fate, eh? The star of Tiflis, Our Girl, now belongs to this sort of—" He had been about to say "little Jew" but corrected himself in time. "—this sort of little Sandro!"

He sat down in a chair. "What a pleasure to come into a Georgian home! Imagine, a *kakhetin* table like that in the middle of Moscow. I say, I wouldn't say no to a glass of wine."

The glass of wine trembled in his hand. Nina noticed this and broke out in a sweat. "What's going on, Nugzar? Have your people . . . arrested Yolka?"

He laughed good-naturedly and drained the glass. "On the contrary, on the contrary—she has arrested one of ours, and just imagine which one!"

Munching on a radish and breaking off a piece of cheese, he once again eyed Nina in seeming amazement. "Ah, Nina, I swear by the Rion, how good it is you're so thin. A certain Englishwoman said, 'You can never be too rich or too thin.' Or was it the other way around?"

Nina slapped her hand on the table in a fury. "Stop playing the clown! Tell me what's wrong!"

"All right, friends, let's get down to it," Nugzar said, pushing away the bottle and sitting down again. His service cap with its oval MGB insignia lay on the table all by itself like a sort of icon; Sandro noticed this automatically. "Think of it, friends, as winning the lottery. The fact is, Yolka made a tremendous impression on one of the leading statesmen of the Soviet Union, to be precise, on my boss, a man whom I respect with every fiber of my being: Lavrenty Pavlovich Beria. Believe me, he's a complex, interesting man, a man of great erudition and artistic taste, wise and generous—in a word, an extraordinary person. I could have told you nothing about this whole business, no one sent me here. However, I considered it my duty as a friend to tell you about this event, so that you wouldn't get the wrong idea about it, that it's some sort of unpleasant trivial thing. In fact, this event is a deeply human, emotional occasion. Please, don't interrupt me! First of all, let's talk about what this all promises for our Yolka, whom I'm not honored to know, but whom I love like a daughter. As a result of this event, she receives support from the most powerful quarters a young girl and aspiring pianist can dream of. A brilliant finish to the conservatory, a concert tour abroad, winning competitions, those are the events that await her after *this* event. Then, all sorts of perks, like the best studios and shops Moscow has to offer, complete material security, a wonderful, spacious flat, first-class holidays on the Black Sea—anything you can name will be offered to her as a sign of gratitude for this event. I know what I'm talking about, because I know this man like I know myself. He will know how to thank her for this deeply emotional event. Moreover, he will think of you now, my friends, as his own. I know he's not indifferent to poetry, and undoubtedly, after today's exciting event, any book of your verses, so long as it's not of an anti-Party or oppositionist nature—which is what some of the comrades of the Writers' Union tell us though I personally have never believed it; you can't hold a person's youthful errors against her forever—any book, even if it's not easy reading, will be able to see the light of day. And your orangerie, my dear Sandrik, will receive its just due, and this whole fantastic home of yours will be completely secure after this event, even though we have gotten reports about it to the effect that suspicious poems are read here to the accompaniment of church music. My friends, you will now be in complete security after this favorable and exciting event, which dirty tongues may say all kinds of foolish things about—dirty tongues, though, that we will have cut out!" A convulsion passed diagonally over his face, starting in the upper left-hand corner of his forehead and ending in the lower right-hand corner of his chin, and he finally stopped talking. As he had been saying all of this, Nina had sat with her fingers interlaced beneath the table, without taking her eyes from the criminal face with its bluish shaved surfaces, and was astounded by her own obtuseness: she didn't understand what he was talking about. What "event"?

She turned helplessly to Sandro. "What's he talking about? Sandrik, do you understand what he's saying?"

Sandro took her by the shoulders, his face, threateningly aflame, turned in the fearsome general's direction. "He's saying, dear, that they've taken our Yolka away for Beria!"

Finally everything came together in Nina's mind, and the phrase "after this favorable and exciting event" stood out particularly; she realized that everything had already been done, that there was no getting anything back. Her daughter, her one and only, the child of her love, defiled; Beria, a statesman of the Soviet Union, had used her to his heart's content. With a shriek, she tore herself loose from Sandro, then snatched up a knife from the table and rushed at Nugzar. The astounded general watched agape as the object, that same object with which he had just cut himself a piece of cheese, flashed near his throat. At the last moment, Sandro managed to grab Nina's hand. At the noise the bodyguard came in from the entrance hall on the run, pistol in hand. "Nobody move, or I'll shoot!" he screamed; obviously, he had received a fright himself. Nugzar, who had turned a cyanotic pale blue, restrained his man with one hand. "Take it easy, Yurchenko, put your gun away!" He reached out with the other to Nina, who in her dazed fury looked not only her age, but even ten years older, her slight goiter, the pouches beneath her eyes, and her flaccid cheeks suddenly apparent.

"How can you put this interpretation on things?" Nugzar appealed to them. "Let's talk about this, friends, I'll explain everything again!"

"Where is she?" Nina wailed in a frightful voice.

"She's perfectly safe," muttered Nugzar.

"Give her back! Now!"

"Friends, friends, what's all this Shakespearean passion?" Nugzar remonstrated. "You simply don't understand how lucky you are. In our serious times—"

Sandro seated Nina in a deep armchair, then strode decisively over to Nugzar and handed him his "icon," his service hat with the insignia.

"Get out of my house, you scum! And take that idiot of yours with you!"

"How narrow-minded you are!" a wincing Nugzar said. "Listen, Pevzner, at least you should think practically." The hat, thrown by the hand of the artist, sailed toward the door.

"For that, you'll pay," Nugzar said, and the sharp features of the Tbilisi bandit of the old days showed on his mercantile cheeks.

☆

By morning, Beria already knew everything about his chance "guest." During the night they had even raised the director of the Merzlyakov School to get the information they needed. She was an excellent student, a great musical talent, successful on the playing field, but a bit haughty, spoiled by her family, had too high an opinion of herself. The Devil has jerked me around again, getting me mixed up with this cherry, thought the chief. I'm not at an age when I should still be fooling around with cherries. I've swallowed enough humiliations as it is! She had been shrieking and looking at him in horror, as though it were a crocodile touching her rather than a middle-aged man. We're not bringing up our young people properly, that's the whole problem. Beautiful girls grow up without the slightest notion of eroticism, a whole frigid generation. Particular attention will be paid to this area in the society of the future. Even drugged, after the right glass of mineral water, she was still trying to protect her pussy. A great treasure, ha, ha! Even proud nations, in the end, give in and surrender their pussies under the pressure of superior forces. Unfortunately, such pressure had been unavailable. This last circumstance had plunged him into gloom. What's happening? Can it be impotence creeping up on me? Where was this tension and this psychological barrier coming from? Holding in his hand the distressed object, for some time he watched Yolka, who had finally fallen into a drugged stupor. The naked beauty only trembled and soundlessly cried in her sleep. How beautiful she is, though! For a Helen like that, one could start a war!

Perhaps in the future, I will be condemned for having treated girls a bit unceremoniously, but will they make an effort to understand? A Don Juan lives inside me, but I also have to run a huge government, such are the dictates of fate. I can't court girls while I'm in the middle of these vile peasants, the Bolsheviks, pretending to be one of them. No one will dare say a word to me, of course, as long as it's all under a shroud of secrecy—but if I were to approach these girls openly, I'd be accused straight away of bourgeois decadence. In the future, the heads of government will always be surrounded by a group of the most outstanding girls in the country, just like this Elena here.

If only I could bring her close to me in public, there wouldn't be any hysterics in the Gradov clan. What's to be done with them now? The whole bunch of them has to be wiped out. I'll entrust the job to Lamadze. When she's left alone, this Elena will cling only to me. That old fool the professor—who has so much nerve, how do you like it!—will go up in the "doctors' trial." The presence of a Russian in the criminal band of Jews will be a politically sound step. His Georgian old lady is obviously growing old, it will be easy for her to settle a bit ahead of time in the next world. The poetess will be sent to the Taimyr, and may or may not reach her destination. Nugzar himself will take care of the artist, of course—he knows how it's done. My beauty's uncle, we can stick down a uranium mine, and in six months there won't be so much as a scrap left of him. There's still one more kid, the marshal's son, a motorcycle racer. He has Vaska covering him, but it's a dangerous sport he's involved in. He loves danger so he has only himself to blame. His mother, a spy in America, could have the same sort of danger lying in wait for her, and her daughter, alas, would share her fate. We'll have to run a check on their roots in Georgia, though—you have to expect any sort of dirty trick from my countrymen, any kind of vendetta. Well, when everything's finished, I'll have to part with Nugzar—he's related to them, after all. I'll be damned, the sorts of things you think about when you can't sleep!

Toward morning, Beria had already begun showing the signs of a fierce hangover, but he still could not take his eyes off the sleeping Elena. If we were the same age, I'd be in love with her for the rest of my life. A ray of sunshine emerged from behind the high chimney of the building across the street and, like a gently stroking finger, fell on the face of the girl, on her bare breasts with their pointy, slightly swollen nipples, on her stomach and inner thigh, where several red spots had formed: maybe the result of recent menstruation, maybe some damage he had inflicted during their fruitless battle. She smiled in her sleep and coyly waved her hand, as though she wanted to say to someone: stop talking nonsense! In the meantime, the distressed man was showing no signs of activity. This dawn is my sunset, Beria said to himself, his thoughts now plumbing the depths of ugliness. My wife doesn't sleep all night, the bitch, she listens to the sounds coming from my half of the house. He took out a notepad and began to write a note for the sleeping nymph: "Delightful creation! Our meeting has turned me upside down, like Ludwig van Beethoven's *Appassionata* sonata. You are my last luv! The luv of an old warrior. Dark forces are around me, they are many, and they need to be fought against, yet I can think only of you. For now, rest, feel completely comfortable, and know that you are in no danger. We will see each other again soon. Thank you for your luv.

"L. Beria."

Leaving the note on the table where his captive's clothes had been thrown, he embarked upon one more attempt to improve his mood. He sat down on the bed and began kissing and caressing Elena's enchanting breasts. Alas, the distressed object still was not showing enough energy. To hell with it, *dzekhneri,* he cursed to himself, and left the sleeping girl alone.

He had a difficult day before him. He was supposed to chair a meeting of the Council of Ministers on the question of the transfer of manpower to the Far East, where, north of the Amur, a pipeline was under construction, along with a railway of the greatest strategic importance. The deputy chairman doused himself for an hour or two, taking now coffee, now century-old cognac. Finally, he went out into the entrance hall. There, among others, a downcast, puffy Lamadze was already sitting. Greeting him politely, the marshal ordered him to take Comrade Elena Kitaigorodsky to one of the secret dachas, to see that she had every comfort, including a swimming pool, a tennis court, and a grand piano—particularly important is the piano. She's not to be allowed to use the telephone. Take special measures to see that all of this is kept in the utmost secrecy. Then L. P. Beria left for the meeting.

Riding along Gorky Street, he suddenly remembered that one of his protégées, Lyuda Sorokin, had been living in this lane behind the Moscow Soviet for three years now and was even nursing his child— he couldn't remember if it was a girl or a boy. At the thought of her, the distressed object suddenly sprang up mightily, shaking off all the affronts of the previous night. He dropped in at Sorokin's place and for half an hour screwed the greatly surprised and happy beauty in the bathroom, which was where he found her.

What does it all mean? he wondered as he continued on his way to the Council of Ministers. No, Friedrich Engels, you weren't right about everything. Somehow or other, Lyuda Sorokin had contributed greatly to making his colloquium go forward under the sign of historical optimism; otherwise, things might have ended badly for several of its, er, members—the colloquium, that is.

★

On the afternoon of the same day, Nina and Sandro arrived in a taxi at the most ominous building in Moscow, on Dzerzhinsky Square. The driver wanted to have nothing to do with stopping at the main entrance to the MGB, where two sergeants were posted, carrying pistols on their belts. Their round buttocks protruded jauntily, and it seemed as though their thin boots would burst any second from the pressure of their fat legs. "They'll take down my license plate number! Better I drop you off on Sretenka Boulevard." Nina, however, insisted that he stop right where she had been told to, at entrance number one. The driver became nervous as she tried to convince her husband not to wait but to go back to the studio on Krivoarbatsky. Sandro refused: he had to be by her side. Finally, almost shouting, she shook her fist under his nose: "Get out of here! Now!" There was no particular reason for her insistence other than the fact that she wished to confront this calamity on her own. I won't share this disaster, this unimaginable humiliation, with anyone! She had been haunting the thresholds of the Writers' Union bosses' offices all day, and now she remembered with disgust the change that had come over these Aleksandr Fadeevs, Nikolai Tikhonovs, and Aleksandr Surkovs at the mention of the MGB, how they had suddenly been plunged into a state of panic when she mentioned Beria's name in connection with the disappearance of her daughter. At the Union of Soviet Writers, she went to the office of the general secretary, whose blue eyes had lingered on the poetess Gradov with sincere masculine interest more than once. No sooner had he understood the nature of the affair than he let his hands dance across his desk like a pair of wounded woodcocks that had just been shot out of the sky, barely managing to soothe them in their agony by gripping the arms of his armchair, he said "That, Nina Borisovna, is not our department, not at all."

Fearing for her parents, she had decided to say nothing to them, although the only man who could really be of any help was her father. She had raced to Boris IV's place, but he was out of town, had just headed off for the Caucasus. What could he do anyway, this sportsman and ex-paratrooper? The Georgian spirit in him would immediately drive him to take up arms, but that could be the ruin of us all, and Yolka would be the first to go. In the evening, if nothing has happened, I'll have to go to Silver Forest and take it up with Father.

Suddenly there appeared a building manager, scared to death, who handed her a note that had arrived by special courier from the MGB and said that Major General Lamadze wished to receive her. On the vile scrap of paper were written the words "on a personal matter" in parentheses.

The antechamber she entered immediately put the lie to any notion that one might enter there "on a personal matter," at least of his own accord. The heavy official style that had been established at the end of the 1940s and enshrined in the 1950s—seemingly forever—reigned supreme: heavy curtains, massive chandeliers, copper door handles. A huge portrait of Stalin wearing gold-trimmed shoulder boards hung next to a padded door. At the end of the office, on the stairs, stood a black stone Lenin, like Mayakovsky's "Negro getting on in years." Still making jokes, Nina thought to herself, and sternly presented the note along with her identification and her membership card in the Writers' Union to the guard in the glass booth. He picked up the telephone indifferently, though not without sliding a curious, greasy little glance over her. He's probably just remembered "Clouds in Blue," she thought. A young officer soon appeared. "General Lamadze is waiting for you, Comrade Gradov." Nugzar came toward her in a friendly manner, although one that hinted at the past rather than any present amicable relations. He touched her elbows and then sat down across from her in an armchair. The last time they had been alone together had been when she was pregnant with Yolka, that is, almost twenty years before.

"Well, have you calmed down?" he asked soothingly. Then he laughed pleasantly. "You're more like one of our people, Ninka, than like a Russian! What do those Georgian princesses sing? 'I know how to handle a knife, I was born in the Caucasus!' Like some wine?"

"I don't want anything except for my daughter," she said, under-lining with her voice that she would not stand for any sort of intimate tone nor for any joking. "I demand that my daughter be returned to me immediately!"

He squinted slightly, as though he had a migraine. "Listen, there's no reason to make waves. Why do you turn to those silly union bosses? After all, they immediately come running to us and tell us everything and turn it to their own advantage at that. She won't go anywhere, your daughter, believe me. No harm will come to her. She'll come back even more beautiful than she was before."

Nina could barely control her rage. Another instant, and her insane act of the previous night could be repeated. There was no knife in sight, but one could pick up that marble paperweight and split that miserable forehead, on which gray fringes crept so pretentiously from the temples. The worried Lamadze followed her glance and shuddered when he fixed his eyes on the paperweight.

She leaned forward in her chair and, looking him straight in the eye, said quietly, "Are we all still serfs, then, if our daughters can be hauled away at any moment to be violated?"

Fear and desperation. The idiot. It's the end. She's heading for self-destruction, and taking with her . . . and taking with her . . .

"You know, Nina Borisovna, this is already more serious than a kitchen knife! This is ideological terrorism!" he said in what was al-most a roar, but then added right away, "I'm exaggerating, of course, but only so that you'll choose your words more carefully." One more (final!) attempt to turn her from this rush toward doom. "Let's drop the official tone. Why won't you believe me? After all, I'm not a stranger to you Gradovs."

The final attempt failed. She spat on his extended hand. There was now no stopping the enraged woman.

"If my daughter is not returned before this evening, I—I'll— Don't narrow your eyes and make fun of me with your giggling! You scum! You always were from the gutter, and you've become miserable scum, Nugzar! Don't think your boss is omnipotent! I'll go to the Ministry of Defense, to my brother's friends! I'll go see Molotov, I know him personally! Voroshilov gave me a medal! And my father, after all, doesn't occupy the lowest position in the country! We'll find a way to let Stalin know!" she cried, gasping for breath, turning instantly, now into a terrible Fury, now into a little girl so pathetic as to move one to tears. In a cloud of gloom penetrated only by the benevolent, inhuman glances of Lenin, Stalin, and Dzerzhinsky from the standard portraits, Nugzar went to the office doors. Sadness had expelled all the oxygen from his once-so-living body. It was all over, there was no saving her now. He opened the door of his office slightly and commanded, "Call the guards!"

★

From the semicircular window of the studio on Krivoarbatsky Lane a view opened onto the vast village that was Moscow. Today, in the windy evening, it had the appearance of an antique hand-painted engraving. Cupolas and the windows on the upper floors of buildings gleamed in the setting sun. There was no government to be seen save that of the good graces of the elements. Below, a floral blanket cover hung out to dry, flapping like a royal flag over the courtyard. Even lower, through the intersecting relief lines of the city, a patch of sun-drenched pavement could be seen with its poster kiosk, against which a girl eating an ice cream pie was leaning her back and the sole of her left foot.

Sandro was impatient to sit down before a canvas. He was ashamed of himself, though: I don't have the right. My wife is there, in their hands, and I'm working. No, I don't have the right. He walked about the studio, moving his brushes from place to place. I haven't worked the whole day because of this dreadful business, he thought. Last night I didn't work because of the pleasant company, and then came this horrible thing. A few more days will probably be lost, too. I have to spend time with Nina, support her; we have no choice, we have to fight for the girl, you can't run away with your paints and a canvas. They say a pianist has to give his hands a workout every day, yet no one says an artist has to work every day, if not every hour. If I take up a brush now, however, I'll despise myself as a heartless egotist. He sat down at the Baltic radio, which, quick to warm up, began to hearten him with its green, fluctuating eye of the free elements. "Don't sleep, don't sleep, artist, don't give in to slumber. . . ." Sometimes one has to do more than just sit with a brush. Living through a lot helps with painting. Radio Monte-Carlo was playing an exhilarating waltz called "Domino." He could see the dark green alleyways of well-tended trees, the bright dots of the dominoes, the Somov motifs. How far that radio station's signal flies: from *World of Art* magazine to the world of Socialist Realism! Slipping even into the shortwave band, he picked up still another waltz, this time Khachaturian's score to Lermontov's "Masquerade." It was a program of waltzes. Lermontov, his greatest hero, the poet who had written about acts of his own doing, a champagne-soaked young man who had yet to sit down to work—even in the partisan detachment they had sucked down champagne, they would never have taken the Caucasus without it—who had better captured the Caucasus than this Scot with the Spanish eyes? We're all contemporaries: Lermontov, Pevzner, Khachaturian, Radio Monte-Carlo, dwellers on the earth in those days when flowers grew. Sliding further on down the dial, he heard the wail of jamming, and right next to it a calm male voice: ". . . that was when I started to work as a surgeon in the Hôpital Saint-Louis . . ." Without even turning around, he sensed that someone had come into the studio.

He turned and saw three men dressed in the Marina Roshcha fashion—small caps with the brims cut off, striped naval undershirts beneath their shirts, wrinkled boots—but they obviously weren't really from Marina Roshcha. How had they gotten in? There hadn't been a sound, not even the noise of a key turning in the massive lock. The three powerfully built types were approaching, wry smiles on their faces as though they were about to settle a score.

"What do you want?" Sandro shouted bravely, like Lermontov. "Who are you? Get out of here!"

"Stand up!" one of the men said quietly, coming right up to him.

"I won't!" the artist exclaimed. "Get out!"

"If you won't stand, then you'll lie down," said the other and gave Sandro a tremendous blow between the eyes with some iron object that he had concealed in his hand.

That one blow was enough. His face streaming with blood, the artist crumpled to the floor powerless, nearly unconscious, yet the plainclothes agents continued to kick him in the ribs with their leather boots and pulled his shirt up to whip his bare back with their rubber truncheons, perhaps the very same ones their fathers had used to finish off Meyerhold in the purges.

"That's what you get, you dirty Jew, when you're not polite!"

All this took ten minutes or so, and when it was over a voice from the Baltic, which was still on, reached Sandro's rapidly dwindling consciousness: "This is Radio Liberation, and you have been listening to an interview with Doctor Meshchersky, a former Moscow surgeon, now head physician at a well-known Paris hospital."

☆

In the isolation cell inside the MGB prison to which Nina had been taken, a bright bulb burned beneath the high ceiling and a peephole in the door opened slightly every ten minutes, permitting the all-encompassing eye of the guard to be seen. Every time, every ten minutes, she wanted to spit into that eye. I'll never give in to them now, Nina assured herself. They still think they're dealing with a weak woman, some pathetic creature, but I'm not a woman anymore, not a human being at all. I'll never yield to them, no matter what they do to me. Everything that has been building up inside me since the days when they beat us in Bumazhny Passage, when they shot Uncle Lado, when they left Uncle Galaktion to rot in jail, when they tortured my brothers in the cells and in the mines, when they shot Mitya in a ravine . . . everything that has built up inside me, now, when they have kidnapped and raped my only daughter, all of it will help me not to give in to them, to withstand any torture, to frighten even them with my insurmountable fury.

The cell had been designed only as a holding tank, and therefore Nina had not been taken down for disinfection, nor had they taken away her handbag containing her personal effects, among which was a notepad on which she had scribbled snatches of lines and words for poems. Still shaking with rage, she began to tear pages from the notepad without looking at the notes, shredding them into fragments. I'm not a poet for them anymore! No one can be a poet in this country! The line "The wind took up its moonlit shift" flickered in her mind. She had written it in April while waiting for Igor on a breakwater at Gagra. To hell with it! What rubbish I've filled my life with: silly little poems, lovers, "Clouds in Blue." After all, how can anyone live in a gigantic concentration camp, a leper colony stretching as far as the eye can see, where everyone is doomed to see his own features warped and deformed? Why is it we offered practically no resistance to them after 1927? We should have gone underground, so we could strike at them with terror. To perish, of course, to perish, but not to waltz and look on as the killing hammer slams down all around! We should have shot at those demons, like the one and only heroine, Fanny Kaplan.

Horror shook her like a high fever—to talk to the point of mentioning Fanny Kaplan! I just hope I didn't shout the name out loud! Instinctively, she clapped a hand over her mouth and then realized she needed to go to the toilet, and right away; another moment, and she, with all her rage, would be transformed into a stinking laughingstock.

There ought to be a *parasha,* a latrine bucket, in here! There has to be a *parasha* in a jail cell! In the hole in which she was sitting, there was no toilet, only a washbasin. If she had even been able to get her backside into the sink by climbing up onto the chair, it wasn't likely anything would come of it but ridicule, and after all, it was probably Nugzar, the erstwhile dashing bandit who was now a murderous scum, who was watching her through the peephole.

The door opened, and a portly, indifferent women in a military blouse with a sergeant's shoulder straps came in. On the small table she laid a tray with dinner: jellied perch, meatballs with buckwheat and even a bottle of something called "cherry drink."

"I have to go to the toilet," Nina cried threateningly.

"Then let's go," the woman muttered in a listless voice not entirely devoid of goodwill. The path along the corridor was covered with a green carpet. Two officers were sitting smoking in a niche beneath a portrait of a most benevolent-looking Lenin reading a newspaper. Both of them followed with expert eyes the individual in the tapping heels who was being kept in the holding tank.

When she had relieved herself, Nina was paraded past Lenin again. Instead of the two officers sitting there, there was now one, elderly and with a drooping, horrible face. "If you want to piss or crap in the night, better to knock on the wall for me," the female sergeant said. Nina surprised herself in the thought that after a successful alleviation of one's needs even the hermetic world of a secret police dungeon seemed to have its good side. In particular, she had nothing against eating the jellied walleyed pike, the meatballs, and the buckwheat kasha, drinking the cherry liquid, and smoking her Albanian cigarette. My God, what sorry creatures we are! What sort of creatures are we with our influxes and outpourings? she thought. What is humanity, really?

Chapter 10

———☆———

TABULADZE
THE ARCHITECT

"Oh, what a moon is hanging up there, Jesus, Mary, and Joseph!" cried Maika Strepetov. "Just like . . . just like . . . just like some sort of Tatyana!"

Boris laughed. "What sort of nonsense are you talking? What other Tatyanas are you going to come up with?"

Their traveling companion, Otar Nikolaevich Tabuladze, a local Tbilisi architect, smiled. "You know, that's not bad! The moon is like Tatyana. Did you remember that from *Eugene Onegin*?"

"Maybe," Maika said.

Otar Nikolaevich smiled again. "The important thing here is that it's not Tatyana but 'some sort of Tatyana'—that's what gives it its flavor. The moon is always compared to other objects. A friend of mine, a poet, in the old days used to call it 'a basketful of mold.' Pushkin, of course, compared Tatyana with the moon, not the other way around."

They were walking slowly along one of the humpbacked cobblestone streets of old Tbilisi. Maika kept hanging on Boris's shoulder and whimpering, as though she were tired. In fact, though, as he already knew, she could fly up any of the hills like a winged mare. Otar Nikolaevich, powerfully built and elegantly dressed, the sort of man who would be called "imposing," was walking slightly in front of them, seemingly in the role of tour guide.

"You're interested in poetry, Otar Nikolaevich, are you?" Maika asked him rather coquettishly.

What a little beast, Boris thought about her affectionately. She's already flirting with men of the world. What he meant by "already," only the two of them knew.

"I used to hang around with poets," said Otar Nikolaevich. "Way back when, when we were your age, we used to all wander along these old streets. We were all one band, Boris, me, your aunt Nina and her first husband . . ."

"With Aunt Nina's first husband?" Boris asked in surprise.

"Well, yes, haven't you heard about Stepan Kalistratov? He was a well-known Imaginist."

"I've never heard of him," Boris replied.

"Sad," Otar Nikolaevich said in such a way that it was impossible to tell what he was referring to: the fact that a well-known poet had been forgotten or the years that had gone by. He stopped by an old iron lamppost beside some sort of basement from which the sound of drunken voices emerged on a wave of dry, intense heat. "By the way, Boris, you know, I may be as much a relative of yours as Uncle Lado Gudiashvili. My mother, Diana, is your grandmother's sister. Perhaps you've not heard of me for the same reason that you haven't heard of Stepan. It's not the thing to talk about us. He was lost entirely, while I was saved only by a miracle. Still, it's considered bad form to talk about me, just as it was before."

★

Boris had met the likable architect a couple of hours before at the home of the famous artist Lado Davidovich Gudiashvili, to whom Grandmother Mary was distantly related, and with whom she had had a very friendly correspondence in which she took pride. The competition in Kolkhid Valley was already finished. Boris had defended his title as 350cc champion in motocross and had taken third place overall. The Air Force Club, of course, had trounced everyone else.

The feeling of triumph was intensified when, toward the end of the competition, a MiG jet flew over the peaks of the Caucasus with Vaska himself at the controls in the company of his latest love, a young swimmer whose body had a positively dolphinlike slickness. Royal gifts were showered on the athletes: suits of the best material were ordered and almost immediately tailored for everyone, each man was given a gold watch with a gold bracelet along with a hefty packet containing a bonus. A huge evening banquet was arranged in a restaurant on Mount King David, where once upon a time the poets of the Blue Horn group had feasted—something about which, naturally, no one in the present day knew anything or wanted to know.

Before dinner, Boris decided to fulfill his grandmother's request and drop in at "little Lado's," as she put it. You can call my cousin that, since I'm fifteen years older than he is, even if he is a major—the greatest, in fact—artist in Georgia, Mary had said. You simply have to meet him, Babochka, if only to see that there still exists something in the world besides your smelly, noisy, and oh-so-dangerous scooters.

He had expected to find signs of decay, of things vegetating, in the old private house on the shady street smelling of hot leaves—how else would an artist who had been criticized for formalism live?—but he came on a noisy feast. A long table was laden with fresh vegetables, berries, dried fruits, dishes of steaming food, and bottles and jugs of wine. There were no fewer than thirty guests, the men in neckties and bowties, the women in evening gowns and low-cut dresses, all energetically engaging in the main occupation of Georgians: feasting. Maika leapt back in fright. What business did she have in a group like that in her sundress bought hurriedly at a bazaar? Hold on there, you little twit! Boris took her by the arm. This was the sort of relationship that had developed between them: he played the strict father to his disobedient little girl. No, she wouldn't go in, she'd never been in a place like that. "Go on, Borka, I'll wait for you here, I'll sit in the garden." "Shut up, you little savage! This is not the only thing you're doing here for the first time!" She flushed with joyous shame and went into the house. They made for a combination of bright colors that delighted the artist and man of the house even more than the unexpected meeting with his "nephew." It turned out that almost half of the guests had met Mary Vakhtangovna at one time or another and that many were even distantly related to her. Many, if not all, knew "Auntie Nina," and everyone, of course, had great respect for the fallen hero Marshal Gradov, in whose great feats one circumstance had played a quite important role: he was half Georgian! "He's Georgian on his mother's side, so that makes him a Georgian," declared the most important guest, the "people's writer" and "living classic" Konstantin Gamsakhurdia. Boris was surprised by the fact that none of those at the party was in the know about the most important event of the season, that is to say, the motorcycle competitions that had just taken place; no one knew that young Gradov had defended his title as motocross champion of the USSR in the 350cc class.

The host insisted that he call him "Uncle Lado." Slight, long-haired, with a billowing, peonylike foulard beneath his chin that gave him the appearance of a Parisian artist, he guided his young guests along the walls, showing them a series of works he had just completed called *Serafita's Promenade*. He kept on looking at Maika and muttering, "I have to paint this child! This child has just my colors. I want to paint her!" He opened a door to an adjoining room and turned on the light, triggering an explosion of artworks. He turned the light off immediately and closed the door. "What's in there?" Boris asked. "Nothing, nothing, just some foolishness from my youth," replied Gudiashvili, for some reason winking strangely with both eyes at him and at "this child."

Suddenly there was the sound of someone loudly striking a fork against a vase. At the head of the table, Konstantin Gamsakhurdia had assumed a statuesque pose—a monumental pose, in fact, if one can imagine a monument of a figure holding a horn filled with wine in his right hand.

"Dear friends, I'll speak in Russian so that everyone can understand. We've already drunk to great Stalin and the Soviet government. Now I propose a toast to our countryman Lavrenty Pavlovich Beria. I personally have met Lavrenty Pavlovich several times, and I have always found in his person a great patriot, a connoisseur of our national culture, and a real reader of literature. Lavrenty Pavlovich upheld my reputation in the years of Yezhov's crimes, and this gave me the opportunity to create a series of new works. He backed my novel *The Abduction of the Moon* when the clouds of unjust criticism had begun to gather over it, and not long ago—" At this point, Konstantin Simonovich paused and made a majestic sweeping gesture with the horn of wine, carrying it through a large semicircle and even a bit back over his right shoulder. "—recently he gave *The Right Hand of a Master* to Iosif Vissarionovich Stalin himself to be read, and he—" During the pause, Boris noticed that everyone present was flabbergasted by this clearly unexpected toast. No glances were exchanged, all eyes were riveted on the writer. Gamsakhurdia went on. "—and he expressed his satisfaction with what he had read. Comrades and friends! In the ancient history of our neighbor Greece, there was the golden age of Pericles, when literature and art flourished. I drink to the hope that Lavrenty Pavlovich Beria will become the Pericles of Georgian literature and Georgian art! The . . . *alaverdi* is to you!" He sought out the glance of the proprietor of the house, whom the toast caught by the wall beneath a large painting showing tea pickers in the midst of their inspired labors. Boris saw the large drops of perspiration that had appeared at the painter's temples. Gamsakhurdia smiled faintly and shifted his eyes from Gudiashvili in order to look at another of the guests, whose back was encased in a raw silk tunic too tight for him and showed signs that the guest was somewhat irritated, perhaps by his constricting clothes, perhaps by something else, maybe even the living classic's toast. "Here's to my friend Chichiko Rapava! *Alaverdi* to him!" Gamsakhurdia concluded triumphantly, and, throwing his head back, began to drink the *kakhetin* nectar.

Everyone clamored, "To Beria! To Lavrenty Pavlovich! To our Pericles!" Someone began to pass goblets of wine to Boris, Maika, and "Uncle Lado" standing against the wall.

"I'd just as soon drink to Dynamo as to Beria," Boris whispered into Maika's ear. She laughed, but both of them managed to drink the cup to the bottom. Lado, when he had finished his, put his hand to his brow for a moment and whispered, "What's he doing? What's he doing?"

"Who's Rapava?" Boris asked. He was trying to remember as much as possible to tell his grandmother later.

"He's chief of the MGB," the artist whispered into his ear. "Let's go to the table, kids!"

The jacket was even tighter on Chichiko Rapava in the front. His blue undershirt showed through clearly. His rows of decorations were askew over his pocket, from which protruded three fountain pens.

With his Charlie Chaplin moustache, Rapava maintained the style of the dawn of socialism, the golden thirties. So the *alaverdi!* had been passed to him, and according to Caucasian custom he had to continue the glorification of Beria.

"With all my heart, I support the toast proposed by our master of ceremonies—I drink to the man who gave me—" He paused and then suddenly began again with a terrible roar: "—EVERYTHING! The man who gave me ALL of my life! To Lavrenty Pavlovich Beria!" Having emptied his horn and taken a few hors d'oeuvres, Rapava did not sit back down but immediately refilled the horn and raised it over his head while still chewing on a bit of Satsivi chicken. "And now, comrades, the time has come to drink to our master of ceremonies, to a living classic of Georgian SOVIET [a few of the words in the man's speech had the peculiarity of being delivered in a deafening howl] literature, my friend Konstantin Gamsakhurdia! And if he, resorting to mythology—isn't that right?—compared our Lavrenty Pavlovich Beria to Pericles, I would compare him to Jason—yes?—who sailed his whole life in the quest for the GOLDEN fleece! *Alaverdi* to Iosif Noneshvili!"

The guests again raised a hubbub. The round, frightened face of the young poet Noneshvili flashed into view. He put his hands to his chest and muttered imploringly, "What did I do to deserve such an honor, Comrade Rapava?" The artist and host waved a desperate hand. "My word, I don't know how this is all going to end!"

Boris pulled Maika toward the door. "Come on, kid, let's get a move on! Some sort of scene is brewing here!" One of the guests left with them. "Where are you young folks going? Do you want me to show you the old town?" It was none other than the architect Otar Nikolaevich Tabuladze.

☆

"I wanted to show you this old bakery," Otar Nikolaevich said. "Our little company of poets used to spend a lot of time here. It hasn't changed a bit since those days, though now it belongs to the State."

They went down a flight of narrow, uneven steps into some sort of netherworld, where intense heat radiated from a stove in the depths of the cellar and large lumps of dough made from a mixture of wheat and corn flour were being transformed into fragrant loaves. Two men with bare, hirsute shoulders in white aprons withdrew finished loaves and shoved baking pans containing dough into the oven. One of them, stopping work for a moment, tossed a hot, almost scorching round bread to the new arrivals and set a pitcher of chilled wine and three tin cups before them.

They were sitting on a mound of earth that ran the length of the wall, and all around them voices were chattering away excitedly in Georgian. The glow of the bread oven lit up their faces and hands, while everything else remained in darkness. "This is a place where poets can be found," Otar Nikolaevich explained. "Young ones, old ones. . . . Over there in the corner, some of the talented young ones are having an argument: Archil Salakauri, Dzhansug Charkviani, the Chiladze brothers, Tomaz and Otar—the new generation."

Suddenly someone burst into song in powerful, gloomy tones that drowned out all the other voices. Boris could not understand a word of the song, yet it seemed filled with a sort of inspiration that was unknown to him. He had the feeling of approaching some sort of border beyond which his understanding would know no limits. "It's an old song about the Svetitskhoveli Temple," the architect whispered. "It's only the second time I've heard it." He was obviously in a state of great agitation as well; his hand holding a piece of bread was trembling in the air as though he were offering it up to an altar. "No, Georgia is still alive," he murmured.

All this must have something to do with me personally, thought Boris. This life, which at first seemed to me so exotic and distant, is in fact going on in me, at some subconscious depth. It's as if I'm not a motorcyclist but a horseman; as if my horse is flying along some rugged terrain; as if a raven with the evil eye is squawking behind me, "You won't live through it, Mr. Airborne Commando"; as if all my thoughts will soon become mixed with the roar of wind and past centuries; as if I died fighting for the Motherland, not for the one I "operated" for in Poland but some smaller Motherland, call it what you will, Georgia or Russia or even this girl who is now hanging so trustingly on my shoulder.

He tenderly stroked Maika Strepetov's luxuriant hair, and the girl's eyes sparkled gratefully in return. His hand made its way down her emaciated spine. Her fingers suddenly disappeared downward into the darkness, in the direction of his crotch. Passion and an endless desire to, let us say, torment her combined with a tenderness he had never thought would be his lot to feel. In point of fact, there was something almost paternal about his feelings, as though he were leading a little girl into a new world, introducing her to stunning new things: here I am, Boris Gradov, a man of twenty-five, and this is my member, the male member of Boris Gradov, twenty-five years old as well. She will make the acquaintance of both of us, and it's clear enough that she will have trouble understanding that they are parts of a single whole.

Today, she, too, Maika Strepetov, a woman of eighteen, with everything that she possesses, will lead him into a new world he had never known before, into a world of tenderness that would stagger him. These were the sorts of foolish thoughts that suddenly stuck in their minds.

When they emerged from the "poets' bakery," the night seemed cool. The wind was blowing in gusts, ruffling and silvering the leaves of the chestnut trees. Boris threw his jacket over Maika's shoulders. Around the corner of the crumbling house with its slanting terrace, a panoramic view of Tbilisi, with the ruins of the illuminated Narikal Fort and Metekhi Temple on the high slopes, opened before their eyes. Around the next corner, the whole panorama disappeared, and they began to descend a narrow street going in the direction of a small, cozy square with a plane tree in the middle and a pharmacy with its globular light fixtures: a closed-off, quiet world, the way it used to be.

Along the way, Otar Nikolaevich said, "Boris, please tell Mary Vakhtangovna about our meeting, and tell her that some time ago everything in my life changed in the most decisive way possible. I work in the city architectural directorate, I've received my Ph.D., I have a wife and two children . . ."

He was silent for a while and then added, "I'd like Nina to know about it, too."

Again he fell silent. Then he half turned to Boris. "You won't forget, a wife and two children?"

"I'll try not to forget," Boris promised and thought he probably would. It's hard not to forget about somebody named Otar Nikolaevich when a girl like Maika Strepetov is hanging all over you.

"It's so good to be with you! Everything's so great!" she whispered hotly into his ear.

Behind the shop window, a woman with a large nose, the after-hours pharmacist, sat beneath a lamp reading a book. Her shoulders were covered with a flowery shawl that didn't belong in a pharmacy at all. On the wall hung a portrait of Stalin and a clock, attributes of stability: time is in flux, and at the same time—that's correct—time stands still.

"My most beloved friend used to work here—Uncle Galaktion," Otar Nikolaevich said. "Did you ever hear about him?"

"And how!" Boris smiled. "Grandma and Bo—Grandpa, that is—used to talk about him so much! A man with a volcanic temper, wasn't he? I feel sometimes like I remember him myself."

"It's quite possible," said Tabuladze. "After all, you were two years old when he was killed."

"Killed?" Boris shouted. "Grandma said he died in prison. He was slandered during Yezhov's terror and—"

Tabuladze interrupted him with a sharply unraised palm, as though he were slicing the air in front of his own nose.

"He was killed! The worst thing hanging over his head was seven years in the camps, yet he was killed by a man who wanted to suck up to the bosses—and we here in Tbilisi know the name of that man!"

God knows I don't want to know the man's name, thought Boris and then asked straight off, "Who is he?"

Otar Nikolaevich shifted his eyes in Maika's direction: Is it all right in front of her? Maika noticed the gesture and seemed to shrink. Boris nodded: you can say anything in front of her. Maika immediately relaxed and felt currents of gratitude pulsing through her body.

"Come on, let's sit down beneath the plane tree," Otar suddenly switched to a familiar tone. "Pardon me, but I'm nervous. I can't talk about this calmly, maybe because it all came to light only recently. A certain woman who worked *there* wanted to get revenge, and she revealed how it really happened. Uncle Galaktion was killed by being struck over the head with a paperweight during an interrogation. A marble paperweight right to the temple, by the strong hand of a young man, you understand. Damn it all, it was my cousin who killed him, which means it was his own nephew, Nugzar Lamadze. Ever heard of him?"

"I have," Boris said. "My mother used to talk about him. He's a bigwig there, isn't he?" Otar nodded.

"Well, yes, he's a major general, but that won't save him!"

God knows I don't want to talk about this, thought Boris. What's all this to me now, in old Tbilisi by the light of the moon, after a championship victory, and with my arm around Maika?

"What does that mean? What can you do to a guy like that?"

Otar Tabuladze suddenly smiled, but it was not at all the smile of a respected architect with a Ph.D. "See here, Boris, some of the old ways of the Caucasus are still alive. It wasn't only Uncle Galaktion that Lamadze killed, he has quite a few other Georgians on his conscience, too. He began his career as a hired gun, after all. In the end, it all accumulates, drop by drop. Even now, some of the relatives won't forgive such things. I'm not talking about myself, understand? Others besides me will appear. One will show up, or another. Rumors go around, a lot has been confirmed. This scoundrel would do better to make an end of it on his own, rather than wait."

The gusts of wind blew through the leaves over their heads and tossed Maika's mane about. The moon, leaned to the side like Pushkin's Tatyana, reading the courtyards of old Tbilisi by its own light. The hand brake of a taxi coming to a stop on the narrow little street could be heard. A burly man rang at the pharmacy door. The lady minding the store removed her shawl and went to open up. Can it be these quiet lads are up to all sorts of mischief? wondered the moon. However much I try to put this business out of my mind, thought Boris, it always catches up with me. In the end, after everything you've been through, you have to figure out once and for all where, when, and with whom you will live your life.

Chapter 11

——————————☆——————————

AIR AND FURY

The curves on Boris IV Gradov's road, meanwhile, were becoming ever sharper, and he had no time left over for any reflections on "where, when, and with whom." He had to rely on his racer's intuition. When he returned to Moscow, he immediately went to Silver Forest with Maika Strepetov. He was looking forward to seeing Mary, who was enjoying the company of "the new Kitushka" and who would now be happy to meet "the new Veronika." For some reason, there was no doubt in his mind that the old folks would like Maika. Alas, peace had once again deserted the Gradov nest. Horrible, incomprehensible news was waiting for the motorcyclist: Yolka kidnapped by Beria's men, Nina arrested, Sandro savagely beaten and blinded, with two detached retinas, the studio on Krivoarbatsky turned upside down, many of the paintings ripped down the middle with knives.

Shaken, he collapsed into his grandfather's armchair and covered his face with his hands. In the silence, only the sniffling of the stunned Maika could be heard, along with the coloratura singing of birds in the garden. The first thought that came into his mind was: How can grandmother and grandfather stand it? He opened his eyes and saw that Maika was sitting on the carpet, her face pressed against Mary's knees, while the older woman, with the same stony expression she always wore in times of crisis, stroked the girl's hair. Old Agasha was moving around somewhere in the depths of the house, playing with Kitushka.

In the garden, two men in striped pajamas were ambling around: Slabopetukhovsky and Shershavy, former subordinates of his father on the staff of the Reserve Front. In reply to an invitation from Auntie Agasha, which was just like being invited by the family, they had come to have a few days' holiday and breathe fresh air. They had not forgotten to bring their guns with their names inscribed on them, so as to be able to boast about their military pasts.

Grandfather was standing by the telephone in his full dress uniform with its rows of decorations. He was pale but stood perfectly erect and even seemed younger. The sound of his voice reached Boris as though from a television set with the volume turned down: "This is Academician Gradov speaking. I'd like to know the condition of a patient, Alexander Solomonovich Pevzner. . . . Yes, report to the head physician immediately. I'll hold the line."

It was only now that Boris felt his strength coming back to him, and with it, or even overtaking it, rage was beginning to course through him, a rapid, undisturbed current. The cold stream squeezed the air out of him and filled his body. Soon his surroundings would disappear, his body would be encompassed by and filled with fury. One can, however, live in that icy cold, act, and even form ideas in one's mind. So that gang of thugs thinks it can get away with anything, even raping my little sister? They're wrong!

"What hospital is Sandro in?" he asked calmly.

"Helmholtz," said Mary. "Where are you going, Boris?"

"All right, now," he said. "Maika, you stay here. I'll go to Ordynka Street and tell your people you're okay. Don't worry about me. I'll be back late, maybe very late. I'll call from time to time."

Maika joyfully nodded through her tears. "You can be sure, Borka dearest, that everything will be all right here—I'm a nurse, after all!" She was evidently filled with a feeling of participation, of usefulness, of being needed, of her own inseparability from this fellow Boris

Gradov, to the point where it nearly took her breath away. Mary, for all her impassivity, lovingly stroked her straw-colored head: anyone could see she was delighted with this new member of their just-destroyed family. Grandfather, waiting for a line to the head physician, waved his hand in a gesture that said, Come here!

"First of all, Borka, under no circumstances are you to show your face in Gorky Street, it's not safe," he said to him, gripping the speaking end of the receiver more tightly. "Second, can you tell me where you're going?"

"To a place where I'm still on the reserve list, you might say," answered Boris IV. "It might be the only place where they can help or give advice. In any case, I can speak freely there."

"A sound decision," nodded Boris III and looked with great attention into Boris IV's eyes. "Be careful!"

He suddenly switched the receiver from his right hand to his left and with his right hand, shaking slightly, made the sign of the cross over his grandson.

★

To tell the truth, Boris did not go anywhere near the place where he was "still on the reserve list," that is, the GRU. All of the secrecy and independence of this organization notwithstanding, he doubted there was one man there who would dare to go against a member of the Politburo and the deputy chairman of the Council of Ministers. He had quite another plan of action, one that was more elegant, not as cumbersome. First, he got onto his motorcycle and rode deep into Silver Forest, where he found one of the hiding places in which he had been keeping things since his childhood days, when he had played with Mitya Sapunov. It was where, after his return from Poland, he had stashed one of his pistols, a smoothly operating Walther 9mm. The weapon was where he had left it, oiled and ready for action. He felt the same way—oiled and ready for action. He was almost sure it would not misfire.

Next, he drove at full speed to Helmholtz Hospital. He rode with precision, stopping at every red light and making proper turns. Once he reached the Belorussia Station, policemen began recognizing the heroic figure and saluting: congratulations on your victory, Grad! In the hospital, in spite of the long line of visitors, he was handed a gown immediately, and he headed for the postoperative ward on the second floor. No one stopped him: the staff, obviously, thought that a young man who looked like that must have some reason for being there. He recognized Sandro by the end of his nose and his mustache. With his bandage-swathed face turned to the ceiling, the artist was lying flat on his back in bed. Approaching slowly, Boris whispered, "Sandro!"

The artist replied in his normal voice: "Ah, it's you, Boris!" Sitting up on the edge of the bed, he groped with his feet for his slippers. "Give me your arm, and we'll go out to the staircase to have a smoke."

"The pain's almost gone," he said on the landing. "I can tell you everything," he said and began to recount how they had waited for Yolka and how, instead of her, Nugzar Lamadze had shown up at midnight with a story about some "emotional event," and what had happened next.

"You talk about it so calmly, Sandro," said Boris. He had long been accustomed to addressing the artist, who was twice his age, by his first name alone, like one of his friends.

"I have nothing else to fight them with," the artist replied.

A cool head isn't a bad weapon, thought Boris, especially if it turns out that there is still another in reserve.

"Yesterday I had a visit from a supposedly ordinary policeman," Sandro continued in the same measured tones. "He said he had been assigned to investigate the assault on the studio. In fact, of course, he was one of them. When I asked him directly where Yolka and Nina were, he said that although he personally was "not up to date on the matter," he supposed that everything would turn out well for them in the end, so long as the family—well, you know the expression—'doesn't make waves.' All things considered—" It was only now that Sandro's voice began to tremble. "—I had to go through the whole war . . . one bombardment after another, and everything else . . . and now . . . one stray bullet . . . and it's the end for everyone that's dear to me . . . and the end for my flowers . . . ."

Boris emerged for a second from his fury. Unable to restrain himself, he put his arms around the comical, lovable man who meant so much to him.

"Come on, I'll take you back to the ward, Sandro. Just lie quietly and get well. You don't have to worry anymore, I'm here."

"What can you do, Borka?" Sandro muttered. "Who can do anything against them?"

"I know what to do," answered Boris, plunging back into his fury that was at once burning and as frigid as the Arctic.

Maybe it's burning too hotly? Maybe the risk is too great? Maybe after this they'll simply wipe all of us out? He made a few futile attempts to gulp in normal air. No, you'll never be able to breathe in enough of it. Breathe in fury and do what you decided to do. He had read somewhere that you couldn't beat a cobra until you had stuck its head into a dark bag. He even remembered what the action was called in the Boer language: *kragdadigheid*.

He stopped at a kiosk by the Red Gates metro station, bought several chocolate bars, and stuffed them into the pocket of his "Stalinist" jacket. He'd need them if he was to lie on the roof for a few hours. The sun was already reaching its highest point in the sky. Above him, from the window of a building, came the sounds of a piano lesson. A feeling of colossal world-weariness suddenly overwhelmed him. Endless repetition, the boredom of *solfeggio*. Not a very welcome visitor at the moment. To hell with everything, nothing makes any sense anymore. He went back to his motorcycle and saw a dozen large, sleek thugs arrayed in a half circle around the entrance to the metro so that everyone could admire them, the leaders and bosses. Beria was one of the most prominent among them: his sleek snout and bald spot looked so convincing that it seemed as though everyone ought to be bald. Again Boris's rage spurred him on, and he raced down the Garden Ring, across Samotyoka and Mayakovsky Squares, turned onto Vorovsky Street, and pulled into a courtyard adjoining the House of Film. He left his motorcycle next to a small, dilapidated truck beneath a spreading elm tree in this patriarchal corner of Moscow and then proceeded to carry out his not terribly patriarchal plan, in the sense that it was directed against one of the patriarchs of the Motherland.

He knew where to find Beria's massive gray stone mansion, surrounded by a high, solid fence the height of two men. The problem was how to get closer and take up a position on a nearby rooftop without being noticed. Strange as it may seem, he had noticed just such a roof once before. One moonlit night, he had been driving along with the chief of the Air Force Club. Vasya, as usual at that hour, was drunk. Nodding with his chin in the direction of the mansion, he laughed. "That's where Beria and his gang have dug themselves in!" He had no love for Beria, neither as the head of Dynamo, his chief rival, nor as a man who was too close to his father. At that moment, Boris, who was not particularly sober either, looked the surroundings over with the eye of a commando and almost immediately spotted a roof from which one might take up a sniper's position. Well, theoretically, of course.

Practically speaking, he had to go down quiet Vorovsky Street first, then cross Herzen Street, which had more life, then lose himself in the maze of communicating yards leading to that roof, and at the same time double back in such a way that he would not be spotted by a passerby, much less by one of the policemen at the entrances to the foreign embassies. Let's bring our Polish experience into this. Two pool sharks he knew were coming in his direction, toward the House of Film. A step to one side, into the shadow of a poster kiosk. The pool players walked right on by. The monotonous stroll of a potbellied sergeant (who obviously had a set of major's insignia at home) by the gates of the Swedish Embassy. A soundless and lightning-fast glide along the dark side of the street. The sergeant, who was professionally trained to memorize faces, saw nothing with his backside. Now you walk along Herzen Street, past the trolley stop like any other pedestrian, as though you didn't have six chocolate bars in your pocket and a Walther 9mm under your belt. Turn calmly into the gateway and, right after the arch, blend in with the surface of the wall, make a note of all of the footholds in the brickwork, the iron rods on the small balconies (just like Warsaw!), check whether the drainpipes are solid or crumbling, all the gutters, the branches of an old elm you could swing from in case of an emergency—you'll turn into a cross between a sloth and a chameleon when you've merged with the branches and leaves. Then there are the varying roof heights, all the inclines and ridges of the rooftops, along which in the end, according to your calculations, a part of the yard of a vile property on Kachalov Street, once called Lesser Nikita Street, will open up before you.

Two old ladies walked right by Boris on Herzen Street, formerly Greater Nikita. One of them was saying, "Let the army draft him as soon as possible, I say, the parasite . . ." They passed without noticing him. He took off his heavy boots and hid them behind an iron drum full of rainwater. He got his grip and commenced climbing the wall. No, he hadn't lost the knack, his fingers and toes made excellent use of all of the rough surfaces. He had almost reached the gutter when to the right, just at the level of his knee, a window opened and the sweet voice of a singer came from the apartment: "On the other side of Gorky Town / Where a keen eye can always be found / In a workers' village lives my love . . ." A permanent wave poked out of the window, and a voice hissed in the leaves, "There's no one, not a fucking goddamned thing, nothing." The window closed. He pulled himself up, jumped across to the roof, lay low in the gutter and probed the tin roof with his palms, trying to determine where it might sag or bend and then straighten out again with a clatter he didn't need. A large dark brown cat, its tail like a smokestack and with white spats, a drooping mustache, and a high white fluff of fur on its chest, like an English general, padded along the ridge of the roof. It seemed as though it had taken no notice of him, although maybe it was just a demonstration of its complete neutrality. Somehow or other, a quarter of an hour later, Boris IV Gradov, former officer of the GRU now retired to the reserves, third-year student at the First Moscow Order of Lenin Medical Institute, master sportsman of the USSR and national champion in motocross, 350cc class, was lying behind a tall chimney faced with prerevolutionary—that is, excellent—tile and observing the inner courtyard of the city house of the deputy chairman of the Council of Ministers and member of the Politburo of the Communist Party Lavrenty Pavlovich Beria. The first thing he noticed was the surprisingly small number of guards and how relaxed they were. It was obvious that they had nothing to fear, that they had decided long ago that there was no one in the city to be afraid of. One MGB agent was sitting in a booth, a second was patrolling around the house, a third was trimming the hedges, looking for all the world like a gardener in an apron but with a pistol in a holster at his backside. There was no one else outside. There were two ways to get into the house: through the gate with an iron door that gave onto a side street or through the main door, which had a semicircular asphalt drive in front of it. It'll be difficult, or almost impossible, to get him if he comes in or leaves by that gate. From here he'll appear for just an instant. All the windows in the house were tightly shuttered. They live like owls, never seeing sunlight. It isn't people they're afraid of, but rather the light of day. There must be at least thirty rooms in the house, and in one of them might be the bastard's prisoner: Yolka. He's turned her into a concubine. He's fucking our child, a Gradov daughter. He gets drunk on cognac, of course, to give him greater staying power and drags out his animal pleasure, drags it out, violating a young girl, drawing all her youth out of her, and pouring his puss into her. Even if you were Stalin himself, you'd deserve a bullet in the teeth for that, or under the chin!

The sun was now at its zenith, directly over the chimney. In an hour the shadow of the chimney would lie on the sharpshooter, but at that moment the sun was beating down unbearably, the tin all around was heating up like a baking pan for meat pies, and it was impossible to move: the position chosen at the start would have to be the one to stay in. Must keep up my level of fury, so that I don't get smeared all over this red-hot roof. It's not only Yolochka he's violating, but all of the women in my life: my mother, transatlantic Veronika, Vera Gorda, Auntie Nina, Maika Strepetov, who has chosen me for herself once and for all, and even all of our Air Force team sluts and all of the girls in my classes, even Grandmother Mary, even Agashenka and Taisia Ivanovna Pyzhikov, the mother of little Kitushka. He had thought everything through, but he had left his cap on the motorcycle and had nothing to cover his head with; so now my skull will pop at the seams and melt down, there won't be anything left to hand over to an anatomy museum. A man has not only to consume but also to sacrifice something for posterity. Is there any sense in this at all? Maybe there is, maybe there isn't. So here's a deadlock, just what I needed. Sashka Sheremetiev, who has read plenty of Schopenhauer, would say that it all leads nowhere ultimately and that everything is part of a vast collection of copies, everything in the past and in the future, not to mention the present, the very place where a dolt of an avenger lies melting on a red-hot roof with a pistol burning his fingers. Within the endless repetition exist the tiled chimney, the sun in the scorching, cloudless sky, and the aria from Strelnikov's operetta *The Heart of a Poet,* which is reaching my ears: "As autumn came, I said to Adele, 'Farewell, my child, don't hold it against me, we have parted friends' "; and the hysterical shriek of a woman drowning out the aria in the Muscovite subjunctive mood: "Go fuck yourself!"

Inch by inch he drew a handkerchief out of his trouser pocket, tied it into knots at the four corners, and pulled it over his head. He felt a bit better. Through the waves of heat, he once again surveyed the yard of the town estate. There was now no one there at all. The gardener with the pistol had disappeared, but in a shady corner of a flower bed there shone the white bones of some large animal: vertebrae, ribs, fortress of a pelvis, seemingly from an elephant—yes, there are the tusks. It all has a certain beauty about it—the remains of an elephant killed with an antitank gun, the apotheosis of a Masonic ode to liberty. On the other hand, there was something alive down there, a large toad moving along the smooth grassy carpet with a soft slapping of its flat belly, its cold eyes observing the shuttered windows with almost conscious reproach: Why do they treat me this way? I never thirsted after anything, you know, but infallibility.

Suddenly the yard and garden filled with people. Two flunkies in civilian clothes ran to the gates. From the main doors came several more men, some in uniform, their service caps topped with bright blue, some wearing sport coats with heavily weighted pockets and flat caps from which carrotlike noses were suspended over Caucasian mustaches like tufts of rook feathers. The gates opened, and two black limousines with cream-colored curtains drove in. Another collection of the same sort of people got out. There was a great of deal of conversation going on, even some laughter, men standing with hands on their hips. Maybe they're laughing about Yolka? Boris raised the gun, and at that moment everything superfluous disappeared from his mind, as though the sun had stopped beating down. There remained only the fifteen yards that his target would have to cover between the impenetrable house and the bullet-proof limousine. In those fifteen yards, he would have to kill him at least three times. One hit, a second, a third, and all of the sections of his murderous incantation would come asunder.

The gang that had gathered in the yard now drew itself up. A few were standing at something like attention. From the doors, Beria emerged onto the porch in a gray suit and a straw hat. One of the lenses of his pince-nez directed a beam of greeting at Boris. Go ahead, pull the trigger, rooftop sniper! At that moment, the trajectory of the unfired shot was suddenly obstructed by a middle-aged woman in a silk dress patterned with blue violets. She was saying something to him, gesticulating mildly with her arm, which was bare to the elbow, as though she were advancing gentle but incontrovertible arguments. Her pleasantly shaped head with its samovar gold hair pulled back in a ponytail swung back and forth in time with her hand. Beria's bald spot protruded slightly from behind this brass serpent. Why stand on ceremony? It's time to strike! Innocent people often get killed in such situations. If the first bullet takes out the woman, the second will go home to its target. All the subsequent moments stood still before Boris like targets on a range. Beria said something that made the woman's head jerk backwards, as if she had been slapped. Boris lowered the gun, he could not shoot through the woman. Beria walked away in the direction of the limousine—that's the end of him—and at that instant the woman did the same, wringing her hands imploringly. They took another three strides together, in perfect step as though they were in a ballet. The small lenses of Beria's glasses directed a mocking gleam at the rooftop sniper: aha, so you can't do it, you gutless coward! Two flunkies stood on either side of the limousine, one in uniform, the other in civilian clothes. Beria rudely pushed away his wife, whom he had obtained from the respectable Gigechkori family by some sort of blackmail, and then dived into the bulletproof darkness. His extended leg could still be hit, but there would be no point in that: a scoundrel with a wound in one extremity is even worse than a scoundrel with two sound legs. The doors slammed, and the limousine moved off. The yard and the garden emptied almost immediately. The reproachful toad continued to flop around in its hiding place in the grass, the bones in the corner had danced a sad sailor's jig and were now standing still, and the woman flopped her flowery backside down onto the marble steps of the front porch, the snake twining from her head to her shoulders. "Farewell, my child, do not hold it aga-a-a-a-ainst me," came the sound from next door as the needle on the record got stuck. The failed Gavrilo Princip began to slide down from the roof. A smell of cooking meat emanated from his palms. There was nothing else to do here: the scoundrel, in all probability, would be gone for some time.

He did not find his boots behind the barrel. He felt himself getting hot under the collar, if that is the right expression to use for a man who has lain on a hot tin roof. Had someone spotted him hiding his "shit stompers"? If not, what in hell had prompted someone to look behind a barrel full of rainwater? For whatever reason, there were no boots there, and there was no point in looking for them—you can't ask fate to give them back! Time to disappear, but quick!

He went out onto Herzen Street. At first, none of the passersby paid any attention to a slight imperfection in the outfit of the extremely noticeable young man, although it was usually the way of Muscovites to size up the clothing of everyone they met, as if trying to decide whether they should stay out of his way or give him an elbow in the side. Then some enraptured young girl eyed him up and down, trying to remember him, and her jaw dropped at the sight of the two shoeless feet with large holes in the socks caused by Boris's habit of neglecting to cut his toenails. Then someone else gaped, and soon his whole path turned into a series of pink caves. As for the potbellied clown in front of the Swedish Embassy, even though he was trained for the most unexpected situations, including a young man parading around in his stocking feet, he immediately dashed into his booth and picked up the phone: Send a regiment of cavalry!

The motorcycle, unlike his boots, was still where he had left it. With no further reflections, as though it were all part of the prearranged plan, Boris raced down Plyushicha Street to Sashka Sheremetiev's place. Blown along by a wind at his back, he realized all at once that he had emerged from his world of sheer fury into his usual airy milieu. I must go and see Sasha now, he thought, I can't stand being alone any longer. I have to find Alexander, he'll think of something!

★

Sheremetiev, fortunately, was home, lying on the sofa with, naturally, a dubious book in his hands. His artificial leg stood nearby like a sentry. Three strips of flypaper were hanging from a chandelier. This age-old battle between two forms of life was raging in the adjoining room as well, where the swats of a flyswatter could be heard.

When he saw his friend come in and noticed, of course, his stocking feet, Sheremetiev smiled ironically and asked, "What is one supposed to understand by this?"

Boris sat down at the table and reached out for an Albanian cigarette. Diamond, a strong brand, had only recently gone on sale in Moscow but had quickly become the favorite brand of Moscow's strongest young people. Some even called it "Dia-Mat," short for "dialectical materialism."

"First of all, Sashka, I'd like to drop this stupid business of talking like snobs," he said after his first drag.

"What's happened?" Sheremetiev asked, sitting up quickly and putting his book down.

"Trouble has come crashing down on our family again," said Boris.

He began to recount what had been happened while he had been racing his GK-1 motorcycle through the Caucasian hills.

Listening attentively, Sheremetiev went about putting on his prosthesis. Suddenly, even before he had fastened all the clasps, he went pale, bit his lip, and turned toward the wall, eyes closed. He remained that way for no more than half a minute before the color returned to his cheeks. "Go on!" he said, a new, incomprehensible, and intense expression in his eyes.

"So," he said when Boris had finished, "what do we have at the moment? Sandro blinded, Nina in jail, Yolka who-knows-where. You know, we ought to do something about that four-eyed cobra." He passed his hand knifelike across his throat.

"I've already tried," said Boris and thought, We're beasts of the same blood after all. He told Sashka the story of his rooftop vigil.

"Well, well, Bob!" was all that Sheremetiev said in reply to this story. His artificial leg creaked along with the floorboards as he stood up. He strode to Boris, clasped him strongly by the shoulder for a moment, and then disappeared behind a curtain that had been hung to create a small storage space. A pair of army boots immediately flew out from behind it. "Put them on, they're your size!" Then he emerged with a pistol in his hand.

"You should have gotten that woman, that broad who got in the way," he said crisply. "All right, now, let's give some thought to this business. From everything you've told me, I gather we need to have a heart-to-heart chat with Comrade Lamadze as soon as possible."

On the stairs, Sasha Sheremetiev's mood suddenly changed to one of buoyant excitement, and he began asking Boris again and again how he had taken aim, had been standing where, and how the whole setup had looked.

"Sasha, why did you go pale back there?" Boris asked.

Sheremetiev came to a stop. He was looking straight ahead at the decrepit wall of the stairwell. Something close to his earlier pallor came over him, but only for a moment, as though someone had waved a white towel over his face.

"Out of hatred," he answered laconically and then limped onward.

Out on the street, on the way to the motorcycle, he suddenly took Boris by the arm, a gesture wholly out of character for a modern devotee of Byron.

"I have a confession to make, Bob. Lately I've been thinking a good deal about your Yolka. No, it's not that I'm in love with her, but . . . probably something very close to it. She more or less personifies the ideal young woman for me, understand? Of course, I've never done anything about it, and maybe I never will. Think about it, okay? Not a word to anyone, okay? It's just that I've begun to find myself hanging around on Gorky Street around Bolshoi Gnezdnikovsky too often and that the whole center of Moscow has taken on a different color somehow. I never thought anything like this could happen in my life again after the lesson I learned in the Far East. . . ."

At the mention of his "far-eastern lesson," that is, of that grisly farce that Sasha had poured out his heart about one night during a drinking session, an unpleasant feeling cut through Boris. His far-eastern lesson was somehow not relevant to Yolka. Sheremetiev seemed to notice that his remark had irked his friend.

"I realize, of course, that I'm not the man for her," he said.

"Why not?" asked Boris somberly.

"You don't understand why I'm not the one for her?" Sheremetiev replied, without annoyance. He already regretted that he had spoken so openly. And yet whom else could he speak with that way, if not Borka Gradov?

"Let's drop the subject. Your cousin is my dream, that's all. . . ."

"That sounds like something out of Lermontov," Boris said with a smile. His momentary irritation had passed, and he was happy to have Sashka by his side. Everything seemed almost perfectly natural to him: two lads with pistols stuck in their belts, what could be simpler? This is the big city, why shouldn't there be two avengers like them walking around?

"You know I've always been afraid of your ironic sense of humor, you son of a bitch," Sheremetiev said suddenly.

"And I of yours," said Gradov.

They nudged each other with their elbows and then began to talk about "the operation." The first thing to do was to find out where General Lamadze, our esteemed gendarme of an uncle, lived. Boris was almost sure that it was in one of the three new buildings on Kutuzovsky Prospekt. It was said in Moscow that these massive towers with their marble façades were occupied almost entirely by the men of the "organs." In any case, they asked at a MOSINFO kiosk. They were told there, of course, that no one by that name lived in the city. Some names were close, but not quite the one they were looking for. "For example, there was a Eliezar Ushangievich Lomanadze or, here, Tengiz Timurovich Nugzaria, but your relative, young seekers, we don't have. Ask at a police station." Alexander proposed that they make inquiries at the Aragvi Restaurant: they've probably heard of their distinguished compatriot there. They immediately rejected the idea: the flunkies at the Aragvi would run straight to the "appropriate authorities" and tell them that two guys were looking for the general. Suddenly an idea dawned on Boris: Gorda is the one to ask! He remembered that she had once mentioned General Lamadze, who, unlike many other representatives of the state, she felt was a real gentleman. Vera herself answered the phone.

"My goodness, Borenka, where have you been hiding?" Yes, of course she knew where Nugzar Sergeyevich lived. They had gone out together with a big company once, and he had invited everybody back to his place to play music, sing, and so on. He apologized for the mess, the family was off somewhere, at their dacha, I think, but he still served me wine, fruit, some chocolate, and there was a piano, a grand piano. Borka, you've got a one-track mind. What nonsense! Boris told her he had brought a package for him from Tbilisi but had lost the address. No, she didn't know the address—what would she want it for?—but she remembered the building. Yes, yes, it's on Kutuzovsky, there's a large delicatessen at street level. I think he's on the fifth floor, or is it the eighth? They say you're in love, Borka! How do I know? She laughed wistfully. A little bird told me. . . . Boris had already put the phone down before he realized that the blocks of flats on Kutuzovsky Prospekt had been built after the beginning of their tempestuous and selfless love affair. Verochka Gordochka. . . .

There were three entrances to the building with the delicatessen down below. Boris chose entrance number one at random and went in. A bulldog-faced cop sat yawning over the crossword puzzle in the *Moscow Evening News*. Without removing his riding goggles, his army boots clattering on the tiles, Boris approached him.

"Is General Lamadze in?"

"What's it about?" asked the cop with a slight start.

"I have a package for him."

"From where?"

Boris smirked. "You ask too many questions, Sergeant."

Just then the elevator came down, and out of it came General Lamadze himself, in a suit of the best gabardine and a dark blue silk shirt. The sergeant was going to open his mouth but did not utter a peep: his tongue must have stuck to the roof of his mouth. He merely indicated with his hand the back of the general, now passing through the exit: there's the man the package belongs to, respected secret comrade.

Boris couldn't have asked for a better situation. Lamadze was standing beneath a young linden tree. He glanced at his watch, obviously waiting for his car. At his back, just below the shoulder blades, he felt through two fine layers of fabric a quite familiar object that nevertheless always surprised him by how it categorical it was. At the same time, a young man in a beret and with a serious, understanding smile on his face loomed up in front of him. In an instant, he opened his sportcoat to reveal the butt of another categorical object protruding from an inside pocket. An order was whispered directly into the general's ear from over his shoulder: "Walk on ahead, and then turn at the corner of the building!"

So he betrayed me after all, the general was thinking as he walked forward and then turned the corner. What did I do to make him dissatisfied? Can he read my mind, is that it? Or is too much loyalty no good to him? Who turned me in—Kobulov, Meshik? . . . What department are these two from? They don't look like our people. Are they from external intelligence? The strange, closely grouped threesome, noticed by no one in the hustle and bustle of the rush hour, passed by the scaffolding of a building under construction on a side street. Here was where General Lamadze was expecting to see the usual black automobile, which would haul him away to be beaten up, disgraced, and thrown onto the scrap heap. However, no such car was anywhere to be seen. Somehow all this doesn't look normal, he suddenly realized. Are they just ordinary muggers? The joyful thought surged within him. If they take his suit off, they'll find a wallet with a thousand. . . . What a joke—a general in the state security robbed right outside his own house! He still had not managed to get a look at the one threatening him from behind and to the right, who was keeping the hard snout of the "categorical object" sticking in his ribs. When he tried to twist his neck, however, the one behind him said roughly, "Don't turn around when there's a gun on you, you idiot!" The side street offered a view of the back of the Ukraina Hotel and the edge of a vast square on which there stood trash bins designed like antique vases and benches with leonine curves. Several nannies were already there, looking after the children of various bigwigs.

"Where are you taking me?" Lamadze asked, with a slightly threatening note in his voice. "Who are you? Is it money you want?"

"This isn't a robbery, Nugzar Sergeyevich," the first creep replied with a smirk. "Here we are, have a seat on the bench!" Lamadze's heart was striking hammer blows throughout his body. His thumping heart was trapped in his arms and legs, in his head and chest, and everywhere in his stomach. They know me by name, and they're acting with a professionalism our mongrels would never dream of! What sort of hallucination is this, anyway? He made it to the bench on his humming, pounding legs and fell onto it. It was then that he saw the first kidnapper, a lad in a leather jacket and riding goggles pushed back onto his forehead. Hair the color of copper, a sun-burnished face with almost Caucasian features and large, bright eyes. There was something almost familiar about him, he might even be related. . . .

"I'm Boris Gradov," said the kidnapper.

Nugzar suddenly burst out sobbing. "Borya, Borya," he said through his sobs and sniffles. Then he muttered through his handkerchief, "You've gone out of your mind, Borya! I'm begging you, stop this now! Don't you understand that they'll literally skin you alive? Literally, Borya, literally, I tell you, for attacking a general in the MGB, they'll literally skin you alive. Borya, Borya, I was a friend of your papa's, I saw your mo—mother off to America. . . ."

"Cut the crap!" Boris growled quietly. "Not a word about Mama! Why all the hysterics, General? Don't you understand that we're serious? Don't you know what this is about?"

Nugzar blew his nose and buried his face in his handkerchief for several seconds before he began to speak in an entirely different, harder voice. "The best I can do for you young people is not to report to the competent authorities what has happened. Just go about your business now, and leave me alone."

Boris sat down on the bench next to him and spoke across the general's chest to Alexander Sheremetiev, "You see what mood swings he goes through."

His friend nodded. "The general is depressed. However, he doesn't understand everything yet. He needs to have a few things explained to him."

He abruptly seized Nugzar by the throat with his right hand, putting pressure on the carotid artery just for a moment—a moment that seemed infinitely long. In the light of this endless moment, the sunset dimmed, and his reflection in the windows of the colossal hotel, and in those reflections, the quintessence of Nugzar's childhood—the tender essence of a future killer—could be seen. All at once, an October evening in 1925 at the Gradov dacha in Silver Forest rose before his eyes and obscured everything else. The pine trees and stars turned out to be the embodiment of a Lezginka dance that opened up into that same path he could have followed but had not. As the moment progressed, as the flow of fresh blood to the arteries of the brain became slower and slower, Nugzar rushed forward headlong, like a patrol boat throwing up white breakers in the darkness, moving farther and farther away in the direction of the true sense of things, until Sheremetiev let up the pressure. Then the blood rushed back to where it belonged, life and reality were restored, and in the place of true meaning there appeared only pure and unending terror.

After that, he swore to tell the young men everything he knew, and straightaway began to lie. No, he wasn't up to date on this matter, not at all. On the whole, he didn't know anything about the details of operations, only the broad outlines. Some of the comrades had asked him to reassure the parents, that's all. And now he didn't know where Elena Kitaigorodsky was being kept, neither in detail nor in general. But he could try to find out. If you like, Boris, and you, comrade, who nearly killed me just a moment ago, I'll try to find out. Generally speaking, I'll try to throw some light on whether she is in the city or at a dacha and what the prospects are for reuniting her with her family. Tomorrow we can meet here again. Your safety is guaranteed, you know, by the word of honor of an officer. How else could he talk to these madmen, how could he not lie?

"That's fine," Boris said. "Tomorrow at this time, that is, a quarter to eight, you'll come here with my cousin. If you show up without her, Nugzar Sergeyevich, you'll be killed, you son of a bitch. You're 'unmasked,' you're a swine and a bastard! I know you killed Uncle Galaktion with a marble paperweight. And I'm not the only one who knows, you murdering scum! You crippled and blinded Sandro the painter, and for that alone you deserve no mercy! You're from the Caucasus, you know how these things are settled. In this case you'd become just a smear on the wall in an instant. The only thing you can do to save your miserable life is to bring Yolka here tomorrow. Her mother has to be let go, too, and you'll do everything you can to see to it because Nina is hanging around your neck as well. We won't forget her! And one more thing: don't try to scare us with torture. And if anything happens to us, there will be two more behind us."

The terrible general again dissolved into hysterical sobs, putting his fingers into his ears so as not to have to hear the cruel words. "You don't know anything about it, Borya," he mumbled. "You don't know how it really was."

"Let's have a smoke, comrades, one each," Sasha Sheremetiev chimed in the words of a popular war song, pulling out his flat cigarette case decorated with the dark silhouette of some eastern building, either a palace or a mosque.

A slightly curious policeman, walking slowly, was approaching. All three of them took a cigarette. "They're strong," said Nugzar Sergeyevich with a cough, at just the right time: the cop smiled as he passed by. And there was reason enough: a well-dressed citizen who hadn't even waited for it to get dark before getting drunk.

"I promise to find out as much as I can," said Boris, returning to a tone of politeness. "And now go home, Nugzar Sergeyevich, and don't forget—the clock is ticking."

For several minutes they watched Lamadze as he walked away, with an unsteady gait that really did make it appear that he had been drinking.

"That guy is in shit up to his neck," said Sheremetiev, though not without a certain amount of sympathy. "We can't count on him."

"I still have an alternate plan," Boris said. "You can probably guess what it is."

"Oh, hell," Sheremetiev muttered. "This one is already more dangerous than your rooftop adventure. Maybe we should wait until tomorrow? Maybe he really will bring Yolka? Technically, as a someone close to Beria, he could."

"I need a drink," Boris said suddenly. "I feel like my nerves are shot. I'm sorry, but I just don't have the strength to sit and wait while they're there. I feel as though I've just become the head of the Gradov clan, you understand, and everything inside me is shaking. My hands aren't trembling yet, I can still shoot, but what sense is there in that? Sashka, Sashka, they used us all! We shot the wrong people at the end of the war."

Sheremetiev stood up briskly, winced slightly at the usual pain just below his knee, and took his friend by the arm. "Come on, I know a little place not far from here where they pour a good cognac."

★

That evening, the party at the Air Force Club was in full swing. They had rented the entire House of Culture of a rubber-processing plant. Oleg Lundstrem and ten of his jazzmen had been brought in from Kazan. The best young girls Moscow had to offer were on hand. The tables were groaning beneath the weight of bottles of champagne and cognac. In a heap just beside the shish kebabs from the Aragvi Restaurant lay boxes with cakes in them. Have a good time, friends! Want a bit of meat? Chew away! Want something sweet? Get yourself stuck in the cream! Deputy Commander of the Moscow Military District, Lieutenant General of the Air Force Vasya Stalin was setting the pace.

He had reason to celebrate. Air Force had without doubt become the most powerful sports force in the country, crushing beneath its feet both Army and Dynamo, not to mention Spartak, those pathetic trade unionists. Among the members of the Olympic team that would be heading for Helsinki in two weeks were a number of Air Force people—soccer players, basketball and volleyball players, boxers, wrestlers, gymnasts, track and field athletes, water polo players, swimmers, marksmen, and so on and so forth; their work hadn't been for nothing, there was someone to defend the glory of the Motherland.

★

The upcoming unheard-of event, the USSR's first-ever participation in the Olympic Games, had all Moscow buzzing. Until quite recently the newspapers had been calling the Olympics a shameful perversion of the physical education of the toiling masses, a bourgeois imperialist pseudo competition intended to stultify the proletariat, to distract it from the vital problems of the class struggle. As a counterweight to this abomination, "Spartakiads," true celebrations of physical culture and moral health, had been held with great pomp since the 1920s. In fact, the use of the word "sports" had not been particularly encouraged; it was too English somehow, that is, un-Soviet in principle, and it was only now after the war that it had come more and more into common usage, until finally the sensational news had broken: the USSR was joining the Olympic movement! And now the jaunty American Avery Brundage, the president of the Olympic Committee, who so recently had been called a "lackey of Wall Street," was flying to Moscow, and a huge team of athletes from all disciplines was forming to give battle in the stadiums, to show the superiority of Soviet sports and our way of life in deed and not in words. The cunning Western journalist with a bent for sensationalism could only guess at the significance of this move of Uncle Joe's: the opening of the Iron Curtain or a rehearsal for World War III? One could imagine the conversation between Stalin the father and Stalin the son taking place in this way: "Are you sure we won't lose, Vassily?" asks the father. "I'm sure we'll win, Papa," the young lieutenant general exclaims heatedly. "And you're not afraid of America?" the Leader asks with a sly squint. "It's they who should be afraid of us, Father!" Then begins Stalin's famous pendulumlike pacing about the office. Is he thinking or just nursing some deep and basic emotion? "Well, then let them play," is what the old *pakhan* suddenly comes out with. Why shouldn't they play with others, anyway? Let Vassily have a bit of satisfaction, after all. He's better than my other son, Yashka, at least he didn't get himself taken prisoner. He's like his mother, the girl I squeezed in the corner that day at the underground apartment in Sestroretsk. Let this lieutenant general play his games. A Soviet citizen had no trouble imagining this scene, and the funniest thing of all was that this was, of course, exactly what had taken place. Crazy about sports, Vaska had caught his father in a good mood and wormed his consent to take part in the Olympic Games out of him. How else would you explain this improbable decision made at the height of the Cold War against American imperialism and Yugoslavian revisionism, when East and West were already banging each other over the head with red-hot frying pans on the Korean Peninsula?

★

Boris and Maika Strepetov pulled up to the factory at eleven in the evening, when the party was going full blast. The backwater Kazan jazzmen who had been brought in for the occasion were hammering out forbidden rhythms to their hearts' content, specifically, at the moment of the arrival of our heroes, those of "The Woodchoppers' Ball," by "the progressive composer Woody Herman!" as "the East's King of Swing" with his slicked-back hair and thin mustache introduced it. The athletes and their girlfriends were all doing their own dances. A few *stilyagi* who had gotten into even this gathering showed them how it should be done, according to American films of the 1930s.

Boris looked at himself and Maika in the mirror. I've got a mug that looks as though it's sailed the seven seas, and you, my dear, are a shining product of the wheatfields of our Motherland, where cornflowers and forget-me-nots grow like weeds. When he had shown up at Silver Forest after dark, virtually grilled by the sun, his palms scraped, to drag her off to some secret nocturnal party, she had barely had time to pull on the little dress she had gotten in Tbilisi and run a comb through her haystack of hair and pin it up. On the whole, she did not produce a bad impression: a wheatfield with a few weeds in it. Boris, in a wrinkled suit and twisted necktie, looked like a savage and, all things considered, was a fitting companion.

"Gradov has a new chick!" the whispers raced throughout the hall. Grisha Gold, the water polo player who was the embodiment of east Baltic elegance, kissed Maika's hand, causing it to twitch like a frog shocked with an electrical current.

"You look like you just crawled out of the hay, friends," said Gold with an enchanting smile and then headed off in search of his date.

"He looks like Tarzan," Maika said in delight. "A regular Tarzan in a stylish suit!"

They sat at the far end of the U-shaped table, where Boris poured himself, and immediately downed, a large shot glass of cognac. Maika, who was simple at heart, did not bat an eyelash: the thought of what it might lead to never even entered her mind. She was overwhelmed by the recent events in her life—the appearance of her prince and their flight to the Caucasus, her first erotic revelations, her entry into the Gradov clan, where she had fallen in love at first sight with "Grandma Mary." She didn't quite understand what misfortune had befallen the family, but of course she had already come to love and sympathize with "Auntie Nina" and "Uncle Sandro," sight unseen, and with Yolochka, who had been kidnapped by somebody. The most important thing was that she had shown up at Silver Forest at just the right moment, when these people needed her both as a new member of the family and, not least, as someone with medical training. For example, when the much-loved Agasha had suddenly felt ill because of her nerves, Maika had immediately given her an injection of camphor monobromate.

And now she was at this strange dance, where Duke Ellington's "Caravan" was being played openly by bourgeois instruments—saxophones—where slender girls with doll-like faces were unashamedly embracing strapping young men, where everyone was looking at her with strange curiosity. And how wonderful it is to sit next to the man you love and be the center of attention!

Boris dragged her out onto the dance floor and enveloped her slight frame in a powerful embrace. He purposefully began to cut a path through the crowd, making his way to a table standing apart from the others in a niche, which was clearly a gathering place for those who wanted to talk rather than dance.

"How do, boss?" Boris yelled insolently, clicking his heels at the table.

"Hey, Boris, you fucker!" someone in the middle of the table said with a wave of his hand. "Where have you been hiding? Come sit with us, we'll have a drink!"

In an instant, Maika was sitting among a very high-class crowd: some were wearing officers' shoulder boards, others conservative ties. In the middle, next to a hefty, rosy-cheeked woman, was a young man in a dark service jacket. His face wasn't too bad to look at; as a matter of fact, he was the one who had shouted to Boris, using an expression not generally heard in polite society. Now he was winking at him like one of the boys and nodding at Maika.

"I see you've got a new comrade!" He looked Maika over as though he were evaluating her. "Quite a suitable comrade." Now he was winking at her, too.

"What's your name?"

"Maya Strepetov. What's yours?"

There was a deafening roar from the table. The young man burst out laughing as well.

"Call me Vasya," he said and poured her a glass of champagne. The conversation at the table resumed. The topic, surprisingly enough, was not sports but the TB-7 bomber, also known as the Pe-8, legendary in some limited circles. It was aircraft designers and test pilots who were sitting around V. I. Stalin that night. One of the designers, Alexander Mikulin, a man with a shaved head and a big nose who was wearing a jacket with two Stalin Prize medals on it, was asserting that in all its characteristics the bomber was better than the American Flying Fortress, and even the Super Fortress. It had a ceiling of 35,000 feet and a top speed faster than German fighters'. That alone made it invulnerable; just ask Pussep, who had flown it so many times over Germany. Lieutenant Colonel Pussep, smiling modestly, nodded. "He's right, antiaircraft shells are spent by the time they get up that high, and interceptors float around up there like sleepy flies, just waiting to be targets for my cannons. As far as Molotov's flights to England are concerned, Vassily Iosifovich won't make a liar out of me when I say that the most recent data show that the German air defenses couldn't even register us—they simply didn't know that we were walking all over them. Isn't that right, Vassily Iosifovich?" Stalin the Younger nodded and immediately raised his glass: a toast to this modest fellow Pussep! One of those present asked Mikulin about the fifth "secret" engine.

"And how do you know about this engine?" Mikulin asked, squinting over his schnozz. "Everyone knows about that engine."

"But no one is supposed to know about this engine."

"Well, everybody knows anyway."

Everyone began to laugh and nudge one another. And now something curious happened: the motocross champion of the USSR in the 350cc class entered the discussion. Theoretically, it's quite interesting, you know: If we had such a plane at the beginning of the war, why the hell didn't we scorch Berlin? All of a sudden, everyone stopped laughing, because the champion—in his naïveté, of course—had touched on the most sensitive aspect of the failure to mass-produce the TB-7. The production order had been canceled, as everyone present knew perfectly well, by an order from the very top, and therefore was not open to discussion.

"Borka, you'd be better off not trying to get involved in high strategy," Vaska said to him with a certain kindliness, which, as everyone knew, frequently alternated in him with fits of uncontrollable swearing and the swinging of fists. "Don't fuck around. You're a great motorcyclist, and for that, all honor and glory to you! Let's drink to Borka Gradov! You know, it's a shame there are no motorcycle events at the Olympic Games, you could win a gold medal!"

"Is shooting still in the program, Vassily Iosifovich?" Borya Gradov asked, leaning his elbow on the table and turning his shoulder toward "the chief." "Why don't you take me along as a marksman? You know I won't bring disgrace on the Air Force in that area. After all, you've seen what I can do with a semiautomatic. And I know a few other little things, too, as any of the boys in the commandos can tell you." He thrust his hand into the inside pocket of his jacket. The people at the table began to feel uneasy somehow. The champion was hanging over a good selection of zakuski, his tie was swimming in a glass of Borzhomi, and his Gradov eyes, shining with a cold drunken flame, were fixed on "the chief."

"I thought I told you not to fuck around!" Vaska screeched from across the table. "Well, take out whatever it is you've got in your pocket!"

With a smile, Boris pulled out his pistol and showed it to everyone. "A Walther 9mm," Pussep pointed out in a whisper.

"Put your cannon on the table!" the son of the USSR said, continuing to shriek. He slammed his fist down on the table. "Lay down your arms!"

"Only if you answer me one question. Can I consider you my friend?"

"Hand it over with no conditions, you drunken asshole!" Vassily Iosifovich stood up and pushed the table away.

Boris Gradov stood up as well and even took a step back from the table. He simultaneously accomplished three actions: he made gentle, restraining, and consequently reassuring gestures in the direction of the dazed Maika; grinned in a strange, inebriated way at "the chief"; and finally, with his right hand holding the pistol, he swung it back and forth in a gesture of warning intended for the rest of the group—don't make a move! The part of the dance hall that could see what was happening froze, but the rest continued to sway languorously to the rhythm of "Bésame Mucho."

"The question is still there, Vassily Iosifovich: May I consider you my friend?" Boris said.

This went on for a few seconds. Several boxers and a decathloner who looked like a symbol of the working class had already begun to make their way forward from the crowd behind Boris's back. The son of the USSR, it must be admitted, was already thoroughly drunk himself. Rage was boiling up in him, though not because of Gradov, not at all. He even felt a certain amount of smirking sympathy for that idiot, as if Borya were part of his own fury, which was directed not at anyone or anything but at things in general. Already on the point of tumbling down the slope, so to speak, he suddenly seized on the thought that everything now depended on him, only he could save the situation, and this whole lousy people, and the whole fucking Air Force, and the whole fucking sporting system. Then he suppressed his rage. He went around the table and went directly toward Borka.

"All right, let's say we're friends. Put your piece away, you fucker! Let's go have a chat!"

The Walther immediately disappeared from the scene. Boris buttoned up his jacket and pushed back his hair with his palm. With a gesture Vassily Iosifovich, quite content, stopped the boxers who were offering their services. Mikulin the airplane builder, currying favor, said loudly, "There's a man who knows how to restrain himself!"

☆

In the office of the club director, Boris told his "friend" that his cousin had been kidnapped by Beria. Vasya laughed out loud. "You're not alone in this city, you know, you're not alone! Lavrenty is hot for every pretty girl." Boris countered that he didn't give a damn about "every pretty girl" and that they were talking about his own cousin. Vassily Iosifovich must know the kind of work that he, Boris, had done in Poland, and if Yolka wasn't returned immediately, he was ready to repeat some of his feats. The son of the Leader was more amused than ever. I can just imagine your meeting with Lavrenty! I never knew what a naïve kid you were, Borka! What have you whipped up all this drama for? So your little cousin has lost her cherry, so what? Maybe she's having a good time with our bespectacled old fart, how do you know? Lavrenty is our government's champion in this discipline.

Boris smacked the director's desk, the glass top of which shattered beneath his fist into as many fragments as a porcupine has quills. Somehow he had imagined the conversation with his friend going differently! "I'm afraid I'll have to leave the premises now. Through a given window onto a certain street, just like we had to do at school. Disappear without a trace into the jungles of the big city."

The son of the Leader hammered the star-shaped porcupine with his own fist. Fragments of glass went flying, exposing the club director's marked cards.

"Who do you think you are, Gradov, you goddamned disgrace, banging around with your fist? Who made you a champion?"

They were looking each other straight in the eye: three-quarters Georgian and one and a quarter Russian.

"The Motherland made me a champion, the Communist Party and the great Stalin, and now I don't give a damn about any of it!"

"You don't give a damn about any of it? Do you want to end up in Kolyma, you dumb son of a bitch?"

"I won't be taken alive, Vassily whatever your father's name is." Ferocious drunken laughter from both sides, face to face. "It wasn't for nothing that they trained me to go behind the lines!"

The Leader's son suddenly leapt from behind the table and opened the three windows in the office in rapid succession. "All right, Boris, let's sober up! Lay out for me everything you know, in order."

The night air of the stars cleared the fetid atmosphere of the room. After five minutes, the Leader's son interrupted his champion. "Everything's clear now. You understand, Boris, that I'm your only chance. Let's shake on it, you bastard, I promise I'll help you. These are my conditions: you'll hand over your gun to me personally, and you won't leave this room until I come back. Three guys will sit here with you. Got it? If you don't accept my conditions, I'll call the patrol and I'll have your name struck off the roll of the glorious Air Force teams forever. Got it?"

The conditions were accepted. Vassily Iosifovich Stalin crossed the banquet hall with crisp, sober—almost not drunk, that is—strides. "I'll be back in an hour," he told his friends. "With Borka," he added, directing a glance at Maika's alarmed blue eyes.

Vassily Iosifovich's wife, a swimmer in a silk dress that hugged her delphine body, rushed after him. "Vasya, I'm coming with you!" His first reaction was to repulse this outburst of loyalty, but then, laughing loudly, he took his spouse by the arm. Two bodyguards from the wrestling team were already bringing up the rear.

"Just who is that Vasya?" Maika asked, resting her cheeks in her palms.

"Stalin's son," someone answered.

"Good grief!" she gasped.

There was something disproportionate about it all. The people were all Stalin's sons, a gigantic sea of heads, but now it turned out that there was one head that stood out from all the rest, Stalin's very own son, the fruit of his amorous delights. But could Stalin ever have occupied himself with that sort of thing? Maika Strepetov took her hands away from her cheeks, which were burning. Everyone at the table—or all of the men, in any case—was looking at her. They're all staring at me as though I have something to do with them personally, she thought. There are some honest-to-goodness old men among them, guys who are almost fifty. This is one of the strange things about life: old women in their fifties have nothing to do with guys my age, while old men in their fifties have quite a lot to do with eighteen-year-old girls. At any rate, they're looking at me as though they're inviting me someplace. They're nothing but old farts! At any rate, they're looking at me like they want to play. And as though they're sure that I have nothing against the idea.

One of the old men, an old uncle if ever there was one, with protruding ears and lips, a swollen, prominent nose, and eyes as tiny as two drops of sunflower seed oil, sat down beside her.

"I don't believe we've met yet, my beauty."

"Maya," she muttered.

"Misha," said the old man by way of introduction, and added, "Academician. General."

Then, carefully, he took her by the elbow and the hand, as if he were picking up a fish.

"Let's dance, Maya!"

They danced to the slow, sugary music from the puppet show "To the Rustle of Your Eyelashes." On the turns, the old man pressed himself against the furiously blushing girl. He had a round but hard belly, with a stone-hard clot of something just below it. In a voice that wobbled slightly and constantly emitted "eh"s and "my, my"s, he told her about what a terrific dacha he had in Yalta, which he sometimes, my girl, eh, my, my, wanted to run away to. Maika suddenly jumped back from the football-shaped stomach and slid out from beneath his greedy hand. "Get lost!" she shouted in a shocked voice as though she were scandalmonger Alla Olegovna in their communal kitchen. "Where's my Borka? Where have they hidden my Borka?"

Working with her elbows and shoulders and occasionally even butting with her head, the girl plowed her way through the dancing crowd.

☆

The son of the Leader headed directly for his father's so-called near dacha, located in Matveevskaya, on the road to Kuntsevo. He was driving a Buick convertible, his dolphin of a wife sprawled beside him. In the back sat his adjutant and two wrestlers. The car roared down its lane, paying no attention to the traffic signals. Inspectors of the traffic police drew themselves up to attention: the Son is passing! In barely ten minutes the Buick had pulled up at the gates, behind which the unseen security guards immediately drew a bead on all those who appeared.

While they were flying along through nighttime Moscow, the Leader's son had sobered up entirely. A question suddenly came into his still-whistling head: What am I doing this for? Father might go into a rage. This thought, however, flew out of his mind as quickly as it had flown in. Here we go! He left the car and its passengers on the small square by the gates and walked toward the dacha. "Comb your hair, Vasya!" his wife said behind him. She was right. He did need to comb his hair. The guards recognized him immediately. A door next to the gates opened, and he entered the grounds. He saw right away that the light was on in his father's huge study—not only the table lamp but all the chandeliers as well. That happened when the inner circle of the Politburo gathered: Beria, Molotov, Kaganovich, Malenkov, Khrushchev, Voroshilov, and Mikoyan. You've really put your foot in it this time; you're going to rat on Beria, and the four-eyes himself is sitting in your father's office.

Vlasik and Poskryobyshev came running up as soon as he reached the porch. "What's happened, Vassily Iosifovich?"

"I need to see my father," he said with an intonation that gave them little chance to refuse.

"But we have a Politburo meeting here tonight, Vassily Iosifovich!"

He pushed back the general's sturgeon- and caviar-stuffed belly. "Don't worry, it'll just be for a minute!" Passing through the rooms and approaching the study, he saw reflected in a mirror a row of chairs occupied by a row of high-ranking flunkies awaiting a summons, including Dekanozov, Kobulov, and Ignatov, Beria's gang of Dynamo supporters.

Poskryobyshev dashed forward and came to a stop before the door of the study. "Vassily Iosifovich, you can't interrupt them, you know!"

The Leader's son scowled and said, pronouncing the words in his father's voice, "Stop playing the fool, Comrade Poskryobyshev!" The faithful bodyguard reeled back in terror beneath the wave of alcoholic breath.

★

In the study, meanwhile, a rather important question was under discussion: the mass resettlement of Jews to a "Jewish Autonomous Oblast" with its capital in Birobidzhan. Specifically, they were debating the problems of transportation. Lazar Moiseevich Kaganovich, the man who held the portfolio of communications—it was not without cause that the people had called him "the Iron Commissar" in his time—was asked a question: Will enough rolling stock have been assembled by the appointed date? All things considered, we're talking about the resettlement of two million people almost simultaneously.

Lazar Moiseevich assured the Politburo that a sufficient quantity of cars and locomotives would be freed up by the date needed.

"Well, what else?" Stalin asked him, his eyes narrowing. "How do the prospects for development of the territory look to you, Lazar?" He sucked at his empty pipe: the damned doctors were still insisting that he not smoke.

Kaganovich's massive face trembled slightly, as though he were sitting not in his friend's dacha, but in the compartment of a train traveling at top speed. "I think, Iosif, that the workforce of the Jewish people will do its utmost to transform the autonomous republic into a flourishing Soviet territory."

Stalin smirked. "And what if they elect you as their Jewish president out there?"

All the leaders roared with laughter, including Molotov, who would have done better to keep quiet on this subject: everyone remembered the tricks his Jewish wife, Polina, had gotten up to with Golda Meir and with the now-unmasked Anti-Fascist Committee, and how on orders from Joint she had called for the new Israel to be set up in the Crimea. Kaganovich jerked forward, as though the train he was in had come to a sudden stop. "What's the matter, Lazar, can't you take a joke?" Stalin said reproachfully. Then he turned to Beria. "In your opinion, Lavrenty Pavlovich, how will our friends in the capitalist world receive the news of our action?"

The deputy chairman of the Council of Ministers and "curator" of the state security forces was obviously ready for the question, and answered swiftly and buoyantly, "I'm sure, Comrade Stalin, that the true friends of the Soviet Union will not fail to understand the actions of the Soviet government. In light of the approaching exposure of the group of conspirators, this action will be viewed as a measure to protect the Jewish working classes from the entirely understandable wrath of the Soviet people. Consequently, this action will be added confirmation of the unshakable internationalism of our Party."

Very good, thought Stalin, he's thought it through very well, the Mingrel. "And what actions will you take to make clear the true nature of this internationalist act?"

Beria was ready with an answer to this question as well: "We are presently working out a series of measures, Comrade Stalin. We are of the opinion that we should begin with a collective letter from prominent Soviet citizens of Jewish nationality who approve—"

Just then Poskryobyshev came into the study, literally on half-bent knees. Expressing reverence for all those present with his entire body, he went over to the boss and began to whisper something in his ear. Straining his not-inconsiderable capabilities to their limit, Beria was able to catch only "extremely urgent . . . for a few minutes." He felt an almost irresistible urge to go out of the study to see who was daring to interrupt this historic session. He managed to rein in this desire, however, and a good thing, too, because the Man himself suddenly stood up and walked out of the study with Poskryobyshev. He didn't even excuse himself, Beria thought. He didn't so much as look at the leading figures of the State. How rude of him! These types from the Cartlean Mountains suffer from a certain lack of breeding, after all!

Stalin came out into the dining room and saw Vassily standing by the window. Recently he had been getting signals—undoubtedly through Beria, or at least with his knowledge—that his son's drinking was out of control. Supposedly, he often lost his head, got into brawls, and wandered about in a generally indecent state. Now Stalin was pleased to see that the rumors were obviously exaggerated. Vassily was sober and stern, with all his buttons buttoned and his hair slickly combed. Not a bad lad, all things considered. He loved his son—not the other one but this one—loved him for not being like the other, and often regretted that the Marxist worldview prevented him from handing down power by inheritance.

"Well, what's shaken you up?" he asked in a rather good humor.

Recently, under pressure from his confounded doctors, among whom, fortunately, there were fewer and fewer Jews, he had started taking longer walks. As a result, his irritability had lessened, and the perspectives of history stood before him in clearer outline.

"Father, I know you've been getting reports about me," Vassily said, "but I've come to you tonight anyway with an important piece of information about an unhealthy situation. . . ."

Ten minutes later, Stalin returned to the study. The leaders had not said a word to one another in his absence. They were waiting in a stupor to see who was in hot water this time. He took his seat, burrowed

in his papers for a minute or two . . . it was as though a flock of net-
ted birds were trembling in the quiet of the leaders' hearts. . . . Then
he suddenly shoved all of the papers to one side, directed a terrible
glance at Lavrenty's lustrous features, and said fiercely in Georgian,
"*Chuchkhiani prochi,* what do you think you're doing, you scum?
We're working on historic decisions that the happiness of the human
race depends upon, and you, you *dzykhnero,* can't even tie a knot in
your cock, *gamakhlebulo.* Take off your glasses, don't try shining
your lenses at me! Let the girl go immediately, and leave all the
Gradovs alone, *dzykhneriani chatlakhi!*" Only Mikoyan among those
present could understand any of what was going on. He exchanged a
glance with Khrushchev and then closed his eyes: I'll explain later,
that meant. We all ought to learn Georgian, thought Khrushchev. Oh
well, Russian laziness . . .

★

Flying back along the same traffic lane, panoramic views of Moscow
opened up at each curve. Vaska, proud of himself, was grinning
broadly: the conversation he had just had with his father had been
tougher than any test flight. The swimmer was whispering tenderly
into the Dzhugashvilian ear, "How brave you are, how highly you
value friendship!"

He laughed heartily. "What does friendship have to do with it?
Whom can I put in the fall cross-country cycle race besides Borka
Gradov?"

★

Two days after the events just described, Major General Nugzar
Sergeyevich Lamadze was found dead in his office on Dzerzhinsky
Square. He lay across his desk with a bullet in his head. The entire
right side of the green cloth covering the tabletop was steeped in his
blood, and in the middle of it stood a small glass full of impeccably
sharpened pencils. On the clean left-hand side of the green fabric, a
note containing just five words was held in place by a heavy marble
paperweight: "I can't stand it anymore." The pistol from which one
supposed the fatal shot had been fired seemed to fit into the dead

man's hand in a strangely tidy fashion, leading one to think that it had been put there after the fact. No inquest was carried out, however. The incident may have been atypical, but it was by no means rare on Dzerzhinsky Square.

FIFTH INTERMISSION
The Press: An Olympic Chronicle

Time (February 18, 1952):

Last week, Avery Brundage, President of the Olympic Committee, agreed with the leaders of the Olympic movements of other countries—or, more accurately, they agreed with him—that Soviet athletes should be allowed to participate in the competition at Helsinki. "It will be good for the lads to get out from behind the Iron Curtain," he said. "Sometimes they don't go home in such circumstances."

Time (July 28, 1952):

President Juho Paasikivi of Finland declared the 15th Olympic Games of the modern era open. The celebrated Finnish athlete Paavo Nurmi lit the Olympic flame. The Russians are taking part in the competition for the first time since the 1912 Games in Stockholm.

Emil Zátopek, two-time Olympic champion and captain in the Czechoslovakian Army, ran his distance with a face twisted into a grimace and holding his stomach as though he were trying to keep himself from disgorging sour apples.

The American and Russian yachts are moored at Nylandska Yacht Club. Yesterday, the two teams met on the pier. The Russians stared at the Americans, who stared back at them. They went their separate ways in silence.

Russian officials, scorning the Olympic village, have housed their athletes and those of the satellite countries twelve miles away from the Western rivals, not far from the naval base at Porkkala.

Life:

To everyone's surprise, the Russian athletes have begun to display friendliness and good humor; they laugh, clown around, gesture animatedly. . . . One Soviet swimmer said of these oddities, "We're here on a mission of peace."

Soviet Sports:

The XV Olympic Games. Triumph of Soviet gymnasts. V. Chukarin, overall champion of the Olympiad, said, "The victory of our gymnasts convincingly demonstrates the superiority of the Soviet school. The Soviet style, strict and concise, with carefully worked-out choreography, showed itself to be the most progressive."

N. Romanov, leader of the Soviet delegation, spoke of the mass character of Soviet sports, of its basic goal, which is to make the workers healthier, of the exceptional protection provided by the Party and the government.

Three scarlet flags of the land of the Soviets are hoisted on the poles simultaneously in honor of the remarkable victory of three Soviet sportswomen. Nina Romashkov, Elizaveta Bagryanin, and Nina Dumbadze proved to be the strongest in the discus throw. The victories they won fill the hearts of Soviet people with pride and joy.

Life:

Compared with the Soviet muscle machine, the Nazi efforts to produce athletes under Hitler are like a few gentle raindrops compared to the roaring Volga.

Built like a tank, Tamara Tyshkevich put the shot. Together with discus thrower Nina Dumbadze, these powerful women represent the main Olympic hope of the Soviet Union.

A meeting of athletes in the Soviet village. Fraternization proceeds with relative elegance before the attentive eyes of official representatives and portraits of Stalin.

A Soviet official said to one American who was trading souvenir pins with his Russian counterpart, "They'll put you in the electric chair if you walk down Broadway wearing that pin."

The New York Times:

The Russians have suddenly become friendly. Their camp has opened its gates to visitors. Clearly a change in official policy.

Rower Clifford Goes says, "We were at their place yesterday. I thought they'd bite my ears off, but instead everything was fine, they were great company."

The Russians did a job on American diver Major Sammy Lee. They gave him a pin with Pablo Picasso's "dove of peace" on it and photographed him holding it. The cheap dove pins have now become as much of a Communist symbol as the hammer and sickle. When Sammy Lee, a man of Korean ancestry, realized what was happening, he said to a Soviet correspondent, "Hey, buddy, what're you doing? I'm in the army, just like you."

Pravda:

. . . outstanding success of Soviet sportsmen. The mastery of Soviet athletes, their moral and volitional qualities, their discipline and comradely relations with their rivals are a source of delight for the whole world.

Soviet Sports:

Demonstrating a high level of achievement, the Soviet team has achieved overall superiority. In the opinion of many western journalists, the American team will now be unable to catch up to the Soviets.

The New York Times:

The Olympic spirit has won a victory, albeit a small one, demonstrating that the Cold War can yield to friendly cooperation, if Mr. Stalin and the other narrow-browed tin idols in Moscow will allow manifestations of human nature.

The Russians invited the Americans to lunch at their camp. Preparations were meticulous: cooks and chefs brought in for the occasion, uniformed waiters, copious quantities of magnificent food. Portraits of Stalin and the members of the Politburo hung on the walls of the large dining hall. . . . Glasses were filled with strong cognac and vodka. . . . "Gee, I've never done anything like this before!" a swimmer named Stevens was heard to exclaim. "It's got potential, this drink!" "What about the steaks?" asked an impressed runner by the name of Fields. "There's a piece of beef for you!" A rower named Simmons put in, "It's too bad we can't invite them to our cafeteria."

Soviet Sports:

The gold medal in the middleweight division was won by the Negro F. Patterson (USA). . . . The winner in the light heavyweight division was the Negro N. Lee (USA). . . . The Olympic champion in the super heavyweight division is the Negro E. Sanders (USA).

N. Romanov, leader of the Soviet delegation, underlined many instances of biased judging, particularly in the last days of the competition. The judges conferred undeserved victories on several American athletes.

No lie of the venal bourgeois press was of any help to warmonger ideologists in concealing the truth about Soviet people, about their love for peace, about the desire of all honorable sportsmen to steadfastly carry on the struggle for peace in the whole world.

The New York Times:

The most significant event of the just-ended XV Olympic Games of Helsinki was the participation in them of a huge Soviet team. . . . Despite their isolation from the world of modern sports, the Russians managed to take second place overall, slightly behind the American team.

Pravda:

The outstanding triumph of the Soviet team was to be expected. It was the natural result of the Party's enormous concern for and attention to the physical education of the Soviet people. The Olympic victory became one more triumph for our Soviet system.

SIXTH INTERMISSION

Night of the Nightingales

By the middle of the summer, the toad had flopped its way from Kachalov Street to the Tsaritsyn Ponds. It moved at night for the most part, so as not to be crushed by traffic. It may not have been much, but at least it was endowed with an exceptional instinct for self-preservation. Sometimes scenes from nonexistent reminiscences slid by: virgin snow banked around the yellow hue of empire, a tree-lined walk swept clean by a servant kept especially for that purpose, calisthenics that were necessary to maintain the muscle tone of the well-fed father of a city that was besieged and breathing hard. By night, the toad perceived the streets of Moscow as a vast, porous, steaming surface. One morning, it ensconced itself behind a fire prevention barrel, beneath someone's abandoned boots or a pile of scrap metal, and opened its oral cavity. Of course, Moscow's insects, a fairly plump lot, immediately began responding to the invitation. Having had their fill of some of the inhabitants during the night, the insects themselves became a meal for the toad.

One day, a panorama of great achievements unfolded before the creature: the growing teeth of charts, powerful flywheels, wheels of various diameters, the ledges of glistening buildings with steeples, figures of metal and plywood—all of this was inedible and none of it living, in the sense that it had no protein, yet it still inspired anxiety in the toad over some other essence from the past. Among the objects of the panorama were faces the size of buildings that flashed up here and there, the tops of the heads even with the spires. The toad wanted to address a great and substantial rebuke to them: Why have you been so violent to me, not like friends? I never wanted anything but ideo-

logical purity. Maybe you yourselves one day will be flopping or humming your way around Moscow as toads, or as insects, and perhaps
you will learn a few reptilian, slimy truths. I could stay here with your
faces, thought the toad, but I feel drawn to the nightingales. It was not
hard to understand why it felt drawn to the nightingales, if one fa-
miliarizes oneself with the Party documents of the postwar period.

So the toad continued on its way, drawn through the whole huge
city, through the vapors of bakeries, dining halls, morgues, slaughter-
houses, garages, and dye works, by the moldy odor of the Tsaritsyn
Ponds.

One night in the ruins of some ancient structure the toad met a
large male rat. The rat had been dozing in the ruins for some fifty
years, feeding on a bit of mold from time to time, which meant that it
was existing on a diet of almost pure penicillin. Sometimes in its
dreams it drifted far away from these ruins, into some fading expanses
over the North Sea, over which some ashes had once been scattered in
order to provide proof of the materialist worldview, ashes which
somehow had a direct connection to this good-natured rat. Startled by
the work of a bulldozer on the night shift, the rat crawled forth from
its drowsy crevice and perceived three planes of being all at once: a
distant constellation; not very far off, a sprig of lilac overloaded with
flowers, a bird's head poking from its seething mass; and nearby, a
toad, a brown, piebald creature with clear, reproachful eyes. What
strange forms bodies of protein can take, thought the rat, an idea
flashing through its mind for the first time in fifty-one years. It had
never thought that such different things could unite in such an enchanting combination. For some reason, the constellation seemed to
it at that moment the embodiment of the protein molecule. The bulldozer quieted down, and then the strong, insistent singing of a
nightingale absolutely convinced of its right to self-expression was
heard. It was then that the toad realized that it had reached its goal
and that the ruins lay on the banks of a large, watery, silty expanse
that was overgrown at the edges with sedge, shrouded with duckweed, and a bit polluted by the city, but nevertheless delightful. Having said its farewells to the rat, that is, having breathed in the direction
of the latter with its own swelling and falling sides and chest, as if to
say "Perhaps we'll see each other again in this phantasmagoria," the
toad flopped downward along fragments of the two-century-old

brick, fell into the first small gulf reflecting a many-meaninged combination of stars, and immediately and involuntarily gobbled down a
mouthful of duckweed together with some of the larvae of the insects
mentioned earlier, and prepared itself to listen.

As a matter of fact, no preparation was necessary. The strong, sure,
and meticulous singing did not cease for a moment, regardless of
whether a toad had moved from one place to another. To the toad,
however, it seemed as though the singing was addressed to it and that
it had finally attained the purpose of its existence. It was not to deliver
a reproach to the comrades on the Politburo, in fact, but rather repentance before the nightingales. Here they are bursting into song, he
thought now, her Tsarskoe Selo voice is heard, filled with age-old passion and a thirst for singing, with him cooing his mockeries alongside
her and together what harmony there was! Forgive me, nightingales,
all intentional and unintentional insults. After all, in those days I almost sincerely thought sometimes, Why don't they sing together with
all the people? It was not easy to understand right away that the
nightingales were not singing but sobbing. Now he had screwed up,
though he considered himself fairly educated. Who? What? A member, of course. When he sat down at some black-and-white-toothed
object, throwing back his tails and amazing all the other members
with his rounded buttocks that flashed into view, with his ten flashing fingers he would extract *Pictures at an Exhibition* out of the given
object. He considered himself first among the vermin for having sat in
judgment upon the nightingales. Serpents gave their endorsement by
way of a full glass of poison. In principle, there were no complaints:
if I hadn't given my due, I would still be sitting in the secretariat, humiliating nightingales, and now here I am sitting in the dark and sati-
ating water, right next to a trembling reflection of stars and to walls
of lilac blossoms fluttering beside the ruins of the walls. There they
are, Comrades, don't you understand, *Pictures at an Exhibition* come
to life; I'm listening to the flowing sounds of nightingales with my
body, which is cold-blooded and yet not provided with base instincts.
With my body I ask forgiveness for something from a previous life, for
that round, belching being constantly protruding from my trousers.

The toad, incidentally, was mistaken, addressing itself in the
nightingale evening of the Tsaritsyn Ponds to those two who had
fallen beneath the boots of the Party. First of all, those two still re-

tained their previous offended appearances and sang not with their throats, but with scratching Pushkin quill pens; in the second place— well, our toad had nothing to do with the fact that some other birds were singing that night above the reflected sky and the ruins of the castle. Then again, however, if one considers that there is nothing in the universe that does not have at least some connection to everything else, that connection was very, very distant, almost entirely cosmic, if not actually extragalactic. On the other hand, the person singing that night with the throat of a nightingale was in fact the former owner of the place, the poet Antiokh Kantemir, who looked down from the lilacs and thought, Listen to me, toad, listen to me!

Chapter 12

———— ☆ ————

THE ENGINEERS' CAMPFIRE

In Kirill and Cecilia's room there were three windows in which they took great pride: three full-fledged windows with sturdy frames plus a magnificent transom window. One of these radiant rectangles looked out directly onto an honest-to-goodness Soviet-style Soviet Street with a transformer shed; another gazed on a hill of the sort peculiar to that part of that country, with its flat and even summit closing off the western approaches of the Magadan skies, reminding one of the Iron Curtain; and finally, the third opening provided a vast perspective of the land to the south, the expanse of the sky, a gently rising slope marred by a rash of rooftops, beyond which was the sea, or at least Nagaevo Bay, whose existence could only be guessed at from that point because it could not be seen. "Sometimes you have the feeling of being in the south, almost in Italy," an engineer named Delvecchio would say with a smile. He had done ten years in Kolyma for having "followed the Comintern line." "Good old Italy!" the Parisian Tatyana Ivanovna Plotnikov laughed. A onetime professor at the Institute of Eastern Languages of the Sorbonne, she worked in the city laundry. "Sometimes such a howl comes through these three windows that it seems like every witch in Kolyma is up and raging. Three big glass windows like these are just too rich for the blood of our brother from Kolyma."

The medic Stasis was in a state of bliss, his powerful shoulders outlined against the backdrop of the "Gradov seaside window." "Every window is an icon," he said. "If you don't have icons but you have three windows, that means you have three icons." Having been released from the camp, Stasis was now working as a medical assistant in Seimchan and made stops in Magadan from time to time, always bringing with him an air of solidity, discretion, and good common sense, as though Seimchan were not a land of camps and jackals but some sort of Switzerland.

"Well, that's just foolishness, Stasis Algerdasovich," was Cecilia's usual reaction to such pronouncements. "Sources of light have nothing to do with your icons." Usually she pretended not to take part in the conversations of the former zeks and sat in her "study," that is, behind the curtain screening off the marital bed, preparing lectures and immersed in her own primary sources. She could not restrain herself, though, and was always coming out with replies that in her opinion "put things back into their proper places."

On this particular day, a fine January evening of 1953—however strange it may seem, there was some fine weather in the midst of the witches' sabbath of the winter—this group had gathered at the home of Kirill Borisovich Gradov, stoker at the city hospital: Luigi Karlovich Delvecchio, an auto mechanic; Tatyana Ivanovna Plotnikov, a washerwoman; Stasis Algerdasovich, a medical assistant whose surname no one could ever pronounce correctly, though it was in fact quite simple: Ionaskiskauskas. Also looking at the fire was Stepan Stepanovich Kalistratov, a security guard at a large garage. In his spare time, he roamed the streets of Magadan like a member of the Bloomsbury Group. The conversation turned on the pleasant subject of cremation. Sprawled on the so-called divan, that is, on a rickety couch with a few cushions, Kalistratov was cheerfully holding forth, saying that in his opinion cremation was the best means of sending the perishable remains back into the natural cycle of substances. "Even when I was young, I was attracted by the poetic aspect of cremation," he said, sipping his tea and scooping up a heaping spoonful of sugared cowberries. His pharmacological experiments had not reduced his sweet tooth. "I'll never forget the impression the burning of Percy Shelley's body made on me. He drowned in your blessed Italy, Luigi Karlovich, more precisely in the Bay of Lerici—a lyrical body of water, isn't that right? And the body pulled from the lyric was burned right there on the shore, in the presence of a group of friends, including Lord Byron. How magnificent it was: 'All the larks of the world are cleaving the sky,' " as Akhmatova wrote, 'the sea and hills of Italy are all around, Lord George is there, torch in hand, almost the entire body is sublimated into the skies, and a silvery mound of ashes remains, instead of the disgusting process of decay, and transformation into a heap of bones . . .' no, no, comrades, cremation is magnificent!"

Kirill objected thoughtfully, "Maybe you're right as a poet, Stepan—there's no arguing with a poet!—but I'm not sure we can accept cremation from a Christian point of view. Bodies are to be resurrected not in a figurative but in a literal sense. Isn't that right, Stasis?"

"Quite so," the medical assistant replied with a smile.

"Listen, Kirill!" Stepan exclaimed. "Do you really think a pile of bones is necessary for the miracle of resurrection?"

At this point, naturally, everyone began talking at once. Tatyana Ivanovna managed to break through, saying that in Paris she had read Fyodorov's *Philosophy of the Common Cause,* and if one is talking about the scientific "resurrection of the fathers" the bones might be necessary.

"This scientific resurrection, if such a thing is possible, cannot be anything other than a great and divine miracle," Kirill said. "In that sense, Stepan may be right in saying that the presence of the remains in the grave will hardly do anything to accelerate the process of resurrection and that the scattering of the ashes, or even of some other elements of the human essence unknown to us, into the world . . . well, you see what I mean."

At that point, Stasis Algerdasovich banged his spoon against his teacup. "I, nevertheless, take a literal view of the articles of faith. What about you, Luigi Karlovich?"

The Italian or, as he often corrected people, the Venetian, clapped his hands and rubbed them together vigorously, as though he had never been in the camp at all. "See here, you cat fucker, I love any manifestations of Utopia, damn you!" Camerata Delvecchio had enriched himself in Kolyma with at least a thousand proletarian interjections.

Just then, Cecilia sprang out from behind the curtain with a copy of Engels' *Anti-Dühring* in her left hand and an ominously trembling pair of glasses in her right. "What are you going on about, you sorry people? Cremation, resurrection—what sort of nonsense are you talking? No, it wasn't for nothing, it wasn't for nothing that—"

She had not finished what she was saying when a tremendous blast nearly tore from the earth the sixteen-flat building that served as their refuge. The sky in the seaside window gleamed blindingly for an instant. They were not even able to look around at one another and at the fragments of cups and dishes before another blast roared, even more terrible than the first. In all probability, it was even more unexpected than the first, because, obviously, after the first unexpected explosion that tore the blameless sky to pieces, a second one seemed even more unexpected and absolutely dumbfounding.

"Down!" Stasis the medic shouted and threw himself down in the middle of the fragments of the dishes, raising his face and his hands to the wildly flickering window. All the participants in the peaceful conversation fell to their knees as well in the expectation of a third explosion, which might be final and apocalyptic. Even Cecilia went down on her knees with her copy of *Anti-Dühring*.

A third one did not come, however. A few minutes later, gigantic mushroom-shaped clouds, white and seething at first and then deep crimson, appeared over the near horizon, that is, right over Nagaevo Bay. The house rang with the cries of its inhabitants, cars roared down the street in the direction of the port. "Could it be war?" asked Kirill. "An atomic bomb?" Everyone began to get up, embarrassed. Nuclear war, though terrible, already seemed like a perfectly normal, almost everyday occurrence compared to what had just so rapidly dawned on all of them.

"Rubbish. Do you think they'd waste an A-bomb on a shitty little port like Nagaevo?" Stepan said. Kirill switched on the radio. The Voice of America was broadcasting a jazz program. It soon came to light that it was just some heavy cargo hauler in the port that had popped its boiler. Along with the freighter, two boats moored nearby and numerous structures on the shore had been destroyed. Fires were blazing everywhere, and a large number of people had been killed and injured. Judgment Day, however, was still far off, in the sense that it was neither near nor far away. As the Savior said, "For as the lightning cometh out of the east, and shineth even unto the west; so shall also the coming of the Son of man be. . . . But of that day and hour knoweth no man, no, not the angels of heaven, but my Father only." So Kirill had read in the contraband Gospel that Stasis the medic had brought to the camp.

☆

An hour before the blasts, at the other end of the city of Magadan, in the Karantinka camp, boredom, dead boredom, reigned. Foma from Rostov, alias Zaprudnev, alias Georgy Mikhailovich Shapovalov, alias another fifty names, including even the one he had been born with—that is, Mitya Sapunov, his real name—was sitting like Vrubel's demon on a crate in the toolshed and looking out beyond the zone, to the endless stony waves of Kolyma. It had been a long time since such a thing had happened to him, to be shut up in the zone without the slightest prospect of a free passage in the near future. He shouldn't have come back to the camp from Susuman a month before. Instead, maybe, he should have slipped back out onto the mainland and perhaps even disappeared altogether. The "bitches" had succeeded in driving the "monks" into a herd here in Karantinka, and there wasn't a fucking thing else to do: everything was falling apart. In the gloomiest of moods, the Rostovite looked out on the nearby decay, over which the sun hung low in the sky like the eye of a prison guard.

Just over a month before, the authorities had begun a cleanup campaign in Karantinka. The funniest thing of all was that the initiative had been taken not by a guard but by a lousy doc—Captain Sterlyadev of the Medical Corps. At first this walrus with a mustache of three whiskers had called for a struggle with "corruption" at Party meetings. The agents of Cleanup Duty had reported back that the captain was screaming at Party meetings like a hysterical woman, saying that everyone had been bought off, intimidating that "Ivan and a Half" had become the real boss of the far eastern camps, and insisting that the noble aims of the corrective labor system of the USSR must not be allowed to be disgraced! Sergeant Zhuriev, trembling like a little whore, reported to the Rostovite that Sterlyadev was off his rocker. Why, the comrade captain had almost mentioned by name those who had been "bought off" and "intimidated." His woman left him, that's the problem. Left him for a former zek, an operetta artiste, and got herself knocked up. So, you see, the Captain has shifted the misfortunes of his personal life onto the staff. He's calling for inspections, he's scribbling out reports. The Rostovite immediately realized that this was serious business. One day he waited for Sterlyadev in an alley behind the infirmary. He called out after the walruslike figure with the spindly legs that seemed to belong to someone else, "Captain Sterlyadev!"

The doctor trembled all over, his boots slipping on the piss yellow ice. He clutched at his holster with one hand and with the other tried to keep himself from falling. "Who's there? Who's calling? What do you want?"

The Rostovite with a sense of humor boomed from the darkness, "It's all right, Captain. Just a hearing test." It was clear that the flustered Sterlyadev could not figure out where the voice was coming from. Then the Rostovite asked him almost point-blank, "What's with you, Sterlyadev? Do you want to be bigger than everyone else, is that it? You don't want to just live quietly? You want to play the corpse?" Then he vanished into thin air, losing himself in the jungles of Karantinka with all its hundreds of beasts with shivs tucked away in their trousers.

The warning had no effect. One fine day, sure enough, a commission showed up. They sorted out almost a third of the prisoners to the huts, straight away, but then stopped work on account of a "banquet" with the local officer corps and the other human puke. After a three-day hangover, the reassignments began again; not at the same tempo but stubbornly and insistently. The best people, the "monks," were marched off to the mining sites, and, most important, Cleanup Duty was broken up. Nevertheless, the backbone of the band had managed to survive, in particular Fomka the Rostovite himself, who had clung to a job as shift timekeeper in the tool warehouse. It was clear, however, that the organization was on its last legs: at any moment there might be a sweep of the camp and they could all be exposed. The new commandant, Major Glazurin, following the example of all Bolshevik scum, walked around the camp, his person reined in with straps and accompanied by three men carrying submachine guns. Not infrequently, the "one who needed to be bigger than everybody else," Captain Sterlyadev of the MVD Medical Corps, was to be seen prancing along beside him. It looked as though the captain was beginning to display the symptoms of goiter: his skin was darkening, his limbs shaking, his eyeballs swelling. After his wife left, the captain had begun drinking himself into a stupor on a regular basis, alone, scooping up handfuls of week-old cabbage soup as his diet. His books, medical and literary alike, had been abandoned. The captain had formerly been known as a connoisseur of the modern literary scene, but now he had thrown all of the new volumes of *Novy Mir* right from the doorstep into a corner of a room, where they piled up in absurd configurations. As for going near the House of Culture, where he had once walked around as nicely as you please in the clothes of an intellectual with Yevdokia, it was out of the question, because in that very same pagan temple of sin the good woman had made the acquaintance of that little operatic Trotskyite, who had bleated the Stanley Matthews aria from *Eleven Unknowns:* "In the morning, everyone's shouting about it, and it's all over the screens! The radio, newspapers, popularity, the law—not bad!"

One pleasure remained to Captain Sterlyadev: masturbation. The wall to the left of his bed was covered with his revelations, and sometimes in his fantasies he even hit the ceiling. At the beginning of a drinking bout, after the first glass, he would write a letter to I. V. Stalin. "Dear Iosif Vissarionovich, my beloved! Under your inspired leadership in the time of the Great Patriotic War, the Soviet people taught Adolf [sometimes it would come out as 'Albert'] Hitler, that lackey of world imperialism, a good lesson. However, Germany not only gave us Hitler, she also gave us Karl Marx, Friedrich Engels, Lenin, and Wilhelm Pieck. She also garnered good and fruitful experience in the cause of the health of mankind. As an employee of the MVD of the USSR and as a representative of the most humane of professions, I consider that we should make use of the most positive features of the German experience in the matter of sorting out the prisoners of the Directorate of Northeast Corrective Labor Camps (Dalstroi). Otherwise, dear Comrade Stalin, we will find ourselves confronting the implacable law of the dialectic in the near future, when quantity changes quality."

He was firmly convinced in sending these letters that he would eventually receive a reply. In fact, he wasn't far wrong: had there not been an uprising, he would have been arrested for sending provocative letters to the Leader. For the time being, he walked through the camp accompanying Major Glazurin, rolling his bulging little acorn eyes and giving orders for the fumigation of entire barracks, that is, for the evisceration of everything they contained and the burning of the mattresses, in which the "fencing fans" of the camps hid their homemade, well-sharpened blades. The zeks sullenly followed the incomprehensible activity of the cops with their eyes. Everyone, of course, was wondering: Why isn't "Ivan and a Half" saying anything?

These were the events leading up to the moment in the present novel, in which there is nothing left for us to do but to display the leader of the once mighty Cleanup Duty in the pose of a Vrubel demon in a hiding place in the tool shed. I shouldn't have come back to Karantinka, Mitya said to himself with a gloomy yawn. There's nothing to keep me here. Thinking this way at this evening hour, it seemed that, above all, he had in mind the absence of Marinka "Five Corners" Schmidt. It was already a year since Marinka had been shipped off to Taly, where in the camp maternity ward she'd produced Mitya's child in a litter of one, which now—he didn't know if it was a boy, a girl, or some taiga wonder—was in the camp nursery, where Marukha had managed to land a job as an orderly. The Rostovite had not managed to get to her the last time he had made the rounds of the camps, and it was a pity: it's not likely you'll be able to reach her now. She was a good kid, Marukha, this Marinka Schmidt: you go into her, and it makes you feel like a human being again. He had taught her to call him "Mit-Mit," and from then on that was what she had called him, seemingly guessing that it wasn't just the sort of thing you mutter when you're screwing but his own name. Alas, as his ancestors used to say, some are no more and the rest are far away, and the lousiest thing of all was that there was no way to call up another Marukha from the women's zone: acting on tips from his informers, Major Glazurin had stopped up all channels, some even literally, with cement. These stool pigeons will have to be dealt with. "Ivan and a

Half" is going to stay silent for a third week running, and then everything will come down to one final slaughter.

The last time they had been cutting up the "bitches" at the Greater Seimchansk camp, Mitya, together with a group of his friends, had gone before an internal court and had received another twenty-five-year sentence under the name of Andrei Platonovich Savich, who had in fact gone to his eternal rest in the permafrost long ago. And even though everyone—the judges, the accused, and the guards—knew perfectly well how little one more "twenty-fiver" meant to this dreaded, good-looking fellow with an obviously assumed name, Mitya himself had felt the quiet but firm handshake of fate and melancholy at the moment when the sentence was being pronounced. How many twenty-fivers had he already received under different names? They amounted to at least five hundred years. Hey, isn't that a bit too much for just one farm boy? Isn't that too much horror for one kid? The Sapunov place goes up in flames, near death from starvation, and then, after the brief period of Gradov sanctuary, all the doings of the twentieth century: Junkers aircraft, tanks, flamethrowers, prison camp, that whole business with Vlasov and the partisans, the whole endless cycle of slaughter. And then surviving shootings and killings and Fomochka Zaprudnev and his eleven cigarettes, and getting further and further into crime and . . . He recalled a song from the camps: "Greetings from the far away camps and from all of our comrades and friends, Lots of love and kisses, your Andrei." And even if you have become the "king of shit and steam" around here, isn't it all too much? You're about to turn thirty-two, and that means you'll never get out of your thief's skin, you'll be a sort of ataman forever. You'll die in it—thanks to fate for arranging such a pleasant trip! But what if I try it the Michurin way, not waiting for fate to offer its favors to me, but taking them? To get out of Karantinka, take Marinka and our bastard, and go to the mainland in the guise of a happy family of specialists out on a contract. Technically, it wouldn't be difficult: the money and the letter he had stashed away in various holes both in Kolyma and on the mainland would be more than enough. There, on the vast, densely populated mainland with well-made MVD documents, a Party membership card, and references, we'll find work in administration. If I managed to hold this whole camp in my fist, I'll be able to deal with those bastards out there. The most important thing is to get your courage and your back up, to believe again that you're better than the rest. We'll move to Moscow, and we'll go to Silver Forest to drink tea with Grandpa and Grandma and listen to Chopin. I'll teach Marinka to stop swearing all the time and swiping valuable things. He pictured an evening in Silver Forest, Grandmother playing away at the piano in the study, Grandfather with his nose in a book, and himself, a kid bringing a grown woman in a silk dress, the irresistible thief "Five Corners," into the house. Once we've set ourselves up in Moscow, we'll write a letter to Magadan, to Soviet Street. Hello, dear adoptive parents Cecilia Naumovna and Kirill Borisovich! Maybe you thought the wolves gobbled me up a long time ago, but I'm alive and well, and I and my young family hope with all our hearts that you are the same.

And I never forgot you, dear fools. I never stopped loving you, my dear pair of idiots. Well, I won't write that, of course, I'll catch myself at that point. Anyway, it would be better to settle in the northern Caucasus than in Moscow. There's more thieving going on there, there's a taste for big money, and the mountains are nearby: if the spotlight ends up on you, you can go off with a gun and stay hidden for a long time.

It may be that Grandma Mary doesn't even play the piano anymore. She's over seventy, after all. And maybe Grandpa Boris doesn't take strolls with books anymore, reading as he walks. Maybe he's already departed for the place where the saints are and where you don't need IDs. Twelve years have already gone by since I left that house. When this thought occurred to him, he immediately slid from the sparkling prospects of his new life down into the present impassible cesspool. If I take off without doing what the gang came here from Kazakhstan to do, they'll never let me live. It'll be curtains for "Ivan and a Half." Our jackals won't spare a minute from looking for me, they'll track me down wherever I go, pull out my guts, and wrap them around my fist. What a sucker, letting your imagination run away with you like that. There's no other road for you to take but the lowest and bloodiest one.

Just then someone sighed noisily beside him. "Ah, Mitya, Mitya," said the muffled, almost inaudible voice that followed the sigh. On a crate nearby sat Vova Zhelyabov, alias Goshka Krutkin, known in the camp by his old wartime nickname of "Runt," strange as it may seem.

Mitya seized him by the nape of the neck. "How did you find me here, you bastard?"

Goshka twisted his head around as though he found pleasure in the grip of Mitya's hand. "By accident! It was an accident! I was just walking along and feeling sad, and suddenly I saw you looking down in the dumps. We're kindred souls, you and me." Thrusting a paw into the depths of his many layers of rags, Goshka suddenly produced a thick glass flask of "patent medicine." "Come on, old buddy, let's have a good time like in the old days in Dabendorf, what do you say? Remember how we used to go to the pictures?" He laughed and with his free hand made a gesture simulating masturbation that recalled a great deal.

"Where did you get stuff this good?" a surprised Mitya asked suspiciously.

"We were in town today, on a painting detail," Goshka explained eagerly. "You know me." He winked, as though hoping to remind his comrade in arms of something else, maybe just everything they had belted down together once upon a time. "Well, go ahead, have a snort!"

"No, you take the first one!"

"Ha, ha, don't be afraid, Mitya, it's not poisoned." Goshka took a swig and trembled from head to toe. "Pure fire! Beautiful stuff!"

Mitya followed his example. Sure enough, it was pure fire, first class, youth in liquid form. Even though he understood the falseness of it all perfectly well, he went on gathering courage, and things kept looking better, swallow by swallow. He was filled with good feeling toward the informer and passive queer sitting next to him. He even put his arms around his comrade's shoulders and shook him. "Hey, Runt, you're my runtiest one of all!" After all, he's the only living soul around who knew me when I was still a kid. Goshka licked him strongly and passionately on the lips in reply. Dusk was gathering in the shadow of the volcano. Mitya felt his prick rise, mighty and implacable.

Goshka Krutkin takes hold of the old rod just as well as Marinka Schmidt ever did, he has manners just like a lady. Have you lost your fucking mind, or what? Mitya, Mitya, my dear boy, I didn't get you wet, after all, even though I could have, right? Remember the song: "The languorous sun was parting company with the sea." The fucking sun, looked as though I were still running away to Italy. If you get me wet, they'll cut you up into chops right here. Oh, Mitya, Mitya, my lovely, stupid boy, oh-h-h, what a fool! Let go of my cock, Runt, you'll choke! Oh, Mitenka, you're my sweetheart, I've been in love with you for twelve years, this is the thirteenth now. The dialogue turned into a monologue: Goshka, you suck dry, bitch, you diseased bastard, what do you know about love except how to suck cocks? Don't you ever clean your teeth, you goddamn scum? Swig after swig, the fire flowed into Mitya, passing through everything, right down to his capillaries. The current in his body was moving along high-tension lines, while down below some sort of snake was sinking its teeth into him, according to the principle of interlinking vessels, a constant flow of fire and sugar.

At moments like these, Mitya didn't guess that he had been betrayed again, that he had been politically uncovered by the fear of the formation marching to the uranium mines, that the working out of things had begun, and that soon his trousers would fall down as the play went on. That's fine, dear boy, that's fine, enter me, please. I'm a pure woman, believe me. Who knows, he may be sent up on a political charge soon, maybe even off to the uranium mines? Here at least is some real happiness, to be able to say good-bye like human beings. What a playful little hole you have, Runt, and how did it get so tender? It's for you, Papa Rostov, oh, oh, it's for you that it's that way, like always . . .

It was just at that moment that two explosions, one after the other, shook the darkening vault of the sky and the earth, already plunged into obscurity. Goshka and Mitya flew apart, fully convinced that this was their punishment for the sin of "interlinking vessels." The thunder in the skies continued to reverberate and walk among the decaying buildings for several more minutes. Over the horizon, over the gates of Kolyma, through which the earth had been sucking in Stalinist human fertilizer for so many years, columns with steaming hoods towered up and black smoke poured out along with the glow of the fires that were breaking out everywhere.

Goshka, pulling up his trousers, was already crawling toward the secret hatch. Looking back at Mitya, he laughed soundlessly. Sirens were wailing in various locations. Shots were heard from the checkpoint guard tower. The thunder of feet. Panic-stricken wails. Mitya raced to his cache, tore away the boards, flung the bricks aside, and pulled out his friend, a Kalashnikov. Goshka squealed, "It's you, right? Tell me, Mitya, it's your doing, isn't it? It's an uprising, right? Anarchy is the mother of order, no? Talk to me!" Mitya rammed a clip into the Kalashnikov and stuck three others into his pockets and in his belt. He had prepared for any eventuality. One thing was clear—it had started, and now let it play out, unroll its whole reel.

Goshka had already begun to introduce his sinful backside into his clever hiding place. His face alternated between grinning like an idiotic greasy pancake and withering up like a sopping wet mushroom. "Answer me, Sapunov, are those your monks tossing bombs? Are we going to play the silence game? Answer me, you Fascist bastard!" Mitya raised the submachine gun. "You're going to give yourself away, you stool pigeon! Want a few bullets?" At the last moment, he decided not to pull the trigger and let his friend with the sugary ass slip away. But his friend would not accept the gift of that instant, the swine. On the contrary, he pulled himself back up out of his hole, shouting our secret passwords and nicknames which no one, except the Rostovite himself, had ever heard all together, even in Cleanup Duty: "Tell me, who did you get to work for you in the port? Ishak? Concentrate? The Stakhanovite? Naked? Moroshka, Catfish, YBK? You see, I know all your wolves. Come on, confess, 'Ivan, and a—' " You're asking for a bullet, you spy, so here, take three! A short burst smashed Krutkin's pulsating features to bits. Now weep for the Runt, weep for his alluring youth! No time to mourn, everything's falling apart.

Mitya ran out of the tool warehouse yard. A crowd of zeks was racing by in some unknown direction. "Hey, stop, orders of 'Ivan and a Half'!" But no one was listening to him anymore. Where are they running to? He took off with the rest of them. A window of the infirmary flashed by, and Mitya glimpsed Crimea and Ishak cutting Captain Sterlyadev's throat. The crowd gathered around was brandishing homemade knives made from sharpened pieces of iron bedframes. They were rushing to knock over the guard towers, to tear weapons away from the guards, and, most important of all, to break the locks and get to the alcohol. The Kolyma tribe, bastards of the permafrost, even without alcohol they were already high just from the great excitement, from the explosions, fires, wailing sirens, crackling gunfire, and they all wanted just one thing—not to lose this intoxication, to pour drink into it, to slash, to stab, to shoot and run wild. "Ivan and a Half" 's carefully worked-out plan for the instantaneous wiping out of all of the "bitches," the disarming of the guards, and then the seizure of the vital points of Magadan—all of that was up the stack now. Now the initiator of the plan himself, drunk on what he had poured into himself and on the sugar he had not yet poured out, did not understand where the crowd was carrying him, a crowd in which they were all mixed together, "bitches," "monks," the special convict brigade, "socially harmful elements," "socially dangerous elements," all of the trustees and the doomed cattle of the workforce—everyone was rushing for the checkpoint, for the guard tower, for the machine guns.

The MVD's iron embrace immediately begins to break up under the blows delivered by the human mass. The gates are already cracking, they've burst open. The mass of zeks streams through. A searchlight has been turned on in one of the principal guard towers, and a machine gun has started up. "Hey you, the Rostovite!" someone shouted in the crowd. "Where's that crooked rifle of yours?" Mitya, without a thought about anything, sent a spray of bullets cutting through the searchlights and the machine guns. The mob spilled out into the zone again. Someone had already seized some trucks and jeeps and thrown out the bodies of the guards. The horde raced toward Magadan, which by now was seized by panic. Roars, howls, whistles—guests are heading for your warm shelter, dear little town! In their burst of enthusiasm, of course, they had forgotten about the commandant, Major Glazurin, who had been stunned by a brick to the head. They had forgotten to cut the telephone lines in his office. The dazed major, true to his Cheka oath, called General Tsaregradsky at Dalstroi. The latter, also stunned, not by a brick but by the events in the port, managed at the last minute to send a rifle company, which took up a position across the Kolyma Highway, at the very entrance to the city.

Thus the monotonous existence of the capital of the Kolyma penal system exploded in one night, only to return to its habitual drowsy cradle, rocking back and forth to the pumping rhythm of manpower and technology once the storm had subsided.

★

When night fell, the wounded and burned from the port were driven past the Gradovs' window in trucks. Shots and occasional volleys, a sound similar to the ripping of a tightly stretched canvas, were heard from the northern edge of town. Celia and Kirill were extracting jagged pieces of glass from the window frames and trying to cover the gaping holes with boards and pieces of plywood, even to stuff pillows into them. In spite of the fires outside, a glassy cold was enveloping the entire coastal plain, promising at least a week of unyielding frost. Their neighbor lady, Ksaveria Olympievna, popped in again and again. The women conferred about what was to be done to protect the house from the cold and whom they should talk to first at the housing authority. Cecilia always greatly enjoyed chatting with Ksaveria Olympievna. It gave her a feeling of having a normal life in a normal city. Sometimes she would try to understand how it was that an ordinary woman from Moscow had ended up in Kolyma: maybe she had some relatives in the camps or, on the contrary, working for the guards. Ksaveria Olympievna, it seemed, had no idea what Cecilia was talking about. She was interested only in new operettas, shopping, the gossip about the staff at the House of Culture, and holiday plans. Only over a bottle of good liqueur from the mainland was it revealed that the lady, like Cecilia, had come to Magadan upon the release of her husband. A situation had grown up that was, even though a bit piquant, more or less entirely normal. It wasn't anything political or anti-Soviet, just a good situation straight out of everyday life: her husband had managed to come out of one of the isolated camps with a new Yakut wife and two children. That, my dear, is what I mean by a piquant situation. *C'est la vie,* my dear. That's just it, it's like that, *la vie,* a strong, spicy business, and it doesn't matter whether it's happening on the Arbat or in the taiga in the shadow of the guard towers—*la vie!*

Finally, everything in the apartment seemed to be shaken out, covered over, and stopped up. The dreadful explosions with their apocalyptic illuminations went off to the land of fresh memories, then to depart for a destination even further removed. The crackling of gun-fire on the perimeter of the "permanent settlement zone" would be easy to get used to. Kirill turned on the radio just in time to catch part of the Voice of America news summary: ". . . a strange incident in Berlin. This morning, a Colonel Voinov, commander of an artillery division in the Soviet Army, arrived in the American sector at the wheel of a Soviet military vehicle. He asked the American authorities to grant him political asylum. The Soviet administration came forth with an announcement in which they claimed that Colonel Voinov had been kidnapped by Western intelligence services and demanded the immediate return of the officer. . . . There is a temporary lull in the Korean theater of operations. The so-called Chinese peoples' volunteers are transferring new armored units to the Panmunjom sector. United Nations aircraft are continuing to strike at targets in the enemy's rear." A record was heard playing in Ksaveria Olympievna's room: "When autumn came, I said to Adèle, 'Farewell, my child, don't hold it against me. . . .' "

★

Fomochka the Rostovite had three caches in the city. He hobbled up to one of them, holding on to collapsing fences and to the beams propping up the crumbling walls of the abandoned barracks, crying, laughing, drooling, his nose running, blood and lymph flowing from the wound in his upper stomach. There, in the stomach, in the kingdom of the intestine, alongside the mighty slopes of the liver, was where that goddamned miserable fucking beast of a trichomonad had lodged like a barbed perch. While it was sleeping, he could walk on for a minute or two, but as soon as it woke up, the dirty goddamned good-for-nothing began crushing the defenseless internal kingdom like a tank, blowing up intestinal arches and burning with Fascist—Bolshevik, that is—fire. Weren't there at least some partisans around to lay a mine that would blow all of this outrage to kingdom fucking come?

The door to the cache turned out to be covered with boards, and, to top it all off, a heavy lock was dangling from the door. Just try to break through that metal, try to pull your guts through those metal clamps! The street wound around into a dead end where a stockade of well-pointed lances met the cripple who was dropping great gobs of thick blood and dragging behind him the pride of the Soviet armed forces, a Kalashnikov submachine gun, designed to blow the asses of any transgressors once and for all. Mitya crawled along the iron fence. He was still trying to stop up his needlessly squashed and jumbled stomach with his leather winter cap. In the meantime his head was covered with secretions that had frozen and turned it into a sort of glazed icy pineapple. Suddenly, beneath the fence, he spotted a tunnel in the snow, and he immediately rolled in that direction, into the blessed land of snowy fur coats of well-endowed larches. I'd like to turn into one of these coats and take it easy. To stand there and quietly, through the branches, talk with the innocent goddamned bullet—fuck it!—that was going cold inside him. He made his way beneath the larches, tumbling now and again into the snow and dirtying it with his presence. It feels like I'm going back to the time when I was a kid—I can already hear the grand piano, Granny dear. Suddenly he saw a man with a rifle up ahead. He immediately cut him down. It turned out that it wasn't a man with a rifle but the statue of a Young Pioneer with a bugle. Where do I go? Not far from the distorted figure of a boy scout stood other sculptures: a girl with an oar raised in a salute, a girl throwing a discus. In the distance, the chief thug, Lenin, stood on a pedestal with his back turned to those present and a winch-like arm extended in the direction of the city. There's the one who ought to get a couple bullets in his ass; let him find out what it's like to stand up with bullets in his guts!

"Hey, you from Rostov!" someone called out loudly with a smile. "Look over there, boys, our Foma is still alive!" The Stakhanovite, Moroshka, and Som, the finest snouts that "Cleanup Duty" had produced, were sitting, quite drunk, in a columned gazebo, keeping a small fire burning on a sheet of iron, pulling from a box vials of what looked like the stuff that Mitya and his stinking friend had sucked down not long before. The assholes were laughing. "An engineer's campfire! It's an easy life here in Gorky Park! A whole crate of the hard stuff and sausage out the ass! Climb on up into the hut, Foma, we'll play 'defenders of Sevastopol' for the cops! Take a look at what we put on the head bastard's skull!"

Indeed, on the head of the statue, covering its view of historical perspectives, was a latrine bucket. Smiling sadly, Mitya limped on by his colleagues. "What sort of Foma am I to you? Foma, he's a kid that's still alive, he walked by, smoking and whistling a tune—me, I'm just a corpse full of bullets." Politely refusing a glass that was offered, he walked through the snowdrifts to the main path of the Park of Culture, which had been cleared, and stood facing the statue with the foul bucket on its head. The bucket made the features of the figure appear even more unshakable. "Here, you lisping cocksucker, take what you deserve," he muttered and, forgetting even about the iron perch in his belly, began to spray the statue with fire from his submachine gun. At the moment he was firing these bursts, it seemed to him that he was no longer connected with the ground, that some sort of scorching stream was carrying him away from the earth and holding him suspended in a state that felt wonderful. The first-class bullets that had been tempered in Tula riddled the alabaster shit. Moroshka and Som were roaring with laughter in the hut at the sight of this bit of theater. The Stakhanovite drowsed off, leaning his back against the column of the rotunda. When there were no more bullets, Mitya fell from ecstasy and came crashing down on all of the spots where he was hurting. Goddammit to hell, where the fuck are you now, you bitch death? Throwing his gun down on the spot where he had stood and left a stain, he shuffled off in the direction of the exit from the park, where Soviet Street lay peacefully in a frosty rainbow beneath the streetlights and alongside houses painted the color of human flesh and a transformer shed. That's where I'm going to make my way to—to the transformer shed. It looks like that's my destination: those very same windows.

Dragging himself up to the shed, he wanted to sit down with his back to it and his face turned to the windows, but he slipped on the ice and fell flat, lacking the strength to stand up again. Now he lay beneath a streetlight, young and handsome, almost the same way that Fomochka Zaprudnev had lain, only a bit frozen, glazed over, and oozing a little from the belly. He still had enough strength to cry out "Celia! Kirill!" But who could hear anyone through those windows stuffed with pillows? I'll throw myself down right next to the house, he was still able to think. At least I'll be next to people who are family. When the door banged, he could no longer hear it, nor could he see two dark figures coming out, and it was only in his last moment that he became aware of the two beloved faces bending over him. "So they must have recognized me after all" rustled in his head like a leaf from Tambov, after which the hot current began to flow out of him. And that very current lifted him up, and he was going away, higher and higher, leaving the icebound Kolyma coastal plain far below.

Chapter 13

———————☆———————

A MEDICAL SCHOOL
MEETING

They really are a wonder, these new long-playing records: Mozart's
Fortieth Symphony, twenty-five minutes long, on one side! It was the
blessed Mozart hour in the loft in Krivoarbatsky Lane. Sandro was
sitting at a canvas, working with a brush, so intent on what he was
doing that he might have been a conductor. At moments like these he
forgot he was nearly blind and brilliantly captured one of Nina's flowers in a rendition that was clear and vividly bright even if a bit
smeared around the edges. "Well, at least he won't see me getting
old," Nina said to Yolka at times like these, when they were both
lying on their backs in the loft smoking. "Or he'll see almost nothing,
let's put it that way." Stretching out with cigarettes on the broad set-
tee covered with a Tbilisi-made blanket had become the favorite pas-
time of the two women, who had become friends after the calamities
of the previous year. They could now talk for hours on end, turned
toward each other, having between them an ashtray, the telephone,
cups of coffee, and often a pair of excellent Napoleons from the
Prague Restaurant. If Nina had a call, Yolka would pick up a book

and read, listening with half an ear to her mother's sarcastic intonations. These tones would immediately appear in Nina's voice as soon as any of her "brother writers" called. No matter what the subject of the discussion was, she would, without even being aware of it, seemingly try to get a fundamental idea across: "All of us are nothing other than absolute shit, respected colleague."

Six months had gone by since Yolka had been brought back from the Nikolin Mountains in a black automobile, and it was only on this gray, windy January afternoon, with snow streaming along the roof and windowpanes of the studio, that she began to talk about Beria.

"If you think he tortured me, you're completely wrong," Yolka suddenly said to her mother. "He always spoke to me lovingly, you know. He'd switch on his American record player and read poetry with classical music in the background, quite often the verses of Stepan Shchipachov—"

"A torture worse than most," Nina put in.

"He'd take my arm and kiss it from the palm of my hand to the elbow," Yolka went on, "reading, 'Learn to treasure love, and to treasure the years twice as much again.' Sometimes he'd read something in Georgian, and it even sounded beautiful. When he had been drinking, he'd go off into some muddled confession, like 'You're my last love, Elena! I'm going to die soon! I have so many enemies, they're going to kill me! I've had a thousand women, but I never loved any of them until you!' And so on in that style, if you see what I mean." Elena's voice was shaking, and she put a hand over her eyes and lips.

"My little one," Nina whispered and began stroking her daughter's head. "Tell me everything. You'll feel better."

"You know, the whole time I was there in that dacha, I felt strange, somehow," the former captive went on, now calm. "A sort of apathy, a sensation of being held back. I was glad to lose at tennis, I would start reading plays and then put them down, and I would wander around the garden in some sort of half-conscious state under the gaze of that kindest of swine. He didn't have to watch me, though—the idea of running away never entered my mind. And I wasn't angry with him at all. It sounds disgusting, but I even came to look forward to his visits. He would say to me, 'Elena'—with a Georgian accent, of course—'forgive me for having taken you away. Look at me and decide for yourself: Do you really think I can court girls the way normal people do?' At times like those, I even laughed: he was funny, bald, plump, glasses on his nose, like a comic figure in a foreign film."

"My God," whispered Nina, "they must have put something in your food, something that weakened your will."

Yolka sighed, bit her lip, and again tried to cover her face with one hand. "You're probably right," she muttered. "Oh, Mama, why didn't I think of that myself?"

Nina again caressed her long-legged "little one," her one and only, stroking her hair, tickling the nape of her neck, even kissing that most tender piece of flesh, the supposedly ageless earlobe.

"Listen, my little girl," she said, "Let's talk about the most intimate subject of all. As far as I can gather, you were a virgin until then, yes? Tell me, did he—well, did he sleep with you? That is—forgive me for such a crude word, but did he fuck you?"

When she had asked the question, Nina seemed turned to stone: in spite of everything, she had refused to believe that the first man for her "little girl" would turn out to be a monster. Yolka buried her face in her mother's breast and began to sob. The two women had finally come to the subject they had been so carefully approaching during all those months of lying in the loft with coffee and cigarettes. Both of them realized that without such a discussion, they would never overcome the estrangement that had grown up between them several years before, when Yolka had only just been entering the "age for love."

"Well, Mama, I don't know anything about that," Yolka murmured. "To this day I don't understand what happened out there to . . . I don't remember a lot of things, I just don't remember. . . . The first morning I woke up without any clothes on, my underwear was ripped, and I felt like I was burning *there,* and then, at the dacha, he played with me like a kitten, stroking me, feeling under my bra and in my panties, and then he would go away looking gloomy—tragic, you might even say. One day, when he was drunk, he jumped on me, covered my mouth with his hand, slobbered all over me with his lips— there was an unbearable smell of garlic, it was like a nightmare. . . . He started trying to tear my legs apart, trying to stick his hands in *there,* and maybe something else besides, but I had my—my—well, you know, my—"

"Your period, dear," Nina said. My God, she thought, if only she knew what I was like at her age, what all of us were like, little bitches with our heads full of Alexandra Kollontai feminist rubbish, with our anthroposophy and the glass of water we were supposed to be able to carry on our heads without spilling it. Why didn't I ever tell her about all these things? Why didn't I just do an anatomical drawing for her on a piece of paper: here's a penis, here's a vagina, the clitoris, the hymen. . . . It's all so simple and all so . . . so what? I myself don't understand a thing about how all of this . . . about what we're supposed to do with it all. . . .

"Well, yes, my period," Yolka went on. "There was blood, and stains, everything around was soiled. I felt sick when that toad expelled from himself. Everything shifted, the smells were just like vomit, and he was pushing up against me, crying out something disgusting in Georgian. All I can remember is *chuchkhiani, chuchkhiani.* That's how it was, Mama, and the next day they took me home. So I didn't understand anything then, and I never will, because there will never be another man in my life as long as I live."

"Don't be silly, sweetheart," said Nina.

"Never talk to me about it again," Yolka said, in as decisive a tone as before the "events." "It's already decided, once and for all. You know, I left the tennis courts that day with a boy. I liked him an awful lot. In fact, I was waiting for him at the metro when they pulled me into the car. You know, I felt such joy waiting for him, life all around seemed to be trembling for me and for him, too. The sensation of everything was keener than usual: the sun, shadows, the wind, leaves, building stones. Nothing like that will ever happen again for me, because I'm *chuchkhiani*—'dirty.' "

Suddenly there was a crash downstairs, and Sandro called in a frightful voice, "Listen! There's an announcement from TASS!" He turned up the volume, and the dramatic tones of the announcer filled the entire loft: "Some time ago, a terrorist group of doctors was discovered by the organs of state security, doctors having as their aim the shortening of the life of leaders of the Soviet Union by means of damaging treatment. Among the members of the terrorist group were Professor Vovsi, internist; Professor Vinogradov, internist; Professor M. B. Kogan, internist; Professor B. B. Kogan, internist; Professor Yegorov, internist; Professor Feldman, otolaryngologist; Professor Ettinger, internist; Professor Greenstein, neuropathologist.

"The criminals confessed that they made use of Comrade

Zhdanov's illness, incorrectly diagnosing his complaint, concealing the fact that he had had a heart attack, and prescribing treatment that was counterproductive and thereby hastened the death of Comrade Zhdanov.

"The criminals also shortened the life of Comrade Shcherbakov.

"The doctor-criminals tried first of all to undermine the health of the leaders of the Soviet armed forces and to weaken the defenses of the country, to put out of action Marshal Vasilyevsky, Marshal Govorov, Marshal Konev, General of the Army Shtemenko. The arrest put an end to their evil designs.

"These doctor-murderers, monsters of the human race, have trampled on the sacred banner of science, they have worked as hired agents of foreign intelligence. The majority of participants in the terrorist group—Vovsi, Kogan, Feldman, Greenstein, Ettinger, and others—were linked with the international Jewish bourgeois organization Joint, a creation of American intelligence. The arrested Vovsi confessed to the investigators that he received a directive 'for the extermination of the leadership cadres of the USSR' from the USA, from Joint, through the Moscow doctor Shimelkovich and the well-known Jewish bourgeois nationalist Mikhoels.

"The investigation will be concluded very soon."

Silence followed. Yolka and Nina looked down from the loft. Sandro was standing in the middle of the studio in a paint-spattered smock.

"That's it?" Nina asked.

"Seems like it," said Sandro.

"Strange somehow, this long pause," she said.

He shrugged. "What do you mean, Nina? It's just an ordinary pause."

"No, it's too long," she objected insistently.

He waved his arm in an exaggerated fashion, like a penguin fitted with the wings of an eagle.

"Go on!"

Suddenly, they heard the familiar, mellifluous female voice of the announcer for All-Union Radio. "We have just broadcast an announcement from TASS. We will now continue with the concert our listeners requested: 'Song of the Indian Merchant' from Rimsky-Korsakov's opera *Sadko*.

"Turn it off!" shouted Yolka.

"Take it easy, guys!" Nina commanded. "Get your things together, we're going to Silver Forest!"

★

A general meeting of the students and staff of the First Moscow Medical Institute was scheduled to take place in the main auditorium three days after the announcement by TASS. A blizzard was raging on the Khoroshovsky Highway. Visibility was approaching zero. Two Boris Gradovs, III and IV, were driving through the snowy obscurity in the Horch on their way to the next turning point in their destinies. Fate, however, was offering them several choices. For example, they could simply not allow themselves to be carried up to this turning point. They could stop the car in the middle of the road, carefully turn the steering wheel, which was already grunting in spite of repeated greasings, put the already grinding gears into reverse, and then turn around and go back in the direction from which they had come; have a lunch of borshch and pork chops, reinforced by vodka, with the family; and then in the evening, when the storm had calmed, go to the Kursk Station and head south for a well-earned rest. In the name of fate, these options were proposed to the grandfather by his grandson. In the name of the same, the grandfather cut off the grandson: "Stop chattering and drive!"

"Don't be a fool, Grandpa! This meeting is a pile of shit—what do you want with it?" Boris glanced over at the noble profile of Boris Nikitovich in alarm. "Can't you see what weather we have?" Fate clearly seemed to be accepting his arguments. Up ahead on the icy highway was the aftermath of an accident: a car had skidded into a ditch, several trucks had piled up, a crane was growling, and the flying echelons of snowflakes were burying everything more deeply by the minute. "There, you see, Grandpa," Boris IV said. "Let's turn around before it's too late." Boris Nikitovich III waved his grandson off again, by now considerably irritated. Trucks and vans soon bunched up behind them, making it impossible to turn around. Having sat in the traffic jam for three quarters of an hour, they arrived at the meeting late. Boris Nikitovich immediately took his place on the presidium. For want of an unoccupied seat, Borya sat down on a step. He caught the perplexed expressions of several students and the alarming and enamored glance of Eleonora Dudkin, the Komsomol organizer. What was the champion doing at a meeting to condemn the "killers in white gowns"? Trying not to pay attention to these stares, he looked at the pale face of his grandfather in the second row of the presidium. Grandma's right, he thought, something strange is happening to him. This affair could cost him his life. Maika, who had by now become a frequent guest at Silver Forest, had watched the day before as Grandfather had opened his newspaper and had seen his signature beneath the letter of the academics condemning the clique of saboteurs and conspirators of the Joint organization. Boris Nikitovich had taken the newspaper, gone into his study, and called to Mary to join him there. For a long time they had been together behind closed doors. Maika had taken little Nikitushka and Archi-medes out for a walk, and when she had come back the old couple's conversation was still going on, sometimes in raised voices, but indistinctly. She had spent a long time helping Auntie Agasha with the washing and the cooking, and the old people had still not emerged. The telephone had rung frequently, and the muffled tones of Boris Nikitovich's "official" voice had been heard. Auntie Agasha had flung a towel away in a fit of anger and banged her fist on the table: "Why does he answer the phone? Why does he answer the phone, tell me!" Finally the doors had opened, and Grandma Mary had emerged, saying loudly, "There's no need for all that!" Then Boris Nikitovich had appeared. Strange as it may seem, he had been in good form, even invigorated. He had asked Maika where she thought his grandson might be at the moment. Maika had said that in all probability the legendary sportsman was at his residence on Gorky Street, preparing for an exam in the company of Eleonora Dudkin and several other female students who were in love with him. Boris Nikitovich had burst out laughing: "You, Miss Maya, can afford not to be jealous about a few students." It had been a remarkable compliment, given in a gentlemanly fashion. "And then suddenly you turned up in that Fascist jalopy of yours, Borya Grad, and we all had dinner together, and it was wonderful, even though Mary and Agasha couldn't stop their fingers from shaking, something you didn't notice in the end. And then, I want to remind you, you had your way with me for a long time, right here in your mother's room. I think I may be pregnant." That's all I need, thought Boris, and then had his way with his beloved, just a bit, the

way one does in the morning, as though it took the place of calisthenics.

At breakfast, they had discussed the various options involving the
absence of Boris Nikitovich at the general meeting of the institute.
Suddenly, the old man had wiped his mouth decisively with his napkin and said he would be there without fail, "if only to see it with my
own eyes." Mary and Agasha had immediately gotten up from the
table and run off in different directions, and Boris had run after both
of them simultaneously; that is, first he had patted the cook on the
shoulder, and then he had made his way quickly to the piano, not even
suspecting that he was repeating exactly the movements of his father
a few months before his own birth. "Something strange is happening
to him," Mary had announced through her dampened handkerchief.
"This business may cost him his life. Isn't it enough, that signature of
his—which they put there without even asking him? And now this
meeting! Can anyone live through such disgrace?"

Moving through the blizzard, constantly turning "in the direction
of the skid" and braking with the accelerator, Boris noticed that the
closer they came to the institute, the more the blood drained away
from his grandfather's face, as though that face had become frozen, a
bas-relief. What was making him go to this meeting? He could go
south, take a room in Sochi, stroll along the shore. Maybe it sounds
naïve, but at least that way there would be a chance. Even speeches at
large meetings now can't save anyone, it seems. The same witch-hunt
is raging, just like in 1937. Sashka Sheremetiev is right: the way to go
is to take up arms and to fight one last, decisive battle. Only, who will
take up arms? The fifteen members of the Dostoevsky Circle?

The assembly's presidium had clearly given up waiting for Professor Gradov. The whole body lit up with smiles when he arrived. The
surviving non-Jewish pillars of medical science exchanged glances.
The chairman wanted to squeeze down one place to make room for
the professor to sit next to him, but Boris Nikitovich modestly took a
seat in the second row of chairs. At the lectern, meanwhile, Doctor
Udaltsov, topographical surgeon and member of the bureau of the
Party Committee, was winding up his speech: "And on those who be-
smirched our noble profession, we say: eternal shame!" The last
words soared up to the chandelier almost like a descant in a church,
striving for resonance in the crystal as well as in the hearts of the au-

dience. Udaltsov was leaving the speakers' platform to applause, when all of a sudden a student stood up in the third row. Boris knew her—Mika Bazhanov, from the third year.

"Tell us, Comrade Udaltsov, what should we do with the textbooks?" asked Mika, whose voice was just like that of a child.

"What textbooks?" the doctor replied, taken aback.

"Well, after all," said Mika, "these saboteurs are great scientists and teachers. We study from their books. What are we supposed to do with them now?"

With his left hand, Udaltsov clutched at the lectern, while with his right he began to grope strangely at the air. Some incautious person in the hall snickered. Udaltsov subconsciously noticed what he was reaching for, a long classroom pointer, which he had laid on the table to the right of the lectern without thinking.

"Their books?" howled the professor in a demonic voice, and then he showed why he needed the pointer: he brought it down sharply across the tribune like a Red cavalry sword. "Burn their stinking books and scatter the ashes to the four winds!" Another blow to the lectern, and then another; the pointer, to everyone's surprise, stood up to it all. "We will banish the slightest mention of their names, all of the Kogans, from the history of Soviet medicine! Let the bones of these killers rot in the Russian earth as quickly as possible, so that no trace of them remains!"

The terrified Mika gave a sniffle. The professor himself was shaking almost to the point of convulsions; he was obviously having some kind of nervous fit. Approaching cautiously beneath the swings of the punishing pointer, two members of the Party Committee led Udaltsov away from the podium with great sympathy and comradely warmth. "Well, well, what an outburst of emotion," said Borya Grad while the rest of the hall sat in embarrassed silence. Then suddenly, the chairman turned the floor over to Boris's grandfather, distinguished professor and member of the Academy of Medical Sciences. By yielding the floor to Gradov immediately after Udaltsov, Professor Smirnov clearly wished to demonstrate the respectability of the gathering; to say that we have here, taking part in this patriotic action, not only young associate professors about whom it might be said, or thought, that it is unhealthy careerism rather than righteous anger that moves them to hysterics but also renowned representatives of the old school who have already had every title and award imaginable bestowed upon them: no, no, respected listeners, Soviet medicine has not been decapitated, not at all, and how good it is of Boris Nikitovich that, in spite of some problems with his health, he has found it within himself to. . . . As often happens in such cases, Professor Smirnov was deliberately deceiving himself in mentally ascribing Udaltsov's hysterics to "unhealthy careerism." In fact, of course, he understood that careerism had not entered into the matter but that it had had to do with a monstrous fear that paralyzed the whole nervous system; a fear that shackled everyone present, that had dragged old man Gradov here and that is pulling him up to the podium now. It made even him, the chairman, force a smile, which made him feel as though he were stretching his facial muscles to their limit.

Boris Nikitovich, mounting the speakers' platform, adjusted his tie and tapped the microphone with the middle finger of his right hand. Everyone immediately noted with attention that the seventy-seven-year-old Academician was not enfeebled at all. On the contrary, he was composed, stern, extremely precise in his walk, his movements, and his facial expressions; there was a light in his eyes and a slight flush to his cheeks that offset his graying hair perfectly.

"Comrades," he said in an even, sedate voice, whose overtones, however, made it seem as though "gentlemen" lay behind the word "comrades." "We are all shaken by what has happened. It has now become clear what the disappearance of these leading medical specialists has meant. Who can believe the absurd stories about the terrorist activities of Professors Vovsi, Vinogradov, Kogan, Yegorov, Feldman, Ettinger, Greenstein, and many others mentioned in the TASS bulletin? I have worked side by side with most of these people all my life, I consider many of them my friends, and I have not the slightest intention of renouncing my friendship and my high esteem for their irreproachable professional actions just because of these absurd and disgraceful—yes, yes, comrades, I say again, disgraceful— accusations! To a man, every one of those named selflessly labored at the front during the Great Patriotic War—how great is the value alone of the first therapeutic service in a field army in history, organized by Miron Semyonovich Vovsi! All of them were awarded military ranks and decorations, and now such shame comes down on their heads! It is perfectly clear to me that our colleagues have become the victims of some sort of muddled political game. It is obvious that the people who approved this action striking down so many prominent physicians and scientists are not thinking about the fate of Soviet medicine, are not even thinking about their own health. Furthermore, I want to say that I have been absolutely dumbfounded by the openly anti-Semitic character of the newspaper campaign mounted in connection with this affair. I have not the slightest doubt that someone is trying to provoke our people, our Party, and our Soviet intelligentsia, faithful to the ideals of scientific communism. As an old Russian doctor, the son of a doctor, the grandson of a doctor, and the great-grandson of a regimental physician in Suvorov's army, I protest this persecution of my colleagues!"

The audience was so stunned by Professor Gradov's speech that it allowed him to finish and even to leave the tribune to total silence. It was only when he had returned to the floor and hesitated, unsure of which way to go—back to his place in the presidium or toward the exit—that a wail, panic stricken, as though striving to make up for the delay, was heard: "Shame on Professor Gradov!" Then the dam burst. The portraits of the historic luminaries decorating the auditorium fairly shook in the face of the malevolent roar. "Shame! Shame! Down with the Zionists, cosmopolitans, and killers! Down with the accomplices of reaction!" After that, everything merged together into one massive howl, from which one ringing Komsomol slogan managed to break out: "Down with the Jewish parasite Gradov!" The Komsomolists and the other students were on their feet, brandishing their fists: *"No pasarán!"* Lecturers and associate professors also joined the attack, and the full professors expressed their dissociation from the outcast with sharp hand gestures. Running down the aisle in the direction of the stage, Boris noticed that even Mika Bazhanov, who had asked the unfortunate question about the textbooks, was waving her little fist indignantly. Alas, so was the love-stricken Eleonora Dudkin, who seemed to have fallen into line with the rest. Leaping up onto the stage with a powerful spring, Boris embraced his grandfather, then took him by the arm and led him to the exit. After a minute, they found themselves in an empty corridor and getting further and further away from the still-shouting auditorium.

"Grandfather, you're a hero," said Boris IV.

"Leave it alone," Boris III said. "I was only following the dictates of my—"

"All right, all right," Boris IV interrupted. "I understand, enough rhetoric."

Boris III was ever so slightly choked up with some sort of strong emotion—happiness, perhaps. "Done!" he virtually exclaimed and set off in a precise, young stride, seeming to play with the cane that he had only just before been leaning on heavily.

"That's the way things are," said Boris IV. He was doing everything he could not to give in to his feelings, not to press his beloved grandfather to his chest, not to burst out sobbing. "What's done is done and can't be undone. Now we have to decide where to go from here. I propose we immediately head south. The two of us will go to Georgia or Sochi, to the Crimea." Then he remembered the women and corrected himself: "Actually, you'll have to go alone, and I'll join you after taking my examinations. We can stay in touch through Maika.

"Stop it, Babochka," Boris III said lightly. "How can anyone hide from them?"

"We not only can, we have to," said Boris IV. "We're certainly not just going to sit and wait for them to come!"

They stepped out onto the porch and saw that, while passions had been raging indoors, the snowstorm without had died down. Accumulating in the distance over the roofs of Moscow, heavy clouds, stained dark blue, seemed to hold out the promise of flight. Janitors were flinging the snow aside with broad shovels.

"Escape? What the hell, I guess it's worth a try," Boris III smiled. "Tomorrow you'll take me to the train station."

"Nothing doing, you have to leave today, immediately. You can rely on my instincts after all that experience in intelligence."

"Don't panic." Boris III slapped his grandson on the shoulder with a fur mitten that must have been sewn in 1913. "There's no sense exaggerating the danger. Decisions about arresting people like me have to go up the chain of command. It takes time. At least two days or so. They won't be in a hurry, after all, because no one ever runs away. No one runs away from them, no one, not ever."

Suddenly the euphoria passed, evaporated, and Boris Nikitovich

leaned heavily on his cane. It suddenly seemed to him that the "janitors" were only pretending to be taking a smoke break and were in
fact watching him. Several faces appeared in the windows of the
neighboring clinic: spies, maybe? Two colonels got off a streetcar—
colonels—from where? A group of preschoolers was coming along the
well-trodden snowy path, each child holding on to the waist of the
one in front of him. None of the children even smiled at the old man,
and their teacher looked directly at him with remarkable hostility.

"No one has ever run away from them."

"No one has ever stood up to them the way you have," Boris IV
said quietly. "Maybe no one else will ever make a speech like that."

The professor laughed somewhat unnaturally. "Someone has to
create a precedent." He looked at his grandson with a tenderness that
almost suggested a final parting. I have to see to it that he's not around
when they come for me, he thought. Otherwise the lad will fight back,
start a shoot-out—it's no secret that he has a gun—and he'll be killed.

"Let's do it this way," he proposed. "I'll go to the department now
and put my papers in order: there's a good deal I'll need to take with
me. You go home and wait for me to call. While you're waiting, look
over the train timetable. In the evening we'll go back to Silver Forest
and decide everything there."

They went their separate ways, the two figures that were so different: Boris IV in his leather jacket and wolfskin hat, Boris III in his long
black overcoat with its caracul collar and a typically professorish fur
hat that went with the shawllike collar. One of the "doormen" picked
up the receiver in a telephone booth to make his report.

★

As he approached Gorky Street, Boris was thinking about his grandfather. What do you know about that! Everyone had thought he was
going to that sickening meeting out of cowardice, and it turned out he
had done it out of an inner nobility—if that was the right word to use.
I don't know if I'd be capable of doing a thing like that. I was hanging on a roof over Beria, but that was something else entirely, something like a vendetta in the Caucasus. Grandfather has done
something colossal for society. Forty years from now, when these
times are remembered, it will be said: the only one who spoke out
against the lie was Professor Gradov. The condescending pats that we,

the young generation, give them on their shoulders are just shit. We think that a man of seventy-seven doesn't think about anything anymore except having warm underwear, and yet it turns out he has passion boiling within. He must have something on his conscience, something from long ago, maybe he's been waiting his whole life to atone for it, and now his dream has come true: he's going out like a knight. They won't forgive him his courage. They wouldn't forgive anyone a hundredth of what he has done, they never forgive the innocent for being innocent. For Grandfather, it's the end, no matter how much I daydream about fleeing to the South. Maybe a miracle will occur, but the chances are equal to n^1. And this old man is the person I care about more than anyone else. He's more of a father to me than a grandfather. My father was always someplace far away, while Grandfather was nearby. He was the one who taught me to swim—Grandfather, not Father. I remember that moment in an inlet of the Moscow River perfectly. I was five years old, and suddenly I was floating, and Grandfather was standing in the water up to his waist, happy, and drops of water were flying from his goatee like they were coming out of a drainpipe. What's to be done? Damnation, it's a law of nature, after all, that strong grandsons are supposed to help their weakening grandfathers, and I can't do anything for mine in this confounded society. At that moment, a treacherous thought occurred: It would be better if they take him away when I'm not around. If they come for him when I'm there, I'm liable to snap, shoot all the bastards, and that would mean an end for all of our women, and me too. No, no, what am I saying? In the end I have to defy them. Sashka Sheremetiev is right: maybe racing a motorcycle here and winning cups is amoral.

Life drags on in a customary monotone, while events pile up, only to crash down on you like a shovelful of snow tossed from a rooftop. Opening the door to the apartment, Boris was not even particularly surprised to see Vera Gorda coming toward him out of the study. She had a key, although she hadn't been around in more than a year. Something's happened, that's obvious—so go ahead, events, do your worst.

"The entire Dostoevsky Circle has been arrested," said Vera. She was standing with one hand resting against the doorframe, her dress clinging tightly to her figure. Bright lips, shining eyes. It was like a scene from a foreign film.

"Sasha too?" Boris asked.

She grimaced, her lip twisting. "What do you think? Nikolai, Sasha, everyone. . . . Oh, Borya!" She dissolved into sobs. In her weeping she clattered with her heels directly into his arms.

"Borya, Borya, I can't stand it. . . . I'm just dying, every minute I die a little, Borya. . . ."

He had her sit down on the sofa and then took a seat beside her, trying meanwhile to keep at least a slight distance between them; he felt an entirely inappropriate desire rising within him.

"Well, tell me everything you know."

It was Vera's opinion that it had all been the fault of the Romanian Jew Ilyusha Verner. Walking along Gorky Street near the statue of Yury Dolgoruky, he had made the acquaintance of an attractive young woman with a child. He had begun, naturally, with compliments to the child and then moved on to paying compliments to the mother. Then he had begun courting this beauty. For some reason she lived alone in a surprisingly nice flat not far from the place where they had first met. "Well, you know how these things go, and a mad romance blazed up." Verner would run, beaming, through all of Dostoevsky's heroines in his mind: Polina, Grushenka, Nastasya Fillipovna. Suddenly, he had been met one day in the entrance hall of her building by two squarely built muscular types who worked you-know-where. They had given him a good shaking and warned him: if you want to live, don't show your face around here again! It had turned out that this beauty was the kept woman of some member of the government. Can you imagine?

This story, with a laugh at first, had been told to Vera by her husband, Nikolai the Giant. It had soon ceased to be a laughing matter, however. One after another, the "Dostoevskyans" had begun to find themselves being tailed. "It was quite possible Ilyusha didn't stop with his visits, which you can understand—a man in love forgets about reason, doesn't he? Obviously, the 'organs' began to do some digging to find out what this fellow's story was, and in the end they came upon the club."

Over the next three days, everyone had been arrested. Sheremetiev had been one of the first to go. Something dreadful had happened there, supposedly a shoot-out. Vera and Nikolai had run all over town like hunted animals, and thought about running away—but where can you run? "This morning they came for him. Now it's the end, my whole life is over! Of course I ran to you, Borenka, who else can I run to? You're my best, my closest friend, after all . . . and you weren't here all day. I've been puttering around in desperation here. I'm sorry, but I drank half a bottle of cognac . . . well, I know you've got this girl now, and I wish you both happiness. I've seen her, by the way, she's quite pretty. Borya, I don't know what to do now, everything's crumbling and scattering, they might throw me out of the band now as the wife of an enemy of the people!"

Once more she fell against his chest, her arms draped around his neck, sobbing on his shoulder. He sat there, afraid to move, feeling engulfed by gloom and by his ever-growing "inappropriate desire." Finally, he was able to free himself from her arms, delicately enough.

"They didn't call you in, Vera?" he asked, not imagining what a forceful reaction the question would bring. Gorda put her head into her hands and let out a wild scream like the piercing call of a Mongolian horseman. Her entire body was seized by convulsions. Boris raced to get the bottle of cognac.

When she had had a drink, she said with almost perfect calm, "Oh, it's so horrible, my makeup is running, everything is smeared. Don't look at me, I know what you're thinking. It's not true, Borya! I didn't inform on them. Of course they called me in. I told you frankly at the beginning of our not-very-long affair that it's me they're watching. So why should it be any different this time? They called me in this time, as well. That snot-nosed bastard Nefedov yelled as though he were talking to a serf, and Konstantin Averianovich, that swine, showed his version of severe restraint—you know. They already knew about everyone and everything by then, though. I couldn't believe how much information they had about things that even I had no idea about. Did you know, for example, that the Dostoevsky Circle was planning a terrorist action?"

"Stop it, Vera," Boris said, his face contorted. He was thinking about Sashka. If they don't shoot him, how is he going to get along in a camp with an artificial leg?

Vera began hanging all over him again, pressing her breasts and one knee against him. Perhaps it was not intentional, maybe it was still just because he was her "best friend," but it was almost unbearable. Her voice now became a whisper.

"They asked about you, of course, Borenka. Bring your ear closer. You know, I've always been afraid this place was bugged. They asked if you went to the meetings of the Dostoevsky Circle. I told them I thought you couldn't stand them, that you almost got into a fight with them when you were courting me. It was no secret to them, of course, that we were dating. Borya, tell me—" She was sniffling like a little girl. "—tell me, you don't consider me an informer, do you? Tell me straight out, I'm begging you. Believe me, I didn't squeal on anyone, not one single person! Maybe they got something out of me, fool that I am. Maybe just the opposite. I protected some of them. Do you believe me? Tell me, do you? Do you mean you don't find me attractive anymore? Well, go on, fuck me, darling!" There was not enough room on the sofa, so they lay on the carpet, which, fortunately, Maika Strepetov had recently vacuumed. Looking at Gorda's smile wandering beneath him, Boris thought, maybe this is the only way she can free herself. From *them*, from all of the other ones who fuck her, from everything—these are her only moments of freedom.

"Thank you, darling," she whispered once she had caught her breath. "Now I see that you believe me."

"Since when has fucking become a symbol of faith?" he muttered morosely. He wanted to add something else, something of even greater cruelty, like "Maybe I screwed you just now as if you were a stool pigeon," but he did not say these harsh, ugly words, which would have been untrue anyway, and instead kissed his old lover on the cheek and on the ear.

"I would have believed you without it."

Sure enough, she felt insulted. She picked herself up from the carpet, walked over to the table, took a swig directly from the bottle of cognac, lit a cigarette, and said defiantly, "And I don't believe anyone without it."

"Fine, then." He stood up too. "For the moment, my dear, just pull yourself together, and be quick about it. The fact is that I'm going to answer your remarkable news with news of my own. Events are starting to unfold as fast as in a track race on ice."

In reply to his "remarkable news," she exclaimed, "Oh my God!

Where will it all end?" She said it in a tired voice, and even seemingly without interest. The thought immediately occurred to him that if Maika had said something the same way, it would have meant only one thing—that which was contained in the words and nothing more; with Vera, however, there was, as always, some other hidden sense that lay behind her words, a sense of which perhaps even she herself was not aware. Maybe by the time Maika gets to be her age, a fair number of these meanings will have accumulated within her, too. It was already 5:30, outside it was getting dark, and only the decorations on the main post office left over from the New Year's celebration were shining. In fact, they might as well have stayed on all the time: there was nothing festive about them, it was just more propagandistic bombast. Boris called his grandfather at the clinic. There was ringing, and then silence on the other end. Maybe he's on his way here? Maybe it . . . already? No, it's not possible! Vera was sitting on the sofa smoking a cigarette. Her face was turned away, showing her wounded dignity.

"Listen, did they notify you officially what charges have been brought against Nikolai?" he asked.

She smirked. "Officially? No, they didn't 'notify me officially.' " The word "officially" trembled on her lips with hurt feelings.

"I absolutely have to see Sashka's mother today," he said.

"Absolutely have to?" she queried. "So now it's 'absolutely have to,' is it?" Her voice was throwing off sparks of some incomprehensible mockery, like an artificial diamond.

And you absolutely have to get out of here, thought Boris. He felt almost trapped. Grandpa isn't calling for some reason. It's possible that Maika, following her habits, will burst in here without ringing first. After one look at Vera, she'll know what happened on the carpet. Meanwhile, I have to do something—go look for Grandfather, go to see Sashka's mother, maybe go begging to Vaska again; after all, Sheremetiev was coach in the Air Force Club. . . . But that's nonsense! What does the Air Force Club and all that have to do with it? It's 1937 all over again, and soon we'll all be in the camps.

He kissed Vera's cheek, shook her gently by the shoulders, and said in a falsely amicable voice, "Let's keep in touch, Vera. But now let's go. I'll see you to a taxi." Vera put on her luxurious fox coat, in which she looked almost stately, like the wife of some Stalin Prize winner.

The huge thermometer on Gorky Street, with its Slavic flourishes, was showing a temperature of minus 15 degrees Celsius. More lights had come on, as well: the constantly revolving globe over the main entrance to the post office, posters proclaiming Soviet achievements, signs reading CHEESE and RUSSIAN WINES, and a radiant portrait of Stalin. There's the one who should have been taken out, Boris Gradov, officer in reserve of the GRU of the USSR, thought about Stalin, clearly and distinctly. He's been begging for a nine-gram dose of lead for a long time.

They were standing on the sidewalk trying to hail a taxi when suddenly Maika emerged from the crowd. In her unbuttoned fur coat— Aunt Nina had not long ago made her a present of an old but still serviceable fur—and her lush, disheveled locks peeping out from beneath the kerchief on her head, she rushed up to the building entrance. "Maika!" Boris shouted. She came to an abrupt stop, saw Boris and Vera, and slowly walked up to them, her eyes wide and her half-opened mouth apparently murmuring something.

"Maika, Maika, what are you doing?" Boris muttered. "Meet my old friend Vera. Something terrible has happened to her—her husband has been arrested."

"And our grandfather has been arrested!" Maika screamed as though she wanted all of Moscow to hear it. In tears, she threw her arms around his neck.

Chapter 14

———☆———

PAIN AND
ANESTHESIA

Why did I say those pathetic words at that meeting about our Soviet
identity, about "our" Soviet intelligentsia, faithful to the ideals of scientific communism? Everything was clear, after all: I knew what I
wanted to do, everything was planned out; I signed the arrest order
and the death sentence myself; and most of all I gave them permission
to torture me. There's nothing more terrible than torture! They didn't
frighten everyone with the threat of execution. The entire population
knows, or guesses, or suspects that behind those doors things are
painful, very painful, unbearably painful, and then painful again. No
anesthesia. It no longer exists, even though a man cannot help but
think about it. My Soviet words with a such a false ring to them were
nothing other than an attempt at anesthesia. See here, chaps, I'm one
of your own—don't hurt me, at least not so much as all that, not so
much at least by a little bit. Let it hurt a great deal, if you want, but
don't make it unbearable: I'm a Soviet man, faithful to the ideals of
scientific communism! Instead of that, though, I should have said,
"Down with the government of bandits! I renounce your scientific

communism!" It was a naïve attempt in a world where the very idea of anesthesia is rejected. It is said that "He who endures to the end will be saved." Strange as it may seem, this idea is the antithesis of torture. Pain is suffering, but it is also a signal. By giving a patient anesthesia on the operating table, we shut down his signaling system: we have no need for it, and it's clear what we have to do. We take away the suffering. If we don't take it away, only endurance is left, the adoption of another system of signals, of holy words. To endure to the end and go beyond the limits of pain. That means going beyond the limits of life, does it not? But pain and life are not necessarily synonymous, are they? Going beyond the limits of pain does not necessarily mean death, does it? They are threatening me with pain—me, a seventy-seven-year-old fighter against pain. "Either give evidence, you old fucker, you Jewcock sucker, or we'll use other methods." Their faces were like nightmares from Goya paintings. Out of the whole crowd, only Nefedov—the most hateful thing of all was that instead of just one interrogator, a whole crowd of the mongrels had come in—only this one young captain still had something human about his face, even though it's possible he was told, "As for you, Nefedov, try to keep a bit of goddamned pity on your face for this yes-man to Jews. We'll get the son of a bitch in condition, and then with you and your pity we'll split him open like a cunt!" That's the sort of language they use. Obviously, they don't just talk like that to people under interrogation, but among themselves as well. Why aren't they beginning my "surgery"? Perhaps they're waiting for orders from higher up? After all, Samkov blurted out that "Comrade Stalin himself is running the investigation!" It's difficult to imagine they would use that name to frighten a prisoner. For most people in our country, Stalin is the embodiment of power, not just a bandit chieftain; he's the ultimate authority, the last hope. All tremble before him as before the holder of the scepter, the ruler of the mountains and the seas, and of herds of human beings, but not as though they were before a man who gives orders to torture people. They don't intimidate people with his name. Still, I don't exclude the possibility that he is personally going into all of the details of my interrogations, especially since I've been more than just a hollow noise to him these many years. He remembers, of course, not only our first meeting, which was benevolent and revealing, but also our last, which was so unpleasant. All this antimedical hysteria has been thought up and put into practice by him personally. It's clear that he has become paranoid as a result of arteriosclerosis. There were rumors that Bekhterev noticed signs of it as early as 1927 and that it cost him his life. It's entirely possible that Stalin himself gave the orders to have me handcuffed. That's just too much, though! Aren't I developing a case of paranoia myself? And isn't it ridiculous that a seventy-seven-year-old prisoner in an isolation cell, wearing these handcuffs that dig into my flesh, is afraid of becoming paranoid? I never thought things like these handcuffs existed. The worst thing of all is that you can't scratch with them on. In other words, you're deprived of the pleasure of touching yourself with your own fingertips. What a great pleasure it is, too, it turns out, in the fleeting moments of self-treatment I've had here. The impossibility of touching yourself reminds you of the worst nightmare of all—waking up in a coffin. The handcuffs were designed by a great specialist—torture is itself a science, after all. Willingly or not, the hands twitch in a futile attempt to free themselves, to scratch. But with each such movement, the screws become tighter, and the hands swell and become blue cushions, like some species of deepwater monster. Don't get desperate. You could tumble into hysteria, which itself is a form of anesthesia, after all. For the time being, repeat to yourself that you're ready to hold out to the end, to the end! Repeat it, repeat it, repeat it, and finally you'll forget about your hands. There, I've forgotten about them. They're no longer a part of me. They're nothing but two underwater frogs caught in a trap. Or turtles, crawling out of their shells to take some fresh air and falling right into a snare. Whatever the case may be, these frogs, these turtles, no longer have anything to do with me. I used to have hands, that's true. They didn't work too badly: they operated—not badly at all sometimes—they could perform an anastomosis, they could feel a patient beneath them. They also did a fairly good job of scribbling with a pen, one of them, almost literary, worked on the nature of pain and anesthesia, while the other drummed its fingers on the table, as though counting out some rhythm. They were also good in their time for caressing my wife, her shoulders, her breasts and hips, her belly. They did a few sinful things, too, these hands of mine, particularly the right one, but that doesn't matter anymore now. The most important thing is that they possessed a rich store of memories. Now they will no longer exist. Once they cease to exist, these steel teeth will no longer have anything to bite into. A soldier who has lost his hands in a war can't scratch his nose, either. What makes you any better than that soldier? Learn to scratch your nose with your shoulder, your knee, against the wall or the bedstead. How many days has it been since I found that I can no longer remember my hands? Seven, ten? Samkov bellowed then, "Well, Gradov, what were you doing with Rappoport in the Tarasevich State Scientific Institute for Antiseptic Compounds?! Don't you see, you old son of a bitch, we know everything! Admit it, you rotten stooge, didn't you and that Jew cook up false data on the autopsies together?" Then someone called for him, and he went to the door, brandishing his fist threateningly as he walked by as if preparing to deal a fatal blow. Of course, they could have killed the one who was listening to all that shouting with just one such blow, yet for some reason that one—myself, that is—didn't even blink at the fearful raised fist. The only one left in the room with me was Nefedov, a pale little fellow in an officer's uniform, who just kept on filling out a report without even looking up. When we were alone, he raised his head and said quietly, "It's better if you confess, Boris Nikitovich. Why are you being so stubborn? Everyone confesses, after all. Why do you want to go through all these tortures? Come on, now, I'll write down right now that you conspired with Rappoport or, even better, that Rappoport drew you into the conspiracy, and then they'll transfer you to the normal regimen straight away." It was the other me sitting there like a ghost of the Russian intelligentsia, kept awake for twenty-seven and a half years—or had a week passed since the moment when three fat men in heavy overcoats with caracul collars, which were probably just horrible coats lined with cotton wadding, burst into my office in the surgical faculty at the hospital (the scoundrels were fortunate that they didn't come upon my boy Borka). I shook the chills out of my head, and said to the other participants in the crude melodrama: "Write this down, Captain. I met with the distinguished scholar Yakov Lvovich Rappoport at the Tarasevich Institute to discuss the question of the possibility of countering with medication the process of rejection following an organ transplant. That is all I can say in reply to the groundless and wild accusations of Senior Investigator Samkov."

"What kind of accusations?" Nefedov asked.

"Wild."

"And what else? 'Mild'?"

"No, I said 'wild.' Even 'barbaric,' if you prefer."

At that point Samkov came in and ordered Nefedov to put the handcuffs on "the old cunt." And Nefedov went even more pale. He went to call the sergeant.

"Put them on him yourself!" Samkov roared.

"But I—" Nefedov began.

"Learn your job!" Samkov shouted even more loudly. "Or else what fucking good are you to me?"

Even in the trenches of the Second World War, the Second Fatherland War, that is, the professor had never heard so much swearing. The year 1885. Mama and Papa and my sister Dunechka—may they rest in peace—and I are going to Yevpatoria. An enchanting voyage! I stick my nose out of the window and get covered in soot from the train's smokestack. "You'll get tanned as a Negro!" Father laughs. Not in all of the surrounding expanse of Russia were so many curse words spread about. "What a clown we have!" Mama laughs.

"We're going to make you into a clown, you fucking old professor," Samkov promised, bringing his fleshy face with its small cross-shaped scar above the corner of the jaw closer. Someone had done a fairly good job of removing a boil. "Then, you scum, you'll forget about your intelligentsia and its dignity, you parasite on the working people!" His face came even closer. Maybe he wants to sink his teeth into what remains of my flesh? "Maybe you've forgotten about your friend Pulkovo? Let me refresh your memory. Your little friend has been working for the American atomic bandits for ten years now. Did they recruit you at the same time? Answer me!"

My God, how happy that makes me, to hear news about Leo for the first time in so many years! So he's still alive? He managed to bring up his Sasha in America! Where's my Mary, why am I thinking so little about her? It's my mother who keeps coming back to me, right up to my memories of infancy: my mother's large breast, the focal point of the world, the desired nipple. I had hands then, I took all that richness into my hands. But where's Mary? Why is it she never appears? We were two halves of one whole, after all. She moved her legs apart and took me into herself, and in the end swelled up, filled with the continuation of the line, and then spread her legs again to reveal Kitushka, Kirilka, Ninka, and then another, unnamed, stillborn. A man is a banal creature, but a woman is a pulsating flower. Remember Mary. Even if she doesn't come to mind, remember her anyway! The same way that you forced yourself to forget your hands, remember your wife now. When did you see her for the first time, and where? Well, it was in 1897, of course, on the balcony of the main hall at the conservatory. She was late for the beginning of a Mozart concert. They were already playing *Eine Kleine Nachtmusik* when a young, slender, un-Russian creature, whom one might be afraid of injuring with a look, passed down the aisle and looked around at the twenty-two-year-old student sitting at the end. Princess Dream! She assured me later on that she had noticed me long before I had seen her, that one day she had even followed me in the street, sure that I was some young poet from a new branch of the Symbolist movement, and that she had never guessed that I was a medical student. So, you've re-membered the young Mary: there she is, slipping into the babble of voices of the crowd at the conservatory, looking at me questioningly as mountains of furs float by in the arms of the checkroom attendants. Well, go on, approach her; I didn't have these hands then, these swollen, ossified frogs of a later time. . . .

The clank of the locks of an isolation cell opening in Lefortovo prison broke into the year 1897, and Boris Nikitovich shook himself out of his half-fainting state. He realized he had committed a brazen violation of the rules: he had dared to lie down on the cot during the daytime. Now the warder would start shouting at him and threaten-ing to have him moved to the punishment cell. He was not the worst of the lot who came in, the one whom Boris Nikitovich called "Jonah," to distinguish him from the others. He didn't even shout at him today and pretended he hadn't seen a thing. He put two bowls onto the small table, one containing watery soup, the other porridge. The fish soup, nauseating as it was, smelled appetizing, and the por-ridge gave off an odor of ripened perfection. In his first week of prison life, Boris Nikitovich had come to feel a revulsion for food, caused, obviously, by psychic anorexia that had turned into cerebral cachexia. The bowls had remained untouched, and the prison authorities had concluded that Gradov was on a hunger strike. Any form of protest there was subject to immediate repression. A fat colonel with a med-ical insignia on his shoulder straps had come into the cell—for some reason, the majority of the MGB agents around were fat, with large backsides and bellies, like real pigs—and threatened him with forced feeding. Boris Nikitovich had then begun to empty the contents of the bowls into the latrine bucket, until he suddenly realized that his symptoms were clearing up and that he was beginning to feel an interest in food again.

"Here, let me take them off." Jonah unlocked the handcuffs and with some effort pulled them from the prisoner's wrists. For the ten-minute period allotted for the taking of food, Boris Nikitovich would indulge in the sweet sensation of being able to feel his hands. He tried to pick up the spoon but found to his dismay that he could not: the puffy sardines that were his fingers would not even consider bending. He would have to slurp the soup from the edge of the bowl again, like the last time, and then dig up the solid matter, using his hand as a shovel. "Rub your hands a bit first," Jonah said to him as though he were speaking to an unreasonable child. Then he whispered, "Take your time!" This unexpected display of humanity had almost the effect of a thunderbolt on Boris Nikitovich. He burst into tears, shaking all over, and Jonah turned away, perhaps in another display of humanism, perhaps in embarrassment over the humanism already displayed. The handcuffs remained off for twenty minutes altogether. It could not be said that his fingers were able to control the spoon, but they could at least hold it, so that he no longer had the appearance of an animal. Putting the educative devices firmly back into place, Jonah snapped the handcuffs closed on the last bracket, which, in a clear violation of the rules, permitted the wrists an ever-so-slight, unlawful degree of movement. As he left the cell, Jonah winked one of his fleshy eyelids at the prisoner and made a gesture of putting both hands next to one ear: get some sleep if you want, it said. Laying his head down on the pillow, Boris Nikitovich thought that perhaps in his entire seventy-seven years of life he had never experienced such utterly satisfying postprandial bliss. He dreamed of absolutely nothing during this sleep, experiencing only complete relaxation, nirvana. How much time passed, he did not know, but he was woken by the hysterical shouting of another warder, whom he called "Tamerlane" in his mind.

"You, you motherfucker on four legs, you're lying down, you son of a bitch, in comfort, snoring even! I'm going to file a report on you for violation of rules! You're going to the punishment cell, you bastard, you'll stand in that closet until there's no shit left in you!" Boris Nikitovich leapt to his feet. All at once the nightmare of the days and nights of his captivity, and maybe all the piercing nightmares of Lefortovo prison squeezed him more tightly than the punishment cell. "Kill me!" he howled, raising his manacled hands and thrusting his head between the two hands that did not exist, as though he were trying to wriggle out through some narrow loophole. "Kill me, kill me, torturers and devils!"

Tamerlane took a step backwards. The sudden explosion from this "enemy of the people," usually so taciturn and withdrawn, left him gaping in surprise. "What's with you, Gradov, are you off your nut or what?" he sputtered out in criminal slang. "Fine, fine, to hell with you. Dinner's over, eat up. Then I'm taking you for interrogation. Stop being so fucking nervous."

Boris Nikitovich's arms fell. His entire body was shaking now. Unexpected infusion of adrenaline into the bloodstream, he thought. It was Tamerlane breaking through the shell of my blessed dream that brought on such a reaction.

In the interrogator's office, they paid no attention to him for a while, as was the secret police custom. Nefedov was engrossed in paperwork, comparing some document with reference books. He looked the very personification of juridical activity. Samkov was sitting alongside in a relaxed posture with the telephone receiver to his ear, giving someone monosyllabic replies, his stomach stirring beneath the uniform jacket drawn over it like a badger curled up into a ball. Finally, he put the telephone down, nodded his round head with a smile, said "piece of shit" under his breath, and only then turned in the direction of the prisoner.

"Well now, Boris Nikitovich . . ." He was pleased to note how the head of the "shitty professor" jerked at the unusual form of address. "Well, Professor, our investigation is moving into another phase. You'll remain alone now with Captain Nefedov, and I'll leave you."

He was staring at his victim with great interest, and it seemed to Boris Nikitovich that the man felt himself under some great pressure: what would his reaction be?

Boris Nikitovich forced a smile. "Well, it was a joyless love affair, so it won't be a sad parting."

"The feeling is mutual!" Samkov barked. He rose from the table,

picking up a few stray papers as he did so. Enraged by these disobedient documents, he glanced once more at the "yes-man for the Jews"
with dark, hate-filled eyes. "Any questions?"

"I have one question," Boris Nikitovich said. "I always expect to
see Ryumin here in your office. Why doesn't he come?"

He could not have asked a more forceful question than that within
those walls. Nefedov went stiff as a poker and clenched his lips, as
though a hot egg had been dropped into his mouth. Samkov dropped
the papers he had just picked up, leaned on his two fists on the table,
then threw his chest out and turned to Gradov.

"You, you son of a . . . how dare . . . how dare you come in here
with your provocations? Have you forgotten where you are? We'll remind you!" Forgetting about the files, he strode off toward the exit,
engulfing Boris Nikitovich in a wave of cheap cologne. You kitsch-
sweating Bolshevik, thought Boris Nikitovich.

Left without the leadership of his comrade, Nefedov sat for another
minute looking at the door that had just banged shut.

"Well, we'll start with the handcuffs, Boris Nikitovich," he said.
"You don't need them anymore, right? What do we want with them?"
he said in a tone of seemingly playful reproach. He came up closer to
the prisoner and jauntily, with deft and experienced hands, removed
the hated bracelets from the man's wrists. With an almost joking expression, as though he were handling a strong-smelling fish, he carried
them to the desk and dropped them into a drawer.

"That's it, then, we're through with all of that. I have no more use
for them, and neither do you, Boris Nikitovich—am I right?"

"They were a help to me," said Gradov. He began to rub one life-
less hand against the other without looking at Nefedov. He had a
strange feeling: the removed objects may have been hateful, yet they
had become an inseparable part of his being.

"What do you mean by that, Professor?" the investigator asked in
a voice that contained both sympathy and interest. Now that the case
was entirely in his hands, he was showing himself to be the embodiment of sensitivity, concern, correct behavior, and even a certain sympathy. They're using the oldest method in the book, thought Boris
Nikitovich. First Samokov the "bad cop," then Nefedov the "good
cop."

"You wouldn't understand, Citizen Investigator. You didn't have to live in these bracelets."

I've probably gone too far, thought Gradov. Now he's going to start screaming his head off. The captain's pale face, however, showed nothing except a momentary expression of fright.

"All right, Boris Nikitovich, we'll forget about it. Let's return seriously to . . . to our investigation. First of all, I would like to inform you that some of the charges have been dropped. For example, the accusation of conspiring with Rappoport has been struck."

Nefedov awaited the reaction to his announcement with keen interest. Boris Nikitovich shrugged.

"The meetings at which you were to be confronted directly by Vovsi and Vinogradov will also be dropped."

"Are they still alive?" Gradov asked.

"Yes, of course. Why shouldn't they be?" Nefedov replied hastily. "It's just your meetings with them that are being dropped, that's all."

Obviously he's waiting for me to ask why, thought Boris Nikitovich, and then he'll tell me that it's none of my business. Nefedov, meanwhile, hunched over his paperwork, gave a heavy sigh and even scratched the back of his head.

"However, several new questions have arisen, Professor. For example: what motivated your speech at the meeting of the First Moscow Medical Institute? Was it a desperate appeal to those who share your views? Were any of your sympathizers in the auditorium, Professor?"

"Of course there were," Gradov replied. "I'm sure everyone thought the same things, only they said the exact opposite."

"You're wasting your time with that line, Boris Nikitovich," Nefedov said with what looked like a pout. "What, are you saying that we produce hypocrites like that? I don't agree. Won't you tell me, though, what drove you to act in such a way? Defying the government is no laughing matter, after all!"

"I had to draw the line," answered Boris Nikitovich with perfect calm and without paying any apparent attention to his questioner.

"Draw the line?" Nefedov put in. "Now just where would that be?"

"You wouldn't understand," said Gradov.

Nefedov suddenly took extreme offense. "Why wouldn't I understand, Professor? Why do you automatically assume that I have a
primitive mind? I'd like to tell you that I graduated from the Moscow
State University Law School as a correspondence student. I've read all
the classics. Just ask me anything about Pushkin or Tolstoy, and I'll
give you an answer straight away. I even read Dostoevsky, though
he's been labeled a reactionary. I read him, and I find it useful, because
it helps us to better understand the psychology of the criminal."

"Whose psychology?" Gradov queried.

"The psychology of the criminal, Professor. We investigators and
jurists need to understand criminals, after all."

"And Dostoevsky helps you do that, Citizen Investigator?" Gradov
had now fixed his gaze upon the face of Nefedov.

The latter, noticing this, flushed slightly and assumed a glum expression. "Now I understand what you're getting at, Professor. This
time, I also understand you, have no doubt about that."

"Very good," said Gradov.

"What's good?" Nefedov asked, the same expression of offense
frozen on his face.

"The fact that you understand everything. However, when I said
you wouldn't understand, I wasn't thinking of your intellectual level
at all, Citizen Investigator. It's just that it would be a long story, one
that has no bearing on the case whatsoever."

"You keep on calling me 'Citizen Investigator,' Boris Nikitovich,
quite formally. Why don't you call me Nikolai Semyonovich? Or even
Nikolai, eh? After all, I'm distantly related to you, in a way." In saying all this, Nefedov had rapidly withdrawn the hurt expression from
his face and put there in its place a certain craftiness, a good-natured
smirk.

"What do you mean?" asked an astonished Gradov. Nefedov the
investigator then made a surprising confession to the prisoner before
him.

It turned out that he was none other than the son of Semyon Nikiforovich Stroilo, so well known to the Gradov family. "The real family name," he explained, making a crude grammatical error, "was in
fact Nefedov, and 'Stroilo,' from the verb *stroit,* 'to build,' was a revolutionary last name, so to speak, in the sense that it followed the
fashion of those days when we were building socialism. Papa was a

great follower of the movement, a crystal-pure Communist, as you remember, of course." Nikolai Semyonovich was twenty-nine, the firstborn of Semyon Nikiforovich and his wife Klavdia Vasilievna. "That is, when Papa and Aunt Nina embarked upon their romantic-revolutionary relationship, I was already around two years old. Well, Aunt Nina didn't even know that the Nefedovs existed because of the huge gap that lay between us. In other words, Papa was like a young bachelor for Aunt Nina, even though my sister Palmira had already been born by then as well. Papa came back to the family then, but he would often think about Aunt Nina and suffer greatly from it." So from his earliest childhood, Nikolai not only had known of the Gradov family but had been drawn into a relationship with them, as it were. "Papa and I even went to Silver Forest and walked around your house, Boris Nikitovich. What are you trembling for? After all, it was all very humane and romantic, the sufferings of a great and proud man." Nikolai had never condemned his father. "A great ship is destined for great voyages. You're surprised, Professor, that I call your daughter 'Aunt Nina,' but what else should I call her, since I heard so much about her during my childhood and adolescence? Maybe I heard about her in a different way, but all the same she became like a relative to me. I always followed her successes in poetry with great interest, and 'Clouds in Blue' became the song of my youth, you might say. Everyone was singing it at MGB school, and sometimes someone would think up a vulgar parody: you know how young people are."

In the 1930s, Semyon Nikiforovich Stroilo had left the Nefedovs, since his star had been rising at a rapid, one might even say dizzying, pace in the hierarchy of the commissariat. Yes, in the commissariat. However, he had never stopped caring about his family, particularly about Nikolai, whom at the height of the war he had led by the hand to the State Security Academy, for which Nikolai wasn't particularly grateful. It was, however, "the verdict of fate," Boris Nikitovich, that is, the external historic circumstances, that Nikolai Nefedov would never have anything but positive feelings for his father. These feelings of his, of course, grew to hypertrophic proportions after his father's heroic death at the very end of the war. The circumstances in which he had met his end had not been announced, but it was known in intelligence circles that General Stroilo, as the man closest to Marshal Gradov, had shared the fate of the commander of the Reserve Front in the very same circumstances. "Well, as a human being, Boris Nikitovich, you surely understand, that this brought me even closer to your family, in an inspirational way, if you will."

"How do you mean, 'brought you closer'? 'In an inspirational way,' you say?" Gradov asked.

He looked at the flat, pale face of the young investigator, and it seemed to him that he could indeed see in him some of Semyon Stroilo, whom he had managed to get a good look at only once in his life—it must have been in the autumn of 1925 . . . yes, at Mary's birthday party, during that silly play the "Blue Shirts" had put on.

"Well, I meant not idealistically, but at least in spirit," Nefedov muttered.

"That is, in a way you became a relative of ours, is that it, Citizen Investigator?" Gradov said.

"None of your venom, Professor, no venom!" the investigator cried in a voice in which there sounded something like suffering, as though the investigator were imploring the prisoner, as though the former had long since foreseen the possibility that the latter might make use of this "venom" and his worst fears seemed to have been realized.

A curious son for that "proletarian warrior" to have produced, thought Boris Nikitovich. He could outdo his father in any number of ways. The professor's hands, in the meantime, had come back to life. The situation was becoming ever more ambiguous.

Nefedov seemed to remember that he was not there to bare his soul; on the contrary. He asked the next question: "So, Gradov, you don't deny that your sympathizers were in the hall?"

Without waiting for a reply, however, he looked at his watch and said that it was now time for Boris Nikitovich to take a little trip. Just like that, they're going to release me, the thought raced through the professor's mind. Just like that, Stalin has given the order to let me go. He made an effort not to betray this mad hope, but something must have shown on his face. Nefedov smirked slightly. It might just as well be—in fact it's much more likely, a thousand times more likely—that they're going to send me to the cellar and put me up against the wall. You know, I'm ready to do what my nephew Valentin did. According to the stories, in Kharkov in 1919, he ripped his shirt and bared his chest just before he was to die, and shouted "Down with the Red devils!" I won't do that, though, because I'm not twenty-one, as my nephew Valentin was, but seventy-seven, and I don't have a long life ahead of me to sacrifice. I'll just fall silently under the onslaught.

An hour later, Boris Nikitovich was removed from the Black Maria and set down before the entrance to a long, blank corridor. On the basis of some indefinable bits of evidence, however, he formed the impression that the guards were from the Lubyanka rather than Lefortovo. This was the extent of his prison experience: after his arrest, they had taken him to the Lubyanka and then sent him off to Lefortovo.

"Where have you brought me?" he asked the sergeant who led him into the "box," the small holding cell the size of a closet.

"To a decent place," the sergeant, his skin puffy and off white from working underground for so long, said with a grin.

The room into which he was put after the "box" also reminded him of his first cell, which had been in the Lubyanka. Everything here was ever so slightly better than in the MGB cell for those under interrogation at Lefortovo: a washbasin, a bar of soap, a blanket. A decent place, thought Boris Nikitovich, placing his recovering hands on the table before him. I'm in a decent place right at the center of the decent city of Moscow, where I've lived through all this. It's like a film about Strauss that begins with his birth and ends with his death, and it all fits into a space of two hours, in this decent country, which I found it impossible to tear myself away from, at this decent time in history. "Where there is a corpse, eagles will gather." Let us mourn the Motherland at the moment when she is at her most unshakable. Someone in the West once said that patriotism is the last refuge of scoundrels. Those whom this Westerner had in mind, however, could not be called patriots, because they had not considered the root meaning of the word but rather only glorified might. In saying "Fatherland," very few thought of fathers, that is, the dead. By forgetting our fathers here in Russia, we made the Fatherland into a Moloch and closed ourselves off to eternity and God; we have been enticed by Antichrists and false prophets, who daily offer us their fabrications in place of the truth. Where was the sense of that monstrous imitation of patriotism that had fallen to Russia's lot? No matter how far you seek, you will find no other answer: the sense lay in the imitation itself. Everything is a substitute, there are no originals to be found. The positive has become the negative. The cosmos is looking down on us with a dark smirk.

And yet, "He who endures to the end will be saved." What else could we come to in the end as a result of all of our Darwinism?

★

One morning several days later, Boris Nikitovich felt something break in his mouth, and all of his lower bridgework fell into his soup in pieces. The thing he had feared so much when Samkov had waved his fists beside his face had happened. He'll hit me on the jaw, he'd thought, and that will be the end of this dental device, which has been unreliable for some time. Then I'll just fall straight into decrepitude. They won't even bother to shoot me. They'll just throw me onto the rubbish heap to rot. And now the bridge collapses when the threats from fists and the torture of the handcuffs are no more. It fell to pieces for no reason at all, really. Evil-smelling, mucus-covered, yellowing pieces. Just toss them into the latrine and let them be carried around the stinking bowels of the Lubyanka; that's where they belong. Almost immediately thereafter, a serious trophic ulcer developed on the roof of his mouth. Disintegration was proceeding at a rapid pace: Boris Nikitovich suffered from chronic dyspepsia and a fierce itch all over his body, a pustulant rash. Now he could hardly speak clearly enough to be understood. Then again, no one was asking him to. The interrogations had almost stopped. He saw Nefedov no more than twice a week and only for form's sake. During these short meetings of no more than a quarter of an hour, his "almost relative" would not ask any questions as such but would just rustle his papers, raising his head from time to time to look at Boris Nikitovich with alarmed and seemingly questioning eyes, like a Stalinist variation on Dostoevsky's Underground Man. Boris Nikitovich, who several days ago had found repulsive the idea that the investigator might belong to his family, now no longer cared. What are you asking with your eyes, young man? I have no answers.

One day, two strangers turned up in Nefedov's office, two broad, padded chests with rows of decorations. All three officers stood with great solemnity as the senior in rank read aloud to Boris Nikitovich from a document:

"In accordance with Article Five of the Criminal Code of the RSFSR, the investigation into the case of Gradov, Boris Nikitovich, is closed. Gradov, Boris Nikitovich, is to be released under guard and fully rehabilitated. Department Head, MVD of the USSR, A. Kuznetsov.

After reading from the document, all three approached him with outstretched hands. He politely shook all three of them. The information had been conferred upon him like an official decoration.

"Where do you want me to go?" Boris Nikitovich inquired.

"To a resort. Go to a resort, Professor," said the padded jackets as they swayed back and forth. "Justice has been reestablished, now is the time to head for Matsesta, on the Black Sea!"

"Where do you want me to go?" Gradov asked again.

"Captain Nefedov will look after you now, Professor, and in the name of the ministry, and of the government of the Soviet Union, we would like to express our best wishes for the recovery of your health, so valuable to the Motherland."

They're shouting as though I'm deaf, and yet my hearing hasn't been affected at all by the advancing decay, thought Gradov.

The high-ranking officers left the office, and Nefedov, beaming in his pallor, went about returning Gradov's identification documents and other personal effects that had been confiscated during the search at Silver Forest: passport, various diplomas making him a professor, an Academician, a military man. Some noncommissioned servants appeared with other belongings, including a relic from the magnificent year of 1913, a fur coat from an English shop on Kuznetsky Street. It had gone through forty years and was showing no signs of decay. Bringing up the rear, a puffy guard flew into the room out of breath carrying a heavy packet. Opening it, Boris Nikitovich found there an Aladdin's trove of sorts: the shining gold, silver, and precious enamel of his state decorations.

"Where are you ordering me to go now?" he asked, holding the package in his hands.

"Right now we're going to go down into the entrance hall, Boris Nikitovich," Nefedov announced in an excited voice. "A few of your relatives are waiting for you there. We could have quite easily taken you to your dacha, of course, and in the greatest of comfort, but they all expressed a strong desire to meet you here, particularly your grandson, Boris Nikitovich, whom I would advise to show a bit more restraint where the organs are concerned."

Captain Nefedov led the procession. Behind him moved Professor

Gradov, with the guards carrying the latter's personal effects bringing up the rear, rather like African bearers. At a bend in the corridor, Boris Nikitovich dropped the package containing his medals into a trash bin.

☆

At this point, respected reader, the author, who, as you will no doubt agree, has so long remained in the shadows in accordance with the laws of epic polyphony, will indulge himself in a whim. The fact is that by means of processes in the creation of a novel, which he himself had not yet studied, there came into his head the idea of telling the story of this package containing the medals. It so happened that, after the liberation of B. N. Gradov, the package was found in the bin by Master Sergeant D. I. Grazhdansky, the night janitor at the headquarters of the organs of state security. Far from ideologically pure, Master Sergeant Grazhdansky decided that his retirement was now taken care of: like many other Soviet citizens, he was sure that the country's highest decorations were made from alloys of the world's most precious metals. Not being very clever, however, Master Sergeant Grazhdansky had not completely thought through the mechanism by which these valuables could be turned into coin of the realm, and thus he died in penury. The idea, however, outlived its creator. In 1991, Grazhdansky's grandnephew, a businessman named Misha-Galosha who was well known on Arbat Street, sold the whole set to an American tourist for three hundred dollars and was very satisfied with the bargain.

☆

Boris Nikitovich slowly but quite steadily descended the last flight of stairs leading to the entrance hall. Just behind his back there hung a large portrait of Stalin, framed with black drapes of mourning. Walking by the picture, he did not notice it and now, of course, was thinking not at all about the fact that his descent by way of this staircase might appear symbolic. Having forgotten entirely that "a few relatives were waiting for him," he thought about how he might warn Mary and Agasha. It will be too much for them if I walk into the house just like that, they'll die from shock. Not even noticing the official telephones and automobiles, he thought that in descending the stairs now, he was finally entering his own house. He went further and further down, Captain Nefedov remaining behind. With each step, Professor Gradov increased the distance between himself and Captain Nefedov, who in the end stopped abruptly in the middle of the staircase and with one hand on the bannister watched the descent of the old man.

"Grandfather!" A young voice thundered the word for all the world to hear. Now Boris Nikitovich finally saw his family rushing toward him: his grandson Borka and the three girls, Ninka, Yolka, and Maika.

Captain Nefedov wanted to burst into tears from a compote of feelings all stewed together, the main ingredient of which, nevertheless, was resentment.

EIGHTH INTERMISSION

The Press
1953

In the end, Joseph Stalin was liquidated by the common destiny of all men.

Henry Heslitt:
The death of Joseph Stalin opens up huge possibilities comparable to those that arose following the death of the Mongol Khan Ogday in 1241.

Time:
The heir of Stalin is the flabby and decrepit Georgy Malenkov, 51 years old . . . a Ural cossack by descent . . . height 5 feet 7 inches, weight 250 pounds . . . married to an actress, father of two children. . . .

Following him: Lavrenty Beria, 53, a Georgian like Stalin, head of the secret police . . . also bosses the Red A-bomb project . . . is quiet, methodical, enjoys the arts, music; can be convivial or merciless. Married, two children, lives in a suburban *dacha*, commutes to work in a black, bullet-proof Packard that looks like a hearse. An old-time buddy of Malenkov. Travel beyond the Iron Curtain: none.

In the window of a Russian restaurant in Manhattan, there appeared a picture of Stalin with the inscription: "Stalin is dead! Free borshch today!"

Antanas Ventslova:

> The name of Stalin is peace!
> The name of Stalin is life and struggle!
> His shining name is the destiny of the Soviet peoples!
> . . . O, my Lithuanian land!
> With the name of Stalin you flourished,
> It was in struggling and building
> That your happiness you found!

Alexei Surkov:

> . . . the waiting was both stern and solemn, a patient air of expectation . . . the doors of the House of Unions opened wide and a living river flowed out gracefully, silently . . . the farewell of a great people to its Great Leader.

Konstantin Simonov:

> And our Stalinist Central Committee of iron
> Which you bequeathed to your people,
> To the victory of communism over the ages,
> Shall lead us forth, as you taught us!

Alexander Tvardovsky, *Pravda* (early March 1953):

> In this hour of great sadness
> I cannot find the words
> To express to the end
> The sorrow of all of our peoples.
> But I believe in a wise Party—
> A bulwark for all of us!

Opinions of Stalin:

Businessman Donald Nelson, who worked on Lend-Lease: "A regular guy all around, in every way, a friendly guy."

Leonid Serebryakov: "The most vengeful man on earth. If he lives long enough, he'll get to every one of us."

Time (March 16, 1953):
Ambassador Joseph Davies: "His brown eyes are exceedingly kind and gentle. A child would like to sit on his knee."

Biographer Boris Suvarin: "This repulsive character . . . cunning, crafty, treacherous but also brutal, violent, implacable."

Admiral William D. Leahy: "Most of us, before we met him, thought he was a bandit leader who had pushed himself to the top of his government. That impression was wrong. We knew at once that we were dealing with a highly intelligent man."

Winston Churchill: "Stalin left upon me an impression of deep, cool wisdom and absence of illusions."

Franklin D. Roosevelt: "Altogether, quite impressive, I'd say."

Lev Davidovich Trotsky: "The most outstanding mediocrity in the Party."

Stalin's mother: "Soso was always a good boy."

Alexander Fadeev:
May the cause of Stalin live long and triumph!

Headlines of Soviet newspapers:

THE DEAR IMMORTAL ONE!

OUR SPIRIT IS BUOYANT, OUR CERTAINTY UNSHAKABLE!

THE CREATOR OF THE COLLECTIVE FARM SYSTEM

MILITARY LEADER OF GENIUS

HE WILL LIVE FOR ALL THE AGES

CHINA AND THE USSR WILL BE EVEN CLOSER!

STALIN IS THE LIBERATOR OF THE PEOPLES

Nikolai Gribachov:

> The Party
> > so dear
> > > holds the banner.
>
> We entrust to it
> > our minds
> > > and hearts.
>
> Stalin has died,
> > Stalin
> > > is with us forever!
>
> Stalin is life,
> > and life
> > > has no end!

Mikhail Sholokhov:

Farewell, Father!

Anatoly Sofronov:

> Let our tears flow!
> Today, as always, we are strong,
> Children of the Party,
> Soldiers of the Revolution,
> The great sons of Stalin.

Headlines:

> STALIN'S CONCERN FOR SOVIET WOMEN
>
> A LEADING LIGHT OF SCIENCE
>
> A GREAT FAREWELL
>
> THE OATH OF THE TOILERS OF KIRGHIZIA
>
> THE SORROW OF THE LATVIAN PEOPLE

Mikhail Isakovsky:

> With his death, the Earth has been orphaned,
> The people have lost a friend and a father . . .
> And we take a vow to the Party today.

More Opinions of Stalin:

Herbert Morrison, Labour Party, Great Britain: "A great man but not a good man."

Indian Prime Minister Jawaharlal Nehru: "A man with a giant's stature and indomitable courage. . . . I earnestly hope that his passing away will not mean that his influence, which was exercised in favor of peace, will no longer be available."

An American GI in the trenches in Korea: "Joe's dead; so they said: hurray, hooray; that's one less Red."

Time:

Artist Pablo Picasso, as a "Communist volunteer," made a considerable contribution to the cause of the Party with his doves. . . . Two weeks ago the Party commissioned a portrait of Stalin from him. Soon after, the portrait appeared in a memorial issue of *Les Lettres Françaises,* three columns wide. London's *Daily Mail* immediately made this mocking comment: "Pay attention to the big, melting eyes, the strands of hair that seem to be gathered in a hairdresser's net, the affectedly concealed Mona Lisaesque smile: why, it's just a portrait of a woman with whiskers!" Two days later the Party Secretariat categorically expressed its dissatisfaction with the portrait. Comrade Aragon, onetime poet and now member of the Central Committee, was given a reprimand for having allowed it to be published. Picasso said, "I expressed what I felt. Obviously, they didn't like it. *Tant pis.*"

Headlines from mid-March:

> LIFE-CREATING GENIUS
>
> IMMORTALITY
>
> STALIN IS OUR STANDARD!
>
> THE GREATEST OF FRIENDSHIPS WITH CHINA
>
> THE VOW OF THE WORKERS OF INDIA
>
> THE CAUSE OF STALIN IS IN FAITHFUL HANDS
>
> THE GRIEF OF THE COMMON PEOPLE OF AMERICA
>
> STEELLIKE UNITY
>
> STALIN ON THE RAISING OF COLLECTIVE FARM
>   PROPERTY TO THE LEVEL OF PROPERTY OF ALL
>   THE PEOPLE AS A CONDITION FOR THE
>   TRANSITION TO COMMUNISM
>
> ALL-EMBRACING GENIUS

Mikhail Lukonin:

>Just as to him,
>>we are faithful to our beloved Party,
>
>Central Committee,
>>we believe you,
>>>just as we did him!

THE PROFOUND SORROW OF THE ITALIAN PEOPLE

TO CEASELESSLY INCREASE THE MIGHT OF THE SOVIET STATE!

Olga Berggolts:

>Blood pours out over the heart.
>Our dear one! Our beloved one!
>With its arms around the head of your bed,
>The Motherland weeps for you.

Vera Inber:

>We took an oath before the Mausoleum
>In the moments of sorrow, at the hour of farewell,
>We vowed we would find a way to transform
>The force of grief into the force of building.

STALIN TAUGHT US TO BE VIGILANT

WISE FRIEND OF THE ARTS

CREATOR OF A NEW CIVILIZATION

THE COMMUNIST PARTY—LEADER OF THE SOVIET PEOPLE

The last headline put an end to the poetic outpouring of grief, and the texts had changed, becoming more prosaic, by the end of March.

KIEV IS GROWING AND LOOKING BETTER

THE COTTON FIELDS OF UZBEKISTAN

IMPROVING IDEOLOGICAL-EDUCATIVE WORK

MAKING FULL USE OF THE RESERVES OF PRODUCTION

ON SEVERAL QUESTIONS CONCERNING THE RAISING OF AGRICULTURAL
PRODUCTION OUTSIDE THE BLACK-EARTH BELT

Epilogue

On a hot, glistening day at the beginning of June, Boris Nikitovich Gradov III was sitting in his garden enjoying being alive. The day was a brilliant manifestation of Nature. How good they are, after all, these annual metamorphoses in Russia! Hopelessly snowbound such a short time ago, the earth was now bringing up marvelous kaleidoscopes of colors; the sky was a striking deep blue; the breezes blowing through the pines brought with them the smells of the heated forest and blended them with scents of the garden. One might have no trouble in calling this whole celebration a "lyrical digression," were it not an epilogue.

The first order of business for Boris Nikitovich following his liberation had been to see to his lower teeth, and he now constantly "flashed his Hollywood smile," as his grandson Boris IV put it. He received a large sum of money for the republication of his textbooks and his principal work, *Pain and Anesthesia*. The family, now grown larger, circled around him with happy sighs, celebrating their "hero" and their "modern-day Titan." The latter term, naturally, was a product of Borka's loving sense of humor. As for the "lesser children" (a term that was coined by our "hero" and the "modern-day Titan" himself), that is, Nikitushka and Archi-medes, they literally laid ambushes for him, in order to fall on him suddenly, snatching at him and licking him. In short, life was smiling on the old doctor during these bright May and June days and even offered him something that was inaccessible to others, namely, an iridescent dark orange cloud that was presently to be found in a state of meek mobility some thirty paces from Boris Nikitovich's chair, beside some lilac shrubbery, swaying as though sensing behind itself a fussy troop of actors embarrassed by a miscue.

Boris Nikitovich laid down his copy of *War and Peace,* which was open to the "hunt scene," and followed the rocking back and forth of the curtainlike cloud that appeared to be either alive or thirsting to come to life. It appeared to want to approach him, but just when it looked as though it were moving away from the shrubbery, it suddenly retreated again in mortification and extreme timidity.

In the meantime, the entire household had spread out and taken their places around the periphery of the garden. Mary was pruning her rosebushes and making the rounds of the tulip beds. Agasha was on the terrace assembling a fresh vegetable salad of grandiose proportions. Nina was sitting in the gazebo in front of her portable typewriter, composing something clearly "unacceptable," if one was to judge by the way a cigarette was clenched in one corner of her sarcastic but still brightly visible mouth. Her husband Sandro, wearing dark glasses, was in one corner of the garden. His nostrils were trembling in time with his trembling fingers. His worsening vision had seemingly been compensated for by keener senses of smell and touch. Kitushka and Archi-medes were racing along the path, sometimes with a ball, sometimes with a hoop, and sometimes just the two of them, without stopping—what energy! Boris IV, in almost the same posture as his grandfather, only a bit more horizontal, was lying in a chaise longue with a book by Dostoevsky—*The Gambler.* The delightful Yolka and Maika were slashing away with Ping-Pong paddles. The dark orange curtainlike cloud, which had moved away despondently, now seemed to be preparing a move through the fence and a retreat to the pines. The only ones missing were those who were far away, Kiryushka and Celia, and of course a large number of those of the human majority: father, mother, sisters, the tiny stillborn one, Marshal Nikita, Galaktion, Mitya. . . . But is Mitya really out there among them? Well, of course, replied the cloud with a rocking motion. Now it turned out to be halfway from the lilac shrubs to Boris Nikitovich's chair, and it stood there in a pose of indecisiveness and waiting: well, go ahead and invite me!

Instead of extending the invitation, he turned his eyes to the slender Maika, lunging after the ball like a straw-colored whirlwind. Not long ago, he had been given the gift of seeing her change her name from Strepetov to Gradov. It was perfectly clear to him at that moment that his family seed was growing inside her. Where is our cloud, then? Ah, it's gone back into the pines, as though it wanted to let us know that it's nothing more than a game of shadows and light. Everything around him was interacting in play, as in a well-tuned symphony orchestra. All in Nature that was rooted in the soil of this world was putting on a harmonious display of its trunks, branches, and leaves to those particles of nature that had temporarily detached themselves from the soil in the form of squirrels, starlings, and dragonflies. In the grass not far from his sandal, Boris Nikitovich saw a large, shiny, magnificent specimen of stag beetle. Beautifully armored, on thin, scaled, but unswervingly sturdy legs, the beetle opened its mandibles, turning them into pincers. Well, my dear friend, Boris Nikitovich thought as he looked at the beetle, if we were to increase your size to the proper degree, you'd be a real juggernaut. At that moment, the curtainlike cloud appeared, passed through the lilacs, enveloped Boris Nikitovich, and evaporated together with him, as though not wanting to be present at the hullabaloo that would be raised when they found the motionless body.

Stalin, meanwhile, in the form of the magnificent stag beetle, his dorsal armor gleaming, crawled off into the sparkling grass. He didn't remember a damned thing and didn't understand a damned thing, either.

Glossary

Abakumov, Viktor (1894–1954): Ruthless minister of state security, accused of plotting with Beria and executed.

abrek: Lad (Caucasian dialect).

Akhmatova, Anna (1889–1966): Acmeist poet who was politically persecuted in the late 1940s.

Aksyonov, Ivan (1884–1935): Poet, critic, translator.

alaverdi: The right to pronounce a toast, a Georgian custom.

Altman, Nathan (b. 1889): Theater decorator.

Anti-Dühring: Work by Friedrich Engels (1820–1895) outlining the bases of Marxist logic.

Aragon, Louis (1897–1982): French writer.

Astafiev, Viktor (b. 1924): Prose writer.

Averbakh, Leopold (1903–1939): Critic who supported "proletarian culture."

batono: Mr. (Georgian).

Bekhterev, Vladimir (1857–1927): Neuropathologist and psychologist.

Belinsky, Vissarion (1811–1848): Radical critic, wrote famous letter to Gogol denouncing him for his conservative religious and political views.

Berggolts, Olga (1910–1975): Writer.

Blok, Alexander (1880–1921): Symbolist poet.

Bloomsbury Group: British literary group in early twentieth century.

Bobrov, Sergei (1889–1971): Poet.

Bogoslovsky, Nikita (b. 1913): Composer.

Bolshakov, I.: Minister for film of the USSR.

Boyadzhiev, Grigory (b. 1909): Theater critic.

Casals, Pablo (1876–1973): Spanish cellist, composer, orchestra director.

Centrifuge of Poetry: Futurist group founded shortly after the end of World War I; led by Ivan Aksyonov and Sergei Bobrov.

Chagall, Marc (1887–1985): Painter, lived in Paris 1910–1914, emigrated in 1922.

Charkviani, Dzhansug (b. 1931): Georgian poet.

chifir: undiluted tea concentrate, drunk to give a caffeine high.

Chiladze, Otar and Tomaz (b. 1931): Georgian poets, brothers.

chuchkhiani chatlakhi!: Dirty whore (Georgian).

chuchkhiani prochi: Dirty asshole (Georgian obscenity).

Corday, Charlotte (1768–1793): French revolutionary, assassinated Jean-Paul Marat.

Davies, Joseph (1876–1958): American ambassador to Moscow, 1936–1938.

Dekanozov, Vladimir (1898–1953): Member of Central Committee of the Communist Party, accused of plotting with Beria and executed.

Dolgoruky, Yury (1090–1157): Prince of Kiev, sixth son of Vladimir Monomakh.

Drda, Jan (1910–1974): Czech writer.

Duclos, Jacques (1896–1975): French Communist and labor leader.

Dzerzhinsky, Felix (1877–1926): Chairman of the Cheka (the secret police).

Dzhugashvili: Stalin's original name. "Stalin" was a pseudonym meaning "steel."

dzkhneri: Shit (Georgian).

dzkhneriani chatlakhi: Shitty whore (Georgian).

Ehrenburg, Ilya (1891–1967): Prose writer, poet, critic, journalist. Lived extensively abroad as journalist and Soviet official.

Exster, Alexandra (1884–1949): Avant-garde theatrical artist.

Fadeev, Alexander (1901–1956): Writer, former émigré who became a sort of government overseer for literature.

Feffer, Itsik (1900–1952): Russian Jewish poet, arrested in 1948.

Frunze, Mikhail (1885–1925): Bolshevik military leader, supposedly killed on Stalin's orders during medical operation.

Futurism, Ego-Futurism, Cubo-Futurism: Modernist aesthetic school of the 1910s, imported from Italy, which proclaimed the arrival of a new machine age.

Galich (real name: Ginzburg), Alexander (1918–1977): Poet, playwright and "bard," emigrated in 1974.

gamakhlebulo: Prick, cock (Georgian).

gamardzhoba: Greetings!

Gamsakhurdia, Konstantin (1891–1975): Georgian writer and translator.

genatsvale: Dear (as in "dear friend"—Georgian).

German, Yury (1910–1967): Writer.

Gershenzon, Mikhail (1869–1925): Literary historian, philosopher.

Gogol, Nikolai (1809–1852): Prose writer.

Goncharov, Natalia (1881–1962): Artist, emigrated in 1915.

Govorov, Leonid (1897–1955): Marshal.

Gribachov, Nikolai (b. 1910): Political conservative and writer.

GRU: Soviet military intelligence agency.

Gumilyov, Nikolai (1886–1921): Acmeist poet, executed.

Gurevich, Lyubov (1866–1940): Theater critic.

Horthy, Nicholas (Miklós Horthy de Nagybánya, 1868–1957): Naval officer and regent of Hungary.

Hoxha, Enver (1908–1985): Albanian dictator.

Ignatiev, Nikolai (1890–1937): Senior political official, executed. "Rehabilitated" under Gorbachev.

Ilf and Petrov: See *Twelve Chairs.*

Inber, Vera (1890–1972): Writer.

Isakovsky, Mikhail (1900–1973): Poet.

Jewish Anti-Fascist Committee: Jewish group, mainly poets, executed in 1949 on Stalin's orders.

Kaganovich, Lazar (1893–1991): Senior official in charge of collectivization of agriculture and purges.

kakhetin: Adjective for Kakhetia, historical area in Georgia.

Kandinsky, Vassily (1866–1944): One of the founders of abstract painting, abroad after 1897, with the exception of the period 1914–1921.

Kantemir, Antiokh (1708–1744): Poet and diplomat.

Kaplan, Fanny (1890–1918): Revolutionary who attempted to assassinate Lenin in 1918.

Kartlians: Residents of eastern Georgia (Kartli).

Kataev, Valentin (1897–1986): Writer.

Kennan, George (b. 1904): U.S. ambassador to the Soviet Union; created the doctrine of "containment."

Khachaturian, Aram (1903–1978): Georgian composer and orchestra director.

khle: Prick, cock (Georgian).

Khlebnikov, Velimir (1885–1922): Poet, creator of "trans-sense" verse.

Khmelnitsky, Bogdan (1593–1657): Ukrainian *hetman* who led a Cossack rebellion against Polish rule in 1648.

Klopstock, Friedrich (1724–1803): German poet.

Kobulov, Bogdan (1894?–1953): Leading official in NKVD under Abakumov, executed.

Kollontai, Alexandra (1872–1952): Politican and theorist of free love.

Komsomol: Soviet Communist party youth organization.

Konev, Ivan (1897–1973): Marshal.

Korneichuk, Alexander (1905–1972): Stalinist playwright.

Kosmodemyansky, Zoya (1923–1941): Partisan during World War II, when captured by the Germans she supposedly died shouting "Hurray for Stalin!"

Kostov, Traicho (1897–1949): Bulgarian Communist leader.

Kukryniks brothers: Political cartoonists during Stalinist period.

Kusikyan (Kusikov), Alexander (1896–1970): Poet, emigrated 1921.

Kustodiev, Boris (1878–1927): Artist.

Kutuzov, Mikhail (1745–1813): Russian general who defeated Napoleon.

Larionov, Mikhail (1881–1964): One of first abstractionist artists, emigrated in 1915.

Leahy, William (1875–1959): American naval officer; personal chief of staff to Franklin D. Roosevelt during World War II.

Lebedev-Kumach, Vassily (1898–1949): Poet.

LEF (Left Front of Art): Literary and art movement 1922–1928 which developed from Futurism, eliminated along with other artistic organizations and fused into a single Association of Russian Proletarian Writers.

Leningrad affair: Purge in the Leningrad organization of the Communist Party that followed the death of Andrei Zhdanov.

Leonov, Leonid (b. 1899): Writer.

Lemeshev, Sergei (1901–1977): Opera singer.

Leontiev, Konstantin (1831–1891): Writer, philosopher, critic.

Lermontov, Mikhail (1814–1841): Poet, killed in duel.

Lissitzky, El (Eliezer) (1890–1941): Artist and architect.

Lukonin, Mikhail (1918–1976): Poet.

Lurie, Alexander (1902–1977): Member of Academy of Sciences, pioneer of neuropsychology.

Malenkov, Georgy (1902–1988): Senior official active in the purges, lost out to Khrushchev in the struggle for power.

Mariengof, Anatoly (1897–1962): Poet.

Marr, Nikolai (1864–1934): Linguist who developed a controversial theory on the development of modern languages; enjoyed support of Stalin for a time.

Mayakovsky, Vladimir (1893–1930): Futurist poet, committed suicide.

Meyerhold, Vsevolod (1874–1942): Actor and director, perished in the purges.

Mikhalkov, Sergei (b. 1913): Writer.

Mikoyan, Anastas (1895–1978): Armenian Communist, supported Khrushchev after Stalin's death.

Mikulin, Alexander (1895–1985): Aircraft designer.

Milyukov, Pavel (1859–1943): Political leader, historian.

Mindszenty, József (1892–1975): Hungarian cardinal, imprisoned by the Communists.

Mingrelia: Historic region of Georgia.

Molotov, Polina: Wife of Vyacheslav Molotov.

Molotov (means "hammer," real name: Scriabin), Vyacheslav (1890–1986): Senior government official.

Morrison, Herbert (1888–1965): British political leader; one of the founders of the Labour Party.

Mukuzani: Georgian wine.

Neigauz, Genrikh (1888–1964): Pianist and musicologist.

Nekrasov, Nikolai (1821–1878): Poet, writer, and publisher.

Neruda, Pablo (1904–1973): Chilean poet; winner of Nobel Prize for literature, 1971.

Nicholas II (Romanov) (1868–1918): Last Russian czar, executed together with immediate family.

Nikiforov, Georgy (1884–1939): Writer.

NKVD, OGPU (GPU), MGB: Predecessors of the KGB.

Noneshvili, Iosif (b. 1918): Georgian poet.

no pasarán: Spanish for "they shall not pass"; Republican slogan during Spanish civil war.

Northeastern Camp Directorate: Agency in charge of Northeastern forced labor camps before Stalin's death.

Novy Mir: Russian literary and political journal which had an especially respected reputation during the Khrushchev period.

October Revolution: The 1917 revolution during which the Communists seized power (as distinguished from the February Revolution).

Pasternak, Boris (1890–1960): Poet, prose writer.

Pechorin: Jaded protagonist in Lermontov's *Hero of Our Time.*

Perventsev, Arkady (1901–1981): Writer.

Petrashevsky Circle: A conspiratorial circle, to which Dostoevsky belonged. All members were arrested.

Polevoi, Boris (1908–1981): Prose writer and literary functionary.

Poskryobyshev, Alexander (1891–1965): Stalin's secretary, wielded great power.

Princip, Gavrilo (1894–1918): Bosnian terrorist; carried out assassination of Archduke Ferdinand, precipitating World War I.

Pugachov, Yemelyan (1726–1775): Peasant leader of Cossack revolt, executed and quartered.

Pushkin, Alexander (1799–1837): Generally recognized as Russia's greatest poet.

Radishchev, Alexander (1749–1802): Writer who exposed the evils of serfdom.

Rajk, László: Hungarian minister of foreign affairs after World War II.

Rimsky-Korsakov, Nikolai (1844–1908): Composer.

Rëkk, Maria: German actress.

Romashev, Boris (1895–1959): Playwright.

Rostropovich, Mstislav (b. 1927): Cellist and orchestra director.

Rotmistrov, Pavel (1901–1982): Marshal, joined Red Army in 1919.

Rudé Právo: Czechoslovakian newspaper, official arm of the Communist Party.

Scanteia: Former newspaper of the Rumanian Communist Party.

Serebryakov, Leonid (1890–1937): Political figure, executed in Great Purges.

Severyanin (real name Lotarev), Igor (1887–1941): Russian-Estonian poet and translator.

sheni deda movtkhani: Fuck your mother! (Georgian exclamation).

Sholokhov, Mikhail (1905–1984): Stalinist writer, Nobel Prize laureate.

Shtemenko, Sergei (1907–1976): Army general.

Simonov, Konstantin (1915–1979): Writer.

Slutsky, Boris (1919–1986): Poet.

Socialist Realism: Literary school officially adopted under Stalin, calling for a depiction of reality in its "revolutionary transformation."

Sofronov, Anatoly (1911–1990): Poet.

Solovyov, Vladimir (1853–1900): Mystic poet and philosopher.

"Stormy Petrel of the Revolution": 1901 revolutionary poem by Maxim Gorky.

Surkov, Alexei (1899–1983): Prose writer, poet, literary functionary, chief editor of *Soviet Brief Literary Encyclopedia.*

Suvarin (Lifshits), Boris (1895–1984): French Communist close to Trotsky, early Sovietologist, lived for a time in Moscow.

Svetitskhoveli Temple: Church in Georgian city of Arsukisdze, erected early eleventh century.

Mikhail Svetlov (1903–1964): Poet.

Tank, Maxim (b. 1912): Belorussian poet.

Tatyana's letter: Letter from heroine of Pushkin's *Eugene Onegin* to eponymous hero.

Thorez, Maurice (1900–1964): French Communist.

Tikhonov, Nikolai (1896–1979): Poet.

Timoshenko, Semyon (1895–1970): Marshal.

Tsarskoe Selo: Small city near St. Petersburg, onetime summer residence of czars.

Tsvetaev, Marina (1892–1941): Poet and prose writer, emigrated in 1922, returned to Russia in 1939, committed suicide.

Tvardovsky, Alexander (1910–1971): Poet and editor of the literary journal *Novy Mir.*

The Twelve Chairs: play by Ilya Ilf and Evgeny Petrov, about jewels sewn into the seat of a chair.

Ulyanov: Lenin's original name.

Vasilyevsky, Alexander (1895–1977): Marshal.

Ventslova, Antanas (1906–1971): Lithuanian writer.

viziga: A dish prepared from fish back.

Vodopyanov, Mikhail (1899–1980): General.

Voroshilov, Kliment (1881–1969): Marshal.

Voznesensky, Nikolai (1903–1950): Political leader and economist; executed in Leningrad affair.

Vrubel, Mikhail (1856–1910): Painter.

Yashchenko, Alexander (1877–1934): Legal expert, émigré editor and publisher.

Yefimov, Boris: Political cartoonist.

Yesenin, Sergei (1895–1925): Russian peasant poet, committed suicide.

Yutkevich, Sergei (1904–1985): Film director and critic.

Yuzovsky, Iosif (1902–1964) Literary scholar and theater critic.

zakuski: Hors d'oeuvre.

zek: Slang for "convict."

Zhdanov, Andrei (1896–1948): Stalinist political leader.

Zhukov, Georgy (1896–1974): Marshal.

Zhukov, Yury (Georgy) (1908–1991): Journalist.

Zoshchenko, Mikhail (1895–1958): Humorous writer.

Zvezda: Russian political-literary journal.

A former professor of Russian literature at the University of Chicago, the University of Iowa, and the University of Maryland, JOHN GLAD was also director of the Kennan Institute for Advanced Russian Studies in the Woodrow Wilson International Center for Scholars. His translation of Varlam Shalamov's *Kolyma Tales* was judged one of the five best translations of 1980 from any language at the American Book Awards.

CHRISTOPHER D. MORRIS is a graduate of the Sorbonne, License et Lettres in Russian literature. He presently resides in Prague, where he is a contributing editor to *Traffika,* an international literary review.

ABOUT THE TYPE

This book was set in Sabon, a typeface designed by the well-known German typographer Jan Tschichold (1902–74). Sabon's design is based upon the original letter forms of Claude Garamond and was created specifically to be used for three sources: foundry type for hand composition, Linotype, and Monotype. Tschichold named his typeface for the famous Frankfurt typefounder Jacques Sabon, who died in 1580.